# COLDHEARTED

## The First Thompson Novel

# MARK DENNIS

# To...

This book is dedicated to my wife, Sandra, for patience, encouragement and enthusiasm, and then probably quite a lot more patience.

Cover artwork and design, and author portrait by Sandra Dennis.

I'd also like thank the anaerobic heterotrophic bacterium, the first organism on Earth, for giving it a real go and without whom I'd not be where I am today.

# ONE

Simon Reid heard the awful rap music as soon as he opened the door. At her hutch, Moonbeam Orinoco knew Reid wouldn't allow that noise to permeate through the room all day, all she got to herself was from when she arrived for work early, until he showed up. After that, they would be condemned to listen to lift music for the rest of the day. Reid's arrival also signalled that it was time for her to keep her head down and keep on looking busy, busy.

Reid knew what she was up to; he saw her log-in times and knew that she only did what she needed to, just enough to keep her head above water in the survival stakes. Her name amused him, she'd always claimed the famous South American Orinoco River was her hippie mother's inspiration for her peculiar nomenclature, he strongly suspected that it was more likely she'd been named after a Womble following some sort of acid trip. It could have been worse he reckoned; at least it wasn't Uncle Bulgaria!

Reid half-nodded to Mo as he donned a pair of neoprene gloves and his lab coat and walked through to the freezer room on automatic. It was just another Monday with another pile of stuff to get done, no doubt involving a ton of Saviour samples. His day would end when all tasks had been completed, the only tangible reward being the adding of a few more pounds to the bank account. At five, it was going-home time and he could forget all about samples, Sample Management, South American rivers and Nash Pharmaceutical Solutions.

The thing about operating entirely on automatic is that you don't notice the little things until it's too late, and Reid nearly went full length when his foot skidded on a broken pen on the floor. He was

1

annoyed that it hadn't been picked up by whoever had dropped it, one of the weekend kiddies perhaps.

As the door opened, air gasped into the walk-in freezer and mist formed on the observation window in the door as warm air met cold. The shelves inside had a winding mechanism that allowed them to roll along either way to maximise the space. They were all wound right over to the left again, despite his asking repeatedly that the freezer be left with all shelves equally accessible. Picking past the unruly mass of boxes piled inside the door, all out-of-hours deliveries with most containing human blood samples scheduled for analysis later, Reid walked to the back of the freezer and there was Marie-Eve Legault.

She was slumped uncomfortably on the floor at the back of row six, her head lolling to her left. Her eyes were open, pale and glassy; her skin was blue-white in places, frosty; almost opaque. She was frozen, she looked dead; Reid presumed that she was.

Not just another day at the ice-face after all, then.

He backed out of the freezer, closed the door then shut down the room. No longer running on automatic, he quickly dialled the company Security Office, asking for the police to be called immediately, a 999, and then telling them to lock down all Freezer Room access doors electronically, by deactivating the card-swipe door pads so that nobody could get in. He told them that there was a body in Sample Management but that was as much of an explanation as they got. There must have been something about Reid's voice that made it clear to Neil Martin on Security that this needed to be done, without undue fuss, because he just said "ok".

He then called Joan Bain, the Site Manager, Richard Greenwood's, PA. There was no answer so he left a message and asked her to relay the information about the imminent arrival of the police with regard to a serious incident in the Sample Management area to Greenwood when she, and he, got in.

Reid, sort-of, assumed that the sole occupant inside the freezer wouldn't mind too much that she was locked in. He might well not have dared assume anything had she still got a pulse, but he didn't stop to check, it never even crossed his mind.

Hand-written notes were stuck onto all Sample Management area access doors, all signed and dated by Reid. Good Laboratory Practice seeps insidiously into everything you do after a while; he couldn't even leave his girlfriend a note without signing and dating it, these days.

Out in the main room, the rest of the Sample Management team had begun to drift in, ignoring the newly-posted notices, either thinking they didn't apply to them or perhaps not even seeing them. Some of them were stood chatting as usual, but on seeing Reid they made to get logged on to their PCs and start working.

Raising his voice above the normal hubbub of arrival, Reid told everyone that the Sample Management room would be closed for a while and to go to the cafeteria until he had more information. The only two smokers in the group quickly rushed out, taking advantage of the unexpected opportunity to sneak in another fag break – god forbid that they might have to breathe oxygen for too long. The rest of them filed out and headed for the cafeteria, leaving just Reid and Mo in the room.

"What's going on, Simon?" She never called him Simon; it was always Reid if she addressed him at all.

"You need to go, Mo, now, just take your stuff and go to the cafeteria please". She sensed the urgency in his voice, he never said please to her, either. She realised that this wasn't a time to argue, something she habitually did, and quickly lumped her scattered possessions into her battered 'Souvenir of Halkidiki' bag, leaving silently. She had contacts around the company, she'd find out what was going on soon enough.

In the corridor, the lab analysts were also starting to arrive to collect their morning samples. Some had already been there a while and were fidgeting impatiently at the closed counter window. Pushing through the throng, Reid told them that there were technical issues, they needed to leave the area and that they'd be told when staff would be available to dole out samples. Inadvertently, Reid made it sound like it was a staffing, and not a stiff, issue that would completely mess up their analytical day,

Reid sat at his PC and started sending out emails to all analytical and related Departmental Heads, Supervisors and to Human Resources (HR) with the same message, vague on details but clear on options, that there would be no samples available for analysis until further notice. He then closed up the main Sample Management room door, locked it and went to the cafeteria to wait for the police and to grab a coffee; it was going to be a long day for everyone-except Marie-Eve, of course.

The police arrived just as the coffee had been poured; pretty quick to get there but then this was a body, possibly even a murder and not just some car break-in wanting a crime number for the insurance.

Neil Martin passed them over to him and, clutching his cup of coffee and quickly sorting out a few formalities, he led them through to the Sample Management room. It was a tricky find for the uninitiated who were not used to picking their way through the maze that was the laboratories of Nash Pharmaceutical Solutions.

Reid didn't know what to do, it was not a normal situation for him so he just kept up a conversation, chattering inanely all the way up the stairs and down the slippery corridors. He didn't shut up until they got to the Sample Management room. The guy who Reid at first took to be the senior officer present, he seemed to be in charge, kept his replies to the conversation to a minimum, only becoming more animated when one of his colleagues called him 'Sarge'. Then he rapidly issued a complex set of instructions, it was a bit like a scene from 'The Bill'.

Soon, some of the other officers were setting up perimeters and crime-related stuff. Reid realised he must have come across as nervous but what could he do? He'd never had a stiff in the freezer before so surely that was not unexpected, not incriminating. He made sure he told them that as a general point, just so that they knew.

It was when they all filed into the Sample Management room that it hit him. If she had been murdered then he might well be in the frame for it. He'd seen enough TV police drama to know how it all works, but even if he got arrested and interviewed, there was no way he could sit there and chant 'no comment'. He had nothing to fear or hide, so why would he?

In no time, the corridor and Sample Management area was a mass of confusion. Despite the signs and the emails, analysts had continued to arrive and they wanted their samples. They were not happy at being told 'no, go away' rather brusquely by the police. Inside, the phone was also ringing constantly. The Sample Management techs then showed up again, having been sent back by HR following complaints from Scientific. Their natural Pavlovian response on arrival at work each day was to fetch their samples, book them out and do an electronic transfer to the lab, a sort of chain of custody transferring them from us to them, and then repeat ad-nauseam until break time. Now they were actually trying to do that process in the middle of a crime scene.

It took one of the police in uniform to light up their brain cells, they could recognise the authority of that but it was still like herding cats. They all wanted to know what was happening, whether they should just go home, would they get paid? As usual, nobody from HR had bothered to try to help out with the practical stuff and it took one of the detectives shouting at them to make them get out, back to the cafeteria. At times like this you can definitely see who the blue sky thinkers are.

Meanwhile Reid just stood patiently, waiting for instructions and trying to look helpful and innocent, especially innocent!

Soon, more official police people arrived, filling up the room. Some were carrying equipment; all had been escorted by Martin from security. He was loving the attention, almost marching and barking orders at people in the way. His face was a picture when one of the detectives, Irish by the sound of it, turned around and told him to "fuck off, now". Sharp, Reid thought, but a joy to watch, nevertheless.

It turned out that Detective Inspector Charnley was the top policeman. He'd arrived just after the main group of plain-clothes officers, almost unnoticed, and then had loudly announced his arrival by telling all present who he was; the other cops all addressed him as 'Sir'. Reid realised that the Inspector had the same surname as someone he knew from school, definitely not the same bloke though; this one looked like a professional lemon sucker!

Until this point, the room containing the walk-in freezer had remained shut from all entrances. At an officer's request, Reid called Security and got them to make live the door catches; then he had to call again to get the temporary cards issued to the police working. When the light came on, Reid swiped his card and prepared to take them all through.

He quickly showed one of the officers how the card worked. She told him that they would keep the cards until they had done with the site, would that be OK? Reid told them to talk to Security later and, as these were temporary cards with full access, they could be swiped anywhere for entry. "What about a finger scan?" she asked.

"Not needed with a temp".

Before going any further, Charnley told everyone to put on the disposable nitrile gloves that were used daily when handling samples. They were company property but they all helped themselves to a handful, Reid didn't care, NPS could afford it. Most of the police present had already done it anyway and there was some obvious eye-rolling going off from some of the plain-clothes people. Reid then gave them all shoe covers and guest lab coats, citing GLP but without explaining in detail what it was. Nobody argued and they found just enough lab coats to go around.

Once they were inside, the door from the Sample Management room through to the Freezer Room was wedged open and tape started to appear, 'Police – Do Not Cross' tape. Reid was about to lead them through to the walk-in freezer when even more people arrived so he stepped back out of the way, or so he thought, but it didn't stop him being unceremoniously barged aside as the new people, all in the sort of anti-contamination suits Sample Management technicians sometimes had to wear for sensitive samples, got to work on setting up an access.

When they gave the sergeant the nod, Reid was told to follow the marked route and to stand by the walk-in freezer and await instructions, which he did, but none came amid the general confusion. Eventually he was asked to open up the door.

Reid felt he ought to point out about the freezer alarms and how the samples needed to stay frozen for stability. It seemed pretty trivial but, as it was he who would be writing memos for the rest of the year if the samples thawed for too long, and he who would get the blame no matter what the circumstances, he thought it worth mentioning.

Having half-listened to him, more activity ensued and, correctly assuming that his help was not needed for now, he backed off and out of it, intending to go back to his hutch where his coffee was getting cold. As he turned, a door behind him that led through to the Shipping Department opened. One of their technicians, Alan Bain, wheeled in a cart with a large pile of boxes on it that were wobbling, precariously. More samples that needed to be dealt with, but not right now, Alan!

Reid intercepted him. Alan was confused by so many new people, they made him agitated and he danced from foot to foot, muttering about the samples. One of the female police officers came over, wanting to know what was going on and why was he able to get in. Security had activated all the card readers, not just the one he'd asked for, and Alan hadn't read the note. He probably couldn't read too well anyway, besides he was not the best at changes in routine so even if he had read it, he'd have just ignored it.

The cart with the new samples was pushed back out of the door, into the corridor and out of the way, they were in dry ice so would be OK with being taken back to Shipping for a while. He explained the situation to one of the officers and was told to come straight back. He then led Alan back through to Shipping where Tracey Mills had just arrived and had not yet read her emails or her new copy of 'Hello' magazine.

Reid explained the situation to her in limited detail, asked her to explain it to Craig when he showed up and went back to join the fray. Tracey called after him that Craig was away today, training in London, but Reid didn't respond. He was a bit preoccupied.

Tracey saw that Alan was upset; he only worked to an established routine and his first job in the morning was to wheel new samples through to Sample Management. Generally, if you gave him a job to do, the instructions had to be exact.

When Alan had first started work at NPS, or 'Blue Sky Research' as it was before the recent buy-out, he'd been told to load the cage wash, a room where equipment was washed in very hot water, sort of like a huge dishwasher that you could walk into. He'd put in not only the cages and carts that needed washing but also the work desk, PC, phone and chairs, everything. They only found out when they came to empty it and passed though the now empty ante-room, wondering where everything was. After that he worked with someone else, always, unless it was a simple case of wheeling a cart from point A to point B.

Tracey felt sorry for Alan, he should be in a home or something but his mum, Joan, had got him the job and while she was still working there, so probably would Alan. Thinking to get him out of the way, Tracey sent him down to the basement to help the other techs load the cage wash. He liked that and she told him that he might as well take the pile of bits and pieces already loaded onto two other carts; that should keep him quiet for a while and they wouldn't need any of the kit until it had been cleaned, anyway. The cart outside would be relieved of its samples, sooner or later, and there was one still in Sample Management to recover, so they'd have at least one to be going on with.

Once back at his coffee, Reid got busy sending out another email, this time to all in the SMC, the Senior Management Committee, a committee made up of those that rarely deigned to talk to the likes of him unless it was to tell him he'd been let go. He explained in simple terms that, due to a serious incident, Sample Management would be closed until further notice. He didn't say why but did include the ominous statement 'on police orders'; that should give them a little bit of a jolt.

Next, he emailed everyone else who might need to know of the ongoing situation, then he called Richard 'Dick' Greenwood, the site manager again, who still wasn't in yet but his PA, Joan, was; she'd already picked up the earlier message and had paged him. Oddly, he liked the idea of being called Dick, apparently taking it as a sign of endearment. He obviously didn't know that it was not born out of fraternity and respect at all, just a statement of what people really thought of him.

The mechanics of a police investigation were new to just about everybody and the Sample Management techs watched with curiosity as the police cleared a space in the cafeteria, screening it off with some mobile panels left over from the failed open-office experiment, another HR triumph, and then started to make inroads into coffee and breakfast. Nobody on the tills knew whether to charge them or not so they didn't, another little job for Human Resources to sort out.

Reid was told by DS Thompson, who was very calm and collected, to remain in the Sample Management room so that he could advise them where needed. They'd also need to have a chat, of course, and so, apart from a brief trip to the loo next door, he was left to stew at his desk while all around buzzed like a wasps' nest that had been whacked with a stick.

He only found out later how the cafeteria had been appropriated, when he'd been allowed to go to a late lunch. He managed to grab the last of the lasagne before they started prepping for afternoon tea. He'd just finished eating when he was asked to give finger prints in one of the booths they'd set up for the purpose. Apparently all of the Sample Management staff had been expected to participate, they were told that their prints were needed in order to rule them out of (or into) the investigation. Nobody refused, why would they?

Reid took pains to point out that staff didn't normally enter the Freezer Room without wearing gloves in order to prevent contamination, GLP again, although that was not entirely true. Only a few of them had a true understanding of GLP. The brain-light ones needed constant reminding and checking, especially the ones who liked a beer or two of a night; one of them, 'Shaking Steven', never mentally surfaced until the afternoons at best anyway, and even then it wasn't always worth waiting for.

After fingerprinting he was called over to one of the makeshift interview booths, only for things to end after a couple of minutes when Thompson came over and said they'd do this later. They had initially told him that they just wanted him to repeat the details of the discovery to one of the officers under more controlled conditions, no doubt checking his first casual description of the events with the more considered second. Having been cut short, he was told to remain in the cafeteria and not to talk to anyone else about the situation.

Despite the instruction not to converse with each other; Reid overheard whispers that the corpse had left through the service bay doors. He found that he still wasn't at all bothered. 'Bye-bye then, Marie-Eve, missing you already!'

The police had told Human Resources that they would release the site by late afternoon and so that information was passed along, piecemeal, mostly from Mo. Nobody really cared about how many pounds, or even dollars, that the company was losing, but everyone took great care to look suitably concerned in public that money was bleeding out of the company in these very unfortunate circumstances.

There was talk that some officers would be visiting the site later in the day. As a matter of priority they'd be interviewing the night people, especially those on the rota who came to receive late samples, all except Craig Shepherd. Reid told the police that he didn't think too many of the cleaners counted English as their first language and they might need a translator, but the officer he spoke to didn't seem to take it in, there was still a deal of confusion throughout.

Later in the afternoon, the reason for Reid's truncated interview earlier became clear when he was invited to take a seat in Conference Room One, the Duggan Suite, along with Detective Sergeant Thompson and a Detective Constable that he'd not seen before, an Asian guy they all called 'Dad'.

It seemed that the general hoi-polloi had given their statements in the cafeteria, for what use they'd be. Those more intimately involved would be interviewed, or maybe that would be interrogated, individually in the splendid isolation of a secure conference room. He was a bit concerned when he realised that it was only him and Mo that this special treatment was being applied to, oh!

The police had actually said 'secure', not to him but to the HR dilettante who had been assigned to liaise. Reid didn't tell them that rumour was rife that NPS had had all conference rooms bugged after

11

the takeover, to help weed out dissenters. Nobody would have been too surprised if the rumour turned out to be true, it seemed to be the NPS style.

Reid had been in Conference Room One many times before. This was where they had to watch the recent compulsory musings of the Company President, James Duggan, 'Jim' to his friends, in selected batches. Each key missive having been recorded from his Ivory Tower in Fuckwit, New Jersey, or wherever it was located, and then relayed to all NPS operations, world-wide.

Usually they got the same old tripe. They were all great, the best, part of a big family but there was stiff competition within the industry and they must keep striving for greathood. He actually said 'greathood'. Then he usually came up with some more twat-speak garbage before ending the mandatory brainwashing sessions with how great the company was and how everyone was equal. He'd almost expected Duggan to lead them all in prayer to close the meeting.

Reid wondered whether he and Mo were being interviewed as suspects. It was hard to judge the mood, but surely a suspect would be interviewed at the station with the radiators up high?

Earlier, Charnley had been brusque, verging rude; his curtness directed at anyone and everyone, so he assumed that that was just how Charnley always was. He was rather glad he that wasn't there now; he didn't seem to be a reasonable type. Thompson was better, more like Reid, easier to chat to without wondering whether you'd said something incriminating, even if there was nothing incriminating to say.

Reid sat back and waited until the room settled down, waited for the fun to begin. He didn't like Marie-Eve Legault at all and had never hidden his dislike. Well, except from her, obviously. He really didn't care that she was in now a box somewhere and he had no intention of hiding anything. He hadn't done it but he was still full of nervous

12

excitement, nevertheless. He wondered whether that was normal, when someone you really didn't like went to meet their maker in suspicious circumstances.

Reid had expected to see a tape recorder and an announcement of time, date and those present, just like on the telly, but they all just sat chatting and occasionally looked at him for a moment or two. It was not for Reid to start things rolling so he just sat and gave them the eye back, not in an insolent way but in an 'I'm from Clifton' way; they'd have come across that before, no doubt.

Thompson introduced himself again and asked Reid to go through the finding from the beginning once more. 'Leave nothing out, no matter how trivial, and don't embellish', they'd know.

He told them again the sequence of events, from swiping in to the company to sticking the 'no entry, closed' signs on the access doors. The rest they knew, he was with them at the time. Despite him being what he thought was thorough, they still pumped him for extra detail, going back to bits he'd already said and asking for further explanation or clarification, more detail, 'The Devil', they said, 'is in the detail'. It sounded such a cliché, but Reid couldn't help but think 'The Devil' was actually on a slab somewhere, thawing out before meeting the rib cutter.

When they'd finished and the meeting, because that was what it had felt like, broke up, Reid caught Thompson alone. "Got a minute?" Thompson nodded and led Reid across the room while Reid almost whispered as he walked "it might not be relevant". Thompson said he'd prefer to decide relevance and to continue, so Reid told him that Marie-Eve Legault was rumoured to be involved, romantically, with Craig Shepherd in Shipping. Thompson just said "rumoured?"

"Well, it's a bit more than a rumour. Secrets here, like anywhere I expect, are hard to keep. I heard they that had a thing but that it was finished. I don't know details and I can't even remember who told me now, possibly Mo. You know, Moonbeam Orinoco Smith, from my department".

Thompson nodded, "OK" and then left the room with the rest of the police, leaving Reid to make his way back to the Sample Management room to collect his stuff.

He shuffled down the corridor; suddenly feeling very tired as the event adrenaline was starting to leave him, when he heard Charnley somewhere bellow "London!", and guessed that his little nugget of gossip wasn't being enjoyed very much, especially with Craig being far, far away. Back at his desk, Reid scooped up his bits and bobs, and checked the call-out schedule on the office wall. So, Craig Shepherd was here last night too, interesting. He thought about chasing down Thompson again, with this new and possibly vital information, but decided against it; they'd find out for themselves. soon enough.

Reid clocked off on-time, amazingly. The road was as busy as ever but the trip soon gets done when you have a bit of music to do it by. He laughed out loud when 'Cold as Ice' by Foreigner came on the radio, the God of Coincidence strikes again! Then for some reason he started running a selection of 'suitable', if not subtle, song titles through his head. The best he came up with though was 'Frosty The Snowman'. He didn't realise how much he was shaking until he parked the car. Was it nerves or excitement?

Once home, Catheryn greeted him with a hug. "Good day?" she said with a glint in her eye. "Anything unusual happen?"

Reid looked at her quizzically. "It was on the news, body in a freezer at NPS, your freezers" she said.

"Right, I wasn't sure it would make the news, it was that Canadian woman I told you about, the one I don't like". "Oh well" she said, "one less".

By bed time Reid had settled down, his body needed to rest even if his mind kept running the events of the day on a loop, now he just had to find a way to put his mind on 'pause'. After a disturbed night, when he repeatedly woke up sweating, the reality of the situation dawned on him. This might go very badly for him.

The previous day, the excitement of the hustle and bustle of the police investigation, as they organised statements, commandeered bits of the cafeteria and set to trying to find out who had stuffed poor Marie-Eve into the big freezer, had carried him along with it; even as he'd tried to force some normality into his day by going to Shipping and taking the new Saviour samples to the Clinical Laboratories freezer. At the time he'd felt mostly detached, but in the clear cold light of a new day it all looked decidedly iffy. The police would ask a lot more questions of everybody and surely the curse of a mouth that said what his mind thought, and that had always dogged his progress when promotion came up, would see his past derogatory comments about Legault come to light.

If he saw Thompson again he decided that he should 'fess up' about his past comments; better they came from him although, as far as he could recall, he never mentioned that he'd actually go in for killing her. With fresh resolve he set off for work, but tripped on the top step. It wasn't the first time he'd done that; a few days before finding the body he'd gone his full length, scattering possessions as he fell.

*Of all the places his car keys could have skittered to, the centre of the one rose bush in the garden was the least convenient. If he'd had more time, he'd have hunted around for a long stick and just poked them back out, but he was pressed and the traffic would be more and more unforgiving the later it got. Reaching in carefully, he managed to scrape the key near enough to get two fingers onto it, and then eased his hand back. As often happens, his concentration lapsed as the task was almost completed and he managed to drag one thorn, possibly the largest thorn the bush had produced, over the back of his hand, shit.*

*The wound only bled lightly. Once in the sanctuary of the Sample Management office, he pulled out a blue plaster and covered it. He thought he might get comments; questions as to why he was wearing the plaster, but nobody seemed to notice and he wasn't intending to go out of his way to explain unless absolutely necessary. Even then he thought that he could come up with something a bit edgier than 'snagged it on a rose bush thorn'.*

# Two

In the Central Police Station Thompson; Tommo outside the public eye, sometimes; sat in the canteen scribbling. He had wanted to be a writer for years, of crime naturally, and since the advent of digital publishing he'd fulfilled that dream and was working on a detective series.

Writing under the nom-de-plume of Jimmy McIntyre, he was collecting snippets for his third book, which was set in Scotland and featured his anti-hero Jimmy McCann, a tough but sensitive cop who was a deeper thinker than his bosses liked. He was the first to admit that it was early days but if you don't try it you don't know whether you can do it so, when he could, he'd snatch time for 'in-life' notes as his 'how to write detectives stories' book had called them, which he'd later write up into something more chapter-like.

To keep his notes in order, he kept a soft notebook for his thoughts, updating it as and when he could, especially when he was on a case with something different. It was a jotter really and very casual, compared to his official police notebook. Facts were easy to remember, especially when they had been studiously written down, but trivia; that was what you needed if you were going to write crime. It also allowed you to either add, or obscure, bits to case details, intuitive bits that you might not want appearing in court undermining evidence, not anything illegal, just opinions really. He wrote:

*We got a report sheet just in and delivered by DI Charnley. A body was found in a freezer at Nash Pharmaceutical Solutions (NPS) on the industrial estate out at Wilford. No further details were offered nor asked for, and we all quietly went about doing our different team bits before heading out to the pool cars. The industrial estate was only twenty or so minutes away, so no time to think of much more than getting there really.*

17

From the outside the largely-glass building could have been anything, only the discreet and unlabelled company logo of blue clouds suggested what might lie behind. Pharmaceutical research was all vivisection, scientists in white lab coats and safety glasses, that sort of thing, wasn't it?

Getting in was something of a pantomime. The entrance had turnstiles that were designed to stop a tank and the minions turning up for work had to scan a card and then stick a digit on a pad before the thing beeped and let them through. We all had to be given our own visitor cards and get a very short briefing about safety and contamination from someone called Neil Martin, just a security guard but who came over as a wanna-be policeman, they always do.

The guy who was waiting to take us to the scene also found the body. Solid but not muscular, a slight accent about him suggesting he might not be local, well at least originally. He was a bit swarthy but he probably loved the great outdoors. It turned out he was a Cliftonite so that first impression was wrong. He gave his name as Simon Reid, no bells rang.

The place was a maze, with offices and what were presumably laboratories, although the doors gave no clues. The floors were clean and slippery, buffed to within an inch of their lives, probably done daily after everyone had gone home although these places rarely slept. There were always animals to tend to and people hanging around late, trying to keep up with their work load and failing, a bit like the police really.

We all came to a stop in a large room where the Sample Management people worked, with hutches along the back wall housing six people. In the middle of the room there were three large desks with two PCs on each and at the end was a small office with a door that could be closed for privacy – that might do as a temporary operations room.

Reid called security and they turned on the card readers so we could enter the Freezer Room, he opened the door and then, with half a grin, let it close again, what was that about? A second call was needed to get the team's cards to work independently, security wanted memos and permission from who knows who; in the meantime we wedged the door open with a plastic tray. I got the impression Reid had anticipated the 'jobs worth' on security being an arse.

The Freezer Room was larger than the Sample Management room. It had three doors in and Reid had posted notices on all three stating no access, oddly clear thinking given that he'd just found a body. The signs were a bit redundant really, given that the electronic pads were the only way in (but not out); still, at least he'd tried, more that we usually got in situations like this. I wondered how he knew what to do, didn't look ex-force, maybe he was a fan of CSI or something similar.

Once the scene of crime people had set up an access, and after being given a selection of white coats and having already taken a pair of nitrile gloves (and several for 'later') from the rack, we were led through to a door with a large stainless steel handle. All around us were large freezers, not chest types but cabinets. He said they were all -80°C. I didn't even know such things existed.

A door in the wall was for a walk-in -20°C freezer. It sounded cold and I wasn't the only one to do an involuntary shiver. A selection of padded winter coats of various sizes were hung on a rack to the left, presumably for staff to wear if they were going to spend any length of time inside. I wondered if it ever got to -20°C in Nottingham, I couldn't remember it doing so; it hardly ever froze up at all.

Reid pointed out a broken biro on the floor. He thought that it had been left there by weekend workers but you never know. We were all gloved up too, so the pen was collected, passed to SOCO and bagged and labelled. It might be nothing; everyone thinks they are a sleuth after playing a character in a murder mystery evening.

Reid opened the door, confirming that he'd been gloved up the same when he'd found the body.

Inside looked cold; there was an icy rime over everything, especially the Dexion shelving. The freezer was set up in rows, six in total, and at the end of each row was a wheel, like a steering wheel. The rows could be wound one way or the other, depending where you wanted to get to.

Reid had mentioned this on the way up, he never shut up. Nervous or just gobby? Too soon to tell yet but he was certainly not upset that a colleague was dead, although we only had his view that that was the case, dead that is.

There wasn't much room inside; two people were comfortable; three required a certain amount of freezer do-si-do. At the end of row six, the furthest row from the door and right at the back, was the body of a woman who Reid had identified as Marie-Eve Legault.

We went to move Reid out of the freezer and out of the way but he said he had to tell us about alarms and thawing samples and stuff, and how there'd be even more problems if the unit temperature dropped below -12°C. Once he was gone this was our space, now and for the duration. He later collared Banks, giving her a lecture again about the samples needing to remain stable, so frozen, and how alarms would be going off all the time if the door remained open for more than a couple of minutes That seemed to be more of a concern to him than the dead woman.

The doctor had arrived by now and, suitably suited, came in and confirmed death, ignoring all questions, as usual. Charnley was heard pushing for a 'when', but the doctor fobbed him off with some comment about how could anyone even tell when a Fish Finger was originally frozen, without then spending time in a lab to find out. A throw-away phrase but a beauty, and so we christened the corpse 'the Fish Finger'.

Having all had a good look at our first ever Fish Finger, Prosser asked the Doc about her colour, bluish, but got no answer. We then started to organise. It turned out that the little office was of no use, too remote from the rest of the facility and too close to the crime scene, if that is what we had. It seems that the Fish Finger was no stranger to working late and could have had a fit or something, and ended up in the freezer then snuffed it. How long do you need to be at -20°C to die?

The Sample Management room had been closed to everyone and all the staff had been told to wait in the cafeteria, a welcoming place of buns and cakes, chocolate, tea and coffee. Perfect.

The two uniformed scene shifters on the team had set up an area at one end of the long cafeteria. They'd found some panels used to separate desks in an open-plan office and arranged an interview area, covering the window side to so that gawkers on the glass-sided end of the building couldn't plague them.

A line of traffic cones with police tape around them marked the 'do not pass' area, mostly to help keep people from overhearing statements. I went off to Human Resources to get a handle on how many people we had to deal with, how to prioritise them, what the work schedules were like and any detail I could get. The guy in charge, Ranjit Singh, would only give basic stuff, no details and no access without a warrant. He was flustered but I wasn't surprised, Human Resources people are only ever comfortable when they run the show and even then most would have withered and died if we still lived our lives through natural selection and the survival of the fittest.

He also bent my ear about the need for getting back to normal; the sample room was an important part of the function of the facility and needed to be back in operation soonest. Deadlines need to be met, samples to process, money would be lost, a tragedy for sure but life goes on. Not if you're a Fish Finger it doesn't.

I did get a list of names of all the Sample Management and Shipping staff. Five minutes later and I'd prised out the full list of everyone who might have access to the freezer, so a list of ten is now a list of 92 including the corpse! I can render that down though. Most would have been off the premises when the death probably occurred and there'll be some sort of electronic list where people used their cards to arrive and leave. We still don't know whether its murder or just unlucky. Has anyone ever committed suicide by freezing, unlikely, or is that what Captain Oates did?

We'll need to push a bit higher for the Fish Fingers personnel file, he was firm on that.

The word is that Fish Finger was last seen between 21:00-23:00 yesterday, in her office -which is where?

Neil, the security cowboy, that might stick too, drags his feet while I get the card reader activity for the freezer room and outside doors. He's wearing some sort of scent, possibly from the 'Maiden Aunt' range. So his rather macho stance, almost a swagger, is a bit bemusing, is he gay? Not sure, but I'd bet a bacon sandwich that his favourite film is 'Reservoir Dogs'. Speaking of bacon, there has to be some with my name on in that cafeteria!

We eventually herded the Sample Management and Shipping staff into one corner of the cafeteria. I keep on wanting to call it a canteen but apparently that does not fit the image they are trying to convey, or so some be-striped creature behind the counter, who could have modelled for Krispy Kreme Donuts, told me. Typically, two of the Sample Management people are missing, the two smokers in the troupe. Charnley is not going to like that if he hears about it; as a manic ex-smoker he is not fond of smokers at all.

DC Banks and DC Prosser are put on statement duty, Sample Management and Shipping staff first. Reid is kept separate; he is in need of a bit more of a detailed chat, he shrugs and goes back to his lasagne, complaining that he 'preferred the poutine in Montreal', whatever that is.

The Fish Finger probably died inside an hour of getting dumped into the freezer. According to Google 'Once your body core temperature hits 27°C, you can become unconscious. Death can happen when your body temperature goes below 22°C. This can take less than an hour. Death can happen faster if you fall into freezing water'. Staff have been muttering that she may have had a pulse of some sort when found. We know that to be untrue but we should keep that to ourselves for now.

So we need to know exactly how long a female, weighing about nine-stones, takes to freeze, then work back from the time of death to find out when she went in. We need to know whether she went into the freezer wet or dry and, if wet, how did she get wet? If wet, it's murder, for sure.

We worked through the list of relevant staff, taking statements and prints. Craig Shepherd, the Shipping Coordinator, is being seen tomorrow morning at home; he's in London today on a course, confirmed. Interesting that he was in last night to receive samples, ladies and gentlemen we have ourselves another candidate!

Reid we did lightly today but will need to do again, although he reckoned the Fish Finger was involved with Shepherd, diversionary tactic maybe? We need to speak with two cleaners – Bangladeshi apparently, not great in English so we need a translator. Maybe Dad can help there, is Bangladeshi and Pakistani the same language or similar enough? They'll be in later or we can call them in early.

Then he did a much more routine completion of his official notebook before grabbing a pre-briefing snack. It might be a late one, it might not.

In the Central Nick, the team and ancillaries all drifted into the main room for the customary close-of-play chat on the big day. The dead board was up, with a few photos and notes.

Thompson handed out the short biography of the Fish Finger, Marie-Eve Legault. The rest of the team and the uniforms all took time to skim through the details.

Marie-Eve Legault, born Hawkesbury, Ontario. D.O.B 31-Jul-1986. Height 5'9", weight 135lbs. Eyes pale blue, hair dark blonde.

Distinguishing features: a scar on her right arm from a fall. Pierced ears, two right, two left. A slightly bifurcated tongue following a childhood accident. *So Fish Finger or Snake-tongue, take your pick.*

Degree from McGill in data management.

No parents (both dead), a brother in British Columbia, has been informed.

French-Canadian. Bilingual, English and French. Identifies as Quebecoise and supports separation (*relevant?*). Worked for NPS for eight years, with a six month break after six years, when she worked for Lemeux BioResearch, Montreal, returning to NPS date tbc. At NPS, which was formerly Heal-Well Contract Research until date tbc, originally a junior in Quality Assurance (which is?), became Head of Department inside four years. On her return to NPS took over as Head of Technical Management.

Arrived in the UK in May as liaison, overseer of transition for technical management and systems, supposed to be here short-term, has now been here just under three months. Has returned to Montreal twice, three days home per visit. Did she have a ticket booked for return; if so, for what date? Tbc.

"Marie-Eve Legault was single with no known serious current relationships in Canada. A brief chat with her friend at NPS Montreal confirmed that, until well before her stint in Nottingham, she was dating one Ben Arjah. It is understood that they split in March sometime. We will talk to Arjah, but it's low priority", Thompson read.

"She lived in Ile Bizard, West Island, Montreal, in her own house, no mortgage. In the UK she was stopping in the Premier Inn, Wilford. Her mobile phone is currently missing; her company laptop is missing too, and we need to find both as a matter of urgency. Off the record for now, there are rumours that she had a brief fling with Craig Shepherd from Shipping. To be confirmed. No known Nottingham relationships, otherwise. The word is that she was a bit of a bitch; not liked, in fact resented".

As usual at this stage, the details were scant but they'd be filling in the blanks over the next day or so. If they hadn't nicked someone for it by the end of the first twenty-four hours, they'd be hearing about it from above.

There was not a lot for the team to go on, no obvious reason why she be stuffed into a freezer to die, or maybe not to die but to be scared off. The stiff was quite young, apparently career-driven, not unattractive but, as per the attached photos, a selfie from her phone, not a stunner either. Having not been around for too long, she must have been pretty quick to climb into bed with Shepherd, if she did, but he was probably just holiday entertainment. She had a decent job and was trusted to come to the UK by senior NPS management. She must have upset somebody, somewhere, though!

After leaving long enough for a bit of speculative chatter, Thompson took the floor. "OK, so now you know more about who she was and her details, such as we have so far. Now we need to find out the 'who, why, where and when' in detail. The 'who' is who put her in the freezer, obviously. She wasn't especially heavy, but it would still take some effort to carry her from somewhere else to the freezer, unless she made her way there of her own accord. It is unlikely that she was killed, or at least incapacitated, inside the freezer, given the cramped nature, but we can't rule it out at this point. The 'why' may be the most interesting bit, and then 'where and when' is down to the autopsy, the answer to that should also help with the 'who'."

Playing Devil's Advocate, Banks asked how they could be sure she wasn't in the freezer by choice when killed. Thompson pointed out the Quality Assurance part of her resume first. If she had been working in the freezer, he thought it fair to presume that she would have been wearing a lab coat and gloves, possibly safety glasses too, all as per Good Laboratory Practice. He'd looked it up on Wiki just to get an idea of it, they'd still need to get more detail though. "Managers don't ignore the rules, they lead by example. True, a killer could have removed the gloves and lab coat, but why bother?"

Prosser asked about the 'Shepherd thing'. "If true, we should look at that in terms of who chucked who, when it ended, and whether there was potentially another lover inside NPS who was jealous or maybe there was another suitor, someone she'd snubbed?"

Thompson told the group that the source of the rumour was Reid. "Was it true or just spite? How did Reid and Shepherd get on, any friction?"

"Work envy, problem staff, anything shady about her in Montreal?" Laura Knight offered to go to Montreal to find out more details, amid lots of laughter, but Thompson said he couldn't see the Nottinghamshire Police funding a shopping trip for her or anyone else; they needed a contact name in the Montreal Police.

"Royal Canadian Mounted Police" said Fasildad, "also known as the RCMP".

Thompson nodded, "I'll let you sort that one out then, Dad", he said.

The door suddenly opened and in strolled the Detective Inspector. "Right everybody, if we can begin". Charnley had growled out the call to order, as he always did. The room hardly snapped to it but, within a minute or two, he had their mostly undivided attention.

"Point one. The deceased is Marie-Eve Legault a Canadian from Montreal. She is on an open-ended secondment to Nash Pharmaceutical Solutions from their Montreal operation. She lived in Wilford in company lodgings. She ran the technical side of the company in Montreal and is here to pass on her experience following a take-over".

Thompson passed Charnley the info sheet which he read quickly. A voice from the floor said "Was, Sir".

"What?" said Charnley.

"She was on secondment, Sir, not is, not present tense".

Charnley looked at the uniform that had commented. "Thank you, Carole-fucking-Vordeman for that piece of astute thinking", nobody laughed.

Three of the older members of the team looked at each other; they were trying to work out who had won the 'Charnley's next crap joke' sweep. Thompson thought he was closest by a week; it tended to go by big margins.

Charnley resumed.

"Point two. The deceased, and I hear you have a nickname for her which will not be used in my, nor any senior officer's, presence, on pain of suspension, clear?" The room muttered a 'Sir'. Was that an attempt at a second joke, no, surely not, two on the same day!

"The deceased was found dead in a freezer with an operating temperature of -20°C. Pathology is not yet in but expected very soon, by tomorrow at least, if not, chase it".

Thompson offered his apologies in advance for interrupting and pointed out that the body had only been removed a couple of hours ago and that it would take some time to defrost naturally. "How long", said Charnley.

"Google reckons two to three hours for 3lb of meat. The fi... deceased weighed around 135lbs, Sir."

"And therefore?"

"A few more hours than normal, we think possibly 24-hours, Sir". Bang! Before Thompson could continue, off went Charnley, ranting and raving and spraying spittle in all directions. Thompson was about to suggest that Charnley faced the office Peace Lily when he went off on one; that way at least it would give the leaves a misting, but he thought better of it.

A few loud minutes passed before Thompson cut in with the news that the body was to be wrapped in plastic and submerged to accelerate the defrosting process but it still might be a while before it was ready.

A hushed, muttered ripple of 'oven ready' went around the room but Charnley still had blood pounding in his ears and heard nothing very clearly. Still, that didn't stop him glaring at the room in general.

Thompson stepped in again, trying to anticipate and avoid any more ranting, and carried on with the briefing. "The thinking is that the deceased was alive when she went into the freezer. There were no obvious signs of trauma initially, but there are lumps on the back of her head that could be from being dumped in the freezer – that aside it is thought likely that she froze to death. The observant amongst you", and he pointed to the corpse photos on the dead board, "will have noticed that her skin and clothing had a blue hue; that may well have been floor cleaner, the lab will tell us. If it is, then she was probably either wet when she went in, or someone threw a bucket of floor cleaner on her; this would hasten her untimely demise. Questions?"

The temptation to say 'please, Sir', was suppressed by all, just. Instead they all trotted out what they knew Charnley wanted to hear, giving a chorus of "suspects, Sir?"

Charnley scanned the room again, rather like a perched owl looking around a grassy field, hoping to spot a slight movement out of place, something to pounce on mercilessly. He'd also calmed down a bit and so took the lead in the briefing once more, without acknowledging Thompson.

"There are 273 suspects, 244 of whom we can reasonably rule out. The scientists, the analysts, the HR people, the management of the facility and what they call 'Quality Assurance'. That leaves those in the Sample Management department, those in Shipping, those in Security, a few cleaners and the sample delivery person, who we have yet to formally identify, as I understand it".

Thompson was about to ask quite how such a large swathe of people, with access and, possibly, a motive that they were, as yet, unaware of, had managed to avoid being suspects when DC Banks shot up her hand and asked broadly the same question.

Again, Charnley adopted the poised-to-pounce owl pose; then he launched into something that, while not a rant, might be thought of as more of an instructional lecture. "Banks, professional people do not commit this sort of crime. They many embezzle, they may steal but not violently, they may even misappropriate with intent to permanently deprive, but they are professional, intelligent, qualified. I see no connection between them and some Canadian woman whom they barely knew, did not encounter in their work sphere and who, to a man, would have no obvious motive for killing her".

The same uniform chirped up again. Thompson shrank back in his seat; he wasn't alone. Still, I suppose this is how they learn. "Sir, she is a French-Canadian and surely the intelligent people at NPS, and elsewhere, are both men and women?"

Charnley looked at the officer, his face showing no sign of what might be drifting through his mind. He picked up the phone and gently punched in a number without removing his victim from his gaze. The room sat waiting, wondering 'what now?' On this occasion Charnley didn't explode, he never even sounded particularly angry, just sort of disappointed that his fellow officers did not immediately understand his perspective. His perfectly correct perspective, as far as he was concerned.

When the call ended, Charnley then looked directly at the rest of the room but ignoring the uniform and just said loudly "Sgt Blaney in Community Liaison is expecting you, now".

And that was it; we'd lost a body on the investigative team and that would mean that any contribution that the uniform might have made was now an added little bonus for rest of them to pull in, great.

The briefing broke up and, as usual, divided up into the regular little units; uniforms and plain-clothes or, for want of a better word, cliques, to chew the cud. Thompson, Banks, DC Laura Knight and DC Ismael Fasildad (Dad) took to a corner of the room and began earnest debate. DC Liam Prosser stood like a lemon in the middle of the room for a while before heading over. Just as well he did, as Thompson was about to go and fetch him. Prosser was a fairly new part of the team and could appear a bit standoffish. Thompson had as good as said so to Prosser, telling him it didn't do to disenfranchise people and that he should make an effort to be less 'Ulster'. Once he'd settled down, Thompson had a hunch that Prosser would be fine, they just all had to get to know him, and he, them.

Meanwhile, Charnley was stood with his hands on hips in the middle of the room, staring at the dead board. "Right", he suddenly announced to no one, "time to start interviewing the suspects properly, but I think we can all see who did it by now". And with that he strode off purposefully, out of the room and into his office, closing the door behind him with a 'do not disturb me' vigour that most of his team knew and loved.

Banter was always a part of these things. Gallows humour too, and so Thompson let the group off the leash to get the jokes and puns out of their system. There would plenty of time for the serious stuff later, although it would be hard not to argue that, with a body defrosting in the mortuary, the serious stuff, for the Fish Finger, had surely already happened.

The discussion, which their HR had told them to call 'focussed brainstorming' in a recent procedural memo, was supposed to end with one name on the table on the red cards, one on the white and the others on the blue. The coloured cards were the new team code for 'Primary Interest' - red, 'Secondary Interest' - white and 'Outsiders' on blue, unlikely but still possible in the suspect stakes. For now they were divided in thought, with Reid or Shepherd on every red card available. Orinoco Smith or Neil Martin were on white. Always take the finder and/or the shagger first, then the next two most likely, then work out the rest; it was a plan, of sorts.

Thompson called time on the proceedings, just as an unknown uniform popped her head around the door, bearing paper. "Tomorrow's case priorities, courtesy of DI Charnley, Sir, sent by email. I printed it for you".

Thompson took it and shrugged, it looks like great minds think alike. Number #1, REID, number #2, SHEPHERD, number #3, MARTIN, really?, and then, in capitals in case it was missed. LOOK NO FURTHER. No mention of Smith though, despite her being there before Reid arrived and found the body, odd!

On hearing the news that Granny was now teaching them all how to suck eggs, again, they went their separate ways.

# THREE

Glad to get home, Thompson climbed the stairs to his 'Bread-and-lard Island' flat. He'd had to explain that one to Rebecca! Coming from a well-to-do southern family, such things as having to eat just bread and lard in order to afford the rent would never have cropped up. Now she knew about it, she sort-of revelled in it, He'd heard her telling some of her friends on the phone, he could almost hear their gasps.

He was luckier than most, he got the rent on the flat cheap provided he acted as occasional caretaker for his mate's father, who owned it and the other three flats; each a part of the conversion of the large Victorian house, originally built to be a home for a family with servants. Thompson was happy for the leg-up; it meant they could save hard for their own place. The overtime helped, especially as Rebecca got nearer to D-Day, called 'D-Day' not because it was 'the' big day but because it was when Rebecca's snooty family would descend on them to take 'dominating' control and he'd be made to feel like a common pauper, which he was, of course.

With luck and no financial disasters, and he tried hard not to think of the now wriggling bump in those terms, they'd be looking to buy a small but perfectly functional terrace not too far down the line. The trouble with being in the police is that little terraced properties in the city came with their own local criminal baggage. There was always a chance that he'd be recognised by the neighbours and it might then result in some unpleasantness, but he had a plan. In a previous life, he'd shared a house in a mining village on the Notts-Derbyshire border. The miners were long gone, most of the properties were being bought by couples similar to them, and so being a Police Officer there wouldn't be quite such an issue. It would be an extra thirty minutes in, each way, but that wasn't so bad and at least they would be on the up instead of treading water all the time. Rebecca could have her dog, too.

He was surprised at how hungry he was. He knew she'd have dinner on the table, like a good northern wife. What that dinner would be depended on how vegetarian she felt. On a good day there would be some meat, on a bad one it would be borderline vegan. Thompson felt he was being corralled into an area of gastric discomfort he'd never have chosen unaided, but he never let on; she tried so hard and he really did appreciate it, really he did.

Result, macaroni cheese with bits of bacon, thank you pregnancy, and there was a tin of stout waiting, not cooled but allowed to adopt room temperature as if it was a fancy French wine that you had to sell a kidney to be able to afford. Thompson was surprised at how quickly you could get a taste for stout, even though it was pretty far removed from the Australian lager he'd been weaned on. He suspected that Rebecca had bought a book, or more likely been on-line, to find out how northern women take care of their men and no matter how many times he'd tried to get her to let him cook, she'd flatly refused. Was the rest of his life really going to be a catering event scripted by the Tingley branch of the Mrs. Beeton Appreciation Society?

The northern thing was something else that perplexed Thompson. She'd decided that, because he was Nottinghamshire born and bred, that he would relate to flat caps, Whippets and stout! True, Nottinghamshire was somewhat further north than Surrey, but it was Midlands not true north. It wasn't that her attitude was meant to take the piss, but it could come across that way if you didn't know her.

Sitting at the scrubbed farmhouse table, bought in expectation of one day having a kitchen to put it in - it would go right in front of the Aga, perhaps bearing a set of butter pats left carelessly on it for authenticity - he tucked into the macaroni cheese while she waddled around the room, with obvious effort and discomfort.

He knew how the next bit went. She'd be looking in hope that all was well and he'd motion that it was the most fabulous meal he had ever eaten, and often it was, pretty much. To be fair, his mother's cooking only just beat raw roadkill, but he'd become very used to it and so the new and fancy menus that were coming his way didn't always sit lightly on the increasingly distended stomach. That was another thing northern, the portions would have fed a football team.

Rebecca grunted as she moved around, the bump was a fair job to haul around all day but she'd never complained. She finally stopped fussing and sat down with a tired exhale, "good day?" Thompson nodded, mouth full. He didn't really like to talk much business at home, mostly because it was so boring that he felt he might be in danger of losing his reputation as her feisty bit of rough. His mate, Alan, called him that all the time, he was only joking but Thompson could see the assumption, well enough.

Dinner over, Thompson stood to clear up and almost had to force Rebecca back into her seat. "We are a democracy", he announced. "We share the load". This time she capitulated pretty quickly, poor sod must have been really knackered to give in without the obligatory light-hearted skirmish.

Generally, Rebecca wouldn't read news that upset her, but she'd seen the body in the freezer story and guessed that Thompson might be working on it, not that he could give her any more than the paper had. "Is it true she was frozen solid"?

"Afraid so, well nearly, it just makes everything so much harder", and Thompson told her all about Charnley and the defrosting. It was a safe enough area and she'd never dream of breathing a word to anyone else anyway. He got that frown from her when he made a joke about Fish Fingers and the chance of the frozen body being dropped on the floor and the poor victim feeling shattered. Not surprising, it was a pretty bad joke for home.

Sticking to public details mainly, she seemed oddly fascinated but then just as quickly turned her attention to pudding, jam roly-poly with tinned custard, just as he liked it. There was a lot to be said for domestic bliss, after a tricky day.

Rebecca turned on the TV, her reality TV show was on and she knew that Thompson looked forward to his hour of writing. She encouraged him, reckoned he was the next Alan Bennett or even D. H. Lawrence. So every night he got his hour at the laptop and she got her witless garbage from the self-aggrandising idiots they found for those things. Would they ever do a police reality TV show he wondered, viewers glued to the screen as the officer spent two hours writing up a report for a crime he knew had been committed and by whom but that the frequently spineless Criminal Prosecution Service would not even look at? Doubt it.

# FOUR

Tracey was half way through her morning croissant when the detective came over, checking her name and asking her to follow him for interview. He was quite gravel-voiced, not loud but forceful.

The rumour that was sweeping the site was that Marie-Eve Legault had been found dead. 'Well good, she deserved it. Best not to say that out loud though', Tracey thought, 'they might think that I killed her'.

"Right" he said "I am Detective Constable Prosser. Is it Miss, Ms. or Mrs. Mills?"

"Do I look like a matronly piano player?" Prosser looked completely confused by that, what the hell was she talking about?

"Sorry" she said, "Just trying to ease the tension a bit. Mrs. Mills was quite a famous lady who played songs from the music hall on her piano. I think she died in the late 70s or something. My Gran had all her records but you've obviously never heard of her."

"No, sadly, now if you'd said Dana or Delores O'Riordan, I'd have been with you but Mrs. Mills, no", and he laughed a bit. It had worked after all, then.

Tracey piped up. "I hear that there has been a body found in suspicious circumstances. You are going to need prints from me and a detailed account of my movements before and during the approximate time of death. You will also want to know what I do here and whether I had any contact with Legault, the stiff, and what my opinion of her and of my colleagues is, am I right?"

"Are you ex-police?"

"No, but my ex had enough run-ins with you lot that I know how it all works. He was doing stuff I didn't know about; I chucked him when I found out. You helped me out there, it should be all on record, you can check".

Prosser was swimming against the stream a bit. Tracey was talking a lot, some of it not making sense, and she clearly had a lot more to tell, he'd better check that he'd got a spare pen in case this one runs out. One thing was pretty clear; she wasn't who they were looking for.

He let her run away with herself for a while, jotting the odd comment as potentially interesting but most of it was yap. When a convenient gap arrived, she may have just been taking the chance to breathe, he cut in. "Well, Tracey, I'm sure you have lots more to tell me about the victim and, since you seem to have decided it is someone we haven't confirmed as involved yet, can we start there?"

Tracey's mouth seemed to work independently of the rest of her, certainly her brain was rarely involved once her jaw had reached top gear. Prosser tried to look beneath the veneer, behind the self-defensive gabbling, but all he could see was Tracey. She was OK; his mum might call her 'blousy', he'd add 'wearing' to that description. She worked with Craig Shepherd though, perhaps closely, she seemed the type, so he'd have to steer her that way a bit, she might have the insights that someone who fancied him might share.

"Are you involved in a physical relationship with your boss, Craig Shepherd, at all?"

"Blimey, that was left-field, as they say! Craig, no, he is a pussycat and pretty easy to manipulate. I only have to mention 'women's troubles' and I can get half a day if I need it. I flirted with him a bit but I cleared it with Jemmy first, his wife and a mate. That Legault woman was a piece of work though, nasty with it, I didn't like her at all. I don't know what men saw in her".

"Men like Craig?"

"I don't know about that, ask him". The last comment had a bit of 'old lag's wife' about it. Prosser knew he'd get nothing else there. He guided her back to her own movements and it all looked fine; when not at work, she was either shopping or at home or with her new boyfriend. Maybe I'll just give her a push in another direction.

"Do you have any relevant thoughts regarding Simon Reid or Richard Greenwood for me?"

"Reid is a bit quiet, he doesn't take any teasing. Greenwood I've only seen once, that was when he was given a tour in his first week. He was unmemorable but he did stare at my tits, though. Men do, but you haven't".

"No, Tracey, when we become detectives we are given tit aversion courses to help us keep our minds on the witnesses or suspects".

"Which am I?"

"As far as I can tell, you are neither but that might change with evidence. If you do have anything you want to tell me, in confidence, that might help us move the inquiry along, now is the time".

"I can't think of anything, Detective Constable but, if I do, I'll be sure to ask for you and I might even try a different top and no bra, just to see how well that aversion training took".

"I think I'll cope alright, Tracey. The training is very rigorous and I've spent my life preparing. Off you go then, and thanks".

As Tracey went back to her table, she wondered what he meant, preparing for what all his life?

Prosser looked at his list, he hoped that there were no more like Tracey Mills out there. Now, which one was Moonbeam Orinoco Smith?

39

# FIVE

The traffic was as bad as usual, that's what came from living down town. Traffic cameras plotted your every move; no margin for error. Getting stopped and your details checked would not be a welcome thing, so the pedal stayed constant, two miles per hour under or less, taking it easy.

At least at this time in the morning everything was moving. An hour later and you can add another 45 minutes to your journey, easy. The car needed cleaning but that didn't hang with Mo's persona, always too busy having fun, hanging out in the hip gay bars, doing shots, on the pull.

Sometimes your head puts up barriers and blocks inconvenient thoughts. For Mo, that thought was that these days she usually preferred to be in bed just after ten, her own bed. She hadn't been to a bar and done shots for the best part of two years and she'd descended into a world of fiction of her own making. She just couldn't imagine being ordinary though, she had to have an edge, that's what people liked about her, what people wanted, expected, so that is what they got.

Work was work. Sample Management was her third department at NPS in three years, somehow she always got moved on and not out. It helped that one of the bosses was a close, personal friend, and that Mo had a history there. But that was done long ago, before the advent of her forties, when she was more Mo than she was now.

For reasons that nobody ever really understood, Mo identified with black. Rap music, a way of talking, crying all day when Michael Jackson died, what was that all about? At times she struggled to keep track of all the false trails laid over the years. Moving departments so often had helped, but a fresh slate of interested minds also added even more complications to what, in truth was not that fascinating a life now.

She breezed through the turnstiles, giving a 'hey' to everyone in earshot, a knuckle touch with Neil and wearing what she thought was her 'enigmatic grin' face, headed to her desk, freshly bought coffee in hand. The first hour was always the best. She could play her own music, have the place to herself and kick back before the orders started to be barked. Her Facebook had the usual stuff, 723 friends but she'd only met about 20 of them and five would be in this room later. Her iPod pumped out some generic rap, the sort where rhyming was more important that content or quality. 'Enjoy it while you can', she thought, 'the beast will be here soon enough'.

A ping from her phone told her that he'd arrived, thanks Neil. Music off just after he appeared, just long enough for him to frown. Log on to the work system, gather paper, set something going on the printer, a couple of emails would do. Reid was early; she'd only had 25 minutes to herself this time, the bastard. It was probably deliberate to wind her up.

"Hi Simon, good night last night?" Always the same question, make them think they are missing out, she knew full well that Simon Reid was not a party person.

"Fine, you?"

"It was a late one, look at my eyes. See, man, I gotta learn to go home earlier, too old man, the old body can't do the business any more".

She suspected that Reid knew, and that her little charade was wasted on him. He never said anything to her though, nor to anybody else as far as she could tell. One of her girlies would surely tell her if he did.

She busied herself doing nothing, ha, working the whole day through, not a very hip song to be today's ear worm but about right.

41

Reid was busy too and she knew she'd have a shit-load of samples to log pretty soon. At least the donkey-work was being done elsewhere now, no more trying to figure out how to make the study design in the sample management software, Clousseau, work. Clousseau, from a software company that couldn't spell Clouseau – perhaps something had been lost in the translation.

Of all Mo's work-related shortcomings, she was aware that her lack of computer savvy was the worst. After being in Sample Management for an undistinguished six months, she still didn't know how to do the basics and she knew it was only a matter of time before she got shunted sideways again. Maybe try the Shipping Department next time, that student Christine was cute!

The room mood, such as it was with only two people in it, was mellow. Perhaps Reid had had a good night after all, maybe he got laid, maybe I should ask? He wasn't dumping stuff around the desks, he wasn't swearing at his emails under his breath, he wasn't even taking time to have a quiet word, something he and Mo did around once a week, usually after another brain-freeze day.

He went past her and through to the freezers, coat and gloves in place like a good little lab rat.

Suddenly the mood changed, everything changed.

Reid came out of the Freezer Room behaving differently. Was he shaken or annoyed? It was hard to tell, he'd be a great poker player. He looked across briefly but there was no clue at all as to what had happened. Was I seeing something that was not there, projecting my inner Wilma Mitty again?

He went to the phone but was barely audible, now what? Then suddenly she could hear him. She thought he'd said "Mo, go to the cafeteria please. Try to stop our people coming up here, get them drinking their coffee down there, you need to do this now". Mo was a bit confused by his karma, besides, the rest of the sheep were all filing in by now, anyway.

She was about to boil over. She always did when he barked orders, 'I don't take no shit from no one', but this time there was something. Not the irritated edge she usually got from him when she'd screwed up, not the frustration when she faced him down, just a clear, crisp instruction that had to be obeyed. For once, she was his faithful dog.

Mo paused to ask what was going on but Reid had moved on. He'd told everyone to go, was on the phone again with one hand and writing notices on A4 sheets with the other. She got her gear and saw that the notices were saying we were closed. 'No Entry'. What the fuck?

In the cafeteria, our lot had trickled down to their regular spots and were more than happy to delay the time when they dipped their fingers into trays of dry ice, nobody asked why, even. Some might have thought it was culling time again, but there was no extra security, no atmosphere of doom.

She went over and asked Neil, he'd know. He said that he couldn't talk right now, stuff to do, important stuff, and then he shut the Security Office door. Well, fuck you too, then, Neil.

So we gathered in the cafeteria, two groups. The older girls were gabbing about kids and stuff, me and my girlies were chatting Khardashians and Lady Gaga. Shots and sex.

Inside fifteen minutes or so, a bunch of suits arrived and were collected by Reid. They went off in what looked like the direction of our room, Reid talking, animated even, the suits following, listening, mostly. Police, Babylon!

After half an hour or so, more people arrived in the cafeteria. Analysts were complaining about not getting their samples, some scientists were asking questions but getting no answers. Then a ripple of chatter went around the room, a Mexican Wave of gossip with one subject, death. Who though?

Mo's phone blipped again, Neil. *'Sorry, body, freezer, more later when I can, sorry'*.

She didn't know where the shaking came from but this was real, a body, in the freezer. She'd sat at her work station not 20 feet from a body, a dead body, in a place she went to 30 times a day, well maybe 10. Who, though? Who had died and how? Mo looked around the room, nobody was missing, none of their group, they were all blissfully unaware of what was happening right where they worked, every day, it was surreal.

Even more suits and some uniforms then arrived and started rearranging the furniture. Mo and her troupe had to decamp to a busier part of the cafeteria. No more rude-talk or someone would complain, again. She noticed Josie from HR looking at her. What did that nosy cow want, another warning? She could hear her sing-song voice in her head now. "Mo, people are talking about you and the students, rumours of inappropriate comments and conversations. Is there anything in it?" The short answer was "no". The longer answer, the one she'd delivered had had a lot of expletives in it and Josie had seemed shocked, as if she didn't grasp every word directed at her. There was no warning this time, just what was supposed to be a friendly comment to not get involved, be careful. Be careful yourself Josie, I know people, important people, dangerous people.

Mo looked away and deliberately avoided Josie's eye, turning back to the girls and laughing loudly at some joke about a man with two willies.

It took an age, but eventually some uniforms and suits started to select people from the Sample Management crew, she was amongst the first. It was just a chat they said, routine, gathering information, background stuff. In her best laid-back voice she said "go for it", loud enough for her girls to hear, maintaining her level of cool with them. 'Hey, mind my stash guys' and they all laughed, the police goon ignored her, leading her to a quieter area.

Behind a partition in the cafeteria was a man and a woman she'd seen earlier, filth, sat there waiting for her. She smiled, despite feeling the involuntary shaking from her feet to her ears. Could they see that? Would they think that she had something to hide because of the shaking?

They took details and started asking questions. When did you arrive, where were you last night, real TV -crime sort of stuff. After a couple of minutes the woman asked if she was alright, the shakes were harder now. Mo brushed off her concern. "Cold", she said, "and I have health problems". Was there a flash of concern, even sympathy from both there, good cop, good cop?

Mo was assured that they wouldn't keep her long and then they continued to ask simple questions, getting mostly simple answers.' Had they spoken to Reid yet?', she thought. Had he mentioned her talking about drinking late shots last night, or her eyes, which he never looked at? She knew he wouldn't, she was sure.

After about fifteen minutes they ran through the statement, just checking details they said. When it got to the part where she'd told them she'd been out, she almost back-tracked, was about to say 'sorry, that was the night before, my brain eh!' but they didn't look the sort to accept a sudden body-swerve as a mistake so she left it.

She shook some more, bad enough that she desperately wanted to tell them that she'd been in all night and only the grumpy guy from Domino's Pizza had seen her, about 6:30pm when he'd delivered to her. She'd paid by cash and the box and receipt were in the bin behind her house, but they'd stopped writing and talking.

After a short while they'd clearly done with her, so she asked about the body. The female suit gave her a sideways look but the man said 'yes, a body had been found', no other details would be released and he'd only told her because rumours were sweeping the facility and they understood that she had lots of contacts and could put the word out for calm. At that she seemed to swell, gifted them her winning smile as she left without wondering how they knew about her.

She went back to her girls, who by now were all deep in a phone-driven world of entertainment. In less than a minute, Mo had confirmed the body story but she couldn't say anything more about the investigation at this time. The police, the stern-looking one and the dull woman, 'Officer Drabble', had advised her not to. 'Officer Drabble', good one. Mo!

It was sometime later that the identity of the body came on her news feed, Marie-Eve. Neil had then texted the exact same information to her moments later. Marie-Eve. Dead.

The Sample Management department was shut for the day, at least. HR assured everyone that they would be paid and those that had already seen the police dispersed. The rest waited impatiently, the novelty of a corpse on the premises superseded by the boredom of having to wait to be seen, even though they were getting paid to do it.

Mo got it together long enough to get home. It was the middle of the afternoon, the traffic just starting to build but it was an easy enough run home. She texted Neil, 'can we talk?' Immediately her phone rang, it was Neil with the scoop. Reid had found Marie-Eve dead in the walk-in. Not an accident, though, in his opinion and no word on the cause of death. The police had shut down Sample Management and the place had gone quiet early, with most people leaving. The management were running around like headless chickens, especially Greenwood and Ranji. 'Beer later?'

Mo didn't want to go out again and Neil wasn't working now until tomorrow, so he was invited over, picking her up a pre-ordered Indian takeaway, he was driving past anyway. They chewed the cud deep into the night, rehashing plots and theories. Neil didn't have a very high opinion of Marie-Eve; he reckoned she had little regard for the likes of Security staff. Mo tried to defend her but trod a careful line between backing up someone she hardly knew and upsetting an old friend, of sorts.

It ended up being a late night. They drank beer then she sipped some terrible Ouzo that she'd kept in a cupboard for six years, a relic of her last foreign trip to Greece, of Halkidiki bag fame. Neil had been careful though, surely under they both thought and he had not too far to go. Tomorrow was going to be an interesting day for her and Reid, but not for Marie-Eve, not now.

"Got to go Mo, do you need anything, you know; to keep you going, keep your spirits up?"

Mo was surprised, "I thought you'd cleaned up your act after last time, I won't help if you get off your head again; I can't, not now".

"Nothing hard Mo, just a little recreational – it helps me at night, helps me keep on the ball on long night shifts, I can handle it".

'Yeah, right', thought Mo. "Well, don't buy around here, there are cameras everywhere, you be careful".

"I have a quiet place I can go, in, out, and away, one of many, no cameras where I go".

Mo shook her head, "slippery slope Neil, I know, I've seen it before".

It was disappointing for Mo to find out that Neil was still using something this way, she'd somehow missed it; she wasn't as sharp as she used to be. After he'd gone and she'd sorted out the recycling she realised in a moment of clarity that anyone who was there at NPS, overnight, like Neil, was a suspect. Might Neil have killed Marie-Eve just because she showed him no respect? He did fancy himself, played up the role. Not a great motive but he might kill in the wrong circumstances, he just might.

47

Hitting the pillow late, her alarm pre-set, Mo giggled. Her eyes would be red from shots tomorrow for sure and she'd make sure Reid saw them, if he was still around.

# Six

For Reid, a frozen Marie-Eve was way better than a defrosted one. He'd have said 'living' but he'd doubted, occasionally vocally, that Marie-Eve had been human at all. She had been cold to most people but particularly to him and he'd tried, really tried, but like so many managers she'd never been one to listen to anything other than her own voice.

It wasn't that she was dead so much as she was dead in one of his freezers, and she'd be stopping them getting on with what made their days pass, structured work. It was this structure that forced each working day along, something that needed to be done, that occupied the time at work. For Reid there was nothing worse than being at work and having nothing to do. Having nothing to do was what you chose to occupy your own time with.

Reid realised that he was actually more concerned about getting behind with the Saviour samples than he was about dead Marie-Eve. He felt a connection to the study because it had been he that had figured out how to work it in Nottingham, he that had set up a system to log the samples into Clousseau, their Laboratory Information Management System, and he that had got the Sample Management team all, or most of them, onside with it. Mentally, he was calculating not just the delays in clearing the analysis of samples that they already had, but also in the processing of those he knew, or at least had come to expect, would be on their way.

The thing with the Saviour study was that it was exotic, and in Contract Research you very rarely got exotic. Mostly it was just batches of samples, put in the system, analysed and the data shipped to the clients. The Saviour samples came from places he'd had to look up on Google Earth. Tashkent, Accra, Bujumbura, Vientiane, Davao, and his favourite, Balikpapan. In all these places and more, nurses would be taking blood from people enrolled in the study, taking the samples along to their shipping services and then they all ended up in Nottingham, via the Central Lab in Mexico City.

At one time even Mexico City would have been exotic.

Reid knew that Marie-Eve dying in the freezer might not just screw up the working days for him but that he had to be in the minds of the police as a strong suspect, too. He rationalised that there were two main suspects, him and Craig, and then perhaps the security on the night, which was probably Neil.

He ruled out the cleaners and anyone else working late. He very much doubted that it would be one of the scientists, there were always a few of them working late, usually the new ones who tended to burn the midnight oil to keep up, make an impression, or just hit the unrealistic deadlines the bosses had agreed with the clients. It would all come down to the time of death.

A fleeting thought jumped into his head. Mo, she was there before him. How quickly would a body look frozen, could she have killed Legault? He cleared it as quickly as it arrived. Mo a killer? Ha, maybe in her own head but not in the real world.

Maybe he should mention his Montreal trip and the Warning thing to the police. It had certainly seemed to sour things a bit with Marie-Eve; if anything, she was more off-hand with him afterwards. Would they think he held a grudge because of that? Surely not, it was a nothing as far as Reid was concerned. Was it in his employee record here? Perhaps, he'd have to ask Ranji, he got on OK with him, even slipped him the odd bit of rogue employee information from time to time, although that hadn't helped him get rid of Mo. If it was in his file, then the police would surely have that now, they'd have the files for all of their suspects. Would the company give them up easily, data protection and all that, would they need warrants? If they had warrants, they'd only get them for 'persons of interest', that would be a clue as to whether he was, or wasn't, in the shit.

Perhaps he should play nice and go and chat with Mo. For all her bullshit stories she did find stuff out, she had her girls all over the company and she usually got to hear the most accurate rumours, she was nigh on 100% right about the rif. Yes, he'd be nice, share the conspiracy, he'd be sure to let her know that she was a suspect too, though, even if she wasn't. He'd infer that they had a bond there, something to team up against. That should bring her onside, into the fold of potential murderers, unless she had actually done it!

It proved hard to get Mo on her own after Ice Storm Marie-Eve, as Reid had started calling her. He'd been mildly rebuked by Bez Dooley for saying that out loud, not to Bez, but to one of his minions, Julie Miller, a lab tech and reckoned to be the Facebook spy. She was the one who always Facebook-friended everyone in the company and then reported back any public comments or discontent to management. Reid had claimed to Bez that it was gallows humour; a way of dealing with the tragedy, and that had kept it off the record, one less blot on the already messy copybook.

When he did get to talk to Mo she was worried, not her usual blah-blah self. No talk of partying late, famous people she knew or who she was seeing. No sex talk, Mo did like to talk sex talk. He'd never seen her like this; smaller, shrivelled, deflated. It was like the shiny, brash Mo had been scrubbed clean of the glamour and was now just as sad as the rest of them, something Reid had seen through anyway but now, seeing it as her public face too, made it all the more real.

The cafeteria had buzzed as usual but Mo was taking her morning break on her own and she never sat on her own. It seemed that there was a force-field around her and people were actively taking a circuitous route to their tables rather than chance being near Mo. Reid arrived and sat next to her, she looked up, she looked like shit. "Not good for us this, Mo, not good at all". She was unfocussed, she usually was, but this seemed much deeper, like there was nothing else in there, the lights are off and everybody has moved abroad. "So what do you know, apart from the fact that you, me and Craig are the potential killers of Marie-Eve in the eyes of the police?"

It came out with a whimper. "Man, we've got to stick together. I didn't kill Marie-Eve, she was my friend, my amigo, we did shots together".

Reid fought hard not to roll his eyes, she might appear dead from the neck up but she was still spouting the same bullshit. "I didn't know you knew Marie-Eve outside of work, I thought she didn't mix with anyone here".

"I told you, we did shots, loads of times. She'd come into the bar, just come in and sit next to me and talk, more and more about stuff as she sank more and more shots and, man, she could do shots".

"That probably means that you knew her best then, Mo, you need to tell the police all that stuff, unless you killed her".

No reaction, maybe she had killed her, then she said "not me, I didn't kill her, but I know she was seeing someone from here, doing the jiggy with them but she never said who. A manager I think, someone high up, Marie-Eve liked high up, she was ambitious. She told me stuff about Montreal, about her men and women there, about her life there, stuff".

Reid was a bit surprised, was it really just him that thought that Marie-Eve's jiggy partner was Craig Shepherd? "Tell the police what you know, Mo, they'll find out sooner or later, you need to talk to them, properly, and on your own terms".

She shook her head, "no, not yet".

Then he asked "who do you think did it or is in the frame, who would have killed her - besides you or me, joke!"

"Yeah, besides you and me, because we are both very much in the police's thinking, I know that, they got everything on us from Ranji".

So, I was right, thought Reid, he was a suspect. "As far as I can see there is me, you and Craig that the police will focus on, at first anyway. I didn't do it so I'm not worried".

Said like that it sounded so simple, but would Dave Thompson and his people see it that way? Reid had seen enough detective shows to know that they wouldn't charge anyone without evidence and, since there could be no evidence other than circumstantial where he was concerned, it was not a problem for him, at least. As he was innocent of all charges, he'd throw himself on the mercy of Great British Justice and take his chances.

Mo swilled her coffee around, it was time to get back to her desk; she'd been surprised that Reid hadn't mentioned it. The anal twat was always on her case. "There are more people on their radar than us, Simon", and with that she creaked into an upright position and shuffled off back towards the Sample Management room.

Talking to Mo had surprisingly helped a little bit, given him a degree of clarity that allowed him to focus on the prime suspect. Craig Shepherd, it had to be. Mo had said that others were in the police thoughts, so logically, they also had the means, the motive and the opportunity. Narrowing down the list was easy, all that he needed to know was who else had been around the Freezer Room at the time of death, which must have been after nine in the evening and 07:10 the next morning. It was a fairly big field to aim at, but he knew how to go about it and just where to look.

Back in the Sample Management room, Reid looked around him. Everywhere was the usual frenzy of activity, all taking place as if nothing had happened. In this little drama, he thought, there are the players and there are the extras and this lot are definitely the extras.

# SEVEN

Phones pinged all around NPS, *'Hey guys, tied up with shit, catch you later, Mo'*. The constant yacking about the murder was getting to Mo and the police attention was getting wearing, too. Not that they were leaning on her, they were just there all the time, a presence, an intrusion and she felt trapped by it. She'd intended to have her lunch away, outside, maybe on one of the nature reserve benches; it was a fine day so why not?

It was such a short walk that Mo found herself irritated, annoyed that she didn't do this more often, on fine days, it was so nice. The reserve was an old, disused clay pit. The whole site used to be covered in borrow pits, places where they dug out clay, things that they did in olden days. It was a real wildlife haven, before the bulldozers came and did their dirty work. The site that was now just a sop nature reserve was easily four or five times larger, originally.

Mo remembered a thing about naturalists dashing to the site when the council gave the 'go' for the business park, on a deadline to dig up hundreds of orchids and try to transplant them in other places, to save them from the tarmac. Did some go to Colwick Park? She thought so but didn't remember seeing them there, not that she got there very often now, not now that her old dog wasn't the motivation to do the circuit of the lakes what with being dead and all. She should get another one, someone to talk to, an 'old lady' dog. Another bullet to bite, sometime soon.

The bench was a simple affair, in keeping with the site, blending in. Just two sections of log and a board nailed across did the job. It was a bit damp in bad weather but OK otherwise, rustic even.

Lunch was not as exciting as she'd like it to be, it was a single person's lunch, made in a hurry and with no real imagination to it. By rights she should be lunching on a yacht in the Adriatic like Shirley Valentine. The aquamarine ocean looking inviting, the food all light salads, olives, Greek cheese and a variety of breads, a glass of local red wine to sip, rough in taste but serviceable. She would feel the sun on her face, her back and her legs and tits, all bare flesh and a tiny bikini bottom. She laughed; maybe 25 years ago she'd have looked good in a tiny bikini bottom, now she didn't think so!

Reid was deep in thought; that was nothing new for him though. He always thought things through and those that didn't know him well enough, formed the opinion that he might be either off-hand or a little bit slow, mentally. He wasn't slow at all, he was just thorough; a planner, trying to look three or four steps ahead, always looking for the land mines. He rounded the corner to find Mo on the bench, also engrossed in some inner thought. This surprised him; he'd previously decided that Mo and any deep thoughts were probably strangers. He knew that she was sharing his anxieties.

The greeting was slightly formal even though they'd been chewing the fat of the case at morning break and had known each other very casually for years. Mo had made that a priority, she made sure she met and talked to everyone who came to Blue Sky Research and now NPS; she had to establish her credentials personally before others, who knew better, did it for her. It was only since working in Sample Management that Mo had rounded off her official opinion of Reid; he was a dick, officious, up himself.

Mostly Mo was annoyed because Reid had seen through her early, he knew who and what she was and no amount of braggadocio was going to drag him into her fantasy of still being the girl, the hip one. Fuck, do people even still even use the word 'hip'?

Reid sat without asking, this was new. Usually he gave her a wide-berth; he'd never sat with her at lunch or on breaks until earlier that day. Actually the 'not sitting with her' thing was not that surprising; her girlies could put most men off. They were young, raucous and not afraid to do willy jokes, making some men, well most men actually, wary of being the butt of them. Now he was sat next to her, on the verge of saying something more. She knew that Marie-Eve, or at least the 'her being dead' part, was haunting him, too.

Reid's delivery was as expected but it still shook her. "I've been thinking about our chat earlier and, even though I think I know the answer for sure, I have to ask, once and for all. Did you kill Marie-Eve Legault?"

Now it was Mo's turn to consider before answering. It came out as a simple "no Simon, I told you, no, never", almost whispered, no special effects added, he really didn't think she could have, anyway. "Did you?"

The "no" was the quickest reply she'd ever had from Reid. He was rattled and she'd never seen him rattled. Her normal tactic, in times like these, was to play cat and mouse and she was very much the cat. Teasing, taunting until splat, gotcha! This time there was no toying with her prey, this was serious.

Anyone passing would have seen two people, quite different in appearance but wearing the same facial expression. Apprehension, nervousness, confusion.

"You know, Mo, I've been thinking, analysing. We are obviously both major suspects here, we both had the knowledge, we both had the access and we both had a reason, if to not kill Legault, then not to be sad that she was killed".

"Her name is Marie-Eve, if we are going to talk about her I want her to be a person, I want to call her Marie-Eve. Why do you think I might want to kill her?"

Reid paused. Maybe he was about to be a bit too insensitive.

"I think you tried to befriend her, like we all did in a way, and she rejected you. You have an ego, Mo, the police might see her rebuffing you as denting your ego badly enough to wish her harm, dead even. As for me, I really disliked Marie-Eve, hated her even. She had me on the rif list, the 'reduction in force'. That was one of the special little duties that she was sent here to do, but Bez Dooley pulled me off, he told me. Why would she want to get rid of me? I'm good at my job, I work hard, I'm loyal and I take on the difficult employees. I don't back away".

Mo turned, her face contorting with anger but the aggression went in an instant when she saw that Reid was actually smiling, at her!

Reid continued: "It wasn't just the rif thing. She undermined me to the management in public, she had the ear of Jim Duggan and Greenwood, and he is such a dumb arsehole that was only a matter of time before he believed her. I think he was hoping to shag her. Craig was, I'm pretty sure of that, he got the smiles and I got the scowls. Don't get me wrong, I wouldn't have gone anywhere near her, Catheryn is perfect for me and we are very happy, but I need the job. I worked hard to get above the floor and that French cow was going to wreck it all and I don't know why. I was always polite to her, I just didn't always agree with her".

Mo put her hand on Reid's arm; she touched him voluntarily for the first time ever. Her inner girly went 'yuk', but she ignored her. That was silly Mo, not really who Mo was now, just a vestige that was hard to shake off. "If it's any consolation, she was after me too, trying to get me out of NPS altogether. You know I'm asbestos but you don't know why and I ain't going to tell you, but my source told me all about Marie-Eve Legault. She was brought in to clean the slate, get rid of the thinkers and the dead wood and install sheep. Before you say anything I'll take being called a thinker over dead wood every time, no matter what you think!" Now Mo was smiling while her mind was screaming 'no, what the fuck is wrong with you, this is Reid, you're being too nice'!

"So, if it is not me or you, who do you think?" A chorus, they both spoke in unison asking the exact same question.

Since they last picked over the bones of the murder, they'd come up with nothing new, so they went with the obvious, Craig Shepherd, he must be the one. His motive was simple, rejection, frustration, fear, revenge. He'd been shagging her, she'd dumped him, he has a kid and an expensive wife plus mortgage, and Marie-Eve was always going to get him out as soon as she could after the fling. It had to be him, he already had several reasons for killing her, each one ticked in Reid's mental checklist.

"But Craig? Craig, the big pussycat, really?" said Mo.

They both knew him well enough to know that he was born without a spine, metaphorically speaking. He'd cave in during any argument with his staff and would always take the course of least resistance. The Shipping crew, especially Tracey Mills, ran him ragged and Mo was pretty sure Tracey had once had it in mind to add Craig to her own personal trophy cabinet, too. Had she given it a go, knowing Craig, he would have been powerless to resist. He'd shag her rather than risk her daily ridicule and even apologise for doing so.

"Maybe Tracey was jealous of Craig and Marie-Eve? She'd wanted in there at one time but Marie-Eve had just waltzed in and got there first. Would that be enough to kill her, is Tracey a possible suspect, as well as Craig and the both of us?" Mo sat there thinking; Reid was right and not being at all smug about it, they were both suspects on many levels. They needed more diversions, more suspects to water down the probability that either one of them did it.

"Neil is a possible, he could have done it" said Mo. "He's big enough and strong enough, and he has a secret that he wants hidden, he's not brave enough to have it known. If Marie-Eve had found out and then threatened to reveal him, or even get him added to the rif list, that might be enough".

"Oh," said Reid, "the being Gay thing? Nah, everyone knows Neil is a left-footer but nobody cares, why would they? He is our comedy security man who thinks he's SAS but is in fact more Graham Norton!"

"Mo laughed. "Sorry to disappoint you, Simon, but Neil isn't gay. True, he is a bit camp, he always has been, but not gay. I know him, I'd know". Mo carried on, she felt she was in some sort of groove. "Think on, though, if you add up the probabilities, the parameters needed to be the killer, then Neil fits the bill for most of them, except that he is Neil".

Reid looked at her. "What? Did you just swallow an Ian Rankin novel or something? Parameters, how often do you use the word 'parameters' Mo?" They both started to quietly giggle, they must have sounded like two old friends sharing a really funny joke and, each time one of them stopped giggling, the other prompted a further burst.

'Was this a turning point?' Mo thought, 'are we going to be better together now or is this the Millwall mentality, everyone hates us, we don't care, so we stick together'. She quite liked the idea of a friendlier Reid, it would be one edge of her work-day experience nicely managed.

Reid glanced at his watch and muttered a whispered curse. He got up to go and Mo expected the look and maybe verbal rebuke for taking too long over lunch but again it wasn't there. Instead, he just said "see you later, take care" and he was gone, walking briskly off back to his desk, back to the samples and back to the place where Marie-Eve Legault and her frozen body had dropped a spanner into so many of their previously quiet lives.

# EIGHT

## Sunday 18 September

Just as Neil Martin reached the security base, a small office set in front of the security turnstiles by the main entrance to NPS, after his late-evening round, the pager went off, telling him that samples were pending. He quickly consulted the printout on the board at the back of the office, tutting only to see that the security guard who'd printed it had yet again failed to sign and date it. He dialled the number at the top of the call-out rota and typed in the message. He loved the new system, no need to engage in conversation, just ping out a page and the lucky guy on duty would have to climb out of their warm pit and drive into the night to receive the samples.

There were still some mutterings from management about moving the late night sample arrival duty to Security. It was, after all, just signing a sheet and shifting boxes onto a cart and into a freezer, not really taxing. He was therefore surprised when HR backed up his insistence that it was outside the remit of Security and was purely a Shipping/Sample Management issue and could potentially compromise the overall site security. Once the delivery had happened, he could get his head down for the night, confident that there would be no more call for his services until 6 am at the earliest, no need for anything to keep him awake, not tonight. In the meantime he wanted to get his printing done. He'd found a bunch of pdf files on the web all about the Napoleonic wars and the night shift was a good time to print them off.

He'd set the printer going and then finish his rounds, well before the samples or Shepherd got there. Apart from the cleaners, who were somewhere finishing off their evening's work, the place was as quiet as a grave, just how he liked it.

60

He'd barely got to the door to start his rounds when the printer coughed and the paper jam sign blinked at him. Following the message on the panel, he opened up the various flaps illustrated and reached into the back of the printer. The evil, bastard thing had trapped a wodge of paper again and he would have to pick bits out, clear the debris completely and then reset it. The printer was a constant menace and Martin hated the thing with a vengeance.

Finally, he'd got most of the shredded garbage out, one last heave should do the job but no, the paper had decided to exact revenge on Martin's prying fingers with the mother of all paper cuts. Holding his hand at arms-length so as to not splash blood on his uniform shirt, well there was no other way really, he edged to the first aid box and quickly bound the wound with an oversized plaster.

Feeling seriously annoyed, he picked up his keys and set off on the last full circuit. Just a quick look-see this time, nothing too deep was needed.

Once the checks were all done, not his best time for the circuit but probably in the top twenty, he got back to base and pulled the report log. They'd left the bloody doors open again, those cleaners. It was always the same, every time they changed the cleaners it took weeks to get them to understand that the heating and air conditioning required all doors in certain areas to be kept closed. He'd closed them of course, not his job but he did it anyway. It made his point nicely if those stupid cleaners went back to do it, it meant that they'd wasted a trip.

His throbbing finger reminded him just how bad the night had been so, after taking a while to admire his first-aid skills even though some blood was now seeping through the dressing, he drew out the accident book and wrote three sides describing the catastrophe. Luckily his writing hand was uninjured, something else to include in the account, he thought. Job done, he took another large plaster from the first-aid box and added to the existing dressing. Bastard, bastard printer, but then weren't they all?

# NINE

Although perfectly bilingual, Marie-Eve Legault identified herself as Quebecoise. It didn't matter that she'd been born in Ontario and that English had been her first language until she went to University, she was Quebecoise and most certainly not Quebecker. It was at McGill that she saw the way that Quebec was going and that she could have a part in its glorious, separate future. After that, speaking English was done with a slight inflection in her voice that said 'I stood in this dog shit but I don't like it and will clean it off my shoe as soon as I can'. She never stopped to consider the irrationality of it all.

It was also while living in the melting pot that is Montreal that Marie-Eve found herself attracted to exotic-looking guys, almost any exotic-looking guy, really. Her friend, Leona, had said, half in jest, that she'd find herself stuck to a seat if she didn't find some way to control herself. But it was hard, she was young and had no responsibilities and she knew that sometimes she behaved like a little doggy in heat, a French Poodle, naturally.

After leaving University, and more by luck than judgement, she had found herself embedded in pre-clinical research at Heal-Well BioResearch. Her data management degree wasn't quite good enough to get in at scientific level there, but there was still plenty of scope in the management side, scope where her type of mind could make sure opportunities arose. Progression through the ranks, from her starting point as Senior Technician to Team Leader took just over a year; to make Supervisor took another nine months and then reaching the post of Sample and Shipping Department Manager took another year. She was, at that time, still only a small cog in the overall machine but the way the technical management in the company was leaning, she was soon to be a vital one.

It had been a genuine surprise to her when she got offered a post in Quality Assurance, so her degree had come in handy after all. The boss of Quality Assurance, English of course, was never very healthy and they needed someone reliable, someone who would be around all the time as much as anything. Inside two years he'd gone and the department was hers.

Quality Assurance was a veritable mine of interesting information and her web-like tentacles soon stretched to all areas of the Montreal operation. Of course, there were problems, but she dealt with them. 'Good Laboratory Practice' was their watchword and guide, but there were always ways to fix a problem, if you knew how and had the experience, not to mention a resolute mindset and some flexibility.

The problem of the then company managers was a double-edged sword. The company, Heal-Well, had originally been set up by an English person, Maureen Whithers, but she had moved on, selling out to a consortium of the existing managers, 60% of whom were English, the rest Anglophone Canadians, no Quebecois; this was troubling to Marie-Eve and to others.

She had actually liked some of the managers on a personal level; they were nice in that English reserved way. They held doors and said 'thank you', and they apologised even if things were not their fault, it was hard to hate them, it took some effort. To effect the changes that her friends had wanted at Heal-Well, and were constantly working towards, the Brits would have to go and then be replaced by more suitable people, for that read 'Quebecois'.

She had understood the aims and the history of the Quebecois struggle, obviously, but still, the Brits were nice people and she found that bit quite hard.

The offer to jump across town also came out of the blue. Lemeux BioResearch was a small contract research outfit in Laval, and only a few minutes from home on a good day. The appeal of not sitting on the highway for an hour each way, each and every day, weighed in when making a choice. That along with the fact that everything day to day, apart from client reports, was in French at Lemeux was enough to persuade her, so she left.

She had expected to be a bigger fish by dint of swimming in a smaller pool, and so she was; a pool that she could touch all sides of if she really stretched. After six months she knew it had been a mistake, but the old company had a policy of never re-employing a former employee, it was a pride issue maybe, or perhaps arrogance. But that policy was founded under the old management; maybe that had changed now, besides, she had an edge.

Marie-Eve knew interesting stuff about Heal-Well, lots of interesting stuff about lots of people, important people, both in Montreal and elsewhere. She also knew a lot of awkward stuff, really awkward stuff, things that the industry publically frowned on and she was well enough known in the industry to be listened to, if she chose to sing her songs. Armed with that knowledge, she'd called her friend in HR and arranged a meeting with Mike Winters, the current CEO at Heal-Well. Mike was a bit reluctant at first, citing the continuing re-hiring unofficial rule but, after half an hour of chatting in the back of an anonymous restaurant in wildest Hawkesbury, Ontario, he'd seen her point of view and she'd been offered a position. She had wanted to be back in QA again, the head of QA, but they had bought in talent from the USA, from Nash Pharmaceutical Services no less, and it was not an option. What she did get was Head of Technical Services, every technician at Heal-Well under her control, in many ways that was even better.

That night she'd met with the rest in a bar on St-Denis in east Montreal. There was no chance an English person would be found out here, they'd more likely get strung up from a bridge the first time they opened their mouth, so it was safe. Between them they talked about oppression and what had the English ever done for them. Amusingly it had descended into something of a Monty Python sketch; it seemed that such humour transcended all things, even language-based xenophobia although even that probably wouldn't save John Cleese from the noose and the bridge, not here.

On her first day back at Heal-Well, after the company orienting session she'd had to do, even though it had only been six months since she was an entrenched employee of fairly high rank there, she'd attracted a lot of bemused looks. What was she doing here? She could see it writ large on their faces. It was then that she got a better impression of her popularity. Because of the regimented structure of science, senior QA people were well-respected because of their influential position; they were the standards police and had a tough job keeping a lid on all of the rogue science that was wont to happen from time to time. Now she was no longer QA but an upstart technical manager. Despised by the scientists might be too strong, but the term didn't require a whole lot of watering down to get the mood of her new associates. 'Well, fuck them', she thought; then she thought 'no, tabernac'. If you are going to swear, then swear in French and 'tabernac' was just about as bad as you could do. Those old religious oaths were always the best, especially in Quebec, even if it only meant 'small table'!

The takeover had been a big surprise, completely out of the blue. One day it was Heal-Well, business as usual, the next they were all called into the main conference room by Mike. There weren't enough chairs for everyone, some stood at the back, none of the men offered up their seats for the women unless they were scientists. Mike had rigged up a large TV and fired up his PC with the help of Janet, his PA. IT stuff was not Mike's strong point and he barely knew which buttons to press to get the thing going.

It was weird that there had been no rumours, nothing in the wind that hinted at a change. Usually even the slightest thing got out; they'd stopped trying to hide the annual 'dead wood' clear-out rif, reduction in force, to the extent that people knew days before it happened whether to bring their own box in to work or not.

66

The presentation by Nash Pharmaceutical Solution's CEO, Jim Duggan, was slick enough. NPS, who of course she knew about - they were a client, had bought the company. Everything would continue as before, the company had been purchased to complement their seventeen other North American operations as they called them and also to gain a foothold in the Canadian market. It was to be a part of a global expansion, Europe would be next.

Everyone in the room knew the purchase was really to up the quality of the NPS brand which, in trade circles, was notoriously low. By taking over a reputable Contract Research Organisation, NPS would up its game, overnight.

Duggan ended the presentation with good news, 'your jobs are safe, people', with the subtext 'so long as you behave and do whatever NPS tells you to do'.

Six months later came the news that Marie-Eve had been selected to oversee the training of yet another company acquisition, Blue Sky Research in Wilford on the outskirts of Nottingham in the UK. She could have turned it down, but her fellow Quebecois didn't want her to rock the boat at that time and her refusal would lead to the management playing their own political games, now was not the time. Besides, other things were now afoot, and so she agreed to the short-term assignment and made plans for her newly appointed Francophone second-in-command to take over her role in Montreal.

She was also told to expect someone from Nottingham to come over and to learn their new LIMS, or Laboratory Instrumentation Management System, Clousseau. The guy, Simon Reid, was a Team Leader, he ran the Sample Management department in Nottingham and she'd need to set up the training and keep an eye on him, guide him, nurture him in the NPS way.

A few weeks before the Nottingham takeover came the news that Mike Winters had, after serious consideration, decided to take an offer to retire and would leave immediately. Janet would go, too. Shortly after, Pierre Belanger, her former CEO at Lemeux BioResearch strode through the door, starting a significant change of dynamic from Anglophone to Francophone in all technical and site managerial posts, the coup-d'état was partially done. Let the ethnic cleansing of NPS, Montreal, continue.

# TEN

## Tuesday 13 September

Craig sat at his desk with his head in his hands. Tracey had popped by and he'd fobbed her off with tales of a headache and so it was, but not the sort that makes your head throb. It was the sort that can be easily cleared up for good with a lead projectile.

He could hear Marie-Eve coming down the corridor, her shoes clicked in a particular way unless she'd slipped her stealth shoes on, her pace was best described as brisk. She entered his office and closed the door, her arms clutching a sheaf of papers and a couple of binders. She turned around and put the 'do not disturb' sign on the door, the sign that Jemmy had made for Craig telling the rest of the world that he was in a meeting and grumpy when disturbed; the little cartoon grumpy Craig was beyond twee!

Marie-Eve said nothing but he could feel the roll of her eyes as she slipped it in place.

Sitting her down and facing her was one thing, dumping her was another but it had to be done, as painless as it could be but done nevertheless. It had been stupid to get involved and, even though they'd only got physical a few times in his caravan, and once in his office, he knew it had been beyond stupid. He wondered what she made of his caravan. She was a Montreal sophisticate and there they were, bonking in an elderly caravan that smelt of boilies, the baits Carp anglers use, and damp landing nets.

Craig waited, not wanting to interrupt. He could see that Marie-Eve was about to talk and he had no intention of talking over her, there was to be no chance of her not hearing him properly or misunderstanding him.

69

"Craig, you're quite sweet but we're done, not that we were ever really anything. I hope you understand, just put it down to experience and we'll resume a strictly professional relationship for the duration of my stay here in Nottingham. It was a mistake for both of us, I'm sure you will agree, so there we are. Now, here are the Shipping Department documents that I asked you to send over. I've taken a look and there is a page or two of comments attached for you to consider. For what it is worth, I copied in Bez, I think protocol or something demanded it. My comments are only observations but NPS is global and we really need everyone on the same page, my page I think you'll find".

With that she smiled sweetly, got up and left, clack-clack-clacking away and out of Craig's life forever, hopefully. 'Well, fuck-a-duck!' he thought.

Tracey came in a few minutes later, carrying his 'meeting in progress' sign like it was the Mona Lisa. "I tell you, Craig", she said. "She is so far up her own arse she can pee out of her ears. Would you like one of my men friends to give her a little fright one night, when she is tucking into her pub dinner?"

"Tracey, I'm going to ignore that you said that. Be patient, and she will soon be gone for good".

"True, but who will she have shot down before she goes? She's planning a rif, rumours are everywhere. You, possibly me, and Reid are all in her sights, I got that from salaries and they always know what's happening, they have to prepare the severance offer they suffocate you with".

She was right, of course, but what could they do, any of them? Marie-Eve obviously had an agenda and was pretty ruthless in pursuit of it. He'd seen that side of her, very clearly.

"She just needs to know that we don't piss about here in Nottingham, Frighten her now and she'll be off back to Canada with her arse on fire in short order, you mark my words". And, having offered her sage opinion, she too left Craig to his thoughts.

Craig got up and put the sign back outside, he needed a bit of thinking time, he was almost in shock. He called Jemmy at home but the machine kicked in so he switched to her mobile number, but it, too, went unanswered. Checking the time, he realised that she was probably out running around Colwick or Highfields, or Attenborough, somewhere out in the open with Small in the buggy and the wind in her hair. For some reason, this made Craig emotionally happy and he slumped back into his chair, exhausted. He'd been so tired lately, especially in the evenings.

He casually flipped open the files that Marie-Eve had left and pulled out the advice sheet. His period of contentment quickly came to an end and, by the time he'd put Marie-Eve's suggestion sheet back in the folder, he was fit to burst with anger and loathing. 'Only observations, my Sicilian ancestors' hairy arses!'

To take his mind off the train-wreck his life was fast becoming, he decided to muck-in and help outside with some boxes for shipping. He didn't get much chance these days and he missed the general camaraderie.

*The trouble with those retractable knives is that they retract when you don't want them to. Mostly it is an annoyance, sometimes they catch you out, just like the one Craig had just fought with, and lost to, and now the blood was seeping through the Elastoplast. True, such plasters were not really designed to fit the cleft between thumb and index finger, you had to use a few to cover the area adequately although they always rucked up, leaving slender gaps for just such seepage. It was not so bad; he'd had far worse when spinning for Pike, and an unforgiving treble on a minnow spinner had shot from the water and embedded itself in his cheek. He called it his duelling scar to anyone who asked, not that many had.*

Minor injuries were pretty frequent in Shipping; cuts, bruises, paper burns and even that time that Tracey reckoned she'd given herself a Brazilian with the packing tape gun, leaving a nasty rash that she'd offered to show him. He'd seen the tape, but he wasn't convinced it wasn't a practical joke involving the hood fur from one of the freezer coats. She swore not, but then Tracey would swear blue was green if the mood took her.

# ELEVEN

## Early September

Lauren Booth handed the little pill bottle to Jemmy with a frown of concern. "You really should go to your GP, you know, he can prescribe some more suitable stuff for you. Flunitrazepam isn't the answer".

Jemmy was ready for this. "I don't want it on my medical record, Lauren, you know how things are going these days, when you want to go back to work they find out everything about you then think you are unsuitable just because of occasional insomnia. This way I can just ride this little rough patch my way. You do understand, Lauren? This really means a lot to me that you'd help me out this way and I promise never to ask again".

Lauren nodded, she was a mate and had been for years, and she'd said her bit, perhaps without any real conviction, but she felt all the better for it. "Any idea what the problem is, Jemmy? You look very well, beaming almost, and I don't remember you ever having trouble sleeping. When you lived with me in that dingy little flat, I had to drip cold water on to you some days to get you out of bed!"

Jemmy left a pause for effect and it worked, as an expression of almost real concern appeared on Lauren's face. "I think it must be Small and the disrupted sleep patterns but things are getting better, I may even end up not using it at all. Should I give it back to you if I don't need it?"

"No, just discard it safely, maybe crush it up and hide it in pills that are out of date, take a batch back to the Chemists and they'll get rid."

Jemmy smiled and said "OK, where did you get this stuff from anyway?" Lauren just tapped her nose, meaning don't ask any more questions, you might be an old mate but we move in very different circles now.   Jemmy took the hint, she was confident that Lauren wouldn't be letting on to anyone about their little secret.

As a new mum, as everyone insisted on calling it, Jemmy was feeling a bit squashed. Craig did his bit when he was home but she had the lioness's share throughout the day, and sometimes Small wouldn't nap and she found that she couldn't either. A couple of hours in the afternoon would be all she needed, and a bit of respite from Craig, too, would be nice. She wondered whether she could ask someone to fiddle the call-out rota at NPS to give him some extra nights and her some extra peace.

The rest of the evening was all girlie talk, babies, clothes, old men, new men, any men really. Jemmy let most of it wash over her, her mind was elsewhere but then it often had been in the past. It made her appear inattentive sometimes. Well it would do, she usually was.

# TWELVE

## Sunday 18 September

In her traditional-style kitchen, Jemmy ground the little pills to a fine powder; three and a little bit or something should do it. From the other room, Craig was cheering on Forest who appeared to have finally scored a goal. She knew that she'd not be disturbed in her kitchen, not in the middle of a game.

Blending the ground pills with the hot chocolate mix and adding a bit of coffee whitener to make everything look a bit dusty, she loaded the tray with the two cups and the Hobnobs and carried them through.

The match was in its closing stages and Forest were now erratically defending their slender lead. Craig took a deep slurp of the right cup; then proceeded to stuff Hobnobs into his mouth virtually whole. The unsolicited treat got Jemmy a little smile of affection and appreciation. Ten minutes later, Forest had scraped the win and the TV was off. Craig drained his cup and finished off the remaining half packet of biscuits, chattering on about how good his beloved Forest were and how they were certs for promotion. It had been so easy. Now at last she'd get a decent night to herself without him clunking and groping around. Good luck to Craig if he ever really pissed her off!

After fifteen minutes, Craig's eyes had started to visibly droop so she suggested he went off to bed, he was on call and might get a disturbed night. The more sleep he could pack in before the pager went off, if it did, the better. She said she had some bits and pieces to finish off, Small stuff, house stuff. Craig nodded, gave her a peck and wandered off upstairs to his room for the night. It had an en-suite so that was the last Jemmy would see of him for a while.

# THIRTEEN

The pager went off and it took Craig a few moments to register what was happening. Hauling his clothes on he set off for NPS hoping for a quick visit, he was so tired.

Andy Mood was waiting for him, so he signed the electronic pad thing and stacked the boxes onto a small cart. He beeped his way through to the -20°C walk-in, yanking the door open. The noise and resistance didn't really register but the blast of cold air perked him up a bit. He dropped the boxes just inside the door then did the bits of paperwork, leaving it in the night delivery pigeon-hole for Reid to deal with tomorrow.

He tried playing music on the way home but his eyes were drooping again and he had to concentrate hard. Luckily the road was quiet, just the odd taxi going about its business.

It was 2:30 am before Craig got home, more bleary-eyed than usual. It had taken him a couple of minutes to register the pager vibrating by his bedside in the first place, at least he hadn't disturbed Jemmy since he'd been in the spare room, de-rigueur when he was on call. There was no real traffic at that time in the morning but that hardly made up for being called in by Security at 1:30 am, the dark hours, to deal with incoming samples.

Surely Security could have signed for them. They could have opened the walk-in -20°C freezer and stacked them by the door, then put the shipping note in the Sample Management pigeon-hole. You'd think so but, to quote Neil, 'it is beyond our role as security personnel, to do anything that might compromise our ability to respond to a true emergency situation'. Still at least the call-out fee was a bit more towards the mortgage, although he'd not need to do it if Jemmy would go back to work after Small's birth. It'd been eighteen months or more now, and Small slept most of the time anyway. Soon they could get a daycare place. He wondered, not for the first time, exactly what did she do all day?

Craig saw that this was his life for the foreseeable. Glorified shipping clerk, fetcher and carrier, general dogsbody and paid as a peasant. Well they all were. No share options for them, no annual bonus that was so secret that you could tell when they'd got their little slips telling them how many more thousands they could expect at the end of the month. They all looked sheepish or sly but at least it was free coffee day if you caught one in the cafeteria queue. Guilt, he supposed.

As someone anonymous but who did stuff that nobody else did, nor would learn about if he had anything to do with it, he felt that he was at least safe from the rif, the dreaded 'culling'! Thinking about it, it was just like something out of the Hunger Games. He'd heard from Reid when he got back from his jolly in Montreal all about how they did things in North America. Once a year, usually in October but they could be sneaky, the rumours would start – lay-offs were coming. For the next two weeks there would be huddled groups, whispered conversations by those who felt vulnerable or those who wanted to go, wanted the pay-off; they would go around loudly proclaiming their desires in front of those who could make it happen.

He'd never heard of it before because it was an American thing and when the Yanks had bought out the old company things changed. Their first one was a shock to the senses despite his being forewarned. In England when people got laid off it was civilised. You got notice, offered help, people had collections – cards saying 'sorry to see you leaving' and 'missing you lots' appeared on desks. Nobody was happy about it but rationalisation had been the buzzword since the 1990s, it all still happened but in a gentle, more British way.

The American way was to hire private security. Set up a room where people were escorted from their desks, given a letter telling them how much pay-off they'd get if they signed the non-disclosure forms and how their pay-off would be a significant amount less if they didn't. The difference was, if you signed then you agreed not to sue. A legally-binding agreement bought with money they could afford easily but, for the victims, that represented desperation. You had no idea when, or if, you'd find another job and, for most, every penny counted.

Once you'd had your 'leaving' interview, you got marched off the premises, stopping only at the hastily arranged table where one of the team of Human Resource Executives would hand you your personal NPS-emblazoned cardboard box full of whatever they decided was yours at your workstation, and a bunch of leaflets offering 'support'. They even put a couple of company pens, a company mug and a card from HR wishing you luck in the box, and all done without a trace of irony.

Usually, if you were liked, your colleagues would arrange for a dinner out later, there might be a gift and another card and that would be it.

While everybody liked to speculate about who would go, the management always sprung the odd surprise. Well-respected people went, hard-working, conscientious, human. The new regime didn't want that though, they wanted sheep; company, corporate sheep, and sheep was what NPS was gradually getting. The thing with sheep is that they are easily herded, made to go one way only, the company way. To some extent that is fine if the shepherd is any good. If not, all you end up with is sheep driving sheep.

Pushing the rumoured second rif out of his mind, the one driven by Marie-Eve Legault or so it was said, he focused on the now. It looked like the next few months would be good for plenty of stand-by and call-out work. The big Saviour clinical study was shipping thousands of human samples their way, at all times of the day or night.

A night call-in normally meant a slightly later start the next day too; you got what amounted to a free hour, something meant to be a sweetener both to do the stand-by and to be family-friendly. Of course, the family functioned to its own time table, as always, so the extra hour was just another hour away from the pc, another hundred emails to answer, phone calls to return, people to motivate, if that is the right word.

Today there was no real later start because today he'd got to go to London for a course.

Exhausted, Craig climbed back into bed. Hopefully Small would sleep through, if not Jemmy would just have to see to it, Craig was way too tired.

He slept well enough; waking to sounds downstairs as breakfast was happening. Jemmy was in the kitchen, Small was in the high chair and Craig's work phone was in the sink, in bits. "What happened?"

"Small happened".

Checking the clock on the cooker, 6 am, Craig saw he had to get his skates on. London was calling and his train was due to leave in less than an hour. Jemmy was on it, a small package of foil was in hand and she was ready to run him to the station.

Small was buffed up to nearly clean, strapped in and they set off in moderate traffic, no problem. Jemmy was a bit quiet, maybe women's things, so Craig just kept it light, even though he was still a bit groggy – it must have been something he ate.

The train was on time but busy, he got a seat though and was at his meeting in plenty of time. He felt stranded without a phone but he'd manage, at least it had been peaceful on the way down and he'd been able to read his Stephen Booth until his eyelids had started to droop.

It was a fairly short course; they could have done it as a webinar. The software had looked useful but he'd have to talk to Marco about it, get his input. He was a colleague after all and it was really his job as an IT bod to know about this sort of thing. At the end of the course they gave him a message to ring Tracey at work. Now what?

All he could muster in response when Tracey told him the news was "oh, really".

He took his time getting back to St-Pancras, picking up a little gift in an expensive shop; Jemmy would like that and perhaps forgive him for breaking the unwritten law. He knew he wasn't thinking straight now but he'd have to soon, the police were sure to come a-calling, especially if his little secret got out. Surely a secret known only to him and the now departed Marie-Eve? How did he feel, hearing that she was dead? The truth was, he didn't.

Jemmy was late picking him up, Small issues as usual, it didn't matter. He'd read the Evening Post while he waited, they had the story about Marie-Eve but little detail, just the same 'found dead in the walk-in freezer' stuff that Tracey had already told him.

He looked forward to dinner and there was no call-out tonight so he could sleep in his own bed, if Jemmy would let him. She might even let him, it was worth asking.

She was a bit cool on the way home; they just made small talk until she mentioned the death. Craig was surprised by how calm he was. She then pumped him for details on the victim. 'Yes, he knew her, worked with her just like everyone in technical had. He'd sat in meetings, chatted in the cafeteria queue but he didn't know too much about her. She was OK.' Then Craig realised, he really didn't know too much about her at all. Well, not her life at least.

There was a Premiership game on the box that evening so Craig lost himself in it while Small was bathed and deposited in the cot, gurgling away on the baby monitor for a while before drifting off, hopefully for the duration.

Jemmy joined him on the sofa for the closing stages, a nil-nil, she never usually did that, was he in her good books now? Not really, she was still a bit distant and he was pretty knackered, what with one thing and another, so he went to bed early, in his own bed, not the spare. Jemmy must have come up later; he was spark out again and heard nothing until the morning alarm went off.

The doorbell rang. Craig reached the front door first. Outside stood a man and a woman, smartly dressed, they were flashing warrant cards. DC Prosser and DC Knight; they needed a word, a quiet word. He invited them in, Jemmy looked through from the kitchen and decided she didn't like the look of this and closed the door. Small made a noise and another mess, as usual.

Although Craig was a big, good-looking lad, powerful even, he was a mouse with zero aggression, literally. Maybe if he'd had an edge, Jemmy would be working again now instead of forging a career as a stay-at-home mum. At work, he'd be further up the slippery pole and he'd have the steel to shrug off those he feared upsetting.

The police made him nervous. Everything made him nervous really, he saw problems in everything and it was the bane of his life, another reason why he always looked like he needed more sleep. Sitting them down in the living room he offered coffee, or tea, whatever, but both were refused. There was a clipped sharpness to the police officers in their conversation. Notebooks were opened, time noted and the questions started.

Craig loved to read crime novels, Stephen Booth, Val McDermid, Mark Billingham, the more baffling the better. Like all readers of the genre, he fancied himself as something of a sleuth although his hit rate at sussing out the killer was less than 50%. Jemmy never read anything but 'Women's' magazines; lose weight, get fit, have more orgasms. Also cooking, home make-overs, fashion, bloody fashion. Why spend fifty quid on shoes when you never wanted to go out like a real adult?

'Where was he between leaving work, at 6:30pm the day before yesterday, and 7:10am the following morning?'

Craig felt uneasy, "why do you want to know, is this about the body in the freezer?" Like he didn't know the answer to that one already!

The curt "just answer the question" came from the woman. Attractive, someone you'd certainly look at twice.

Craig went through his schedule.

After leaving work he went to the local supermarket to pick up a small list of things he'd had texted to him by his wife, Jemmy, and, no, he'd deleted the text. Besides, the baby, Small, had since totalled his phone, anyway. They told him they would want the phone, no matter what the condition. Craig nodded, he'd expected that too. Luckily Jemmy had already scooped the remains of his mobile into a sandwich bag, expecting Craig to have to try to rescue the data on the sim card for the next phone, if he could. It was covered in what looked like baby sick; Small looked to have been creative but maybe had also been given a little help with the distribution.

They asked whether it was his personal phone or work phone. Craig explained in minimal detail how only staff of a certain rank got company phones, his was his but also used for work and, no, there was no financial gain in that, he paid the bills.

He continued with the summary. He left the Tesco Express at around 7:20 pm and was home by 7:50 or so, Jemmy could confirm, probably. He was then home until the pager went at 1:30 am, then he drove to work, picked up the boxes of samples, signed the electronic thing that Andy, the delivery guy, had, put the boxes, seven, in the walk-in -20°C freezer. Went to his office to pick up his phone charger lead, left the building, went home. He was back in bed before 3 am and home until the next day when he headed off to London.

82

"How did you move the samples from the Shipping area to the freezer?"

"We have carts". This comment elicited some lengthy note taking.

Going back to his movements, he told them that Jemmy couldn't confirm when he left and when he got back. After the call-out he'd slipped back into the spare room bed, he normally slept there when on-call so as not to disturb her beauty sleep; that was their call-out routine.

The female officer continued to write the details in her notebook, neither officer speaking to each other, although once or twice they exchanged a look that Craig couldn't interpret. Perhaps they were an item.

The door swung open and Jemmy came in with a tray of coffee but the officers refused again and she left without leaving any. Craig was a bit annoyed by that, it was like he wasn't there; or at least as if she wished he wasn't.

The male officer's phone went and he stepped into the hall, whispering and nodding as some message was relayed from wherever. He entered the room but didn't sit, so the female officer stood up. They were just leaving when she asked what time he would be going in to work. He said he'd be at his desk for 9:30 am.

He was asked for his broken mobile phone's number, which he gave them without hesitating, forgetting he'd not got a replacement phone yet. That was his first job of the morning; that was why he was going in later. He realised later that they'd already have it, so this was obviously a double-check.

Jemmy was hovering by the front door, she opened it without a sound and they left, the door closing so quickly it brushed the heel of the man, but he didn't stop. They must be used to not being very well received, especially if they were so taciturn with everyone.

Jemmy was looking at Craig. "Well?" Craig said he had no idea, they just wanted to know where he'd been, as Jemmy already knew, she was a champion eavesdropper after all. She huffed and went back into the bombsite that was the kitchen after breakfast with Small.

Craig got himself a coffee and shut himself away in his home office. Logging on to his work account via a VPN, he planned to scan the emails for a clue but he couldn't get in. The message said he was denied access and to contact his IT professional for assistance. That would be Marco, then.

The house phone rang. He answered, it was from Tracey, his nominally second-in-command in Shipping. Normally she was a bit flirty, even embarrassing, this time it was straight to the point. Why wasn't he answering his mobile? She seemed mollified when he told her of Small's creativity but something in her voice wasn't the usual Tracey, she sounded scared.

Craig noticed the frost in Jemmy's voice as soon as she entered the room. She could scowl for England sometimes, but this was worse. He knew better than to ask directly. It would come out after the frostiness had thawed and then the following forced niceness and then a few doors would bang somewhere in the house, or they might not, now that Small was around, and then out it would all come, the crime that Craig had committed.

This time the forced niceness slipped into sideways glances of such spite that she'd have a chance of making the England team in that discipline, too. Time to start the countdown, Craig thought.

Sure enough out it all came, was Craig a killer? How could he not know a colleague was trapped in the freezer, dying slowly in the -20 cold? How could he always walk around with his eyes shut, being so lamb-like all the time?

So that was it. Craig was an evil killer now, Jemmy had decided so it must be 100% true.

The only way to play this was straight, so Craig set to convincing Jemmy of his innocence, in the killing of Marie-Eve, at least. She listened, which was unusual. It took a while of covering every angle before he felt he'd made his case, or so he thought.

Then Jemmy suddenly switched tack, she wanted to know the gory details and speculation. Any wounds, how long in the freezer, who did Craig think had done it? Craig had no idea, how would he? He knew he would have liked to throttle Marie-Eve so many times in the past few weeks but that was then. Now he was in another place, somewhere more serene, a pristine riverbank, playing a 30lb carp gently to the net, at least in his head.

Jemmy pressed him and Craig told her bits, enough to keep her happy but not all of the details he knew, or suspected. It sounded like she'd already been on the phone to Mo, they often talked late at night, unlikely friends but they went way back, to a time when Jemmy was happily working in the labs as an analyst and Mo had enlisted her as one of her girls. But then Craig came along and she became Craig's girl, not that Craig had a deal to do with that. A smile and a nod became something else very quickly, then Small started to develop and the route to parenthood lay before them in all its glory.

From the conversation it was clear that Jemmy had heard much the same as him. There had been assumptions. The police had not released the actual cause of death but it was all over NPS, nor had they said where the body was found but the walk-in was the obvious choice. You could easily get a body into an upright -80°C but you'd have to take the shelves out, easy enough if it contained no samples, like the spare freezer. A quicker death too, at -80°C you'd be well-frozen very quickly.

Craig had always thought that there was stuff, personal stuff that Jemmy kept back from before. There had been rumours, but then in a place like Blue Sky, NPS now, with lots of people, rumours are a form of currency. Craig had ignored them. So what if Jemmy batted for both sides at one time, not his business, exciting in a way and besides, now she was a married woman with a family, responsibilities. It was good for her; it would make her grow up, finally.

Jemmy's erratic behaviour was what made him keep the caravan at Calverton after they got together. He'd used it mainly for fishing weekends, night fishing after Carp when he could. Well, one Carp, a 29lb Mirror Carp that he knew was in the lake at the caravan site. Only residents could fish the lake and, at the time when the caravan came up, he had nothing to stop him chasing his fish-related dream. It was only later that the caravan, naturally christened the 'Love Shack' had been used for other things. Trysts, as his mother might have called them, and all but a couple pre-Jemmy.

The thing with Marie-Eve might now come back and bite him, Craig knew that. He'd 'fess up' to the police later, they'd soon have found out anyway, but they would be discreet unless it became relevant, unless he got charged with murder.

# FOURTEEN

## Tuesday 20 September

Jemmy sat in her chair, the one she always sat in, with the baby monitor set high so they could be there in an instant if the now-playing Small urgently needed them. She felt better for having vented. The poor sod didn't deserve it, she knew Craig wasn't a killer, he even carried spiders out when she screamed. She'd have just stomped them to mush but they always seemed to appear when she had bare feet, why was that?

She wondered when would be a good time to tell Craig she thought that she was pregnant again. Now would just put too much on his plate and he'd be off fishing again. She knew he went to get away from them. He'd said he'd all but packed it up but she knew he still had all his fishing tackle stored away ready, somewhere he could get at it. She supposed he was allowed some relaxation but what about her? When could she relax?

Mo hadn't been very helpful. She was less assured than usual, cagey even. Jemmy felt that she hadn't filled in as many blanks as she could. Normally Mo knew everything that was happening, every fact and every rumour, probably because she started most of the interesting ones in the first place. Maybe, tomorrow, she'd be a bit more forthcoming. She'd call her at work, Mo could pretend it was a work issue and they could have a girly chat, just like the old days, before Craig, before Small. She was going to try Tracey again too; she didn't know what to make of her now, she'd changed.

She'd thawed towards Craig a bit now. She'd wanted to rattle him and see what came out. She wondered whether he'd noticed that she had been refusing wine for two weeks. Would he have guessed or is he so self-absorbed that she'd have to get it tattooed across her chest before he noticed? She was quite sure that the new baby would be Craig's, just like Small probably was.

If Craig didn't do it, where would the police look next? Would she be a suspect herself or would they go for someone more obvious? Mo reckoned Marie-Eve had a bloke on the go, someone 'local', meaning at NPS. It would have to be there really, unless she haunted transport cafes looking for emotional truckers, they were never hard to find. Perhaps being Canadian, Marie-Eve looked for other types. Jemmy couldn't think that there would be too many Beaver trappers available in Nottingham, well not the animal kind.

Sensing a return to calm, Craig readied for work. Jemmy appeared at the office door, coffee and breakfast for him on a little tray. She said she was sorry, the pressure of Small, she was scared by the police and panicked. She'd be OK, realised she'd been unreasonable and breakfast was a peace offering.

Craig forgave her for the price of toast and coffee. He always did, he probably always would, no matter what.

Her parting shot as Craig was leaving the house was that she was going to pop down to visit her friend in Northampton. It had been arranged a while, she'd take Small, she'd be gone one night, was that alright? She would be happy to stay, considering.

"No, you go, I expect the police will want to talk to me more than once, these things are often very complicated and there are procedures to follow. I expect I'll either be working or helping them with their enquiries".

She gave him a peck and said "great", and went off to clean up the bombsite that was the kitchen.

Craig went to work. Before her trip, Jemmy was going to go for a run with Small strapped into the fancy three-wheel pushchair. "Perfect for off-roading", as Craig said, every time. All was normal again for now, that would change, soon enough. He didn't mind too much today if there was traffic, thick, crawling traffic. Anything to delay the time when he'd get in to work where all would change.

# FIFTEEN

Small howled in the playpen, but Jemmy was preoccupied with talking to the TV. The 'look at me' designer had painted a crappy council house yellow with brown window frames and it looked like a Saturday night pavement pizza, but the occupants were fawning all over her. Jemmy was sure the victims' neighbours would have something to say, once the cameras had gone.

Ignoring Small from time to time was a tactic, a way of getting the baby to realise that there was reward in being less needy. Jemmy had read all about needy kids and how you have to train them young to be more independent. Small, who hadn't read the article, howled away anyway. It was non-specific howling, the sort kids aimed at any adjacent human because, occasionally, some good came of it.

The house was always more peaceful once Craig had gone to work. Today the disruption he brought was magnified by having strangers in asking him questions. Knowing Craig, he'd not have any answers, or at least not the right answers. You always had to have the right answers for every situation in this life.

She debated whether to tidy up now or later. Things never got too bad, never slipped into the sort of mess she remembered as a kid when her Mum was asleep on the sofa, her Bacardi bottle long since emptied, and her brothers and sisters running riot. She'd tried, hard, but the age gap between her and the little ones was too much and she had her school work to do, it was her way out. Her siblings and their unruly behaviour, had put her off kids for life, she'd thought, but here she was. A kid of her own, and a loud, messy one at that, but she was sure that would change, with training.

Jemmy wondered why she didn't miss her Mum at all. She'd never known her Dad, or any of the Dads of her brothers and sisters, not really. They were just different, temporary faces from different places. Now what was left of her family, those that hadn't perished so very tragically during their childhoods, had grown up, dispersed and gone their own way and she never heard from any of them, there was at least one she'd never even met. Now what should have been her family were all strangers to her and they didn't even know they had a new, tiny relative.

Sometimes, when she was out running, she'd go through the Wilford Cemetery, the big sprawling mass of dead people on the hill and look at the graves. Her Mum had wanted to be cremated and buried with the little ones that went before, as she called them, which was good because they only had the one plot. As she'd died penniless, and Jemmy hadn't got any money at the time either, there'd been no formal burial. Jemmy had kept the urn in the back yard until she'd been able to sneak into the cemetery at night with a trowel and lift the turf enough to pour in most of the ashes. It was windy, and so some of what was supposed to be her mother probably did a tour of the surrounding countryside. She'd have liked that. She'd always wanted to travel.

Death had been something she'd got used to at home, if you ever really did get used to something so final. Two brothers, a sister and then her Mum, all gone in the space of six months. Jemmy wondered what effect it would have on her. At the time she was just resigned and had got it into her head that she would be next, like Death had a list and her family names were all on it waiting for collection. It was a relief to be able to move out, stop with her friends, Mo and then Lauren for a while, find her feet then rent a bedsit.

Before she knew it, Small was strapped into the car seat; soon Small would be swapping the car seat for the fancy pushchair, ready for her little outing. Craig had moaned at the price of the pushchair but there was no way Jemmy was pushing a crappy four-wheel thing around, her off-roader was perfect for the young, active mum lifestyle. Thankfully Small had shut up, so whatever it was that had caused annoyance had gone away and there would be no need to have the music loud in the car now. There was no smell, so the howling wasn't for that, she'd be alright for a bit, until they got back.

Today was a running day. Cosmopolitan had a plan to get in shape after childbirth and she was trying to stick to it but it wasn't so easy. Some days she just wanted to veg on the sofa, not go out, but the thought that she'd look just like her Mum did on the day that she died, spaced out, face stuck to the velour cover, the smell. No, that wasn't going to happen to her. If Death still had his list with her name on it, well then she'd better be up for a fight!

Jemmy loved her hatchback, it was so convenient and she never had to unload it. The pushchair slipped in easily and her travel box with everything she needed for a longer trek where all where she wanted them, when she needed them. Today she'd run though, get the wind whipping around her, smell the river, hear the geese, maybe take some cake for the ducks; not bread, that made them ill, but cake they could eat. She was going to try six circuits, that was about 10k, that would tighten those flabby, child-damaged abs, give her some big muscles ready to shove the next one out, if it came to that.

The park was quiet; it was always quiet once the fishing season had been going a few weeks. Dog walkers and joggers were omnipresent and a few would nod to her as she passed in recognition of her as a 'regular'. They'd smile at Small, strapped in tight as they shot past, seeing the natural world at speed. Most of the dogs were well behaved too, on leads, friendly, but their owners would keep them controlled, just as they should be. There were always a few gits though, their dogs ran wild, chased swans and ducks and bounded up to her covered in mud. She'd complained, told the rangers, pointed the people out and they tried but what could they do? Some people have no respect for others.

Once Jemmy got running, over the initial wheeze, then she found her legs and lungs. The ash-covered track was even and her pace steady, no sprints, not with Small bouncing along in front of her. She passed the park vehicle, a ranger emptying bins, picking the scattered litter. Had it been deposited carelessly or been pulled from the open bins by naughty Magpies? They were everywhere, chattering and cackling like the spirits of old women doomed to roam the park as a bird for their sins. Perhaps that was her destiny, for her sins when she died, maybe her mother was inside one of them, watching her sail past.

The ranger waved as she passed. She felt a flush, she was recognised, that made her feel warm, welcome, she liked to be liked. Or was he just being friendly, did he wave to every pretty jogger? Probably, he was a man; their brains are programmed by their balls after all although his would be quite old by the look of him.

She felt at ease on the park with all its little nooks and crannies. Quiet spots where she'd been shown a Kingfisher when she and Craig had taken one of the park's nature walks, before Small, when they'd had fun. She stopped for a breather after three laps and consulted her list, like a shopping list but different. She'd numbered the park benches on a map, the one in the free park leaflet, and then had her system for rests, never the same bench twice. Today she'd rest on two different benches, number seven and number eleven. She was at seven now, it was off the main track and set in a quiet spot looking over the lake, sheltered from the wind unless it was due south.

Small gurgled, so Jemmy gave her a drink and had her own isotonic, the amount carefully measured and marked in bottle one. Five minutes was all she allowed; then she had to do her stretching before setting off again. Around the top lake she went past one of the Carp anglers, weird men who sat in little green camps waiting to catch one fish. There always seemed to be a hint of marijuana in one particular area and she thought that that must be part of the exercise, fish, drink and smoke dope out of the way. It's a lifestyle of sorts, she supposed. Is that what Craig did when he went fishing? Not dope, surely!

After completing her bench obligations, Jemmy warmed down behind the car. Small was starting to grizzle and probably needed a bath and changing after all the exercise. As she was packing the car, one of the rangers said "hello, enjoy your run?"

She was a bit wary; it suddenly occurred to her that it might be better to be more anonymous, unmemorable, nobody bothered you then. "Yes thanks, lovely park, you keep it well, I'm sure visitors appreciate it". He nodded and went off picking litter, just small talk she thought, he probably spoke to everyone he saw, part of the job, public relations and being seen to be doing something. She'd noticed that he was carrying binoculars and wondered whether you really needed binoculars to pick litter?

*Bastard! Blood was starting to show where the same push chair catch had opened up the wound again. It wasn't dripping but it was very irritating, especially if it got on her top, or her new trainers, or on Small. As the blood started to get some urgency she reached into her little bag for emergencies and pulled out the last remaining Huggie, carefully wrapping it around the affected hand and around the wrist; that would do until they go home. She looked down at Small who'd not budged, fast asleep after the fresh air, she felt a twang of annoyance at Small's lack of concern for mummy. Did every new mum think that way?*

Back home she unloaded everything, bathed and fed Small who went straight off to sleep after. Fresh air, the best way to keep baby happy, the article had said. She went out and hosed down the pushchair, she'd read that fecal matter was everywhere and the amount of dog shit on the park was the bane of her life, they had bins for it, for fuck's sake, but not everyone used them and so she always had to clean everything after, as a precaution.

The time had rolled around nicely to lunch so she pulled her labelled pots from the fridge and built her lunch, then sat all afternoon with her feet up watching makeovers, occasionally swearing at the telly. Tomorrow, thought Jemmy, I should do something different. Next to her, Small started to cry again, so she carried on with the personal development training that the TV show was offering and just turned the TV up.

She'd head off to her friend's place later. No rush.

# SIXTEEN

Reading through their notes to Thompson, Prosser and Knight, who they all called Elkie, waited for questions but it was all pretty routine and it looked like Shepherd had cooperated. They really should have had him held in London but knew that there was little chance of that sort of co-operation based on just suspicion. In any case, Reid was the finder and you always start with the finder first, so they had enough going on without going cap-in-hand to the Met.

Lighting a little fire under him at home might set him simmering nicely anyway, especially if his wife had been straight into his ear as soon as they'd left, as they'd suspected. This was going to be a busy day and Charnley would need a good and detailed report of it, if only to keep up appearances.

"Thoughts?"

Prosser spoke first. "I don't think so. I've met people like Craig Shepherd before, they don't have the edge to be a killer. The only motive I can see is that he was trying to stop his wife from finding out about his physical relationship with Legault".

"What's she like, the wife?" Thompson added "Elkie" before Prosser had the chance to babble. He could sum up a man succinctly enough, but women left him bemused.

"A smart sort, fashionable, got her shape back after having a kid. The house is a bit worn in places, kid-worn though so not unexpected. She offered refreshments, played the good hostess and wasn't flustered. She doesn't think her husband is a killer, she showed no sign of nervousness at all".

"Too good to be true, or just a confident person?"

96

"Confident but in a slightly detached sort of way. I got the impression that we could have arrested her husband for murder and she'd have just gone back to attending the child".

"Did you get his phone?"

Prosser held up a bag of bits of electronic components and what looked like vomit. "The kid totalled his phone, conveniently. His wife kept it bagged".

Thompson checked that everything was arranged for later but he had no fears, his team were pretty thorough. They'd whittled the names down to a few people with access as a minimum and another few just to throw a spanner in the works, decoys to make the killer, if indeed the killer was in the first group, confused. It was an old tactic, a way to make people relax enough to just drop their guard a fraction. It was amazing what could seep out of a fraction of a gap into the daylight.

This time they would see about getting formal statements, including using the 'black arts' to see whether they could uncover a few missing details. Most of the interviewees would be bussed in, Shepherd and Martin being collected by marked car later. If the first batch did have things to enlighten them, then, with luck, they might even make an arrest before bothering to bring in batch two, it had happened before.

When Thompson had called NPS it had been Neil Martin who'd answered the phone, it seemed that his contact number was the direct line to Security. He sounded particularly nervous as Thompson went through the schedule, perhaps they should have lumped him into the first batch after all? He certainly sounded relieved that he wasn't in the minibus. That relief didn't last too long though, once he'd been told to be ready for his turn, too.

Today we get things moving up through the gears.

# SEVENTEEN

It was around midday, the day after Marie-Eve Legault's untimely end, that Reid got the call from Security. Downstairs, the police were waiting for him, wanted to interview him at the station now, formally. It didn't take a clairvoyant to see how this would look. Marched off the premises, not cuffed, but presumably flanked by two big, burly officers. 'No smoke without fire', they'd say. 'Well, they didn't get on', they'd say. 'I never liked him', they'd say and, before long, his name would be shit.

When Reid got to the security station it was not what he'd expected at all. It was explained that further interviews were needed and that they'd be conducted offsite and, for convenience, at the station. Nobody was being arrested or charged, and there would be seven of them, including Tracey and Mo, that they wanted to talk to. They'd be brought over in a minibus. There would be a car for Shepherd and Martin.

Reid was relieved, so he was not going to be the singular object of curiosity he'd expected to be. Five of them would be riding in the minibus, one might well be the killer but he thought, on examining his mental list of those he now knew to be travelling in the minibus, it was very unlikely. Of considerably more interest was the treatment of the two others who had a more direct bearing on the situation, Shepherd and Martin. They'd been on the premises during the period of Marie-Eve's murder and were now being treated to the psychological drip of water that a ride in a marked car would provide.

He had to wait patiently while the rest of the interviewees were fetched. For some reason, Mo came out leading them like a mother leads her ducklings. When Thompson said they'd be transported in a Transit, Reid had all sorts of images in his head, but it turned out to be just an ordinary white Transit, no riot grills or darkened windows, no angry graffiti, deeply carved into the side panels and calling the usual contents of the Transit 'pigs'. A bit of an anti-climax, really.

Reid saw that Shepherd had showed up too, but was told to wait until Martin joined him. They would be travelling separately and he was directed to the lone cop car.

Just as the Transit left, the babble from the group, especially Tracey Mills, reminded Reid more of a group off on a trip to the seaside rather than a bunch of potential suspects, one of whom might be potentially heading for choky.

At the station they were all shown to a pleasant waiting room with magazines to browse and fresh coffee from one of those machines that use little pods, the sort that are responsible for filling landfills with yet more plastic. Tea was more of a green option, hot water and a tea bag, milk and sugar if you wanted it, no biscuits though.

Although the room had strip lighting, it didn't glare at its occupants, it just gave off a warm light with a slightly peachy feel to it. Presumably the warmth was to relax people, calm them down from the trauma of being in a Police Station. The nice room was probably where the non-villains went, people who were not suspects but a useful part of the investigation, genuinely helping the police with their enquiries. There must be something more basic, more sordid and intimidating, something fitting for the crooks to be held in and made to sweat.

Despite the welcoming aura of the room, everyone was nervous. Not conversing naturally but making a few muttered comments, mostly involving gallows humour. The chattering competitions they might have had in their comfort zones had been replaced by more of a guarded acceptance that they were involved, even when they weren't. A mirrored window at one end had Reid thinking that they were being watched, observed just like the techs observed the animals back at the labs, a behavioural study. The difference between this and a rat study was that if any of them showed signs of distress, there was little chance of them getting euthanised and removed from the study, presumably.

Two people went off when called, out of the door and to the left, a different route and away from the way they'd come in. Reid wondered where the cells in the station were. Did they really smell of vomit, pee and disinfectant, just like all the TV crime shows portrayed? Maybe he'd find out for himself by the end of the day when they'd fingered him for the murder and he'd been taken deep into the hinterland of this Police Station

Reid was in the second batch. Those who'd already gone out didn't come back to the rest and there was no suggestion that those remaining would be told where they went. Even money was on a canteen nearby, perhaps with tokens good for a free coffee and a bun. Reid hoped so, he was hungry.

When his time came, he was walked left out of the door and along a not unpleasant corridor. Leaflets, wall-mounted, offered up information about locking doors, getting alarms fitted to your house and not sharing needles. It was a mish-mash of sage advice running the length of the corridor. Reid wasn't particularly inspired though, his mind had started racing and there didn't appear to be a leaflet for that.

The interview room was less comfortable than the waiting room but still not the sort of place Reid had thought it would be, the sort of place with easy to wipe walls and floor, a place where the good-cop, bad-cop routine would work you until you cracked. It was simply functional. He had thought of asking for a smoke-free interview room but then thought better of it, they might think he was a lippy bastard, some people did, it seemed. Maybe he was masking some deep-rooted insecurity that made him appear more confident than he really was; maybe he'd suffered a childhood trauma, something he couldn't talk about. Thinking about it though, lippy bastard was about right. He was nothing if not secure in knowing who he was.

DS Thompson started the interview off, he had a woman with him, someone he'd not seen before. She seemed to be mostly involved in taking notes, doing that despite the fact that the dreaded tape machine got an outing. Thompson tried to smooth the way by telling Reid that it was just procedure, perfectly normal and it allowed them to better review all of the more formal statements later, especially as Reid had played such a prominent role in the investigation so far. It was also for Reid's benefit to some extent, as the tape was indisputable, it was potentially evidence.

Reid asked whether he should have a lawyer present and was told it was his right to do so but that he was not being charged and then interviewed as a suspect, more as a witness. "By the way", Thompson said, "they are solicitors here. You watch too many American cop shows, Mr. Reid".

He was offered five minutes to think about it but decided to go with it. Reid knew that he hadn't done anything and, despite the evidence sometimes to the contrary, he actually had some faith in the police. He was totally innocent of this particular crime and had nothing to fear, so why drag it out?

Thompson told Reid to call him Dave; the woman was Laura, although Thompson called her 'Elkie' twice. She'd take notes alongside the tape, more to get an impression on a personal level, he was welcome to review the notes after if he wished. Never having been in this position, Reid just shrugged and said "fine" and tried not to smile. Well, smirk, but sometimes he knew he had no control. He settled for thoughtful and hoped it came over that way, although smarmy might also have covered it.

"Before we start, I thought that this might be useful". He placed a sheet of computer printout on the table.

"What is it?" said Thompson.

"Each freezer is wired up to a temperature recorder. I mentioned the alarm for low temperature when you first arrived; well the monitor is more sensitive, recording changes by single digit degrees. This is a print out of the -20 walk-in freezer for the relevant period, 21:00 to 06:00 the next day. As you can see, at 11:17 pm the temperature rose by six degrees. At 1:02 am it rose by three. I think the first temperature is when your body was placed in my freezer. The second is presumably when Craig Shepherd deposited the delivery of samples. The temp went higher earlier, and you understand that I'm only speculating here, but is rose higher because the doors had been wedged open by the cleaners, throwing the air conditioning out of kilter. In other words, making everywhere warmer".

"I see, thank you for that. How would we independently check this information?"

Reid was a bit surprised to be asked that particular question but then thought, 'of course, if I had done the dirty then I would use something like this to cover my arse'. "You can go through the company IT people. They can do it for you, show you everything in the system, which is a sealed entity, designed to stop any fiddling with the data, in case you wondered".

'There was that helpful, verging on smarm again', thought Thompson.

"Thanks for that, Mr. Reid, we'll follow it up. Right, so you found the body and had the presence of mind to secure the site, stopping all access until we arrived and you also sent out this email to all those who might need access or something from the freezers. That's very cold and calculating, considering that you had just found a colleague dead, or apparently dead", said Thompson, as he pushed a copy of the first email Reid had sent on the dead day across the desk.

"Apparently?" said Reid. "Do you mean that she was still alive when I found her?"

"We don't know yet precisely when she died, that'll come out in the wash, later".

"That doesn't actually answer my question. Are you suggesting to me that she might have been alive when I found her?"

"Not suggesting that as such, but it is not impossible. If she was, the suggestion from the medical people is that you wouldn't have been able to tell anyway. Her vitals would have been almost beyond detection so don't feel bad that you didn't check, that you didn't try to save her".

"Beyond detection? But what if I'd had a mirror handy?"

"What?"

"Unless, like in an Agatha Christie, I'd had a mirror; in the freezer even a little breath would have misted up a mirror".

Thompson decided to move on from the speculation. "OK. Mr. Reid, did you like Marie-Eve Legault?"

"No".

"Why?"

"She was on secondment from the Montreal site to check up on us and clear some more people out, for some reason, including me. As a part of the takeover transition I went out there, to Montreal, for training to learn the sample management software, Clousseau, so that we could start using it here. People there were suspicious of me at first, but a few of the ex-pats played football, five-a-side, and I got invited. After, in the bar, I heard a few things, not very complimentary. When she came over it didn't take long to see that what I'd heard was true."

"It sounds like gossip or sour grapes. Marie-Eve Legault was an ambitious young woman and some men don't like that, they feel emasculated. Did you feel that way, Simon?"

"No, of course not", Reid replied. "She was a manipulative and devious cow who couldn't be trusted. She'd risen to the top in the company like a turd in a bowl and nobody could figure out why. She had no idea what she was doing most of the time. No feel for how to handle people and no vision beyond the end of her nose. She was in her second stint with the company, having left for a rival but then having returned after six months. Nobody could understand it; nobody of her level ever came back. Once they'd left they were regarded as pariahs".

"Obviously all this has been bugging you, especially what you deem to be her preferential treatment. Nobody who you discussed Marie-Eve with in Montreal had any idea how she got back in, then?"

"No, the only thing I heard was that she probably knew where the bodies were buried, and before you write that down, I'm assuming that they were talking entirely metaphorically, of course".

"Metaphorical bodies, interesting. Can you tell me more about what that might mean? Your industry is not that familiar to us".

"Things happen, especially within studies, things that don't make the final study report that is sent to the clients. Usually it is minor stuff that affects nothing, but not always. Sometimes there is a cock-up that the FDA, the Federal Drug Administration, would take a very dim view of, dim enough to have the company closed down. The FDA start with a 483 notice and it can go on from there. If a Contract Research Organisation starts to get 483 notices, the clients lose confidence and go elsewhere. The sort of stuff that will get you a 483 happens, but a good manager or, say, Head of Quality Assurance, can either head off the issues that might spark one at the pass, or eliminate them altogether".

"So, if I understand correctly, somewhere in the past there may have been one or more such issues and Legault may, or may not, have played a part in burying them to avert a '483' as you call it. They are your metaphorical bodies?"

"Yes".

"This still doesn't explain why you didn't like her, why you have such antipathy towards here even in death".

"We didn't get on".

"She crapped on you, then?"

"More than once".

"Tell me".

And so Reid opened his festering heart up and told 'Dave' all about promised promotions; projects of his that had subsequently become her idea when she presented them to management. Then there was the placing of a spy within the Sample Management group, Dominique Yip, a woman who'd been a supervisor in their failed Chinese operation, but who had wanted to return to Canada, back to her old job in their Sample Management Department. She must have been surprised to find herself sent to Britain for a few months as part of the transition team. There were other things he could talk about, rumours and stuff, but he thought he'd said enough for now.

Dave listened; Laura wrote notes and the tape span away capturing every spat word. Reid felt flustered. He sat back and focused on the red light blinking in the corner, CCTV, of course. Had he said anything incriminating, or had it just come out like the bile of a bitter low-down employee? Probably the latter, he thought.

Thompson turned off the tape. Reid sat waiting, thinking maybe they had to change it or something. Surely there was more to be asked, to be answered. Some of the answers he'd already mentally prepared, but Dave Thompson just said "no, we're done – for now" and Laura offered to read back her notes but he declined.

"A couple of further things, Mr. Reid. We looked into Dominique Yip. I think you were wrong there, she left NPS recently of her own accord and we know that she didn't get on with Marie-Eve Legault".

All Reid could say was "oh".

"The other thing is that you have mentioned the term 'Good Laboratory Practice' a few times, including when you told us, quite correctly, to put on protective equipment when we first arrived at NPS. I'd appreciate a little description of what you mean by it and how it is applied at NPS on a daily basis. This I'd prefer you to do by email, no great rush but it would very helpful".

Now Reid was completely confused. He went in as a suspect and now they wanted to liaise with him. Was this a cunning trick to get his confidence? Probably not.

"I'll do my best, Detective Sergeant, anything I can do to help, really".

Following the interview Reid was guided out through the back of the building to a canteen, yay! By now there were five others in there, so two more to go. Would Shepherd and Martin be riding back in the Transit, or would only one of them be getting home for tea today?

As they waited, everyone was getting a bit impatient, checking their phones, some for texts, some for the cricket score, others just a bit sad that they'd not at least had a missed call. Reid's phone was dead, he'd forgotten to charge the damn thing.

# Eighteen

Talking to Reid was interesting. The stuff about the FDA is plot-thickening, I never knew such stuff existed; I always thought the pharmaceutical companies were squeaky clean or else, seems not though. Legault obviously did the dirty on Reid at some level, and so probably did the same to many more; the potential killers should form a queue! Reid is not our boy but he's been very useful with background stuff, even if he didn't know it.

It is unlikely whether a pharma that is naughty enough to get what Reid called a 483 would fess up to a police investigation, unless the information became public; that would damage them. Legault had her own bullets and it seemed that she used them as needed. The thing is, who was she pointing her gun at?

# Nineteen

Mo's phone blipped, the caller display said 'Crazy Neil', *'The cops are here for you!'* While not unexpected, she found herself feeling nervier than she ought. Reid then also sent her a text warning her, she didn't even know he had her number. Did he want to become one of her girlies?

Sure enough, five minutes later the one called Thompson, accompanied by 'Drabble', came into the Sample Management room. At first they were preoccupied, going around the room identifying people against their names on the list Ranji had given them, Mo had the same list in her drawer. It helped, sometimes, to know stuff about people, old stuff, embarrassing stuff. It helped you to survive.

Everyone in the room got a couple of minutes, confirming who they were, contact details and that sort of thing, but the police didn't seem too interested in most of them. They must have already eliminated them from their enquiries.

Although the pattern the detectives chose when talking to the other Sample Management staff seemed random, Mo knew that she would be last and she would need to give them more details, real details, so she was caught a bit off-balance when Thompson left the main group and headed her way. That's cheating; there were at least three more to go! She slipped into casual, unruffled mood and asked him "what's up?", trying to be a bit gangsta but, because she was at heart a polite girl from Edwalton, ended up with being a slightly chav, horsey deb.

Mo listened intently while Thompson explained that she would be required to give them something a bit more formal than the chat they'd had immediately after Marie-Eve had been found. They'd be doing it at the station, was that OK? If she wanted to, she could have a solicitor. The last word chilled her; before it was casual, no hassle, nothing heavy. Now it was talk of solicitors, serious interviews, probably in an over-heated, dingy room or perhaps one where the air-con had dropped the temperature to uncomfortably cold levels, anything to make her uncomfortable. Anything to get her to squeal.

Her girls were watching, taking mental notes, getting themselves ready for when they would get dragged out, speak to the filth, the pigs, just like Mo had told them would happen. For them she kept her composure, just. Fixing a grin, nodding around the room she stood up holding out her arms and telling Thompson loudly to make with the cuffs. The room laughed, Thompson laughed and she forced the atmosphere down a notch. To everyone around she wanted to give the impression that they wanted to talk to her more as someone with vital information, a part of the inquiry but there was no suggestion of guilt. Man, she was almost one of the investigating team, almost.

The drive down town in the minibus took her almost to her home. Another three streets and she could have been at her front door. Her neighbourhood was edgy; there was menace at night as street girls who lived on the same road set just off the nearby red light zone, worked the kerb crawlers. Guys cruised constantly, either to pick up or to keep an eye on the girls. Cops cruised too, but always in marked cars. Like insurance crime, the street girls were just inconvenient, not really a crime, nothing to bother with in any depth unless a punter got pasted. It happened occasionally when they got rough with the girls or worse, cheap.

Her mind was away with the fairies when they stopped and the door snatched open. Child locks to stop the bad guys fleeing arrest, of course, another layer of fact to give credence to her story when telling it to the assembled girls later. She was surprised that most of the suspects were being ferried to the station together. Whatever happened to splitting people up then getting one to confess?

She didn't speak to anyone at the station while awaiting her turn. Reid was left behind when she was called in the first batch, as Thompson called them, the first of a dodgy bunch.

She bumped into Craig Shepherd as he came out of a room just off the corridor. He looked really guilty in the lights of the Police Station; did he kill her, Marie-Eve? Then she thought for a second and laughed, hadn't she seen that tactic on every police drama ever? Show one of the suspects the other one, imply evidence had been given, incriminating evidence at the expense of the other suspects; to save their own skin, 'they've made a deal, they were a snitch'. Well, she was no snitch.

Craig only glanced at her as they did an intricate narrow-corridor dance. She was shown into a room two doors down, warm but not hot, comfortable.

Coffee arrived, black, "just how I like my men", she said, 'and women', she thought, mostly, well if possible, perhaps at one time.

Thompson and the woman, Jenny she said her name was, sat opposite. No solicitor was asked for nor needed. She had nothing to fear, she knew, but she wasn't going to tell them zip.

Thompson started the 'chat' as he kept calling it by reading back her timeline as it appeared in her statement taken the previous day. She confirmed that that was correct with a polite "yes, Sir". Thompson's face remained set in stone as he said "no need for the 'Sir', call me Dave".

Mo liked men called Dave; she liked the story of David and Goliath. David was smaller but smart and brought the mighty down. She identified with that, the oppression that she had fought and beat. She was a Dave, if you could have a female one. Sure you could, equal rights is why, Davina then.

110

Once the formalities had been done, Mo was asked by Dave about her relationship with Marie-Eve.

After a long pause, made even more uncomfortable because the bastards had obviously turned up the heat further to make her even more uncomfortable, Mo took a deep breath and started to talk.

She had been seeing Marie-Eve since not too long after she'd arrived in Nottingham. Marie-Eve came to her place, they were in love. Marie-Eve was going to move in when the time was right, she already had a toothbrush at Mo's place in case she stayed over, she said, but she never had.

Dave asked whether they could collect the toothbrush on the way back to NPS, just a formality, DNA maybe. "No point", said Mo. "Marie-Eve had never used it, nobody had, it was still in the plastic packaging". Dave said they'd take it anyway; if that was OK? Mo shrugged, fine by her, waste your time, cop-boy.

Dave asked for specific dates, times and places when Marie-Eve and Mo were together outside work. Had people seen them together, could someone confirm her list of dates and places. Anyone?

After going around the block with her stories of snatched moments of intimacy with Marie-Eve, Dave sat back and audibly exhaled. The room went quiet. The digital clock on the wall was a cheap one, no disguising the simulated tick. There was no noise of water going through the radiator, a radiator that was cool to the touch; there weren't even any muffled voices from outside. In the corner of the room a white device sat, were they filming, was she being taped, had they already said that?

Mo plucked up the courage to talk. She pointed to the corner and asked in her best street voice whether they had a good view, those goons who were watching? Dave looked over, stood up and pressed a button; a shrill sound filled the room, a panic button?

"Mo", he said quietly, "it's a smoke alarm and, no, you are not being recorded and I'll tell you for why. We know that you were not involved in any way, shape or form in the murder of Marie-Eve Legault because you were at home when you said you were out partying the night before. You live in what we call a casual crime hotspot, ladies of the night, etc. and the CCTV on your street monitors what happens, records it. You drove up at 6:10 pm on the night before the body was found. Pizza arrived at 6:30 pm, good, quick service by the way I hear".

"Yeah", said Mo, "they know me. We all hang together".

"Yes", said Dave, as if the three-letter word had five consecutive vowels. "To continue, your car was stationary until 6:12 am the next morning when you left the building. Traffic cameras recorded you all the way to NPS until the time you signed in, all accounted for. We know you were nowhere near when the fish...". Jenny coughed loudly, and Dave seamlessly completed the sentence with "Marie-Eve was placed in the freezer".

Fish, what the fuck is fish? Mo thought. He said 'fish' and there was more to follow before drab Jenny had her coughing fit.

Dave continued. "The thing is, Mo, we see you and, while it might be OK for your little group to get drawn into some sort of fantasy world, it doesn't work here. We know you, we see you, who you are so let's just cut the secret world of Moonbeam Orinoco Smith and talk facts, real facts, OK?"

'Fish', what the hell did he say fish for? What could follow fish, what had he not said that completed the phrase? Think. Marie-Eve was dead, dead fish, no, nobody says dead fish. Marie-Eve was frozen, fish fillet, no, sounds wrong. Fish, fish, Fish Finger, yes, Fish Finger, the fuckers were calling her Marie-Eve a Fish Finger, the bastards. Quite funny, though.

Mo looked up just as Dave was finishing saying something, going on about real facts. "OK", she answered.

For the next twenty minutes Dave asked questions and Mo answered, giving the absolute truth, mostly. They seemed fixated on who Marie-Eve had been seeing. Perhaps saying "well, how long have you got?" was the wrong thing to blurt out at that point but, really, if Marie-Eve was all that she'd heard she was, if she'd really had been a bike, then she'd have been a ten-speed racer!

After delivering up the fifth name, Mo paused to let her mind catch up and she had to go back two to try to give them the sequence. Marie-Eve had lots of boyfriends, she knew this because she'd heard all about it; she had girls everywhere listening, all whispering facts back to her. The currency of knowledge, how else are you going to survive?

More silence.

"You were doing so well, Mo", said Thompson. "Then you sort of skidded into a cul-de-sac and now we have to try to reverse out and get back on the straight and true road, OK?"

"OK, so Marie-Eve wasn't a bike but she was seeing someone from work for sure". Mo didn't have a name but suspected it was Reid, or Shepherd, or maybe even Bez Dooley.

Thompson let out a long, drawn out sigh again and thanked her for helping them with their enquiries. At that Mo chirped up, "no worries bro, any time", and she sauntered off out of the room escorted by drab Jenny to her ride back to NPS.

Thompson added a comment as if to the audio, which he would always think of as tape, no matter how digital things got. "I'd contend that the statement of Orinoco Moonbeam Smith on this recording is 60% accurate and 40% fantasy". Thinking about it, the other way around might have been nearer the mark. Then he opened the tape player and inserted a blank tape. "Next!"

If I ever want to write about a female Walter Mitty I have the outline right here. Quite what world she inhabits is a mystery. This sort can be killers, if their delusion becomes a strong paranoia. Not a suspect here though, just a sad, ageing woman grabbing the last of the light.

# TWENTY

Well before lunch, Craig got a call from the Irish officer, Prosser. He would be collected by officers working on the murder, might as well call it what it is, and he was to be in the reception area by the security office at 12:30 pm. Didn't they know he'd not yet had time for lunch, was this a deliberate ploy to unsettle him?

Without telling the rest of shipping where he was going, this was not that unusual where Craig was concerned, he slipped down to Reception, hoping that there would be no fuss but knowing full well that being collected by the police right in the middle of most of the facility's lunchbreak would be all over the company within minutes. When he got outside the building he could see an unmarked minibus, with Reid and others inside and so he made for it, but was eased away to the lone car. It was white and fully marked, anybody seeing him would think he was a criminal. Why just him, on his own?

Craig hated white cars for no more logical reason than that he'd once had one. He'd spent his savings on it when he was in his teens and it had lasted six months before the engine blew. It went for scrap, thirty quid cash, take it or leave it. It had been an ex-police car and he'd not realised when he bought it, another reason to hate white cars, especially white police cars.

The minibus left but Shepherd waited patiently by the cop car. He was surprised when Neil Martin emerged and came over. Another suspect, of course.

The city flashed past as they made their silent way to Central Police Station. He'd been there before, more than once, but not for a few years and usually entering through the main door, not from the underground car park. It was a short climb up some stairs, they were clean enough but with a hint of bodily fluids, these stairs had history.

He saw the rest of the NPS group in a cheery enough room, but he was led directly to an interview room and Martin to another. His head was spinning; did this mean he wasn't the prime suspect?

Once inside, his escort, the Irish one, settled one side of the desk next to an attractive woman, Craig on the other. His first question was whether this was a formal interview and should he have a solicitor present? Reasonable enough but giving away some knowledge of procedure, mind, they'd know that he had knowledge anyway. In that folder the guy was looking at would be a print out of Craig's misdemeanors, first to last.

This was, they said, a fact-seeking interview. Craig could, if he wished, have a solicitor but this was simply to complete gaps in Marie-Eve's timeline, a time line that Craig was a part of as he had placed the sample boxes in the freezer. It was now beyond doubt that Marie-Eve Legault was in the freezer at the time. It was also likely that she was still alive, but they couldn't say for sure, that would be known when they could do the autopsy.

Craig weighed up the situation while trying to look unruffled. He hadn't killed her, he knew that, obviously, but his alibi and proximity to her body were issues that the police were rightly pursuing. Asking for a solicitor now would infer a level of guilt, so he decided to play it cool, not have a solicitor, and to smile.

Although there was a recording device of some sort on the table, neither officer set it going, something that Craig struggled to get his head around. Surely that was procedure?

The attractive woman officer opened her notebook and they went line by line over the notes taken at his home earlier. Here and there she asked for more detail, anything to confirm something. A question about whether he'd had the radio on the way in or out, what did they play? Had he used the toilet during the call out? Had he seen the cleaners, did it look like the cleaning had already been done, bins empty, chairs stacked prior to mopping, that sort of thing? Despite his inner tremors Craig confidently answered every question while trying to think exactly why they'd asked that particular question.

Almost as an afterthought he mentioned that the doors were all left open by the cleaners, so he'd moved their buckets that had been holding them open away. "It upsets the air-con", he said, by way of an explanation.

"Just to clarify", said Prosser. "All the doors from Shipping, where you received the new samples, through to the Freezer Room, where the walk-in -20 freezer is housed, were all wedged open?"

"Yes, all except the middle door, the one with no card reader".

"Was there a bucket there or was the door just shut, as you'd expect it to be?"

"Just shut".

It took a while to get through the seemingly pointless trivia, and part way through he was given machine coffee without asking and the option of buying a Mars bar or something but he declined the chocolate, not his thing. There didn't appear to be anything in the interview to catch him out, nothing he'd not already covered; they just wanted what seemed to be another layer of pointless information.

The female officer closed her notebook and the other one shut the file, he'd kept it just out of visible range but Craig suspected he'd made notes in it too. They all stood and Craig presumed he'd get a ride back. She confirmed that he would, they had another employee to talk to and the transportation team were waiting for a full load. The end of the interview was more of a relief than Craig had realised. He was glad it was over and thought they'd not need to talk to him again, they'd got everything.

He hoisted his jacket off the back of the chair, it had come off ten minutes in, the room was on the warm side and Craig could feel his pits depositing sweat onto his clean shirt – a blue one, so the sweat patch was quite visible, white would have been better.

Craig had one arm in the jacket when the woman officer did the Columbo thing again, they must train watching old videos! Craig very nearly laughed, probably out of nervous tension more than anything. "What was your personal relationship with Marie-Eve Legault, your relationship outside of work?" she asked.

'This must be how people feel when they stand on a high place and look down and can't move', Craig thought. It was probably only obvious for a moment that he was the rabbit-in-the-headlights, but they'd notice, they were trained to and this was probably where the previous lengthy chat had been leading all along.

Both officers played it with a poker face.

Craig stopped, pulled his arm back out of the jacket, hoiked it back over the back of the chair and sat down. "I'll have that solicitor now, if you don't mind".

She only took five minutes to arrive. For Craig it was an uncomfortable time spent in an increasingly warm interview room. She introduced herself as Margaret Bough and asked for five minutes with her client. The officers seemed glad of the break. He was a smoker, Craig could smell it on him, and he was probably gasping.

Margaret Bough was quick and to the point, and satisfied that Craig had been honest with his statement, she seemed to like him. She also seemed a bit put out at not being there from the start but nothing she was told worried her. Now the crunch, Marie-Eve Legault, the physical relationship, everything.

After a generous twenty minutes, the police officers filed back in, took their seats and readied their pens.

Craig knew it would look bad but he really needed to pee. He was escorted to the loo by the Irish one, passing Mo in the corridor but avoiding her gaze, trying to give nothing away. He'd be the last in the station he was sure, everyone else would have been taken back to work. He was getting the extra attention, he knew it, and, based on their last question, he knew why.

Margaret, not Marge, nor Peggy, suggested in firm tones that her client had cooperated fully but there was an issue that needed explanation, also she would like to do the interview formally, on tape, for the record and in case it was needed at some future point. Craig was glad that no mention of court was made; he didn't much like going to court.

And, as the 'record' button finally got some work, so the rest of the story came out.

Craig had had a physical relationship with Marie-Eve Legault. It began shortly after her arrival in Nottingham. Craig had been the company greeter and had collected Marie-Eve from the airport, Heathrow, and taken her to the hotel in Wilford.

"Just the first time or on each of her subsequent arrivals?"

"Just the once, the first time. This is NPS we are talking about!"

He continued. He'd taken her out to dine on her first night and then, for a while the following week, spent time showing her around the city, sorting out financial issues – cash points and the like. Their relationship was conducted outside of work and was irregular. Meetings took place in Calverton, in a caravan on a private site near Springwater Golf Club. His caravan was on plot eight, the keys were in his work office, top left of the desk with a rabbit's foot on the key ring. Marie-Eve also had a key which she'd asked for 'in case'.

"In case of what?"

"She didn't specify but I'd presumed it was so she could go there incognito". She hadn't returned the key to Craig when the relationship ended.

"How and why and when did it end?"

"Marie-Eve came to my office and told me we were done about a week before she died. She said that it wasn't very professional, her being involved with a junior employee, and that it had just been a bit of fun. I was relieved, because I'd decided to end it at the next opportunity but I didn't feel I could just stroll into her office, like she did to me, and just dump her. I was being sensitive".

"Did you love her?"

"No, not even remotely".

"Why did it happen at all then?"

"I've asked myself the same question many times, it just happened. She was willing and I just let it happen. It was stupid, I regretted it".

"How many times did you meet in the caravan, and did you meet anywhere else?"

"No, only in the caravan. Four times, the last time two days before she dumped me", and he wrote out the four dates on the top of one of the sheets of paper on the desk. "They are marked in my Carp fishing diary, which is in the caravan at the moment".

"Marked, how?"

Craig realised that the next bit was going to sound silly. "I drew a little sketch of a Carp with a hook in its mouth next to the date. And, before you ask, I'm the Carp".

"And after, how did you get on with her?"

"We remained on good terms, as far as anyone was on good terms with Marie-Eve, she was spiky. We last spoke about the security issues in the Shipping Department, the broken card reader and the not-yet-installed CCTV, two days before she was found in the freezer. Other than that, we may have passed in the corridor but, if we did, I can't remember it".

And that was it, warts and all. Now, not only was he there when she was in the freezer, perhaps even while she was in the throes of dying, he was also shagging her for some of the time.

The officers said that they would need to check the dates and times for each liaison. They would also need a DNA sample from Craig. They would be seeking further corroboration for the affair time-line, perhaps from her phone or PC, but they would be discreet and, no, Craig's wife would not need to know unless it either came to court or she was needed to corroborate information. That answered the question that had been stuck in his throat since the solicitor had been requested. How the hell does this not reach Jemmy?

Craig then pointed out that Jemmy was away overnight, which made their ears prick up a bit. 'Whoops!' thought Craig, bad move her going on a trip, however short. She was a witness to his movements so, perhaps, they should have cleared the trip with the police, after all.

Reflecting on the afternoon and the unravelling of the whole affair, the cat was not only amongst the pigeons but busy rolling out the pastry crusts. Craig had a feeling that he was probably screwed in more ways than one. Still, it was a relief that they hadn't asked about the others!

At least he wasn't the only one being talked to by the police, there was some hope that somebody else would slip up and change the focus of their attention. He wondered about Mo. In the corridor earlier she'd been her annoying self as she sauntered past. What had she told them? Had she mentioned about her having a thing about Marie-Eve?

He bet she didn't know that Marie-Eve knew all about it and had found it amusing.

"Am I being charged now?" he asked.

"No", said Prosser. "You're free to go, for the present".

# TWENTY-ONE

Neil Martin walked briskly to the parked police car, back straight, eyes front, as if he was heading for his regular seat and not having been collected for interview. As he opened the car door he looked a bit nervous that Craig Shepherd was sat in the back too, but he barely acknowledged him. Once inside the car he shrank, visibly, and barely said an audible word all the way in.

Thompson had apologised for not fitting him in earlier and hoped he understood why. Martin had visions of Reid and Shepherd, battered and bruised, left crying in adjacent cells. Now he was next for the treatment.

In the Central Nick he was led to a little room with a table and three chairs. Steeling himself for whatever they were going to do, he was somewhat discombobulated by being offered a cup of tea, which he accepted. Settling in opposite him, Detective Sergeant Thompson and Detective Constable Banks introduced themselves, not that it was needed. His memory was like a steel blade, sharp.

Reaching into his top pocket he produced a printed sheet which gave very precise details of his movements. A separate sheet included all of the operations his personal electronic access card had recorded, for the period 6 pm to 7 am on the night of the murder. He'd redacted the other card operations on the same day which, when he thought about it, was pretty stupid. He was a bit surprised when they produced an un-redacted sheet with the exact same information on. Where had they got that from or, just as interesting, from who?

"First of all, Mr. Martin, in your capacity as Head of Security, can you tell us what we are seeing here?", and they'd highlighted several rows of card activity and the coded doors accessed.

"Each door has a specific code, when the door is operated the system records who, via their card, and when. Quite simple really".

"Yes, we get that, but there are some cards that do not have any identification but that accessed various doors within the facility, it just shows up as a 'V'. Would you mind explaining those, please?"

"Right, I see. Well, those used between 10 pm and 4 am will be the cleaners. They don't have personal cards; the agency they work for has a generic card with the same access for all the cleaners".

"So they can go anywhere, and who goes where is not specifically recorded, just that it is a cleaner?"

"Yes, and the others of course".

"Others?"

"Yes, the members of the Senior Management Committee don't have personal cards either. They are the senior managers after all, we can't expect them to be tracked the same as those lower down the pecking order".

"So, if we understand this correctly, there are two groups who could move around the facility without being tracked, cleaners and senior managers?"

Martin could see the flaw in the system immediately when they put it that way; the cleaners were being regarded as the same level as senior managers in terms of security. That would have to stop and he'd have to bollock whoever came up with it.

"Was Marie-Eve Legault a member of the Senior Management Committee?"

"Hardly, she was just a visitor. She did attend meetings but only as an advisor, she wasn't senior enough".

"And her card had access everywhere without tracking?"

"Again, she wasn't senior enough for that".

He could see that they were thinking that he was something of a bigoted idiot. He was Head of Security after all though, so he tried to explain further. "The cards don't require a finger scan either. The cleaners return their cards to Security at the end of their shifts, when they don't lose them, that is. During the regular day, those cards become visitors' passes. Remember, I issued you with them when you arrived on the day the body was found".

"Do people lose their cards very often?"

"Some do." He didn't add that Greenwood was on his third, he was the big boss and it wouldn't do for tales to get back to him, tales of how his Head of Security had dropped him in it.

"Is there a list of lost cards replaced?"

"No, the system has no way to record it".

"Do these lost cards get deactivated?"

"Of course, as soon as we are told they are lost".

"All of them?

"Most".

"So someone could enter the property using one of these active cards and, if not seen at the entry point, could then freely move around the facility at will and untracked?"

"The cameras would see them".

"Where they worked, true, but if you knew which ones were faulty, you could avoid them?"

"Yes, of course, but you'd need a good knowledge of the facility, not just anyone could do it".

"Who might have such knowledge?"

What were they, stupid or something? "Obviously Security know which cameras are out, we have to. Listen, we have to check every inch of the site, three times a night, we know the place inside out. We also report the issues weekly to the Senior Management Committee who take the appropriate action".

"I see. So, just to recap, you were on duty, alone, on the night that Marie-Eve Legault was killed. You know where the cameras don't work, which cards cannot be traced, and you know the site 'inside out'?"

A tiny little "yes" issued from the slightly trembling lips of Martin, who had realised when he got to 'inside out' that he would be looking at a murder charge before the end of the day.

The two officers left the table and stood in a corner, quietly deciding what was going to happen next. Then they left the room altogether. Martin was just about to get up and go when a uniformed officer entered and stood by the door. He wasn't especially large but that probably meant he was a martial arts master or something, you could never tell until it was too late.

After a few minutes Thompson came back alone. "Don't worry Mr. Martin, you are not a suspect. We have a record of your movements and we have an idea of the time of death, pending confirmation. Thank you for the information regarding the cards, especially the fact that not all are tracked. Please keep that information strictly to yourself".

Neil Martin was shell-shocked. He checked his watch, he'd been there twenty minutes, it had seemed like hours. He was led to the canteen to wait with the others for a ride back to NPS. His mind raced. Who had he inadvertently pointed the finger of suspicion at?

They all shuffled out of the canteen and climbed quietly into the waiting Transit van. Conversation was muted but then few of the other employees ever chatted to Martin socially, even Mo was quiet but that may have been a ploy. They stopped outside the main doors and Martin briskly walked back in. One of the new security people was sat in his chair, so he got told to move sharpish. He ignored Martin as though he wasn't there so Martin announced that he was going on patrol and shot off out, fuming.

Once he'd rounded the corner and was out of sight, the newbie security man got up and went over to the other chair. Behind him, the monitor covering the camera in the main corridor showed Martin kick a few doors as he passed. He headed straight for Sample Management, to get Mo to one side, away from other ears. He had stuff he felt he ought to tell her.

Thompson made his way to the canteen. He had sandwiches, haslet with mustard. He'd not seen haslet since he was a kid; he didn't actually know what it was apart from that it was a meat. He got a coffee and found a quiet table. Pulling out his current jotter he settled in for some background note taking.

Martin was rattled even before he got into the van. There isn't anything that points to him, apart from proximity. The CCTV shows him asleep for most of the early hours, once the delivery had been taken by Shepherd.

The card reader thing is interesting though. Who has a system that thinks that some are too important to track? I bet that Martin set it up that way, to aggrandise the bosses. What it does mean is that the Senior Management Committee now has to be thought about and checked out, despite what others think about the colour of the perps' collar.

Does the system actually track the card but not show the results? A question for the IT people who installed it. Perhaps there is a hidden log? Now that will be essential reading, if it exists.

We need to know exactly how many cards might be missing, cards with no tracking.

I wonder who he ran to, once he got back to NPS?

# Twenty-Two

## Wednesday 22 June

"Do you mind if I sit down?" Dominique Yip looked up from her book surprised to see Bez Dooley. Nobody ever sat with her at break or lunch, she was a company spy, everybody knew that.

"Sure, not worried that I'll report everything you say to Jim Duggan, though?"

"No, not at all, you don't strike me as the devious type, quite the opposite, actually".

"I see. Was there something work-related that you wanted Bez, or is this purely social? Only I've been here two weeks and so far everything has been work-related, except for Tina's birthday cake thing in Sample Management but that was short-lived. By the way, I think that is a really good idea, letting people off the leash for five minutes to chat and eat cake, something I'll remember if I'm ever in charge anywhere".

"Is that the official NPS position or just Dominque's Yip's view?"

"All mine, I don't think NPS and I think very similarly at all, these days".

After the opening salvo, Bez and Dominique chatted about this and that, the way strangers do, strangers getting to know each other a bit before hiking up the relationship level to acquaintance. Bez was pleased but not surprised. He'd been in meetings with Dominique and seen how she interacted with people, all of whom were certain that she was looking for a reason to report them. Such paranoia is quite normal when a stranger is dropped in your midst, especially so soon after the NPS takeover.

"I can only apologise for not doing this earlier but I had to observe first, just to see how the land lay. Here in Nottingham we were quite isolated from the changes in the industry. Most of the people come in, do the job and go home. As a manager I have to keep an eye on what is happening, read the pieces on Linked-In and try to make sure I am doing the right things".

Dominique didn't expect an explanation, she just shrugged it off as perfectly normal. She'd be the same if Bez, as a manager, had showed up in Montreal for reasons that were not entirely clear.

They chatted about China a fair bit. Bez was interested as much in the reasons for failure as the NPS attempt to expand in to the eastern market. He was pleased that they seemed to be getting on quite well, and was happy to be seen with her publically, despite the sideways look his wife, Wendy, had given him as she went through to join their regular lunch club.

"So Bez, now we have broken the ice, what do you really want?"

"Two things; the first was to break the ice because I wanted to know you better. You might only be here for a short time but I always welcome new ideas and you have lots of experience, your company profile on 'Our Family' tells me that you are someone worth knowing".

"OK, good answer, obviously thought out, a girl always likes a bit of praise. And the second reason, I'm guessing, will be related to the impending arrival of Marie-Eve Legault. Nominally your equal in Montreal but actually something a little different".

"Interesting, and if I show you my palm can you tell me how long I'm going to live and what next week's lottery numbers will be?"

Dominique laughed. "Sadly no, but I can tell that you that Madam Legault is a dangerous person in many ways. She will sweep in smiling but she will be calculating immediately what she thinks NPS should keep and what to discard, and that is not just at technical level. She has some sway at all levels, so the ever-so-slimy Mr. Greenwood had best watch out".

"Funny how all women don't think much of our Dick. If it helps any, nobody here does either, his appointment was a complete mystery to us".

"He won't be here long. NPS will have someone else lined up; they probably weren't available at the right time".

"Cynical".

"No, Bez, just a product of the experience you mentioned".

"And you?"

"Let's just say that my future plans are going to follow a different path. And you, Bez, are you prepared for the conflict to come? You will be one of the first she looks at although, and no disrespect, not at a physical level".

Now Bez laughed. "Relief floods through my veins. I've heard the odd rumour, all negative I'm afraid, so I'm expecting the worst".

"A good plan under the circumstances. Unfortunately, I'll still be here when she arrives and we don't really get on. I know what to expect, she has always been a bit difficult, but these past eighteen months or so she has been down-right painful. Between you and me, and whoever else you intend to tell, she went a bit angry after she very publically dumped her boyfriend, although there have been rumours that they are back together, at least unofficially".

"I don't know anything about her at that level, and I can't say that I really care".

"You may not care too much but information is sometimes useful. Her boyfriend was, or maybe is once again, Ben Arjah. You may not know

131

the name but you will know what his company does because you are dealing with their study samples. He is the head Honcho at Saviour".

"Is he? Well, that is interesting and, as you say, useful".

Bez was about to go for more details when he was paged back to his office for an incoming call from New Jersey; best not to keep them hanging on the telephone.

Dominique smiled, "thanks, Bez. I appreciate you taking the time to talk to me, in public, where all the conspiracy theorists could see us. I promise you I am not a company spy but there is a Facebook spy here. She's in the labs and she friended everyone that they let go in the first rif. I'm sure you can work out who it is. Now, off you go, it might be the mighty Jim wanting to gossip. We'll talk again I'm sure", and she picked up her book, trying to pick up where she'd left off.

'First rif', so the rumour was true, there was another one in the pipeline.

Back in his office, indeed it was Jim Duggan calling and, to Bez's surprise, he was touching base and asking that everything be done to help Marie-Eve Legault when she arrived. Shit, the big boss is in on whatever she's up to.

When the unexpected call ended, Bez made a mental note to make sure he got to spend more time talking to Dominique, she obviously knew more than she was letting on. He even wondered whether she like curry, and whether Wendy would be very happy if he invited Dominique to a working lunch at the local curry house sometime.

# TWENTY-THREE

## Friday 16 September

Marco Baggio wheeled the cart laden with brand new computers into the Sample Management room "Yo, ho, ho, Happy Christmas", he yelled, to little reaction. Simon Reid was talking to one of the techs but, on seeing Marco with his stack of PCs, went over to see why he was there.

"Simon, my friend, I have for you a bunch of the finest computers known to discounted bulk-buying, all bearing the latest fabulous Windows version, specially designed to cope with the requirements of modern computer users or, in this case, your lot!"

Reid shook his head. "We discussed this, Marco. Until we get the software to print labels working on the latest version of Windows we can't take the new PCs".

Marco immediately bit back. "I do as I am told, Reid, as should you, and my big boss babe says I should go and install the new computers in Sample Management now and so here I am".

This was typical, thought Reid, tie one hand and a leg behind our backs, why don't you? He dialled IT and had a short, but by the look of it, animated conversation with someone on the other end.

"Right, that's all sorted, we have another week to sort it, Marco. Go talk to your boss, she'll fill you in on the details", and with that he turned and went back to his patiently waiting tech.

Marco went ballistic and started throwing the new computers around, one for each desk. The entire room, who were only vaguely interested in the show before, were paying full attention now. This was real entertainment, much more fun even than when Reid and Mo got going on their weekly boil-up.

Marco looked up to see Reid had his phone out taking pictures or worse, a video, shit!

Backing down, he started picking up the new machines gently and placing them back on the cart. One had lost a bit of plastic off the front; it lay broken where it had landed.

"Simon, really, is that filming me necessary, mate? My mistake, look, I'll leave these over here, right?" and he eased the re-stacked machines into a clear corner.

"Honestly, Marco, I am not being awkward but if I can't print a label then we can't use the software, and you know how keen they are that we do that. I could do with some help, I've been trying to work on it when we are quiet".

"How far have you got, so far?"

"Nowhere, really, we are never quiet. Isn't there someone in IT who can give us a couple of hours? They will know how to get things working much better than me, although I can't help thinking that we need a software patch from LabSort, they probably need to do one for Clousseau across the board, what do you think?" Reid was offering an olive branch and hoping to get an IT person onside at the same time.

Marco backed off, hands held up. "Not my area, Simon, I install only, we don't have a real software man since the rif", and with that he went to leave the room, with another "sorry", tossed over one shoulder as he went.

Reid put his phone back in his pocket. He wasn't stupid, he knew that he could get in deep trouble using a camera inside a contract research facility; there were company laws. Good job that he'd only been waving it about and that Marco was stupid enough to think otherwise.

Mo hustled over. "Show me the vid, Simon, show me, man".

"Sorry to disappoint Mo, no video I'm afraid. Using my phone in here would be very bad facility security", and he went back to the still ever so patiently-waiting tech.

Once back at her hutch, Mo messaged Marco and told him all about it, winding him up like an elastic band. What was that phrase that people had used to describe her, in jest of course, 'shit disturber'. Yup, that was her, alright.

Marie-Eve Legault was in her office with the door closed despite the company much vaunted 'open door' policy. There was a loud angry knock and Marco walked in without invitation and started his diatribe against Reid. She listened, extracting the bits she needed to know before picking up the phone. Marco stood silently seething while she clearly spoke to Reid.

Expecting to hear that Reid had been fired or flogged even, his face sank when Legault chastised him loudly, citing the importance of the Sample Management software and how IT should be leading on trouble-shooting. He took none of it in, what was wrong with the stupid French bitch, he was the good guy here.

He left without further comment. Once Marie-Eve was happy that he was out of ear-shot she redialled, telling Reid that he had two days to sort out the printing problem or they would find somebody who could do his job, understood?

On the other end of the line, Reid flushed red and then went into the rarely used office and shut the door. Two days to fix a problem that was an IT issue and it was Friday, meaning that he'd be in all day Saturday unless he stopped a few hours after close of play today. There was the little fix that he'd found that was nearly ready, just a bit more testing to be sure, validation they called it, and he was tempted just to go ahead and use it and worry about glitches later, when he knew that

Legault would be gone for good. Why was he was surrounded by bastards and arseholes, or was that 'derrieresoles'?

# TWENTY-FOUR

## Tuesday 20 September

The view from Superintendent Perkins' office was about the best you could hope for, given that the Central Police Station was hemmed in by dull buildings, a multi-storey car park and the top of the old entrance to Victoria train station, now a shopping mall of the impersonal sort. You could, if you stood on the desk, make out a few of the nearby Arboretum trees and, although the place was heavily used by chavs, it still made a leafy place to go for quiet contemplation if the mood came upon you.

The short, loud knock was immediately followed by Inspector Charnley entering the room, no pause for a 'come in'. With Charnley in his current fragile state, Perkins had expected no less.

Charnley sat opposite Perkins with his face set to 'what!' Perkins knew the game and turned on the charm. "Thank you for coming, DI Charnley. The Legault murder, any progress to report?"

"My team are carrying out their enquiries diligently. No arrest has been made, none is expected just yet. Five potentials, three firm, one nearly solid but not supported by evidence - you remember evidence? It's what we need when we arrest and then later allow the courts to successfully convict people".

Perkins didn't bite; he'd been here before so many times with Charnley recently that it was starting to get boring.

"There are aspects to this case, Jock, which are attracting attention from above; indeed comments have been made regarding the need for a quick resolution, if at all possible. The importance of NPS to our local economy and the quality of the people who are involved with NPS at senior levels, have prompted the Chief Constable, no less, to ask me to tell you to get a move on. This must be seen as a simple murder, perhaps a crime of passion and therefore committed by someone involved in a passionate relationship with Ms. Legault. A timely resolution would be best for NPS, best for the force and best for the other unfortunates who have become embroiled in the case through no real fault of their own".

"Craig Shepherd didn't kill Legault, we don't have anything but circumstantial evidence and it doesn't sit right. We've talked to him and he's never tripped up, that tells me he is answering our questions truthfully".

"From where I sit, Jock, he is the most obvious candidate. He ticks all the boxes and the estimated time that Ms. Legault was placed in the freezer is close enough. Charge him, scare him, make the man sing for us but, if you do, make him sing the right song, we are always being watched these days. In times past we'd have had Craig Shepherd shitting himself and willing to admit to being the iceberg that sank the Titanic, just to get some peace. I know the old days are perhaps where they now belong, in the past, but surely he has enough boxes ticked to push on?"

"As I told you, Sir, it doesn't fit and we don't have the evidence for the CPP to make a case. Your call, of course. Your career too, I'd expect".

"No firm evidence, yes, true, but I'm sure you will find some or some will come to light via some other avenue, especially if your people get their bottoms into gear and turn enough stones and lift enough logs. I do wonder sometimes, Jock, whether you have lost your motivation?"

Charnley looked at Perkins, the mantra in his head was chanting 'don't, don't, don't'. He knew that if he just punched Perkins until his face was jam, they'd only put another one in his place, so don't.

Charnley stood up and left, closing the door behind him lightly. "You may leave", said Perkins smiling.

Sitting back, his leather chair creaked slightly, it was an old one that he'd had brought in and it had seen a lot of distinguished posteriors over the years. Of course, the leather that covered it now was not the original material by a long way, but the whole did have a history and Perkins rather liked that. It was only a chair and an old chair at that, but, it was a comfort to him when dealing with the likes of Jock Charnley.

Perhaps, Perkins thought, I should be a bit more hands-on with this one, get amongst Charnley's team and chivvy them up a bit. We don't want this to go on too long, it really wouldn't do at all. After further thought he decided to just fire off an email, copying in the whole team and making veiled threats disguised as observations. Thompson was no fool, nor were the rest of the team, and pressing Charnley didn't seem to be transmitting the urgency for a result as much as he'd have liked it to. He decided to go all melodramatic and give them three days to come up with something concrete, or he might have to bring in some sharper minds to assist.

Satisfied that he had at least done something, he dialled a number he knew by heart and reported progress. He'd bought a little time but, barring a disaster, or another murder linked to the Legault case, he was confident that the obvious, to him, would be the answer and that Craig Shepherd would fit the bill nicely.

Thompson just happened to be at his work PC when the email came through. Conscientiously he printed off five copies, opened his desk drawer and slipped them in. If Perkins looked, if he knew how that is, then the system would say that five copies of a controlled document had been printed, assumed them to have been distributed to those concerned, read and understood, job done.

# TWENTY-FIVE

## Wednesday 22 June

Dominique supposed that the management had taken into account her Chinese ancestry when they sent her out to China to work on the Far Eastern Project, or FEP as they'd reduced it to when making reference in planning meetings (and 'what the FEP' in private!). That she didn't speak Chinese and that her family were Canadians with a good few years in the country didn't seem to matter, she looked the part and so off she went.

In no time at all it was quite clear that the 'venture' was doomed to failure. The Chinese had their own way of working and simply were not interested in taking on board the methods and standards required to satisfy the western regulators. She got the impression that they were actually quite insulted when she tried to train them to GLP standard but they never said as much, they were awfully polite to her, at least at work.

There was also the problem of the imported staff settling, however temporarily. For everyone arriving from Canada this was an adventure, for sure, but also one with a definite end point, a time when they could return to the jobs they knew, where they lived, at home in Canada. Adventure was all well and good but in the long term, the FEP was just a break from the Quebec norm and not at all like their real working world.

Despite regular teleconferences, and her making her desire to come home quite clear to NPS's management, Dominique was still stuck away from home in the UK, although not now in such a difficult spot. She'd been told, sure, there was a place for her back in Montreal but first would she help out in the UK with the new NPS acquisition there? Although it was dressed up as another opportunity to ingratiate herself with the company 'high-ups', Dominique knew she that was just being pushed into something else that she'd rather avoid at that time. The insistence of NPS had helped her to make up her mind.

As things panned out, she agreed to do three months in Nottingham but they didn't know that she'd also lined up something else for when she returned home, they didn't need to know about that either. When the time came, she'd do what she had always wanted to do to the company. She'd give them just a few minutes notice that she was leaving the company and at a time of her own choosing, just like they'd done to several of her friends in various past rifs.

Apart from the occasional despair at not being at home, an upside was the extra money she was earning, this was part of the sweetener to get her to China in the first place, now the Nottingham gig would keep that going a little while longer and her formerly sorry little Registered Retirement Savings Plan was going to get a welcome boost come the end of the year. The financial side was just about enough to lessen the 'Marie-Eve effect': she'd be working in the same area as her again, reporting to her in fact, and that was no picnic. They had a very chequered history, but then who didn't with Marie-Eve Legault?

Thankfully, due to their scheduling, she'd only have a couple of weeks of her before heading back to Canada, but two weeks of Madam Legault was more than enough for anyone and she wasn't the only one who thought so.

Dominique's ex-boyfriend, Gilles, had ended up being one of Marie-Eve's little friends for a while, he still bridled whenever she was mentioned. Dominique quite liked still being on good terms with him; as a friend, he was quite protective. True, he could be a bit volatile sometimes but he was handy if she needed a bit of support. If only he'd asked her about Marie-Eve first, she'd have been able to save him from some severe grief. In Montreal, the girly gossip was rife with her wayward goings-on, as her Granny might have said.

141

Typically, Gilles had been badly chewed up and spat out, and Marie-Eve was one of the reasons why he'd left NPS. He seemed much happier these days, working for Air Canada, the jet-set life suited him and he had a few tales to tell when they had their platonic date nights, infrequent though they were. He said he'd take her somewhere swanky the next time he did a London lay-over and had time to take the train north.

The work in Nottingham had turned out to be quite easy. The Brits were a pretty easy-going bunch, mostly, and would usually just have a little bluster before accepting any changes she felt they should make to align with planet NPS. She'd actually quite enjoyed meeting a few characters, not Dick Greenwood though; slime ball central as far as Dominique was concerned. No, everyone else was quite nice, even though they saw her as a company spy. Well, at least one of them now knew that was not the case.

News of Marie-Eve's untimely demise, or timely if you had a different perspective, came the week she was planning to leave NPS. It wouldn't change her plans at all; she had a window of a couple of weeks between jobs, it had all been very deliberate in the timing, she needed a bit of a break. It hadn't occurred to her that she might have information pertinent to the murder until she had a call from her friend in Nottingham.

Thinking about it, her getting involved would only end up dragging her into NPS business again, something she was intending to get well away from and, besides, it might end up dragging Bez into it too.

# TWENTY-SIX

## Tuesday 20 September

In Neil Martin's world you always had pride in your appearance. Shiny black boots, a crisp, clean shirt and spotless tie every day and you had a crease in the uniform trousers that you could cut cake with, that was the way. Everyone thought that he was ex-military, or had at least spent time in something official requiring a uniform. He encouraged it without actually saying that it was not the case. Neil had been in the Territorial Army but that hadn't worked out too well. He'd only been in for a couple of months before things caught up with him, as they always seemed to. Now he felt that had found his life niche, as Head of Security at Nash Pharmaceutical Solutions (Nottingham).

This business with dead Marie-Eve Legault was bad for him and the company. She'd always seemed OK to him in a 'what's your name again?' sort of way. Busy people are like that though, as evidenced by the same trouble in remembering names that most senior NPS people had. It was nothing personal, simply a matter of rank and water off an old campaigning duck's back.

Martin reckoned that only one person could have done the dirty and that was Craig Shepherd, pretty boy himself, it had to be. He had the MMO, means, motive and opportunity, basic first rule of detection. They all knew Marie-Eve didn't think much of Craig, the way she was so offhand with him, there is your motive. Craig was a vain type of guy, a shallow looker. Martin had seen the likes before, fancied themselves and expected every pretty girl, or boy, depending which way they leant, to fancy them too. Certainly Craig tried to come across as harmless, but it was pretty clear to Martin that he used his looks and physique to intimidate.

Staying with the classic TV Cop thought process, Martin added up the pointers without any trouble at all. Craig had access to the delivery bay and knew all the routes around the company, there's your means and Craig had the cover of a sample delivery to help him kill Legault, probably using chloroform first to subdue her then injecting her with an untraceable drug to make her unable to move. Then he put her in the freezer to muddy the tracks. Quite why that lot from the police couldn't see that Craig was the killer was beyond him. He went back to his word search, doing the easy ones first, CAT.

He wasn't alone in thinking it was Craig. Mo agreed, they'd talked, of course they'd talked, the phone call had lasted an hour; they were soul mates. She'd been out for shots with one of the female detectives, Laura, and she'd told Mo that they all thought that it was Craig; they were just putting together the details before the arrest. Martin hoped that Craig would be arrested at work. He could do crowd control, clear the way as Craig, arms up his back, was roughly shoved along the corridors and into the back of a cop car, his head been forcibly pressed down as he got in, just like on the telly.

Martin did wonder about the other stuff though, the bits even he'd noticed didn't quite fit. Craig was obvious when he was around, everyone knew him and he'd made no attempt to hide or even be slightly furtive on the night of the killing. The police had asked for the CCTV, but the Shipping Room and Loading Bay set were down, pending the installation of a new system. They didn't ask for the other ones though, even though Craig had been on one of them, looking over at me and waving at me as bold as brass when he came in for the shipment, when he killed Marie-Eve Legault. It was good that they didn't ask, so far Martin had got away with not having the cameras set to record, any of them. Besides, it was only a technical error and the night log had an entry noting the equipment failure again.

Then there was the mystery of Martin's keys. For three days, his keys had been missing, probably left in a freezer door or something, so he had to use the spare bunch. It was always happening and this was weeks before Marie-Eve had died, probably nothing to bother the police with. Curiously, it had been Craig who had found them and handed them back. Had the killer, stalking the freezer room at quiet times, found the keys in a freezer lock, made a copy, then put them where he knew that they'd be found? That would mean it wasn't Craig, so it had to be Reid. Neil would ask Craig who had actually found his keys if he got the chance, before they carted him off to the nick.

The phone pinged; a delivery was coming, e.t.a, 2 am. Oddly, Craig was still on the stand-by list so Martin sent him a message. *'Control here, delivery imminent, 2 am, respond in the affirmative'*, send. A few minutes later the phone rang, it was Craig, he sounded wide awake. "Why are you texting me, Neil? It's Reid tonight". Neil huffed that he thought Craig would find he was wrong. The schedule printed and pinned to the wall clearly had Craig, 'despite the circumstances'. "Check your email please, Neil. A revised schedule was sent out by Bez this afternoon. I'm off the schedule for the rest of the week, at least".

"Hold". Neil was such a tosser, thought Craig. "Ah, yes, I see it now, it went to the spam folder but I found it, another IT error". Only Neil Martin could lie with pride!

"Call Reid then", Craig said and was about to hang up when Neil said "my keys, who found them?" Craig was losing patience but tried to hide the frustration, "I did, Neil, they were down the back of the sofa in the reception to HR, OK?" "Roger that, and out", and Martin hung up.

So, the key theory was a bust, a daft idea anyway, one of Mo's crappier ones. He went back to his word search. Fifteen minutes later he realised that he'd not texted Reid so he called him.

"Reid, there is a delivery coming at 2 am, I've been calling for the past half an hour, did you turn the phone ringer down, or off even?"

"No, Neil, I didn't, must be patchy reception here. I'm on my way, I'll be ten minutes". Martin then cleared the call history on the phone automatically, that was one task he had mastered.

Now Martin was in a dilemma. Clearly Craig was not the killer, meaning that the real killer, Reid, was on his way to the facility and only a few cleaners would be around as back-up. If Reid thought that he'd figured out that it was him who had killed Legault, then he'd likely be the next to go, so he locked the Security Office door and awaited Reid's arrival.

Reid came in through the front doors; that was unexpected. "One box, Neil, it will be quicker to carry it up. We are using the Pharmacy walk-in as temporary storage so it needs double-checking when you do your rounds and please keep an eye on the alarm. We had to shift all the deliveries to it so that the police could do their stuff in ours". Martin was stood in a slightly defensive combat stance that he'd seen on a YouTube cage fighting video, except that he kept his shirt on. He nodded at Reid as in the affirmative. Reid just shrugged and went off to Pharmacy.

He was back inside five minutes. "All done, paperwork in Sample Management if anyone needs it. I'll be off, are you alright there, Neil?" Martin still held the defensive pose and just said "fine thanks, just stretching my back using some karate moves from the old days". This time it was Reid's turn to nod before turning and letting himself out. Neil watched the front security camera until Reid's car had left the vicinity, then sat down with a thump. It has to be Reid he thought, he looks guilty.

Settling back into his chair, Martin started to nod off. Double-shifts were getting to him but it wouldn't be for much longer, he had a run of just days after tonight.

He found that he was losing concentration through tiredness, but now that they were at the quiet hours he'd be able to get some desk sleep, a couple of hours at least. Another night without pills, Mo would be proud, if she knew. He didn't know how long he'd been in the land of nod when the beep of the card reader seeped into his consciousness. "Evening, or should I say, good morning." It was Richard Greenwood, what the fuck is he doing here?

"Just resting my eyes there, Sir, been a busy shift and not had chance to take my break, yet".

"Oh, don't mind me, I couldn't sleep again so I thought I'd come in and catch up, always busy, you know that. I like to be here when it's nice and quiet, nothing to disturb you while you go about your business", and Greenwood went off towards his office as if it were 9 am and not 3:30 am.

Martin decided that fresh coffee was needed and set to making it. 'What if' he thought - 'what if Greenwood had done it, he had the means and the opportunity and now he's here, with me, alone.' He checked that the door was still locked, slid the Plexiglas window across a bit more to make the gap a bit tighter and went, reluctantly, back to his word search, FATALITY!

# TWENTY-SEVEN

## Wednesday 06 July

Dave Thompson sat by the bed looking at Jock Charnley, his Detective Inspector, as he readjusted his gown and got back into the bed. He was looking better but still a bit detached.

"Any sign of him?"

"No, Sir, he's skipped the country. It might be a while before we get wind of him again".

Charnley seemed to take it in. Then he was confused a bit again, his face blank before he seemed to snap into focus. "I want him, Thompson, I'll get him".

"Yes, Sir, we all want him, we want to have a good, rough arrest with lots of resisting and some heavy subduing, then he'll know our displeasure, but we've got find the bugger first".

Charnley nodded. Thompson knew that there was no way in this world that he'd ever get his hands on Ray Frost, the man who broke his leg and shut him in the boot of a car before trying to drop it into the compactor at his mate's scrap yard. Charnley had brought it on himself by going gung-ho solo, again. Now Frost was being well-hidden by his associates and he wouldn't chance gracing these shores with his presence any time soon.

Thompson had seen Post Traumatic Stress Disorder before, probably even had a mild dose himself, as a young PC. Experience rounds the edge off your ability to be stressed, but the first few bodies, especially when kids are involved, that should shock anyone. Even Prosser, a battle-hardened bog-trotter from the Shanklin Road, has his moments and he's seen the real stuff of nightmares, so it was not surprising that Charnley was finding it hard to adjust after his near-death experience, he might never get over it, not fully.

Charnley looked tired, too. They must have been sedating him, to help him rest, a dreamless sleep but he'd still been having nightmares during the day, flashbacks. Thompson couldn't imagine being trapped in the enclosed space of the car boot; the pain from the broken leg and the sound of the machinery, the grinding and crunching of the car crusher going about its business, not knowing when you'd be feeling it start to compress your soft body, squeezing the life slowly and painfully from you. That the boot had popped first and then Charnley had managed to scramble out was nothing short of a miracle. A million to one chance, the lads in the scrap yard had said, innocently.

Of course they'd pulled Heard and his associates in, and been heavy with them. Well, as heavy as you can be, but Heard denied all knowledge, he'd been with his wife on a jolly in Amsterdam, and there were lots of witnesses to confirm that. The scrapyard had been empty at the time, none of Heard's lads were there and they too had solid alibis. It was all down to the absent Frost.

Naturally the team had taken it on the chin. They liked Charnley, as much as you can when the boss is a cantankerous sod at the best of times, but he was never malicious, like some. If you did well he expected it of you, if you fucked up you got a bollocking and didn't complain and that was the end of it; that was the system. Like him or not, it didn't stop the wisecracks. 'A tight squeeze in here, Dave,' 'Pressed for time, Dave,' 'Room for a little one?' They really were a bunch of bastards sometimes, he'd be sure to lay down the law when Charnley came back, if he ever did.

"What are we working on at the moment?" Charnley liked to hear bits and pieces from work; it seemed to help him grab back a bit of reality one chunk at a time. "Insurance death, Sir. A bloke called Mike Westland, tried to get a leg lopped off by an Intercity Train at

149

Attenborough. It didn't end well, the draught sucked him under and turned him into a bit of a mess. We think he was helped by a mate, there to call for an ambulance and staunch the blood; a mate who 'just happened to be passing', he said. He's not admitted it yet, but we have a 'friend of a friend' conversation to hit him with, see how he feels then".

"What the fuck would a healthy person want to lose a leg for?"

"Seems he was always intending to retire early, bragged to his mates at work that he'd lose a leg and be on disability for life".

"Twat, he might have been better going for losing the bloody head, nothing but shit for brains by the sounds of it".

Thompson laughed, that was as close to a joke as Charnley ever got; that was a good sign and a bit surprising. In the four years he'd been on Charnley's team he'd only tried what they took as a joke with the team a handful of times before, each one being an inevitable Tumbleweed moment. Did he know that he was a crap comedian or was he just stubborn?

Charnley was going to be discharged in a few days, then have some psychiatric stuff, then an assessment before a return to duty. If all went well he'd be back in a month, if not then they might have to break in another Detective Inspector. Thompson hoped not, much better the Devil you know.

Once Thompson had gone, Charnley relaxed. He'd never been much of a one for role play but now he was method acting for all he was worth. He knew he was being watched and he thought he knew who by. They'd be waiting for him once he got back to work, waiting for a screw-up, a reason to toss him out early. A watch, a card and 'goodbye and don't come back', on the scrapheap you go. He gave a mild chuckle, two jokes in one day, well nearly, I must be going mad.

Back at the station, the team were all eager to hear the news. Like Thompson they didn't want a new DI before time, someone who was out to prove themselves to the world at their expense. Pity nobody in the team had the required yet. Well, Thompson did, but in Nottingham they rarely seemed to promote from within an existing team for some reason.

Thompson decided not to sugar-coat it. Nobody wins that way. He told the team that he thought that Charnley might not come back, that he might find the strain of active police work too much and have to take an early. "You mean bottle it at the vital moment?" It was Liam Prosser, who had a blunt way about him that some found refreshing, others thought it marked him out as an ignorant shit.

"Something like that, and with him going it is likely to be our arses in slings for the duration. I think we have to hope that if, and it is a big if I think, he does come back, he is sound. We'll all have to baby-sit a bit until we can trust him again, agreed?" There was no argument, Thompson had hit the right notes.

A week later, Thompson was summoned to the Superintendent's office for a little chat, as Perkins put it. He got pumped for information about Charnley, his state of mind and body after the assault. It sounded like none of the senior officers had been to see him, not really surprising. Thompson knew that Charnley was lacking in the apron department and everyone knew that a flexible apron was an absolute must if you wanted to reach the heady heights in today's modern Police Service.

Thompson sat with both cheeks firmly on the fence. He told Perkins that Charnley looked and sounded good to him, but he was not an expert, and medical minds would decide. Perkins listened and said little, when he did speak you had the overwhelming desire to wash your ears out thoroughly with Vim. Perkins was the sort of person that Thompson's people would have hidden in caves from, back in the dim and distant day.

151

"I do hope you are not withholding important information from me, Detective Sergeant. A career in the police can be fraught with obstacles, some there to test, others simply to impede movement. Some may even be employed in a negative sense, driving the most promising career in the wrong direction". No disguising the threat there, then.

"As I said, Sir, I leave the complicated stuff to those who have the education and experience. I may think Detective Inspector Charnley is sound in all areas but a specialist might not, only time will tell".

"Very well, but before you go back to keeping our streets safe, DS Thompson, there are a few things for you to ponder. Our friend Jock Charnley will no doubt suggest that the Freemasons are responsible for many of the ills in the Police Service. This is not so, and Jock himself well knows the extent of Masonic influence right here in Nottingham, you should ask him why but he won't say, he can't say. Yes there are people in the force who are Masons and, yes, some try to use the organisation as a way to rise but, I assure you, it no longer works quite that way".

"I'll have to take your word on that, Sir, I don't know or care much about societies like the Masons, secret or otherwise. I like to keep my life simple and free from outside distractions, free to concentrate on my job and my family".

"Very laudable, DS Thompson, and as it should be. However, if you ever did have an interest at some future point in your career, you will be aware that there are ways and means to make your interest known. Thank you Dave, regular reports if you please", and, having been summarily dismissed, Thompson went back to the office trying to work out what had just happened. Was Perkins suggesting that Charnley was a Mason, was he also suggesting that he should apply to join to help his career? Only bits of it had made sense; but that always seemed to be the case when you had a 'little chat' with Perkins.

Thompson had been right, inside a month Charnley was back at work but definitely not his former self. It had been confirmed via the grapevine that he'd be retiring in the near future, and Charnley himself had told Thompson the same but without giving any details. Thompson assumed it was PTSD-related but, as ever, there were other forces at work in this particular game and Charnley's recent 'they are watching me' routine was perhaps not so far from the truth, after all.

# TWENTY-EIGHT

## Thursday 03 March

Ben sat down in the comfortable wicker chair on the deck overlooking the Marina at Key West. He was on a short break with his partner, 'in crime' he supposed. He was using the place of a friend, well at least someone who wanted to be Ben's friend, it was nicely anonymous. The wine was chilled and they'd just got back from an excellent seafood restaurant. It was good to get away from the business of business for a while and he thought she appreciated it, besides there were things to discuss.

Marie-Eve and Ben had been sort of an item for some years. Not living together but snatching time here and there, as and when they could, if it suited them. Ben's work kept him busy, very busy, but he'd assured her that it was only temporary, while he made enough money to make the future financially secure. Marie-Eve Legault always wanted to ask whether that secure future included her, but it never seemed to be the right time or circumstances.

There had been a time in Ben's life when he'd not been secure in any area of his day-to-day existence. He lived on the street for a while, dined on the finest dried cat food, Ocean Treasure with Real Shrimp, and relied on his ingenuity to survive. His looks had helped, he scrubbed up remarkably well and that had got him on the right track via a number of besotted and wealthy girlfriends. He didn't have a single expensive gift of theirs left now; the lot had been sold almost as quickly as they had arrived, watches, jewellery, even a car one time.

He'd pulled it off by always being on the move and accumulating enough as he went. Ben found that he was especially good at persuading people to back him, and the very rich often made for surprisingly gullible people. Not the new rich, the people who had made their money through their own sweat, but old rich, they were careless with money and even more careless with information. Ben had stockpiled both with a single plan in mind, to leave it all behind and live somewhere with no worries of any sort, financially and emotionally secure. And that plan, the work of many years, was almost at the point of fruition.

Marie-Eve wasn't stupid, not by a long way. She'd seen part of what Ben was, knew that she'd never know or even want to know the other parts of him, but they had clicked and she knew he felt the same way. The 'no-kids' option and the 'no recriminations until they reached their goal' was also their choice. Some women used the unexpected arrival of kids as sprung-traps intended to snare a live one, not Marie-Eve, kids were not for her.

The only thing that slightly concerned her was Ben's relationship with Carrie, his PA. They were obviously close, sometimes talked in code and she naturally wondered whether they had just a professional relationship. She wasn't jealous if they didn't, they'd both agreed that monogamy at this stage of their lives didn't always suit either of them.

Ben had often spoken of having a plan without ever elaborating. Now, here on this break, when they could be with each other, indulge each other, she expected to finally hear all about it, but all in good time. You didn't try to rush Ben Arjah.

Ben liked to set moods. Part of his job was getting people in the mood to do whatever he thought they should be doing. His consultancy had done well and she knew that they had enough to live well enough now without working again if they didn't want to. She'd even be happy to move in, make it official, settle down a bit, but he'd be restless unless he'd carried out his big plan, a plan that she was sure that she would be an integral part of, that was how Ben worked.

"I think we know each other well enough now for me to ask you for complete trust and to not make assumptions or judgements", Ben said.

She laughed, "We know each other well enough and, well, yes, I should say that no assumptions or judgements apply".

"I want to show you my plan, or at least give you a verbal description. It is not written anywhere except in my head and, for it to work, it needs to stay that way. It will be dangerous, illegal even, actually very illegal, are you still in?"

That laugh again, "I expected nothing less. Which one of us is Bonnie and which Clyde?"

"Neither, we are Ponzi squared and then some!"

She was intrigued, this must be how Ben's clients get settled and sold whatever Ben is selling. Eased into a position where they are hanging on his every word and, when the whole is revealed, it is almost a relief.

"We need to split up".

She didn't panic, not even a flinch, she just waited for the rest of the conversation to unfold. Ben had tried to shock her, to test her, to see whether she had the stomach for this, whatever it was. It must be big, it might be dangerous, it would be final; the last part of Ben's plan, the key that opens the door to whatever it is he has decided. My part is in there somewhere, and after. She waited some more.

"When?"

Now Ben smiled. If she had been something furry looking into the eyes of that smile, she'd have been shaking to her expensive shoes. "I intend to make us very rich but first I have to appear focused and my focus will be exponentially sharpened by our splitting up in a very public fashion, once we've become very publically official that is. When the split happens, and it will be a while before we are ready, it will be acrimonious, it will make me appear vulnerable, it will give people who know of it the chance to help, to be involved. I want 'poor Ben', I want 'driven by the failure of his relationship'. I need to be pitied at first".

156

"Then?"

"Then I need to be engaged by a project, pour my renowned energy into it, be seen to be determined to drive the project to success, grand success, fortune making success. Easy money for investors' success".

"Then?"

"Put simply, we take the money and run".

'Where?'

"I have a property in Australia and I have Australian citizenship and so will you. We will live near Brisbane and we will live very well. We will develop into well-rounded people with the Australian competitive edge that makes them so special, so successful. We'll be called something different of course but we will be gone, untraceable, lost to all seekers".

"And the plan, do I have to change my name to Sheila?"

Ben ignored the joke. "I have a drug compound, I will get it nearly to the point where it goes to the FDA for approval and to get to that point I will need investors. I will take 650 million dollars out of it, give or take. It will cost 50 million to move the money, it will cost 30 million dollars to set it all up and make everything work, the rest will be ours and there will not be a trail to us or it. The plan will take time, it is already underway and we will be looking at the final phase inside around 18-months, perhaps earlier. We will need to be flexible and ready to act quickly".

"And my part in this involves me using my position within the industry, and specifically within Nash Pharmaceutical Services, to ease the way at minimum cost? I will be the grease that lubricates the mechanism?"

Ben didn't answer immediately, he seemed to be reading an autocue that only he could see, he just continued with the presentation, as Marie-Eve thought of it.

"My plan is, by necessity, very complex and it has many characters. Obviously, I have to play a part. I will vanish after the most expensive phase is underway. You will already have vanished and you will do that soon after our split. Nobody can know anything. No friends, no family. As neither of us has much family to think about, that is not really a problem. Friends will be harder, but necessary".

Marie-Eve took another sip of the very good wine.

"For you to play your part, people have to fear you, hate you even. You have to behave in a way that makes people below and above nervous and you have to have a hard edge in everything. You will have to be many things but, as you rightly surmised, you are integral to my plan and your position within the pharmaceutical industry will be key. You are going to have to be something that you are not, play a part and play it so well that nobody knows any different. Can you do that?"

"So you expect me being on the inside just to help you, to prostitute myself, lose my friends and be a figure of hate just so you can make a killing? You fucking bastard, get out of here, you bastard, I'll fucking kill you!"

Ben sat perfectly still, he'd long known that he'd made the right choice, she was perfect. He smiled that winning smile again and she laughed like a horse. Reaching into his pocket he produced a small, finely crafted locket, silver, cloisonné. It was heart shaped but so tastefully designed that you could ignore the hackneyed 'lovers entwined' crap. It had obviously cost a fortune and, although Marie-Eve usually dressed lightly where jewellery was concerned, it hit exactly the right note.

They didn't sleep much that night, the next day it was straight into the role for both of them.

# TWENTY-NINE

Saviour began as a daft idea, but then many things do. Ben had listened to the banter, punched his Blackberry with notes and then left the dinner table. Conferences were always like this, dull until dinner and then, after a bit of judiciously applied, mouth-lubricating alcohol had been provided - on account, as expected - guards were dropped. It was then that secrets slipped, ideas could be harvested and contacts made. The best ideas came from those who had been indiscreet and wanted their conference activities to remain at the conference. They were always the easiest to manipulate later and Ben always made sure he had the tools.

Once Ben had digested some unexpected information; given it serious thought and examined all the angles, he knew his patience was about to pay off. He'd had a plan in his head for years and had been waiting for the right opportunity to crop up, as he knew it would. It didn't take much work at all, just him and his long-time PA, Carrie, making calls, filling in forms and talking to the right people and soon he was the proud owner of Saviour, a new player in the drug research market. Now he needed some help, people he could work with but then discard once they became less useful; he knew just the people to talk to.

The two stooges he had in mind were only too happy to jump right in. They had dollar signs in their eyes obstructing their view of a few of the wrinkles that Ben had yet to resolve. Virtual they called it, a virtual company. They had no roof, no heating, no parking lot, no water cooler. They only existed electronically, which meant that the staff, the 'three pharmaceutical adventurers' as Grant Lang liked to call them, got to work from home and could have a relaxing morning in bed. It wasn't really like work at all.

In short time they had a company web site, Saviour email addresses and business cards, very professional-looking, too. Now all they needed was a registered office address as a mail drop and they were away. The oil that was going to make the whole machine function would be Ben's insiders in the industry and he was fairly confident there, like minds and all that.

For the two other equal business partners, the early signs were there that this one was going to be the big one. All three Saviour executives had to put up a share of the cash to buy the compound. Gavin Jupp and Grant Lang had even put their houses into the mix to raise the cash to make the investment, Grant was a bit better off than Gavin, but still had to dump the Ferrari in favour of a leased Lexus to make his share. It was a good sign that he was prepared to rough it for the product.

The whole project had a good feel-good factor to it. They'd all made a few dollars trading their portfolios over the years, bought cheap, sold at the right time and now they were ready for the pension play, the last big investment before shutting their filo-faxes, well Blackberries now, and buying the condo in Phoenix and a lodge in the mountains. Grant was something else, not unknown because he'd been around on the fringes for years. He had even given good advice to those he had some respect for, if unsolicited. The Laxo shares he'd put Gavin's way had been a boon, easy money really even if there was a hint of insider trading about the whole thing. Still, when a 'friend-of-a-friend' says it's a good thing and there's no route from them to you, it's your choice if you stick or twist.

Once Saviour became an entity, the industry then knew that something interesting was afoot and it was not too late for some to get involved while others were keeping their investment options open a little longer, just in case. Articles on Linked-In under the pseudonym 'The Pill of Truth' had even mentioned the 'G-spots' involvement. Grant rather liked the nickname, it conjured up an image that pleased him and it took his mind off his ex after she'd dumped him. It was Ben that had first called them the G-spots one boozy evening, right after the Cellux business - now that was a big payout and a leg-up for him and Grant in the industry. Gavin was less keen on the name though; he liked to keep a lower profile and he kept his cards close to his chest, from the team and the players alike.

People called him Ben, or Benjamin when they wanted to be formal, usually depending on whether the people that he was trying to impress and involve were important. Mostly he was just Ben at home and to his friends. He was always a busy man, a bundle of activity and his grey temples showed it. The only time he got callouses on those fidgety hands was when his friends' kids forced him to practice hockey with them. Maybe that was why he was always made a point of keeping out of the way as much as possible but without seeming rude, keeping everyone onside, as always.

The capital venture people also knew something very big was cooking-that was their job after all-but nobody could get inside, not if Ben didn't want you, and everybody wanted to be inside when Ben was doing his stuff. Ben was, historically, 'pure gold', they said.

The research project would, officially and publically, take around to two to four years and patience was of the essence. The irony was not lost on Ben; patience was never something the modern pharmaceutical industry could ever be accused of practicing. Those shareholders' bank accounts didn't feed themselves and so, across the board, the industry had to keep offering a short-term return on what was supposed to be a long-term investment. How they did that was not Ben's problem, just another fish to catch and, this time, a pretty big one too.

And so Saviour was born, or at least emerged from a cave blinking; a virtual pharmaceutical research company, perfect for a virtual world. Ben was the face and he, Gavin and Grant had put their pile into the study money pot. Where the initial study money came from, even if there would be significant casualties, was not something that interested Ben. True, he'd spend wisely of course, wouldn't stint, no need to not make sure things ran smoothly for the cost of a few thousand dollars or more. Not when the end-game was going to be so profitable and, when it inevitably went into a manufactured belly-up, Ben had his own, personal back-door.

He recruited a team of Clinical Research Associates, made sure to pay them well and gave them the enthusiasm that good money could buy. Next he'd had them set up the clinical trials at sites where they could pursue what politicians referred to as 'best value', which meant reduced cost, lower standards, fewer questions and flexibility, always flexibility.

To put a gloss on the project, he needed a clearing house which would deflect a just little any of the questions regarding his choice of clinical sites, somewhere more acceptable to the North American palate, closer to home. He settled on a place in Mexico, a new place but one eager to do business with the respected Ben Arjah. Perfect.

Patient enrollment had been very good but then so had the financial encouragement and they were up and running very quickly. Samples were being collected and shipped and would soon be deluging the analysis location. The whole project now had its own head of steam and was starting to become unstoppable. Now that they had samples and were guaranteed encouraging results, it was time to bring in Marie-Eve and let her do her thing.

# THIRTY

Despite her not feeling too great, Marie-Eve turned up at the posh restaurant on time, Ben was late. This was supposed to be a public performance, a distancing operation to have anyone looking too closely, confused, if only temporarily. There was another problem; one that she ought to mention but Ben didn't seem so receptive to her these days. Was he really acting as they'd agreed? If he was he was very good, Broadway good. Maybe the pressure of the project was getting to him.

Once seated, Ben ordered wine but she stuck with water, citing an upset stomach, maybe a bug or something. "We should eat first", he said, rather coldly. This was probably going to be easier than she thought, just remember this is a fiction.

In the intervening period between Ben recruiting her for the project and getting down to the nitty-gritty, Marie-Eve had more or less decided that this whole episode in her life was simply a means to an end. If it went well with Ben then OK, but she'd do what she always did and ensure that she had an independent option, a fall-back position. For now she'd give this little charade everything, they'd certainly remember this when she'd left Ben to pay the bill. She was pretty sure that she could keep her eyes dry, pretty sure.

Their voices got progressively louder. The well-heeled couple at the table right in the middle of the restaurant were having a real disagreement bordering on violence. The Maître-d was about to step in when the woman stood, swearing loudly at her date in French and threw the contents of her meal onto him. Not content with the effectiveness of her food barrage she then emptied what had been a

163

very good wine all over his head. He just sat there, obviously embarrassed.

Marie-Eve stormed out leaving him to not only pick up the tab but also looking a real mess. At least she didn't use the bottle, there was a palpable fear amongst the restaurant staff that that could happen, such was the bile in her voice, belittling her date.

"Problem, Mr. Arjah? Madam Legault appeared to be in a state of distress".

"Yes" said Ben, "I'm sorry that our little tiff had to happen here, so public. She's very volatile and that, I'm afraid, is that as far as we are concerned, pity".

The Maître-d shrugged, "Ah, the affairs of the heart, so complicated. There are very many fishes in the seas though, Mr. Arjah, I suggest you take up fishing again".

Ben laughed. The Maître-d was only talking English because he thought Ben was anglophone. "Sage advice, indeed. Sorry again about the disturbance, add the cleaning cost to my bill, please".

Ben paid and left. A text pinged in his pocket. *'Good enough?'* His thumbs went to work *'you are a very naughty girl, Madam'*. He pressed send, then deleted the sent messages from his phone; then he ran his deep clean app, just in case.

# THIRTY-ONE

## Thursday 31 March

Ben liked using anonymous little places like the Quality Suites. They were efficient and business-like and there were so many options in the business meeting-type suites across North America that he never needed to use the same one twice. A bonus was the wodge of loyalty cards he had for every chain, never knock a free room, his reward for being such a regular customer.

It helped too that potential investors could stop on-site, not that they ever did. Satisfied that Ben and his company were not squandering their hard-earned capital on personal luxuries, they'd slope off somewhere much more glamorous, on expenses of course. People could be so easy to influence sometimes.

The room was set up, his PowerPoint presentation ready to go and the 18 specially selected people were in situ, ready to be impressed. Some of the people viewing the show worked for Ben, they were dummy investors; they were there to ensure that the greedy sheep mentality prevailed. The ones he was after only numbered six, but the day was set up to catch the lot, use their greed with promises of even bigger piles of cash. They liked the thought of big piles of cash, easy cash, so did Ben.

He made sure to circulate, he knew most of the people to nod to at least, one or two a little better, relationships he had been carefully tending since he first hatched his plan. One who thought Ben a friend, touched his arm and said in a subdued voice "sorry to hear about you and Marie-Eve, Ben. She was an interesting girl but, perhaps, not quite right for you at this time in your life".

165

Ben smiled his hurt but brave smile "You may be right, Bob, she is history now though. My focus is here on the project, no distractions".

Nibble, nibble, bite!

Good coffee and quality hand-made cookies were served, each little snack treat finished with a small, personalised box of specially imported British chocolates, they really know how to do good chocolate, and then they were all ready to go. It was often the little things like free chocolates that hooked the fish.

"Gentlemen", he said, for they all were. "The compound is good, we know that and a summary of the pre-clinical situation is in appendix one of the proposal. For those of you not chemically-minded, the compound works on subcutaneous fat deposits slowly, so the patient loses weight and has the opportunity to work their bodies into some sort of shape - if, that is, we get the drug into their bodies, but before that, onto the market".

One of the plants asked a question, brusquely, as if an answer was expected without questioning their unalienable right to ask it. Just the sort of way someone wealthy and used to getting their own way would behave, nice. "Where did the compound come from and why is it available?"

"Good question", said Ben praising the asker's understanding of the process. "The compound was being developed by a small bio-tech in France but they were the subject of an aggressive takeover and so the owners chose to sell it on before their predator could get at it. They got taken over as they expected, but the company management, they were a sort of cooperative, let it happen and only revealed that the compound had left the building after the takeover had been completed. The company was then liquidated by the new owner and the staff all made redundant with zero compensation, via some legal offshore ownership loop hole. Not our problem".

"Had they completed pre-clinical and were they ready to start clinical?" This time it was a different potential investor asking the right questions.

"Pre-clinical is all but wrapped up; clinical is now set up, the details of which I'll come to".

Ben knew this was true because he'd owned the biotech and had engineered the take-over so that he had cash from the forced sale; he had moved the compound elsewhere long before the new people came in. He was more than happy that they didn't find what they were looking for but they really shouldn't have known about it in the first place. That they did was something Ben had filed under 'pending'.

One of the real money men asked a question. Here we go, thought Ben, bait the hook and they will bite.

"I'm a simple kind of guy", he said, "so let me just clear this in my mind, just to help me along and anyone else who might not get the science jargon". There was a bit of subtle nodding around the room, three bites for real by the look of it. "You have a compound; it is a good one and will hopefully get to the drug stage. The drug is for obesity and we all know that size of that market", there was a ripple of laughter. "Sorry 'bout the pun", he continued. "So you want investors to put up for the clinical trials. How much money is needed, what is the percentage chance of a getting the drug onto the market?"

The question couldn't have been better put if the guy had been one of Ben's plants, but he wasn't.

Ben looked him square in the eyes, prepared to hit them hard. The set up for the trials had cost an initial 2.5 million, that figure is a rough estimate at this time, as it is ongoing". Anticipating the next question he continued, "The cost is relatively cheap because we are using subjects from countries where the costs are proportionally much lower than those used in western-based trials. Investment now buys a chance to be on the inside when the drug gets to market, and I would say it is

75% likely that the drug gets to market right now and based on the results we have in so far. In our field, 75% likely at this stage is very good, but not perfect".

Before there were any more interruptions Ben went on. "The 2.5 million is invested in the parent company, Saviour, who are setting up the clinical trials and dealing with the shipment of samples, analysis schedule and results interpretation. We are a virtual company, which means we don't own buildings; we don't hire more people than we need and we don't have big pharma overheads, everything is spent on the research project. Saviour only has one compound and will only ever have one compound. There are three people listed as Directors of Saviour, these people are paid directors, their salary is in part seven of the document you all have".

Somebody asked Ben to verbally outline the timeline; "yes, it was in the presentation but verbally please".

"The goal is to get the compound approved by the Federal Drug Administration and associated regulatory bodies, then to sell it on to big pharma while retaining an investor interest for a short period. The 2.5 million is the Saviour directors' initial costs, which we have already put up and spent. We will need more and that will be needed after the initial round of clinical trials get underway, when we need to take it further. We can only estimate here, at present, but we are talking around 65 million, give or take, to get it to the point where we can sell it as a viable option to big pharma".

"Are you talking to any of the big pharma companies and, again roughly, what is in it for them?"

Ben had to admit, Carrie had written a very convincing script.

"We have spoken to several of the biggest players but not committed to any at present. Whichever pharmaceutical company buys the compound from us, the receipt from sales would be an estimated 35 billion in the first year. That figure is just the estimate for North America; well the USA, to be precise".

There was no intake of breath at the profit estimate from anyone; that would have been too obvious. None of the crusty old poker players in the crowd would be showing anyone their cards today.

"If we invest with Saviour, how safe is our investment?Are there any safeguards?"

"At all stages investors can review their position and reduce their future liability, but that would also reduce their profit option, too. Investments are non-returnable but, as I said, should an investor decide that they had reached their limit, including before FDA approval for manufacture, so pre compound sale, then their return on that sale will be pro-rata. In effect, you will be betting on a 75% chance that your investment will multiply considerably, and the longer you stay in, the more you will make when, and if, the compound is successful in getting to market".

Naturally, more questions followed, but the gleam in their eyes told Ben that he'd sold the snake-oil and now it just needed to go down the legal route - Saviour's hired business team were all ready to roll and would visit each investor's legal people with complicated contracts at their convenience. Funds would then be transferred on a set schedule to Saviour, not all at once but enough to make it worthwhile, Bingo!

A few days later, Ben visited each of his briefing plants personally, handing over their cash and reminding them of the seriously binding nature of the non-disclosure agreement that they had signed before taking the role. He wasn't worried; they'd all worked like this before. Pay them enough cash, and he made sure that he did, and they would always be willing to go method for a while, and silent thereafter.

# THIRTY-TWO

In his role as CEO of Saviour, Ben Arjah spent most of his busy days in personal meetings. As he prepared for the latest round, he took out the fluffy toy duck from his briefcase and inserted his laptop. Carrie, his personal assistant, was always slipping stuff in there and it always made him smile, just a bit. His next meeting was in no meeting planner nor would it ever be. Carrie knew that she could reach him if needed but otherwise this was as good as a black ops. He was crossing the tracks and going to a sleazy Country and Western dive on the outskirts of town. It had 'secret meeting' written all over it and the guy he was seeing just didn't realise that. No matter, this was business at the sharp and dangerous end and this was another complication that he needed for the project.

He took up a place near a window so that he could see who came and went, and to make sure that the right people came. If not he would go, he had already sorted out his escape route if needs be.

The cab pulled up and a very casually dressed guy got out, a simple flight bag over one arm. Inside the greeting was simple. For the next two hours and over quite a good lunch of fried chicken, southern style, the details of the task that the visitor was expected to complete were discussed. Ben then paid the bill; his guest climbed into another pre-arranged, anonymous cab and was gone.

There was still work to do but Ben had a major part of the initial finance sorted and now he would have his guest run a subtle diversion in Nottingham. He texted Carrie to say 'all done' and went back on the grid, his phone chirping away with missed calls and messages, as he'd expected it would.

# THIRTY-THREE

## Tuesday 26 April

Marie-Eve climbed out of the warm bed, sticky. Ben was asleep, for now, so she took advantage of the lull in activity to grab a shower and a think. What was wrong here? This one was just supposed to be temporary and yet she felt warmth. Just because she'd sealed the Ben deal with a blowjob, there was no need to get all sentimental, business was business and the finder fee, as she had previously thought of it, would set her up nicely.

The shower was hot and powerful; it was a good choice to go for a power shower when she had the renovation done, the ones that just dribble on you like a leaky child were not fit for purpose. Why had she thought 'child'?

It was true that her biological clock was chiming last orders, loud and clear, but she'd managed to hit the mute button on it last time, so why was hit hitting instant reset now? Was Ben more than just another exotic-looking plaything to her? Her instincts had told her to go with the flow and bail out at the right time, but here she was again, and so was he.

She padded through to the kitchen and got the coffee on the go. He'd be off soon, once her allotted three hours had been reached. It suited her nicely, she had things to do, people to meet, offshore bank accounts to put money into. She wasn't too pleased to be stuck out here in Mirabel, even temporarily, but Ben was right. They were supposed to have split up acrimoniously, although both had heard the rumours of a possible reconciliation. Someone must have seen them. Oh well, at this stage of the game it hardly mattered.

Being on the inside of the Saviour thing was not why Marie-Eve had gotten into the drug research business. Her motives had been quite pure when she left university. Help the sick, heal the world, do some good and get paid for it. It didn't take long to realise that drug research is rather mercenary and that most research, especially in a contract research facility, was simply a means to a profit. Once the lesson had been learned, and she'd seen how brutal employers could be, she'd acquired a 'portfolio' of information to help her fulfill her potential. It guaranteed her independence from the whims of the industry, and any men she got involved with, always temporarily, along the way.

Ben had come along at the right time for her and bearing the right credentials though. His Lebanese ancestry had helped, had given him an 'in' with Marie-Eve at a physical level but it was later, when he started to talk about making a killing with a virtual company that her ears had well and truly pricked up. Now, though, she felt she was in the classic mistress situation where she wanted him to be 'the one' but he had no apparent intention or desire to go there officially. What to do? That the wife substitute was actually his big plan that he had left her for was academic, maybe all would be well as he'd said. The feeling that she didn't really know where she stood with Ben, on a personal level, was starting to get to her.

The coffee machine beeped as Ben entered the room. He'd had a quick splash too and was dressed and ready to leave. Suddenly Marie-Eve felt stupid, stark naked at the kitchen counter, making him coffee.

"Off so soon"? She said, thinking she'd got another 45 minutes left at least. "Got to, things to do today, investor meeting too and you know how tricky they can be". Not a flicker from either of them. Ben obviously had no tact where Marie-Eve was concerned and she wasn't going to give him the satisfaction of showing hurt, or, if not really hurt, then annoyance at least.

He slurped half a cup of coffee and made to go. "Are we good with everything?" "Yes, all is good; I don't think there will be any problems.

172

Listen, I am being sent to Nottingham, England to help with the NPS integration, I'll be back roughly once a month for a few days. OK?"

"I know you are, that is where I wanted you; it helps spread a bit of confusion. The samples are all going there from now on, so it adds a nice level of complication, I like it, I can use it". And off he went smiling, but it was the smug smile and not the sex smile, like it used to be.

Marie-Eve was a bit confused, how did he know about Nottingham? She'd only just been told. It seemed that going to Britain and being in the facility that would be holding his Saviour samples had now become an important part of the plan, a plan that she had thought that she was also integral to but was last to know about. Never mind, just think of the dollars, Marie-Eve.

Leaving Montreal and moving somewhere different temporarily, away from her friends, the cabal even, such as it was, would be an irritation. The language wasn't an issue; her parents had foreseen the value of a fluently bilingual daughter and how it would help her forge her place in the world. Sometimes, unless you knew differently, you'd never guess that Marie-Eve was a Quebecoise and that she identified as Francophone strongly, on other occasions it was strikingly obvious.

The language thing was the rock with which some Quebecois intended to break the chain of ties with Canada, Quebec would be a self-determining nation. In seeking sovereignty, they were protecting the values and traditions of the Quebecois but especially the language, especially the language. It was ironic that most of the movers and shakers in the organisation were completely bilingual. Some had even legally attended English school, thanks to their fathers' schooling, ironic indeed.

Like most of the things in Marie-Eve's life, the cabal, and she really didn't think that was a great name but the others had liked it, was a means to an end. There was no way that she was going to remain in

Quebec. Not just because it would get complicated later because of the Saviour thing, no, it was too damn cold and Marie-Eve liked to feel the sun on her back. She had thought that she might just become a wealthy Snowbird. Split her year between a chic downtown, air-conditioned Montreal house in the summer and a swish Miami pad in the winter. Perfect. She might even go for a place in the Caribbean or Central America too, a time share maybe.

Despite the earlier stuff about Australia and being together, she hadn't really believed it. No, being a Snowbird would suit her better, but she would have to maintain plausible deniability where the Saviour study was concerned though, she'd have to be as shocked as everyone else when Ben vanished.

Marie-Eve knew nothing about Nottingham. Google showed it to be a big city but nothing like Montreal. It had a good night life, it said, and a small airport nearby but with no direct flights to Canada. It didn't rain all of the time like the west and it wasn't cold, in the overall scheme of things. They had gun crime, the highest per capita in England, so it was quite like Montreal in that way. It would be an experience and there would be a whole new set of people she could like or irritate at her pleasure. There'd also probably be men, interesting perhaps, but definitely temporary, men.

Ben called the next day, talking about what she'd need to do when she went to England, making sure that she knew the technical details of what she'd do to help smooth things. What he wanted was stuff that she could easily find out, she had unrestricted access to most areas on the company system, for now at least. IT had told her that they were bringing in a new system of central filing, company-wide, and system access would be limited on a need-to-know basis. That would add a layer of irritation but she'd find a way around it. NPS were certainly more security aware than Heal-Well had ever been. She'd better let Ben know about that, it wasn't general knowledge but one of the Anglophone IT guys was a close and formerly personal friend and still harboured hopes of renewing the friendship. Well, elements of it, despite his girlfriend being pregnant.

When Marie-Eve next met Ben, it was a short, social thing, a business conference and, for reasons she didn't really understand given her importance, she'd been placed in a booth representing NPS. It wasn't demanding- smile, listen and do the job of handing out NPS goodies, especially the memory sticks with their service details on. Not a very effective way of promoting what was supposed to be a big player in pharma now, but at least they were trying.

The news of the potential security changes made him quiet for a while; this was something he didn't know. He made an excuse to use the bathroom and it was twenty minutes before she saw him again. Slight change of plan", he said. "We could do with more precise start dates and details of access levels to information". Marie-Eve took in the information but couldn't talk much, her USB thumbs had suddenly become popular and people were hurrying over to get their one gig of free storage, well a bit less after the space for the departmental adverts had been accounted for.

Marie-Eve decided that the best thing was to get her little IT friend on his own, maybe in a quiet restaurant, and use her charm. He would be more likely to give her what she needed if she hinted that she'd reciprocate in kind. She wasn't going to, of course, that boat had long sailed.

She called him when she was back at work. A conversation over an IT issue was good cover. He sounded a bit unsure of the restaurant date but she assured him of her discretion, besides, if anyone saw them it was just two friends chatting. They decided on 'La Belle Province' in Beauharnois. It was far enough out of the way for their meeting to be anonymous, just another couple of travellers grabbing a snack together.

It was late afternoon when they got there; separate cars of course, keep up the pretence. He had suggested Marie-Eve's own place in Ile Bizard, but that was not on, it would be too easy for him to think she was open to more than debate. The waitress came over and Marie-Eve ordered. 'La Belle Province' staff were always happy to hear a Quebecois voice. After she'd brought over their coffees and left them to it, they both started to talk in English, but quietly.

He was nervous, this information was classified, he made out like it was some kind of spy thriller stuff and that he was a special agent. There would only be a couple of people in NPS Montreal who were trusted enough to know what was going on, he was lucky to be one of the few because he was lead IT on it. Marie-Eve calmed his fears. She wanted to know to stay ahead of the game, to show willingness to learn, be the first to embrace a new system. The bosses liked that, it showed leadership, she'd be in his debt for the heads-up.

Pulling a laptop from his case and plugging in a VPN he logged on to the new system via the free WiFi. She was right, it was much tighter. It would make it harder to manipulate anything, any activity would all be tracked; leaving an audit trail that anyone with the right access could follow. He told her that validation was all but completed, this was a priority and it was supposed to be live in two weeks to manager level, then other levels would be trained at intervals thereafter. They were also trialling it in other NPS facilities in North America and Europe. Marie-Eve knew that 'Europe' meant 'Nottingham'.

The waitress brought their food. She must have heard some English words because she muttered something unflattering. Marie-Eve was tempted to give her a broadside, she had the full range of French swearing at her disposal, but it would only attract attention and so she let it pass and made a joke in French to her companion, who took the hint and laughed, without arousing further waitress-based ire. He was a bilingual laugher, after all.

Her stooge made sure she knew that this was a secret; she had to be surprised when the Senior Management Committee in Montreal revealed it, play the part, for me. He tried for a kiss but she diverted, giving him a swift peck on each cheek. She was on her way back to her car when he called after her. "I suppose you ought to know that something called 'Our Family' goes live at the same time too? Look it up on the company intra-net, I just put everything up there earlier".

'Our Family', what the fuck was that and how come she was out of the loop on this stuff? She was going to have to talk to a few people, remind them who she was!

She called Ben while sat under the Mercier Bridge, a nice anonymous place. He listened without interrupting and then there was silence. She knew it was a Ben pause, so waited for him to resume the conversation. "Right, we are going to have to bring things forward a bit. The Nottingham site will get flooded with even more samples and the analysis schedule will be pushed hard. I need to get us to the next phase of investment but I need some tangible, if not terribly representative, results to show before they'll commit further. We can't take the chance of not being able to make the later results suit our needs now, so we need to put up a smoke-screen".

"And I suppose that is where I come in?"

"Yes, you'll be pulling any strings that require a good tug. We can work OK after the new system goes online with what we have but only for a short while". He'd planned on six-months; the new timeline will be much shorter. "Be sure to come back here at least once per month as you said, the company will pay for it, a sick aunt or something will do. We'll arrange for our little reconciliation to take place on your last visit; that will give time for news to bleed out in the drug research community, spread a bit of warmth. I'll get back to you with details of where and when. Have a good trip". She wanted to ask about meeting up at the Mirabel place again when she came back but he was gone, so she probably wouldn't be seeing him before the merde really hit the fan.

The unexpected abruptness in Ben's voice rang warning bells again and the old steely survival instinct began to kick in. She was sure knew where she stood now, she'd made the decision. Pity, there was another outcome she'd been still half-hoping for until today, just a day dream really on the face of it.

# THIRTY-FOUR

## Wednesday 27 April

Lewis looked around at the empty Sample Management office in Montreal, whoever thought that synchronized breaks were a good idea should be boiled in oil. Here he was again, holding the fort while the rest yap and moan in the cafeteria although, thankfully, there shouldn't be too much sample activity this late in the day. Everyone else in the department seemed to be morning creatures anyway, turning into a pumpkin or some other sort of suitable vegetable when the end of shift bell chimed, admittedly a short trip for some.

It was around three-thirty in the afternoon when the first batch of polystyrene cooler boxes started to arrive at the counter, delivered by the guy who shouldn't have been able to get inside what was supposed to be a secure establishment. 'Fat Steve'; was known to everyone though, and was able to wander around at will during any of his several daily deliveries, so it was not really that much of a surprise when his chubby little face appeared at the lab door, bearing multiple gifts.

Normally the boxes in a late delivery would get dumped into a walk-in minus 20°C freezer in Shipping until being delivered to Sample Management and processed the next day, but the shipping guy couldn't find anyone to deal with them. Early leavers had gone, smokers were outside and the dodgers were nowhere to be seen. Receiving looked like a morgue, so here they were, boxes and boxes of samples. It looked like he'd have to beg for overtime again, or more likely just do it and plead to add it to his rack of outstanding hours owed, later.

The paperwork was a mess, only the old waybills, mixed up with the new ones, gave a clue of the shipment's origins. Mexico, India, France, Russia and one of the unpronounceable 'stans', amongst others. This was a big batch of thousands upon thousands of clinical samples, collected in what were probably back-street clinics in some of the world's scruffiest cities. What were they for? Not a clue, nothing was expected to arrive for analysis on his schedule, but then the so-called early warning system they had was useless, much like the guy who was supposed to make it work, where do they find these ass-holes? It was time to delve into the dry-ice-filled boxes for some clues.

The good news was that the study protocol number was consistent on the samples he'd checked so far, even if the rest of the info was a bit askew. They were either plasma or serum vials, all human and originating from 27 scattered sites, and then all sent to a facility in Mexico for consolidation for some reason. After re-boxing and icing there, they'd been sent on to Nash Pharmaceutical Solutions – Montreal, oh good!

Just a quick glance at a few random samples confirmed that the clinical sites had continued the time-honoured tradition of putting the wrong stuff in the wrong tube, a bit of a problem when each tube's bar-code was supposed to be unique to the sample. Much of the tiny scribble on the tubes, even if it was in English, was illegible; this would be a 'double-glasses for magnification' job when he got around to sorting it out.

The boxes held no shipping inventory sheets inside, but no surprises there. Clinical stuff was such a pain, always a mess and it was always time-consuming just to get the samples into their new system, such as it was. The new system, Clousseau, was at least running now, it had taken two years just to sort out the IT glitches before they could then try to make something of it. Now those 'higher up', which meant just about everybody compared to Lewis, were frantically trying to put every one of the tens of thousands of samples scattered around the facility into it, just to show the clients how clever they were. The fact is, all of them had been the managers-in-post when the software had been originally bought, and not one of them had a clue how it worked.

Lewis knew that he'd been lucky to land the Sample Management job at NPS, coming from 'outside' as it were. It had only happened after the project lead had buggered off on holiday, having sat on her hands for six months when she was supposed to be getting something practical working. The fact that she fell for a Panamanian while there and never came back was just a stroke of luck. At least this was better than being a lab pot washer, Lewis's former 'support' role. The software was simple but actually designed for something else entirely. With a little bit of tweaking, and using some functions creatively, they now had a process and a buy-in to the new sample management process from perhaps 15% of scientific. It would take time, but it would be worth it for everyone.

Lost samples were one of the biggest banes of Lewis's life. Hours were spent searching the 20 or so -80°C freezers next door that were packed with samples going back to the Ark. There was a 'do it now, worry about technicalities later' thought process at NPS and its predecessor, Heal-Well, and it had permeated through to all departments. This was most definitely not what Lewis had expected from science. If the world only knew how unorganised it was, they'd think twice before reaching for those pills-well, some would.

The software package had come from LabSort at great cost. For some reason LabSort had thought to use the names of famous fictional detectives for elements of their software, but had not really thought it through. Montreal were using a version of Clousseau for sample management. The analytical software was also Clousseau but a different module. They were planning on a revamp of the system and they were supposed to be getting a training version of something they were thinking of calling LeStrange. The original package had been obtained cheaply from the French software people - France, a country where they never did understand the Pink Panther, why else would they choose its bumbling anti-hero Clousseau, and then spell it wrong, for a product that was supposed to be top of the (economy) range?

The synchronised-across-the-facility clock on the wall said 5:30 pm. Lewis had been digging through the samples for an hour and a half and couldn't feel his fingertips, dry-ice does that to you. With nothing in the system to tell him what they were and only the sample labels to go on, they all got stored at minus 80°C, filling up the emergency freezer. It was going to be frost-bitten fingers crossed that none of the other freezers went down in the night. Sod's law said that one would though, but that was somebody else's problem. It had been six months since the site manager had farmed out Montreal's night security to a local firm. If there was a freezer crash, you just had to hope that the one who could read and write as a minimum, and preferably in English, was on shift. If not, well he didn't hire them.

Lewis sent an email to each of our four heads of the various bioanalytical departments, plus Shipping, and to the dorkus Sebastien Cormier, the shipment tracker, and then made for the exit. Being a Sample Management technician at NPS was the ultimate mushroom job, kept in the dark all the time and fed copious amounts of, well, merde.

It was two weeks before a reply to the emails asking about the samples came back and then only after the fifth reminder. Julie St-Pierre in Immunology replied that the samples were for a clinical study coded S1P1CL500, the client is called 'Saviour', no NPS study number yet'.

'Yes, Julie, I told you that in my email because I too can read a sample label', he thought.

'We have no protocol as yet but it's not a problem, no idea what the client wants to do yet, we haven't even signed a contract but that is not your concern. The only thing we do know is to expect a few more samples but no idea when or how many. Leave them at minus 80°C for now, better to be too cold than too warm'.

Lewis replied giving thanks, he realised that he was being a bit hard on her, she'd probably only just found out herself. Next he'd have to memo the whole thing, so that anyone wanting to follow the sample tracking audit trail had something to refer to. He had little choice in the matter, GLP was something that Quality Assurance monitored very closely and he didn't want to fall foul of them again. Even without Marie-Eve Legault at the helm, they were still incredibly retentive.

Good Laboratory Practice was brought in when TV was black and white, to at least try to set a basic standard for all research scientists to adhere to. NPS was supposed to be a GLP-compliant facility but five minutes with the samples inventory and the FDA would stop the study, dig deeper into Saviour's creative approach to scientific clarity and then they would look at other studies that were also a mess and shut the place down. Or they might, unless directed otherwise, it had happened elsewhere.

Lewis had decided early on, when he first moved to Sample Management, that he'd keep his head down and learn both GLP and how to read a protocol. The latter was important now that they were using Clousseau because each study design, the thing that generated the unique bar codes in the system, was taken directly from the Study Director's protocol. Sample collection points, days, hours, minutes amounts, types, it was all covered somewhere, you just had to know how to read it.

One of the problems was that, at NPS Montreal, fiefdoms were rife and each scientific department had 'its own way' of doing things, as he was told and, when he'd pointed out that they would benefit from a coordinated system that they all used, they asked who was he to question the intelligentsia? He was just a former 'pot washer', now above his station.

Chantal in Immunochemistry had actually said that to him once. Chantal was supposed to be a scientist and therefore knew better than the likes of technicians like Lewis. She was still very upset because Lewis had proved that she didn't understand one of the protocols for a study once. Marie-Eve had naturally taken her side and he'd had to

183

apologise (for being right) while she sat there like Miss Piggy, lording it. She was not one of the 15% of happy scientists. Eventually they would all be using Clousseau, and they would all be following the process, and they would all have to conform because the lord and master, Jim Duggan, had said so and his will be done, or else!

By the 26th Saviour study shipment, they were still struggling. The samples that had been pouring in almost solidly for weeks, necessitating the renting of three more expensive freezers. It turned out that they were for a very promising clinical study into an anti-obesity drug. It didn't take a scientist to know that, if the compound used for the clinical study was any good, it would effectively corner the market in the treatment of obesity; a market that was, both in reality and metaphorically, huge! If they were at the clinical stage then it could even be on the market in three to five years.

It was projects like the obesity one and, of course, needing the job, that really kept Lewis going in the pharmaceutical business. He liked the feeling that he was helping out and, in however small a way, playing a part in getting some effective treatment to market with the Saviour study, for what was a very insidious disease. The one concern here, and it was quite a large one for Lewis, was that the vital clinical stage for this drug was apparently being done on the cheap in ethically-dubious third-world countries, all to make Saviour's research expenses as low as possible.

Perhaps there was a very good reason for the reduced cost route, maybe it was the only way a small, virtual company like Saviour could have afforded to get this far. One thing was for certain, at some point one of the big pharmaceutical companies would be paying handsomely to take the whole thing off Saviour's ephemeral hands.

Given the volume of work the study was going to provide, nobody had delved too deeply into the client, Saviour, for much background. They were, as per their limited but fancy web site, virtual, but this was not that unusual, NPS had dozens of contracts with small, virtual biotechs.

The head of Saviour was well-known in the industry and to NPS, Ben Arjah, and so the contract, Lewis was told, was fairly loose in detail, initially. Aside from guaranteeing NPS the analytical rights, the sheer scale of the project wasn't totally clear. They were all finding out about that factor, now that it was a done deal.

Once Lewis had got the information he'd really needed, he had started to work up a process using Clousseau and then they would try importing the inventory sheets that they would create for each delivery, directly into the system. It would have been plain sailing and he was quietly pleased with himself for coming up with the process, pleased until he was told that there had been a sudden change in plan and that all the samples would be re-shipped to their newest facility in Nottingham. On top of that, his counterpart from NPS in Nottingham would be visiting Montreal for training. That would be training by Lewis, on Clousseau. The email also made it clear that the Nottingham guy, Simon Reid, would need a full briefing on the Saviour study, especially on any processes he would need to use for Sample Management; that is Lewis's processes.

It was almost, but not quite enough for Lewis to get his coat. The only thing stopping him was the fact that getting another job in the area was nigh-on impossible without fluency in French, and Lewis was some way from that level. He got by in science because the world language of science is English and it helped to have a fluent English speaker in-post in a largely Francophone department, especially as all documentation was in English.

Montreal losing a study the size of the Saviour project was a blow - it had promised an element of job security for the duration and Lewis knew that he could quickly have become the study 'expert' on the ground. A status worth holding, even if the financial remuneration didn't quite match the effort required to achieve a degree of indispensability.

Following the Saviour study sample news, Lewis was summoned to the office of Marie-Eve Legault, his boss. She was her usual off-hand self, telling him he was to give the 'Englishman' as she called him, every assistance in learning their ways. She also broke the better news that she herself would later be doing a term in the UK as part of the harmonisation process and, while she was absent, he would report to Luc Roulx, a recently appointed Supervisor who Lewis knew. Roulx had previously been a Shipping rat, the highlight of his duties being allowed to lift boxes, wheel a cart and use the packing tape machine unsupervised. Now he was a Supervisor in one of the minor analytical sections and, surprise, a unilingual Francophone.

There was no point in explaining this to Marie-Eve. She mostly worked in French and only spoke English to him when she needed to be sure that she had been understood fully. "Oh, and expect Dominique Yip back at some point, she is moving from China and will be working in Nottingham for a while. She will be your Supervisor from a couple of weeks after I've started my assignment. I'll send you the schedule so you know who is Supervisor and when. Watch Dominique carefully and don't let her mess anything up!"

No chance of promotion then, still Dominique was alright and much better than Legault any day. She was efficient, bilingual and with a good sense of humour. He'd heard that the China thing was falling apart slowly but he hadn't expected her to come back to NPS. He thought she'd be looking for something better. He knew that she wasn't bosom buddies with Legault and she'd hinted to Lewis about some sort of clandestine agenda held by some of the technical managers before, but without specifying. Lewis had a good idea what that agenda was and he knew it would spell the end of his tenure at NPS eventually. He'd just wait for the annual rif with his name on it and take the cash.

Back at his PC, Lewis sent out an explanatory email to the department, in English only, telling the staff about Marie-Eve heading off soon to the UK and Roulx taking over as Supervisor pending the return of

186

Dominique Yip. He also mentioned that they would be welcoming a Sample Management technician from Nottingham and, finally, that they were basically now on a 'verify, store and ship' routine as far as the Saviour samples were concerned as they were all going to Nottingham too. Over the next couple of days they all read his email but nobody replied.

# THIRTY-FIVE

## Tuesday 24 May

To Simon Reid, the Sample Management room at Nash Pharmaceutical Solutions in Montreal was considerably bigger than its Nottingham counterpart. Other than that, the old adage that everything in America was bigger was largely myth, unless you counted bellies and bums.

The initial excitement at visiting Canada for the first time was soon waning, especially in view of everything he'd seen being in French. He'd not really understood the French thing from afar and so was surprised by how all-pervasive French, both written and spoken, was in Montreal. He later mentioned this to his mentor Lewis, in Sample Management, who'd laughed and recommended a trip to Quebec City to get the full-on French experience.

That was not going to happen. Simon had ten days to see and understand how his department at home had to metamorphose from the occasionally shambolic Sample Management group it currently was into something watertight, GLP-wise. He was shrewd enough to know that, while the company would only be investing heavily in the IT side, it would probably be making-do with everything else. Ingenuity would be needed to make it fly, just like the company slogan now adorning the outside of their otherwise featureless facades, 'We Make Blue Sky Fly!' Sure we do.

After arriving from London late afternoon, Reid was collected from the airport by a bonny redhead called Paula Long. His case just about fitted into her little hatchback and they set off the twenty or so minutes to his generic hotel, right on the side of highway 40 in West Island, Montreal. Paula was an ex-pat who'd been tempted out to the old biotech, Heal-Well, that NPS had bought nine months previously. She was guarded in her comments, neither heaping praise nor scorn, on their now common employer.

Once checked in, Simon was told to be in the lobby at 6:30 pm, she was taking him out for his evening meal tonight; after that he was on his own.  In the parking lot was a rental for him; the rep would be by shortly to fill in the details – he'd need his driving licence and passport. He hadn't expected that, a car, and driving on the wrong side of the road too, that would be an adventure for everyone.

The room was OK, spacious and with a desk, a small sofa, a coffee machine and complimentary Wi-Fi, so he logged on and sent an email to the gang, telling them the adventure had begun and to behave themselves while he was away. The gang didn't actually give a shit, he knew that. Most would not have gone out there, only Mo might have fancied it but there were reasons why she wasn't chosen, being lazy and disinterested in her job being the most obvious of them.

He also called home, just a quick call. It would be expensive to talk to the UK, he thought, and he was unclear who would be picking up that particular tab. Catheryn sounded cheery enough, she reminded him that it was compulsory to buy gifts when you got sent on a trip, just like the rock she'd bought him when she had a seminar in Scarborough, one day. He'd already planned to find her a little something, a suitable budget-end souvenir of Quebec.

The flat screen TV clicked into life and Simon scanned the channels for football, all he could find was Ice Hockey, seven channels of Hockey, as they kept calling it. Flicking on a TV show, he settled back to watch a 'Friends' re-run. After ten minutes, and two ad breaks, he clicked it off, how do they put up with that?

It had been a long day, made up of not just the seven hours crossing the Atlantic but also three to get to London from Nottingham and the three waiting to set off, so he decided to shower then take a coffee before getting ready for dinner with Paula. She seemed nice enough, in a jolly-hockey-sticks sort of way, a sort of five-foot Charlie Dimmock with bigger hips. Simon wondered what her back story was though, there was always a back story.

Refreshed from having washed off the plane grime, he went downstairs to wait. From the Lobby, Simon saw the elderly hatchback bounce over the speed retarders, pulling up outside the front door. Paula had made no move to get out so Simon just walked over and opened the wrong door before realising. Nipping back around the car, he climbed in and settled into the seat, but only after hurling a couple of folders off it and into the back foot well, no apology was made from either side. Paula was wearing the same clothes as earlier, 'once a student', Reid supposed.

It only took ten minutes and an equal number of traffic lights, to get to the restaurant – Baton Rouge. Inside they were shown to a booth, just like on TV, and a brassy waitress with sketched-on eyebrows and a blonde ponytail descended on them within seconds. She was quite attractive but had that 'what are you looking at' demeanour that makes you concentrate on the menu. The food range was a bit different from the Baltimore Diner's menu, the place in Castle Marina that was lauded as almost, but not quite, the authentic taste of North America!

Paula ordered a beer, blond, which seemed a reasonable choice, so Reid went with it. A hefty jug and two tankards appeared, opaque after being wetted and kept in a freezer, quite appropriate given that that would be on him Monday. Well, the freezer bit at least.

Conversation was unsubstantial, had Paula decided he was an idiot already? It normally took women at least a couple of hours - she hadn't laughed when he said that out loud. No chance of a shag then, not that he would.

Food was ordered and beer sipped slowly after the initial decent glug, it was good. Around half way down the pitcher, Paula started to converse, it was almost as if she needed the alcohol to let her mouth say what her mind had been holding back. Reid probed a little, establishing that Paula was an analyst, not a technician, and that her work permit ran out in two months and she had no intention of renewing it. When pushed, it seemed her reason was, in-part, the new American owners of the company and, in-part, a guy who she'd been dating since college and who had now very recently moved on to pastures new. That explained her demeanor, but at least she had perked up a little bit now.

The food arrived quickly, it was piled high. The chips were the long string sort; Paula said we call them fries here, or frites within hearing of a separatist. Reid must have looked especially dumb as Paula launched into a twenty-minute monologue about Quebec, the French and separatists. Who knew that former colonials would get so uppity about a language? Nuts. Hey, he'd only been there a few hours and was talking like a North American, well the English-speaking part at least.

Reid asked lots of questions about the stuff he was supposed to be doing, the Sample Management software and processes. Everything he could take from this trip would put him in a position of greater job security, not that he was too worried. The company at home had rarely shed jobs and when they did it was usually via natural wastage, the lost people not being replaced and their workload being spread far and wide. Paula tried her best, but Sample Management was a bit of a black hole to her. He'd have to wait until he met Lewis, his mentor.

Reid asked about the company, good or bad to work for? Although with Paula planning to bail at the end of her work permit, he guessed that all was not right in the state of Denmark, as far as she was concerned. Paula became more guarded, as if the booth was bugged and that their light conversation was being monitored for naughty words that might denigrate the company. He mentioned the idea to Paula who laughed and said "don't put it past them". The term 'control freaks' then slipped firmly into Reid's frontal lobe.

After the big meal and a huge pudding, Paula called for the bill and Reid noticed that he'd drunk two glasses of beer to her three plus dregs. He could just about see the hotel from the car park; he was finding it hard to remember to call it a parking lot. The road was straight, it was a slow ten minutes or so, they should be fine going that short distance, he thought. After that, well she drank the beer, nobody made her. Not very gallant thoughts, though.

In view of the circumstances he didn't fancy offering her another beer in the hotel bar and she didn't offer any encouragement in that direction either, so they parted on the kerb and she shot off into the night. Exhaustion crept up on Reid suddenly and he decided that the bar could wait for another night, time to get some sleep.

In his room, Reid saw the light on the phone flashing. A message from home perhaps 'how was it going? Was it Catheryn again? Was she worried that he'd been out on the razzle with a local hottie? The maths said it was gone 2 am in the UK, so Reid decided to leave it until morning, he'd get up early and make the call.

The next day was a Sunday and so everything opened a little later. Not feeling the need to rush, he called home only to find no, Catheryn hadn't called, but how was his meal and was she hot or not? Reid laughed, Catheryn laughed. No, she was best described as tepid. All was well with everything, nothing to know yet, more when he actually got to the company, wherever it was. Montreal Island was huge, as big as Nottinghamshire. He was having a quiet day, he might just have a ride around in his Pontiac, and he promised to take a photo to prove that he'd driven one.

Realising that he hadn't actually established who his mystery caller was, he checked the message on the machine and called back. It was from his mum, who berated him for not calling back yesterday. Reid spent ten minutes trying to explain the time difference; 'yes even though they do use the same clocks in North America'. She could be hard work, sometimes.

Later, out of interest, Reid drove slowly over the highway and into the huge parking lot for the Fairview Mall. He'd always thought Broad Marsh and Victoria Centre in Nottingham were shopping malls but this was something classier. The floors were clean, there were no idiots pissed on cheap cider hanging around the benches and the store fronts all had clean glass. He headed for HMV, just to browse, and ended up putting $200 on the credit card, about a hundred quid he thought, worth it though because a CD in Canada was about a third cheaper than at home.

At the bottom of the glass-sided lift, or elevator as he should call it, a little jewellery store was just opening up. Taking the chance to get ahead of the game, he browsed the items on display looking for a pendant. He selected a nice Bee-type of thing; it was multi-coloured with a silver chain, Catheryn was sure to like it.

The rest of the day he explored. He'd got hold of a road map from the hotel, a simple sheet thing with only main roads on it but enough to get around and, anyway, there was a sat-nav in the car, he just had no real idea of how it worked. He drove out past the NPS facility in a place called Vaudreuil, just to see where it was, and then out further off island. At a fork in the highway he had a choice, Ottawa one way and Toronto the other. Suddenly Reid fancied driving over to see Niagara Falls; it might be his only chance.

Pulling off the road and parking up in some truck place, it took ten minutes to find Niagara Falls in the sat-nav. Interesting, Niagara was six hours and six hundred kilometers away, maybe not this time then. Now he had the mastery of the sat-nav he decided to take some back roads off the main highway and ended up in a place called St-Lazare. Everywhere so many places seemed to be saint-something or other in Quebec, he wondered what the original inhabitants of the land called their places before the invasion of rabid religion with all its saints and miracles.

In what passed for St-Lazare town centre was a parking lot and a diner, so he went in and ordered lunch. At first they just asked him what he wanted in French, but when he opened his mouth to explain his linguistic difficulties, the waitress switched seamlessly to English and something called poutine was soon on the way.

After lunch the day sort of fizzled out. He picked up some crisps and biscuits from the local supermarket, and a bottle of wine, cheap Australian stuff, for later. Lunch had been big enough to not need a real dinner, besides tomorrow was going to be almost like a first day at work. The evening was again an exercise in channel hopping and swearing at the TV, ending with him nearly turning the damn thing off until he found The Weather Channel. And they say Brits are obsessed with the weather!

Reid was out early the next day wanting to get in and make an impression; he was also expecting a ton of traffic. Paula had warned him that getting to NPS would be a slow drive in, especially over the I'lles aux Tortes bridge, but the roads were pretty good and he sailed along with the radio on playing something by April Wine, a band he'd never heard of and would immediately forget once he got back to the land of the Beatles and the Rolling Stones.

Safely negotiating the sat-nav directed exit from the highway, and later pulling into NPS, everything seemed very quiet for a Monday. He buzzed the bell at the facility and a security guard dressed exactly like Neil at home came out. He had lank black hair and a thick, almost continuous brow but his uniform was crisp, so Reid made no instant judgement. After a rapid burst of French and a pause, Reid told him that had no idea what he'd just said, sorry. The guy then just turned and stomped off, like a Vogon on silent shouting duty. Moments later another guy came over, small, wiry, hard looking. He spoke English, well American, and asked if he could help.

Reid explained who he was and why he was there. Through half a chuckle, the security guy explained that today was a provincial holiday,

194

HR should have told him that, and that nobody was there to receive him. No, he couldn't go in, not until they had the paperwork which would be tomorrow morning. He should try again then.

For a minute or so Reid stood in a state of confusion, had he read the information wrong? Fumbling in his folder he double-checked. No, he was right, they said to be there at the time and date specified, which was now. Once it all sank in he wondered what to do with this extra day off and realised the timescale for his comprehensively understanding the new company requirements adequately had just been shortened by a full day. It looked like Human Resources the world over were idiots, and he found that he felt strangely sanguine about this, as if it was meant to be, a moment of normality in a sea of turbulence.

Setting off back to the hotel, he managed to get lost and ended up at a place called the Ecomuseum. It turned out to be a small zoo with a few native animals and some recuperating birds. He especially liked the Flying Squirrels in the basement room, it was a diversion and it stopped him fretting that this trip had disaster written all over it.

Out of the blue on the Monday evening, Paula called and asked about his meal plans. He had been previously told, in what he'd thought were no uncertain terms, that he would be on his own after her initial welcoming duty had been done, so this was quite unexpected and not unwelcome. The pile of snacks that were piled on the computer table now looked less inviting than when they'd been bought, so the chance to go out with the lovely Paula to another local eatery brightened his mood considerably. Date night, do they call it?

She put-putted her junk car into the parking lot, more or less on time again. The car sounded awful, like the exhaust has broken in two, but Paula just shrugged it off. She wasn't spending anything on the car now; it would probably just be donated to the Kidney Research people anyway once she'd got her leaving date. Quite what Kidney Research would do with the car that would benefit someone who needed a kidney, he didn't ask, it was yet another Canadian-ism.

As he got in the car, thanking her for the treat, he thought he caught the suggestion of a smile; maybe he was in here, time for caution, Simon old boy.

They took off down another one of West Island's endless boulevards, arriving at something called 'Peche Peche'. So good they named it twice, he thought. It turned out to be a decent fish restaurant, 'peche' being French for fish, who knew.

Paula was warmer than before, although she'd made it very clear that Simon would be funding his own meal this time. Her demeanour suggested that this wasn't a duty but something more, but Simon struggled to read any clear signals, not that he was particularly interested in her as such, but any port in a storm. That thought brought him up sharp - no, he really wasn't interested.

They were halfway through the main course when her motive, if that is the right word, became clear. She wanted to talk work, or more specifically individuals at work. Slightly disappointed, despite inwardly claiming a lack of interest, but also being entirely realistic after a lifetime of disappointment, Simon listened intently. Montreal seemed to have numerous sub-plots going on, especially since the takeover.

Various characters, like players in a production, were mentioned, too many to keep track of but the juicer ones naturally stuck with him. The gossip, because that was really what it was, all centred on a Francophone plot to oust as many Anglophone employees as possible, by fair means or foul. Paula reckoned that a group of six or eight Francophones had got their heads together and worked their way into important and influential posts. The de-facto head of the group was Marie-Eve Legault, Simon would be meeting her and spending time in the department under her. She had Sample Management as part of her overall Technical Management portfolio.

After fifteen minutes of Paula and her explanation of one of the major ills of NPS, the techs-versus-scientist war, Simon felt obliged to cut in. He at least knew how his industry worked. Technical staff worked for the scientists, technical management reported to the scientists, the company product, the research, came from scientists, it seemed crazy that what amounted to support staff would think they had similar status to scientists and, by implication, the power to control the way technical staff worked. There was that enigmatic smile on Paula's face again. It looked like pudding and drinks after still might not be long enough for her to tell all. 'But do tell', he thought.

It seemed that in Montreal, at least, the scientists were treated by the technical staff as something of an inconvenience. True, it is they who carry the can when the techs get it wrong, and get it wrong they do with monotonous regularity, but it is not the scientist's place to interfere in the technical side, it is the technical managers, team leaders, coordinators level one and two and supervisors who do that. The analogy of too many Chiefs and not enough Native Americans sprang to mind, but Paula was in full swing.

Most of the scientists at NPS now had been poached from the UK by Heal-Well, the old company that had been set up by a Brit, Maureen Whithers. Experienced scientific talent was scarce in Canada, she didn't want anyone from the US and so she went with what she knew, using all her contacts in the UK to find the right people. When it was Heal-Well, the technical staff management was done by each scientific department head via a phalanx of lesser management such as Co-ordinators and Team Leaders who reported exclusively to scientific. It worked, up to a point, and often despite some of the technical people, who had been clearly rewarded with a promotion for service and not based on talent.

"NPS came in and changed the structure by running two distinct, and as it has now become, rival, sections, scientific and technical. The technical is made up mostly of Francophones and they are mostly nice people, very easy going generally. In with them are some separatists who are not easy going at all, they spread discord and, amazingly, it is often the younger ones who fall for it and join their cause. So now there's a bunch of people who get all antsy when English is used where they think French should be. Things took a step up when the IT people started buying French language PCs, citing that they had to obey the language laws, which was not actually true. The PC is not really an issue because you can type in English and set the PC to English, obviously, but the keyboard was different because it was a French one and you had to waste time trying to write English language reports and protocols while having to learn the way to change the French keys to give you the English character you needed".

"Surely all keyboards are universal?" said Reid.

"You'd think so but no, the French ones have a different layout and the function keys operate differently, too. In the scheme of things it is minor, but it is also unnecessary and it gets scientific upset".

Paula continued. "As a piece of bloody-mindedness it was superb, but the even stranger thing is that the top brass didn't step in and make them buy the right keyboards. No, they let them get away with it. It got to the point where the Anglophone Study Directors would prefer not to get a new PC, and if they did, they'd go to where the Francophone techs had their PCs and swap the keyboards, because most of them still had English ones. If you were writing a farce, you'd have a first season right there!"

Reid felt he ought to be saying something more, apart from mostly 'really?', or 'that's crazy' but really that was all he could contribute. It was beyond the realms of a joke to make your scientists waste their expensive time, trying to relearn keyboards for fear of upsetting a handful of misguided people.

Paula then darkened the mood a little, lowering her voice and edging closer. "It got worse, Simon, because, almost simultaneously, all new supervisor promotions were Francophone-only appointments. The

English technical team leaders and co-ordinators, some of whom had been at Heal-Well since the beginning, went in rifs as soon as NPS took over. The coup was being orchestrated by none other than Marie-Eve Legault."

Reid cut in. "Sorry Paula, what is a rif?"

"Ah", said Paula. "A rif is a Reduction in Force. You'll like this..."

After a long and detailed explanation, Reid was shell-shocked. He'd been sacked a few times when he was younger, fired they called it here. Thinking about it, that particular phrase was in use at home too but it was usually for a misdemeanor, or if the company went bust, he'd never heard of a company going through a list, lopping people out of the system to please shareholders and then dressing it up as unavoidable. Whatever happened to responsible employers?

"And another thing", said Paula. "I told you that you will meet Marie-Eve Legault. She is the boss of the technical staff as I said, all the technical staff. Expect to deal with an obnoxious cow and you won't go too far wrong. Try not to upset her, she bears grudges and you don't want to be on her rif list just because of a stray comment".

Reid thanked Paula for the nod or 'heads-up' as he'd heard it called in Montreal. "No worries, I can be quite likeable if I try". There was that smile again.

The warning just about marked the end of the evening and Paula soon had him back at the hotel. She'd certainly been warmer than before and Reid took it as one ex-pat helping another. He had the idea that there was something else on Paula's mind but it never came out, despite him giving her plenty of space to open up. If it was anything to do with Legault. he'd probably find out over the next nine days.

# THIRTY-SIX

Marie-Eve breezed into the training room where Simon Reid was watching a recorded presentation by the Clousseau developers, it was boring and not really covering the areas he would be involved with. She sat opposite and said, ignoring everyone else, "you must be the Englishman we have to teach our clever and complicated ways to. I don't suppose you speak French; it would make life so much easier". Then she sat back and awaited a reaction.

"Normally, being British, we just talk loudly to foreigners until they understand us. It's worked well for the nation in the past, you'd be amazed at how many foreigners learn 'we surrender' in English as their first useful phrase".

The room went quiet so Reid quickly piped up, "I am joking, it is the British stereotype, sorry. I thought you'd probably heard that one before". Then he made the right noises about how important it was to sing off the same hymn sheet and how it was good that Nottingham and Montreal embraced the opportunity to learn from each other. He added that, while he did French at school, he was limited to knowing how to count to five, say 'hello', 'goodbye', 'a beer please' and 'the road is broken'.

Marie-Eve snorted. "In terms of learning, I think you'll find this a one-way process and the good news is that I'll be visiting your little town personally to make sure there are no more screw-ups. As for French-speaking, no matter, you won't be around long enough to make any difference and some of my people are bilingual. They say it is a sure sign of intelligence".

Reid held his poker face then countered. "Well, Nottingham is not really so small. By the way, do I call you Marie-Eve or Madam Legault?"

200

"Marie-Eve will do. So you know my name then, what else have you been told about me?" she said, accusingly.

"That you are well-organised, efficient, and effective and that you don't suffer fools gladly, which is lucky for me because I'm not a fool".

Marie-Eve was rather taken aback by this; she actually smiled as if she'd enjoyed the verbal jousting. "Good to see my reputation precedes me, Simon. I think you may be someone I will enjoy working closely with". And with that she sashayed out of the room. The Montreal techs present, having sat with their collective mouths open during the whole exchange, looked astonished.

"That went well" said Reid to nobody, and then carried on watching the boring presentation.

Once Reid was finally in the Montreal Sample Management room, they set him up with a training version of Clousseau and various study plans and protocols to work through. From the general attitude, it seemed that his standing up for himself with Legault had caused a stir, he had gained a reputation already. Later his Clousseau mentor, Lewis, had a little word. "Beware, my English friend. Legault is someone to stay the right side of".

"Thanks" said Reid. "You're the second Montreal-based person to give me that sound piece of advice".

As the day wore on, Reid became at least proficient in Clousseau. He was determined to get the hang of it quickly, it would be a good feather in his cap when he got back to Nottingham, especially if there was to be a restructuring, or even a dreaded rif, as had been rumoured, post-takeover. They hadn't used the term 'rif' specifically, instead, they'd had said that there may be the need for a restructuring to take place. It had occurred to him that Sample Management might even become its own full department now and that they'd need someone competent in charge.

Everyone else in the room eventually drifted off home but Reid intended to stay a while and work through a few training exercises. He was surprised when a faint whiff of perfume broke his concentration and made him look up. Marie-Eve was leaning on the side of a desk opposite. He'd never even heard her come in, so engrossed was he in the rudiments of Clousseau. Glancing at her feet he saw that she'd dumped her heels and was in flats, no wonder he'd not heard her. He looked back at the PC quickly, she might have thought he was looking at her legs and he didn't want to give any wrong impressions.

She hadn't noticed and said "dedication, Simon, exactly what NPS likes to see in its employees".

"Lots to learn, Marie-Eve, and I'm hopeful that this will stand me in good stead as NPS progresses in Nottingham. My girlfriend and I are hoping to buy a house, maybe start a family in time". He wasn't sure why he'd offered those personal details unasked, it just seemed apt in the current circumstances and it had an effect.

"Well, Simon, I hope your girlfriend is behaving herself while you out having fun in Montreal". Was she flirting with him or did she know he'd had two work dates with Paula?

"We trust each other completely, we always have".

That flipped an off-switch and, as Marie-Eve stood up, she just said "lucky her. Lights off when you leave and make sure your workspace is clean and tidy before you go".

Having delivered the thinly disguised rebuke, she was off and out of range when Reid uttered "yes, Miss", under his breath.

Reid shut everything down, he really didn't feel like hanging around now. What was it they were called, thirty-somethings who acted as predators? Panthers? Feral tabby cat more like!

Reid had expected his time in Montreal to be taken up with training, learning the systems, getting a feel for the way they wanted the Nottingham site to operate. As it transpired, the Montreal site had its own problems, not least because they had been naturally struggling with how best to manage the biggest clinical study they'd ever had to handle, however briefly.

Clousseau, the Laboratory Instrumentation Management System was pretty simple, although not really designed to manage samples as such. It was more for the analytical people to manage and, especially, export their data. Reid saw that there was potential for some flexibility but that would come later when he and IT back home had had time to sit down and apply their collective experience to it.

The Saviour study however was a whole new territory. They already had over 23,000 samples in store, packed into their -80°C freezers, which was an awful lot of expensive storage. Nobody had done much more than open the boxes, count the samples and then put them in boxes, all marked with the client name. The boxes were not even numbered or dated. It was a fuck-up.

The next day, Reid had a determined edge about him and, grabbing the bull by the horns, he set to, helping out with the Saviour samples, knowing that he would reap the benefit further down the line and train as he went. The documentation for the samples was sparse; sometimes there was not even a sample listing for a delivery so how were you supposed to know what you should have and what was missing?

The first thing he decided to do was to take each sample and produce an inventory manually in Excel. That way they could generate shipping sheets at least. It was a painstaking job but, in between training stuff and pointless meetings he was making some progress. In a few long days over a tray of dry ice he had perhaps 10% of the samples listed in a spreadsheet.

Reid and, to some extent, Lewis, were not best pleased when they found out that a junior scientist in one of the minor analytical departments had actually been receiving Excel inventory sheets for the study from the start, but had told no one because she didn't know what they were for, the study wasn't on the company listing for ongoing projects and nobody she asked knew anything about it, or so she said. It later transpired that the scientist with the inventory sheets had been told not to pass them on because her department would be doing the Clinical Laboratory analysis and they wanted to be in front.

Until the switch to Nottingham had been announced, a war had been brewing between the Immunochemistry lab and the Clinical Laboratory because it was decided that it should be Immunochemistry who would be charged with producing multiple aliquots of the same sample, each destined to be analysed by a different department for different things. Was this an alien world that Reid had landed in, a pharmaceutical 'Game of Thrones' with House Immunology up against House Immunochemistry while House Clinical Laboratories ran their own version of the kingdom to a completely different set of rules? Weren't they all supposed to be working for NPS?

Once they'd managed to get access to the inventory sheets, well copies, it had then been a further four straight days of constantly sorting out samples for shipping to Nottingham, interspersed with teleconferences with the virtual client.

These were largely unproductive, numerous, very long and winding conversations which got them nowhere. It didn't help that they were continually interrupted by someone called a Client Liaison, Ria Sullemane, who was nominally an NPS employee but appeared to be 'on the side' of the client. Clearly they did things very differently at NPS, North America, or maybe it was just Montreal.

# THIRTY-SEVEN

## Wednesday 01 June

Completing his induction and training piecemeal, Reid soon found that the Saviour study was taking up all of his available time already; he was doing ten-hour days just to keep up. This was supposed to be training but it had turned into hard labour! It was on the seventh long day that he'd been working on the Saviour samples, late into the evening as usual, that Ria Sullemane sent an email to schedule yet another client teleconference.

Reid was not surprised to see that, once again, it was to be with the same guy who had no idea what they were talking about and didn't have access to anyone who did. Reid's short, jokey reply 'life's too short, and these teleconferences are like listening to paint dry' to Sullemane didn't go down well at all.

He was later surprised to find that his schedule suddenly included a visit to Marie-Eve Legault's office. Not really knowing why, but presuming it was to discuss how things were going, he was astonished to find out that he was getting a written, verbal warning.

Mentally the conversation went 'What the fuck is a written verbal warning?' In reality, Reid expressed surprise, genuine surprise, especially when Marie-Eve revealed that Ria had wanted him fired for disrespecting the client. Reid's natural response to the accusation was to be dismissive. It was an aside, a way of dealing with a constant mess after a long day, a long week, just a joke, purely internal between him and Sullemane. Perhaps asking whether they had heard of humour in Canada was a bit naughty, but not as naughty as it could have been.

Marie-Eve's demeanour was odd. In their previous meetings, including the short session that went on about deliverables and such like, she'd seemed fine with him, even seemed to quite like him if he'd read the signals correctly. Now there was an undercurrent of contempt, although her suddenly stronger French accent made the whole disciplinary hearing seem like a scene out of 'Hello, Hello', so what was going on?

Reid had to re-read the written, verbal warning twice before he took it all in. Marie-Eve said that she had persuaded Ria that this warning, which would be placed in his personal company file, was sufficient. What went unsaid was that she'd done him a favour, a big favour and she might want repayment of some sort eventually. Reid placed the warning on the desk, face down. A knock on the door and it being opened without the knocker waiting for answer broke the mood a bit, it was Lewis. He apologised to Marie-Eve only for being late. 'So he was supposed to be there at the start', Reid thought. Lewis took a seat. Marie-Eve turned to Reid, not speaking but clearly expecting something.

More composed now, Reid started to talk, a monologue, almost, but Marie-Eve allowed it to go without interruption, making notes as he delivered the comments that he'd requested be added to the 'case', as she called it. He reiterated that the comment was meant to be a joke, not disrespectful to anyone. It had been a long and intense period, they were getting nowhere even after repeated teleconferences because the client representative did not know what they were talking about when it came to the LIMS, and Ria did not allow any sort of conversation to develop that she was not a constant part of. Reid said he would not be signing the written, verbal warning.

It was thirty seconds or so before Marie-Eve had finished writing on her pad. Lewis said nothing, just looked down at his feet for the duration, clearly one of Marie-Eve's mice. She looked up but not quite into Reid's eyes, preferring to focus on the wall planner behind and asked why? Reid countered that the whole thing was ridiculous, including the warning which contained several spelling errors and, for that reason alone, he was not going to put his name to it. Another joke, well sort of, but perhaps an even more ill-judged one.

Marie-Eve's face suddenly looked like a smacked dog's bottom. Lewis chirped up, asking whether Reid would be willing to sign a corrected version. Seeing the whole thing was getting too silly for words, he agreed. Like synchronised swimmers, Lewis and Marie-Eve stood up, that was Reid's cue to get out of there, back to the relative sanctuary of the Montreal Sample Management department.

What a bunch of humourless control freaks. If Reid thought some of those in Nottingham were a bit anal at times, he now knew he was in arse-clench city.

Back at the ice front, Lewis came over and suggested they go to the cafeteria for a chat. This would be the first time that he'd have a conversation with the not-very-loquacious Lewis, that wasn't just a simple phrase or a brusquely delivered set of instructions - a tone Reid had tolerated because it was probably not worth upsetting too many more people, people he would have to work with, and ask for cooperation and advice from, as Nash Pharmaceutical Solutions' operating process infiltrated the Nottingham site like the tendrils of a Strangler Fig.

Lewis chose a table away from the chatter; it was all in French anyway and, although Reid had picked up a little bit more, and then mainly swearwords, he didn't really catch what they were talking about and he didn't think anyone else would bother to listen in on their conversation either.

Lewis explained that Marie-Eve was under pressure from the site manager and that Ria was his unofficial partner away from work, it was a secret so everyone knew. Marie-Eve was OK, he said, supportive and helpful but within the management structure, which was still fairly new for them too, as they were the NPS acquisition before Nottingham. The talk was clearly designed as a way to get Reid to climb down a bit, maybe instigated by Marie-Eve, or maybe Lewis had thought of it himself.

Lewis was a strange one. Originally from Scotland way back, he was fair skinned, tall and obviously kept himself in good shape. Reid supposed he was attractive, in an earthy kind of way, and picked up clues from the conversation that there appeared to be warmth of a sort between Lewis and Marie-Eve. Was he shagging her or was he just being nice to survive in an obviously hostile environment?

After ten minutes of quiet conversation Lewis stood to go, and reminded Reid that the next teleconference was in ten minutes. Oh joy.

Ria's office, perhaps the best in the facility and with a nice view on two sides, was empty when Reid got there. The fancy conferencing phone was in the centre of the desk but he waited outside, not wanting to go into someone's office without them being there to invite him in, it was an English thing.

Catching him unawares, Marie-Eve breezed past, pulled up a chair and motioned him to come in and sit down. Ria appeared seconds later, closed the door and she set to connecting to the client.

This time the conference call was quite different. The client, actually the third different client person that Reid had telephonically met, had a different guy with him who understood exactly what a LIMS was, and what NPS were asking for. "No problem", he said. Ria barely spoke except to confirm the participants, welcome and then bid farewell to the client and it was all done and dusted inside ten minutes.

Marie-Eve opened her file and produced what Reid rightly presumed was a corrected version of the written verbal warning which he duly signed without checking. Was this being done in front of Ria deliberately to pacify her? Possibly, but she never said a word about it or anything else. Job done they went their separate ways. Back in the

208

Sample Management office, a box containing half a tree and a set of disks was on Reid's desk.

The disks contained electronic shipping manifests for every delivery of Saviour samples that they'd had in Montreal so far, and also disks for those projected to come to Nottingham in the next delivery. The half a tree was the original shipping manifests, which could differ from the electronic version, depending on whether the Mexican facility had had to make changes. This wasn't explained and Reid was confused, electronic inventories that differed from those with the samples was new territory for him, this was turning out to be some learning curve.

Somehow he'd become the de-facto Saviour sample guru, mainly because Lewis and the rest had effectively abandoned the study. He was later given an assurance, by no less that Ria Sullemane, that he'd get the advance electronic inventories directly as they were all very impressed by his willingness to tackle a difficult study. Nothing else was mentioned, it was as if the misunderstanding had never happened.

Two days later and Reid had finished in Montreal. A car would pick him up from the site, the flight was late afternoon and he had to buy a small suitcase to carry back the study documents and copies of disks, some of which were relevant to samples now arriving in Nottingham.

For reasons unknown to technical, the 'higher ups' had decided to move the receipt and analysis of the samples to NPS Nottingham, then use the LIMS to collate the results and then ship them electronically to the virtual client on a weekly basis, downloading the data directly into the client's LIMS database which Reid would have to find a way to set up. It had to be an exact a copy of the one in the NPS system.

The shifting the study to Nottingham answered the question that had been bugging Reid. Why had they spent money on him being sent to Montreal for training and then embedded him inside the study when he was only supposed to be receiving general Sample Management procedural training? Well, now he had an answer, this wasn't just a sudden decision but who had made it?

Just before Reid went down to get his luggage from Security, Marie-Eve came by the Sample Management rooms and thanked him for his help, wished him a safe flight, warned him that she would be looking closely at his department in Nottingham and then she gave him a sort of constipated grin, turned on her heel and went. Lewis watched from the office, impassive maybe, hard to tell from his usual, dour facial expression. Hands were shaken, a couple of hugs from the Sample Management team and even cheek kisses, French style, all happened before Reid was in the car and heading for Pierre Elliott Trudeau Airport. It would be good to get home.

# THIRTY-EIGHT

## Wednesday 21 September

The nickname for the corpse was, despite the questionable taste, in general use in the station although not within ear-shot of Charnley. Nobody worried though, Charnley only ever appeared at briefings or to yell at one of the uniforms. The team worked as an autonomous unit while Charnley caught up when reports appeared on his desk. He hadn't always been absent without leave, he'd been a good cop, had to have been to make DI, but something had changed inside his head, something even his naturally protective detectives hadn't been able to help with. After short periods of circulation he'd retire to his office at every opportunity, waiting for the day his early retirement pension would arrive.

Pathology was finally in. Iain Lynch had done his usual thorough job and the report sat on Thompson's desk. With the next team briefing starting in 30 minutes there were going to be a few twists and turns to the case including one that might give a motive, or at least another motive, for the murder of Marie-Eve Legault.

Banks, Prosser, Knight and Dad filed in, bringing their own chairs in with them for comfort. Now they had a few facts to go on, facts they could examine and then present to the suspects in a way that might persuade them to slip up.

Instead of copying the report and giving the team one copy each, Thompson decided the fewer opportunities for a copy to wander the better, so he'd read out the pertinent facts from his own sheets, item by item.

There was no sign of Charnley so Thompson pressed on.

"The time of death is given as between nine and eleven thirty but this a best guess and the time may go out up to two hours later". Thompson let it sink in, the time of death pulled in two of the current suspects known to be in NPS at the time, known being the operative word. They were Shepherd and Martin.

He continued. "Marie-Eve Legault had died due to hypothermia induced by freezing. She'd likely been unconscious before she died and had presumably already been unconscious when she was put into the freezer because there were no signs anywhere of a struggle. She had also been drenched after she had been placed inside, soaked in a cleaning material/water mixture like that used by the site cleaners. Judging by the spread of the fluid it appeared as if a whole bucket had been dumped on her but none had been found elsewhere and there was no bucket in the freezer. Where is the bucket now? The water would not have been cold, more likely at or close to the same temperature as came out of the hot tap in the nearby toilets, the place where the cleaners filled their buckets, it depends on how long it had stood but this was not something to get hung up on".

Prosser asked about the chemical make-up of the water, was it confirmed as the same as used by the cleaners that night? They would have a measure to use in a cost-conscious operation like contract cleaning. If that was the case, the killer wouldn't be expected to have known this and they might not use the right percentage if they'd fetched the water themselves. It would establish the source of the water used and its deliberate use to accelerate freezing. "Good point, Liam, I'll follow that up with forensics and we'll need to speak to the contract cleaning boss".

Banks asked about the Fish Finger being unconscious just as Charnley appeared at the back of the room. So he'd decided that he could fit us in after all; how nice; thought Banks.

Thompson, ignoring Charnley's arrival, quoted one of the admins statements. "Marie-Eve Legault had complained of feeling light-headed more than once in the days prior to her death. Twice in her office one of the administration staff had found her slumped at her desk, seemingly exhausted. The admin said Legault had just waved away their concerns, claiming to be a bit under the weather, probably in need of a good meal and some rest. Aside from three trips back to Montreal, which themselves must have been tiring, she hadn't taken any time off, including working weekends. She was known to be a regular night-owl, too".

The autopsy report told them virtually what they already knew. There were two, well-defined, impact marks on her head, one at the front and one at the back. The mark on the front was made with a weapon, something straight and heavy. Examination of the expanded scene on the day of discovery had turned up two heel-bars in the Shipping Department, used for opening packing cases. It was beyond reasonable doubt that one of these had been used to strike her, possibly unconscious. One had been recently cleaned and was almost spotless, the other had multiple fingerprints on it. It was fair to assume that the clean one dealt the blow that rendered Legault unconcious.

The back of the head also showed an impact mark, partially created when she was dumped in the freezer, banging her head as she was released. The impact shape was consistent with meeting a hard, flat area, so presumably the freezer back wall, but there were also some irregularities that may suggest another prior impact. Pathology also reported that there were a few odd marks on the body that didn't make a lot of sense. The two marks, that were quite straight, were on her upper legs, like she'd spent time leaning on a small table or something. There was also a mark on her neck, which might have come from a necklace, although one wasn't found.

"Lynch thought that she might have been close to passing out due to a lack of iron, anemia and all that, before she was walloped with possibly the heel bar. This tied in with her being in the early stages of pregnancy. Once the assailant had got her into a freezer, the cold would soon take effect, especially with Legault having been doused with water. The pen they'd retrieved, broken on the floor, may have been used as insurance so that, if she regained consciousness, she couldn't get out with the freezer door being jammed", Thompson added, in conclusion.

The combination of head trauma and soaking confirm that this was certainly a murder. It made them all feel sharper. Now they knew what game they were in, now they needed to find the motive, gather more evidence, agree on a suspect and then pull their boy in and make him cough to it. Two days should be enough on this one.

"One final thing. Reid and Shepherd both mentioned a report that Legault was supposedly writing which was said to include a list for the next rif, due to take place shortly after she left", and then Thompson affected his voice telling them that 'the proposed rif was strictly confidential'. It had to be someone from HR saying that. It got a laugh and the new information was added to notes as possibly a 'why'.

The briefing went quicker than expected and everybody went back to their desks, except for Thompson and Charnley.

"Sorry Dave, I got delayed. Can you do me a recap, please?"

So Thompson covered the same ground again while Charnley listened. He seemed confused, almost sedated. At a natural pause, he rambled on about getting to grips with it and getting a suspect in, and then he went off to his office without another word. He was getting weirder by the day.

Thompson electronically doled out the sheets with the days tasks expected of what was left of the team who'd be looking at checking alibis, dropping them on the relevant desks. They'd nearly finished up the donkey work but there were a few more details to come in that needed checking and other cases were taking people away from the case. Charnley was actually right, they needed to get a wiggle on and make an arrest.

# Thirty-Nine

The idea of starting a Contract Research Organisation in Nottingham seemed to be pie in the sky until a chance meeting between Councillor Ken Murray and Clive Gerrard, where interesting information was imparted and, later, for the price of a 30-foot river cruiser, a deal, assuring Gerrard of a place on the soon-to-be-created business park on the old Wilford Clay Pits site was done. It was the sort of business that only happened if you knew the right people with the same interests. You didn't get in unless you knew someone on the inside. The paint was barely dry when Clive moved in and, with the help of a small group of friends, investors and, perhaps most importantly, scientists, got Blue Sky Research off the ground.

Gerrard had loved the boat, his refuge he called it, perhaps that's why he called it 'Save Me'. It was handily moored in Colwick Marina and he could be out on the river and off towards a favourite watering hole within minutes. All good things come to an end though and, if the new business went as well as his little consortium thought it would, then Clive would be looking at the new narrowboat he'd always set his heart on. One that he could build from scratch.

With the property zero rated for ten years and a start-up tax-exempt status for three, this was really a chance to put that hard-earned Biology degree to work. The actual name had come to him one boozy evening on the boat. His friends had gone and the sun was long-down, but the quiet of the night must have carried its own inspiration and Blue Sky Research had been born.

Gerrard's luck had also been in when it was announced that a large amount of technical equipment was up for auction, part of a recently closed lab that was once Boots on Pennyfoot Street in Nottingham. He got the right equipment cheaply enough to be able to run his first few

215

studies, which brought in enough to invest in more equipment and then he was off and running. After a couple of years they had a friendly set-up, a mostly honest set of clients that were something of a rarity in the industry, and a set of staff who were second to none. Most had been there from the start, or very near, and most had a real loyalty to the company, they all felt like family. They were just coming around to celebrating five years when Nash Pharmaceutical Solutions, the expanding giant of North American Contract Research, got in touch with an offer.

Gerrard knew all about NPS of course, and of their reputation, everyone did. 'Shoddy' was the word that most in the business used - not averse to taking the mercenary approach, especially with staff, and it was that that had made Gerrard dismiss the approach. Then a couple of his good clients whispered in his ear that they were sorry, but commercial pressure might force them to re-think their association with Blue Sky Research. To Gerrard, it was obvious that the commercial might of NPS was being brought to bear, the writing was well and truly on the wall.

Of course there was a critical limit to how much work the company could lose before questions about viability were asked. Gerrard went back to NPS in person, in New Jersey, and with his personal lawyer in tow. Gerrard used the very high reputation of Blue Sky Research within the industry to lever a little more out of NPS, although in hindsight he might have gone even further. He also made it clear that there would be conditions to be met.

The assurances came straight from the horse's, Jim Duggan's, mouth. There would be no job loses, Blue Sky Research would become a valued part of the NPS global operation and would help drive their already admired high standards even higher with its dedication to quality. All bullshit, of course, but what can you do when the Lion comes for the Lamb?

Clive Gerrard had always known that it would happen, it was the way of the industry these days and he hoped, truly hoped, that his disquiet about the way NPS conducted its business was unfounded. His people would be safe as far as he could be assured, and their careers, for those with ambition, would possibly benefit from being a part of a well-funded global brand.

The agreement was for Gerrard to stay on as nominal CEO for a minimum of two years, then beyond, or not, on review, all open to mutual agreement. The shares package alone was enough to retire on, and Gerrard seriously thought about doing it, at 48 he wasn't getting any younger. So the lawyers met, the contracts were signed and Gerrard and his few Blue Sky investors, all close friends, did rather well. There was still a sadness about letting it all go, but at least he'd still be there to steer the ship during the transition, help allay fears and make sure Blue Sky Research in its new guise kept its high standards high.

There was the other thing too, of course, but that wasn't a part of the deal. Even NPS would baulk at taking over that area of chemistry.

Within three-months of the takeover, Gerrard was packing his personal possessions into the boot of his old Jaguar, having exercised his option to leave, his safety net built-in to the contract. He'd not liked the way NPS moved in with heavy hands. Not liked the way that his valued influence, as they had previously put it, was ignored out of hand. He'd not liked the way his employees had all been put on new contracts either. The only concession he actually got for them was for holiday entitlement to be respected for the rest of the financial year, after that, holidays would be whatever you could scrape and, if the company decided it needed you to keep working, they'd just pay you the money and you lost the holiday. Insidious.

With a thirty-five page non-disclosure agreement in his pocket, Clive Gerrard left NPS, his Blue Sky Research, for the last time.

Despite the assurances, it wasn't too long after he'd gone when the culling of dead wood started, a reduction in force. It was probably true that there were a couple of people in the company who recently had barely pulled their weight. Much of that was down to getting their departments running really well and they had gradually, and it must be said somewhat skillfully, reduced their workload to meagre proportions. Everyone knew who they were and so it was not a surprise when they were cut adrift. It was more the way it had been done, but the new contracts had actually said that was how the new people worked. The staff, without any choice in the matter, had agreed to the new conditions with a sweep of a biro and had no recourse to the law as they waived their employee rights big time. At the time of signing they didn't know they had, well not to the extent the contracts had stipulated.

The grim-reaping, as it came to be known, brought into sharp focus how things would be from now on; well, at least for those who understood the situation it did. The tight ship that New Jersey had told us that they ran, turned out to be an old-style slave galley, with everyone on board a slave, and how bad your lot was depended on whether you were standing on deck, telling people to row the boat faster, or were one of the poor sods below decks, shackled to the job and rowing your heart out.

Media interest in the takeover at the time was intense. Nash Pharmaceutical Solutions had bought their way to a contract research empire via a process not without hostility, the feeling on the ground and around Linked-In was that it might be a good thing. No matter how Clive Gerrard the CEO viewed it, Blue Sky Research was rather like a friendly old dog and the scientific staff tended to be a bit head-in-the-lab and nowhere else. They only managed a small, annual profit because their name was gold in contract research circles, and mostly because Clive Gerrard had held it all together.

The changeover was interesting, and certainly something that nobody had any experience of, that is why it caught them on the hop. The company was effectively rebooted and everyone in the company fired and re-employed in one fell swoop. An entire week was set aside for what they called assimilation, including bunches of bewildered people being selected for the almost continuous screening of the video including clips of their new glorious leader, Jim Duggan, telling them how things would be done from now on.

Virtually nobody realised that they had effectively been fired and re-hired until it happened, when they were then presented with a new contract of employment. The document was full of legalese phrases that nobody uses in normal life. They littered the text, making knowing exactly what was involved more of a stab in the dark than a reasoned assessment of your new situation. And it was time-sensitive, effectively sign or go.

Essentially, many of the lower orders, the technical staff, went to zero-hour contracts. The scientific area was a little different. Their new contracts were, they were told, in keeping with the sensitive nature of the industry. What all staff were presented with, was a watertight non-disclosure agreement as a part of their contract. The professional staff also had stringent conditions regarding moving within the industry attached.

Most saw it as a continuation of the norm, a few realised that they were being conned to accept overly restrictive terms of employment, terms denying them some of their expected personal freedoms. About a dozen people left immediately, never to be heard from again as far as the company was concerned, but it later got about that they'd seen the rather complicated writing on the wall, taking the firing as just that, then going to a works tribunal with the hopes of getting compensation. As far as anyone knew they didn't get a bean.

Everyone in Sample Management and Shipping stayed put. Not because they came out of the changeover well, they didn't, but because it was a job. At their level that was better than no job at all. They were just the victims of the responsibility grindstone that slowly, over a life-time, turns your very spirit to dust. After a period of frenetic activity, everything settled down again and the company got on with doing what it always did; only now hiding the cock-ups that bit better. What the client doesn't know about won't upset them, after all.

In Sample Management the lurch into new technology brought fresh terrors. The old paper-trail of accountability was, in part, to be replaced by a digital audit trail, generated from the use of a Laboratory Instrumentation Management System. It loomed before them, and they were expected to 'learn all this new stuff and still do the same old shit', to quote Mo, or Moonbeam Orinoco Smith to use her full, and rather splendid, name.

Simon Reid expected to be handling the changes within Sample Management and he was right. Before the rif, he'd been sent to NPS in Montreal, Canada, to learn all about how the company did Sample Management and then his brief was to implement it in Nottingham, the departments being, he was told, up and fully functional within 20 working days of his return. No pressure then!

There had been some resentment around the department about Reid going on a 'freebie holiday', as it was so succinctly put, Mo again. But really there was nobody else in the department that could do it, so Simon it was. Shipping seemed pissed off too; nobody from there was being sent anywhere but then, as Simon had said to Craig Shepherd jokingly, "how hard is it to learn how to lick a different stamp?"

Like all companies, and takeovers, life did continue to run like some sort of site-specific soap opera. Friendships were made and broken. People met, got together and made more people, and others lived their lives like hummingbirds looking for a better flower all the time. They always said that someone should write it all down and sell it to the BBC, they just couldn't think of a snappy title for contract research.

Across town in Netherfield, where extensions to the industrial park were sprouting up quicker than mushrooms in a field full of horse shit,

Clive Gerrard sat in his car, thinking. His old unit, the one NPS hadn't been aware of, still had a 'for lease' sign on it. He didn't know quite why, but his Montreal contact had suggested that the old place would work and he'd been paid up front so why not? Gerrard called his lawyer, and the next day he got the keys.

Using his contacts, he'd arranged for a short puff-piece in the local newspaper. 'New Blue Sky Research' would be open for business soon as a low-key player in the contract research game. They had intimate knowledge of the industry and, more importantly, an intimate knowledge of one of the main rivals. Sheila Wright, his contact on the newspaper, had done her usual succinct piece.

Gerrard hadn't felt the slightest bit of guilt sending out the emails. If the departure of a few scientists disrupted the Saviour study for just a few weeks, then that would be enough and besides, he'd got his cut. Quite why Ben had wanted the delay was not his business. He just liked the idea that some of the money supposed to be paid to NPS by Saviour, for something that was probably a set-up, had found its way in his direction. All those scientists that had pissed him off over the years, endless meetings where the same ones always told him what he could do, well they were going to find that he had a long memory and his payback was that they'd all be eating humble pie when they went back to NPS, asking for their jobs back.

What he hadn't expected was the text from Marie-Eve Legault. She knew all about Saviour, everything Gerrard knew and his part in it. They should meet up when she came over to Nottingham. Hadn't he heard, she would be working there for a spell? Provided the right amount of US Dollars ended up in her offshore bank account, she'd forget Gerrard's part in Ben's little scheme, nothing personal, just business.

Gerrard realised that there were some parts of the scheme that he wasn't involved in. He speculated that, for Legault to know anything, she had to be inside. If so, why was she playing both ends?

A mistake now and Gerrard's future plans were up the spout.

He texted back, '*agreed*' and contacted his accountant, forwarding the newly received transfer destination details. The money had to come from his special account. The accountant logged the activity as 'sundry services' and sent Gerrard a bill by return.

When news of a potential new rival in Nottinghamshire reached Jim Duggan, he said that he welcomed competition. As a way of heading off trouble at the pass, he instigated a pay rise for analytical staff and above at NPS. As a ploy to keep the best of the best it didn't work, and anyone who bothered to look closely could see that Gerrard had already done his recruitment before leaving NPS.

Each department was slated to lose key staff in important places and HR would have to do a hurried recruitment campaign just to get bodies in the door. The upshot was that the quality level of the scientific staff would suffer, as would the research reporting accordingly. New Jersey, it seems, had already decided to just accept it as part of the cut and thrust of pharmaceuticals and that was that.

Then something strange happened, a couple of months after the announcement. The new CRO seemed to vanish in a puff of smoke, Clive Gerrard had too, and with him the promised posts offered to some.

At NPS, those staff that had handed their notices in, expecting more lucrative posts in the new company, tried to do an about-turn. NPS was sympathetic, of course, and graciously cherry-picked those they wanted, leaving the rest to their own devices.

The news that Clive Gerrard hadn't taken up the lease after all didn't seem to surprise some and that he had simply vanished from the research game, and even Nottingham altogether, was never mentioned again.

As an interference game, the machinations of the New Blue Sky Research situation and the furore it created for a few weeks had worked well. Clive Gerrard had played his part as directed, it was a pity that there had been so much collateral damage though, perhaps he'd gone too far.

# FORTY

## Thursday 9 June

Everyone knew something was going to happen, but this was the first time it was to happen in Nottingham and so nobody had had time to build a thick-skin; the sort you need to grow if you can see a well-liked colleague being marched off the premises just to cut a few pounds or dollars off the costs. Who actually went depended on who you'd pissed off most, more or less. You didn't always know that you had pissed someone off, but when the reduction in force came around they would be there in the background, basking in the glory of getting their own back, having the last laugh, or at least last smirk.

For all at NPS, Nottingham, this would be a memorable occasion. The first one is usually the biggest; the one where they clear out what they like to call the 'dead wood', but what they really mean is that it is generally the little people who go. No matter how long they had worked there or what they had invested in the job, they were always just numbers, and clearing them off the balance sheet meant that some shareholder in downtown New York had a few extra dollars return on one of their investments.

Reid had heard all about the rifs when undergoing NPS immersion training in Montreal but living through one was different, a shock to the senses, uncivilized.

People, technicians, arrived at work on the day to do their low-paid and supposedly unskilled jobs, only to find their coffee barely cool enough to drink before they were led off for the chop. The weird thing was, for a company that prided itself on being employee-friendly, there was no end-plan; nothing set up for those that were left. Sure those that went had a rough time of it, work is not always easy to find, certainly not at the same level and, even after years of good service, you were unlikely to find anything but menial work nowadays. The world of full-time employment had changed drastically.

When the 'big day' came, they lost three people from Sample Management and two from Shipping, plus all the students went. They weren't really employees, everyone was told, but they did count, statistically they made up the numbers. The night cleaners all went too, and they brought in a new contract cleaner for, it was said, a fraction of what they were currently paying. Some of the fired cleaners had been there years, knew what they were doing and took a pride in their jobs. The new lot would end up constantly frightened, they would not be given any real training and when they subsequently fucked up a few things, as they surely would, then they themselves would get the chop.

It later transpired that the department heads had to put their collective feet down and demanded better. The word was that the damage done by the untrained and unfamiliar cleaners in their first few days had cost the company most of the savings made from firing the original cleaners, plus another chunk on top. But that didn't matter because 'The Market' saw none of that, nor did the clients.

When they'd talked about rifs, the Montreal people had been right in every aspect. People were cut, their jobs absorbed; for that read 'done by existing staff for no extra pay and on top of their existing duties'. In many cases, the duties of those lost were left to flap about like some badly strapped-down tarpaulin in a storm, with nobody knowing who should have been doing what.

When the dust had settled, 78 people had been let go, a fair percentage of the workforce. The next week, the compulsory video missive from the Emperor in New Jersey delivered the news that the rif was unavoidable. It had to be done in order to keep the company stable financially, and he wished those that had gone his very best in their new adventure. Like all former NPS employees so affected, they were all in his thoughts and prayers.

225

Not long after the first rif, the odd bit of vandalism happened around the facility. A couple of cars got scratched, one quite badly, but it was a company car and so no individual suffered financially. An office window got smashed and a large number of new shrubs were ripped out of the ground and removed, petty stuff. The police didn't bother too much, nobody got thumped so it was an insurance job; phone the station, take a number and then moan when you renew your own insurance because it has gone up by five percent to cover the losses. The last attack probably should have attracted more police activity. Somebody wrote 'titch' on Richard Greenwood's company car in acid, and he'd not even been in post at the time. That was when they agreed it was time to put some CCTV outside too; security was due for a beef-up anyway, they were just accumulating quotes.

One problematic area of the site was to the rear, where there was no fence backing onto the Wilford Clay Pits Nature Reserve-side of the business park. The pits in the reserve were just two of what had once been ten former borrow pits that had made the site a haven for birds and, particularly, Great Crested Newts at one time. It was a complete mystery where the newts had gone. One season they were there, thriving, the next none could be found despite an ecological contractor spending hundreds of hours surveying the site. Completely coincidentally, once the newts had been confirmed to be absent, there was nothing to prevent the infilling and destruction of the remnants of most of the old Wilford Marsh. Not too long later, up went a spanking new, 'zero-rated' for ten years, business park, which, according to Councillor Ken Murray, the developer, would be good for all of South Notts.

# FORTY-ONE

"Detective Sergeant Thompson, phoning me on the hour, every hour, will not hasten the DNA report on the child in the womb of Marie-Eve Legault. I expect results around 3 pm today when those, along with the results of samples taken from your male lines of inquiry, will reveal whether one of them did, in fact, put the 'tup' in on the Fish Finger". Iain Lynch, pathologist and, he claimed, general dogsbody, hung up. He understood the situation and was not truly annoyed but just a little peeved at being continually pestered when he'd already explained the timeline for results, several times.

Thompson felt a little guilty in bothering him again. He knew that the process had a certain length of time to run and they both knew well that the results could point a massive finger of suspicion towards one of the few, or perhaps it was one of the many, suspects. On the other hand, determining the exact age of the foetus was proving problematical and the conception may have happened in Canada just before she left, on her first return visit or, given the supposed flighty nature of Legault, in the air somewhere in between or within the first two weeks of arriving in England, it was that tight.

Back in the operations room, the core team huddled in one corner. Coffee had been brought in by Dad, along with some strange but delightful fancies made by his wife. Dad's catering, well his good lady wife's, was always the high point of informal discussions because it was the sort of Pakistani cuisine that was kept within the culture and rarely found for public consumption outside of places like 'The Sweet Shop' in Bradford.

On the table top, a sheet of A4 had been appropriated for the latest hanging tree diagram and headed 'The Fish Finger'. Lines had been

227

drawn and then erased and re-drawn several times and no matter which way they approached the problem, the solution always seemed to come to one familiar point, the name of Craig Shepherd.

Thompson had a go at jollying them along. "Right team, ideas - Elkie?"

"Craig".

"Liam?"

"Craig".

"Dad?"

"Don't know".

"Drabble? Oops sorry, Jenny?"

"Don't know". Knight and Prosser let out a low moan, intentional, derisory, hoping for a reaction. "Look, I don't know", said Jenny. "Craig is obvious but he's a pussycat, a good-looking pussycat but still a pussycat. I can't see him squashing a spider, let alone deliberately murdering a woman".

"Who said it was deliberate?" This time Thompson had stepped in as Devil's Advocate. "He might not have any malice but he has brawn, it could have been an argument or even a reconciliation". There was a chorus of "in a freezer?" but Thompson continued doggedly "in a moment of passion, Legault slipped, banged her head and Craig panicked – just saying".

Dad reached over and took the pencil. Writing out numbers one to five he put Craig at number one, Reid two; Martin three; Greenwood four and then Montreal five and then he wrote 'a woman?'

"Montreal and women, Dad? Go on" said Thompson. The rest settled down, this should be good because when Dad had something to contribute like this, it was always thought-provoking. It must be all that meditation and prayer, it gave you time to think instead of endlessly running around with your brains slowly dripping out of your ears as modern life always seemed to require.

"So far we have assumed that poor Marie-Eve Legault was killed by someone local, but have we completely discounted the possibility that her murderer came here from her home town where we have little idea exactly what she was up to, in terms of behaving in a way that might involve individuals who would wish to end her life. While Craig Shepherd is the obvious candidate, I agree with Jennifer that he is too obvious and that he does not have it in him. I think, had he been involved, then he would have told us. Reid, I would also discount. Cold to Legault, yes, but then his personality, such as we have seen, is not particularly warm, perhaps you just need to get to know him before he warms up. Martin is a bit of a Sideshow Bob, Greenwood is not a nice man, but more devious than vicious, and the person we are looking for is vicious. Bez Dooley might also be added to the male contingent. We should also consider that Tracey Mills, Moonbeam Orinoco Smith, Jemmy Shepherd, Lucinda Greenwood, and Catheryn Selys may have had a reason that we are currently unaware of to form a dislike of Legault. A woman scorned and all that. Place six might be filled by whoever Legault's Montreal man is currently attached to, if there is one. We have more work to do there".

Dad looked around the room at the faces of his colleagues, each processing the potential additional suspect. Taking a deep breath he then said, "therefore, I think we should charge Craig Shepherd".

"What, after all that, you think we should go for Shepherd because he is the easiest option?" Banks was almost apoplectic.

"I think we should formally arrest him in public and make it seem that we have our suspect. I think we make it known at NPS that Shepherd is who we are after for the killing and then I think that the real killer might just relax. We also need to know more about the Montreal end of Legault's life and I suggest we start with Reid. He spent time there;

he may have information, even gossip, which might fill in a few blanks". And there endeth the word, according to Fasildad.

Dad put the pencil down and set about tackling his own fancy. He always got the biggest portion but nobody argued in case he pulled the privilege altogether.

Thompson loved it when the team got going like this; it must be something in Dad's fancies that always got them moving. Dad meanwhile had finished his fancy and gone off on his own to do whatever he thought best. Thompson never tried to stop him at times like this, no point really; Dad was the designated free-thinker of the group after all – if only for today.

As the room quietened, Thompson sat back, nibbling a sweet thing while looking at the suspect list. There was little doubt in his mind that the name of the guilty party was right in front of him, goading him almost. The lightweight start of the investigation had been consumed and the stodgy main course had begun. This wasn't any of that Nouvelle Cuisine crap; this was slowly filling all the spaces. Pudding would be just around the corner with maybe a brandy to follow.

Before they broke up to chase their respective tasks, Thompson called them all together. "I just want to make it quite clear that the Fish Finger, Marie-Eve, was a person not a thing. There have been mutterings from on high about this and so we, as the investigating officers, need to set an example. Besides", he added, , "if you lot keep on calling her a Fish Finger, then we'll have to call Jenny 'Officer Drabble' too, and she really won't like it!

A ripple in the space/time continuum told him Charnley was behind him so he continued to stare at the sheet, making indecipherable squiggles in one corner which were meant to convey deliberation in code.

Charnley said nothing, just looked at the sheet nodding slightly. After about a week, although it was possibly just moments, he turned and

230

strode back to his office. Taking advantage of the welcome absence, Thompson heaved his coat on, motioned to Jenny to accompany him and headed for the door on a little mission of his own.

# FORTY-TWO

In the car, on their way to have a look at Craig's caravan, Banks wanted to know where the 'Officer Drabble' thing had come from, but Thompson was never going to let on that Moonbeam Orinoco Smith was the culprit. Banks would only give her a hard time, which would be OK if it was necessary to the case. At this point it wasn't though and besides, he thought, the sad little fantasist had had it hard enough in life already, big soppy that he was.

Naturally forensics had already been all over the caravan but found very little. Craig had been honest about everything and so they hadn't been surprised to find Marie-Eve's DNA at the site. There was traces of DNA from other sources in there too and they hadn't been identified yet. Craig had claimed that he'd allowed a couple of mates to use the caravan for their own purposes. They had the names and rough dates; that was being checked although nobody thought it would be very helpful. Shepherd had assured them than nobody but him and Marie-Eve had used it recently, and not for a good two months at least, but Thompson decided that they still needed another visit, and they were doing that today.

The caravan offered no fresh inspiration and so, on more of an exploratory trip, Thompson and Banks went back to the scene of the crime. Security weren't entirely pleased to see them but signed them in anyway and issued the access cards. At first they just sat in the cafeteria, more to enjoy some coffee, which they paid for this time, and to see whether anyone would come over for a chat, it was low-key and sometimes worked.

After twenty minutes or so they went off around the site, calling in at the crime scene first. The Sample Management room had reopened the day after the body had been found, pressure from above, and was

232

now back to normal, with technicians going in and out and the freezers fully open again for business.

Reid saw them arrive but figured that if they wanted anything they'd say. Thompson caught his eye and nodded but then went into the freezer room after donning a lab coat and goggles. They weren't sure exactly what they were after but as neither had a very good handle on the actual operation of the Sample Management department they just took stock to see what happened. Thompson especially wanted to see the delivery process in real-time.

Nosing around, looking in freezers when techs opened the doors and nipping into the walk-in -20 to see them in action proved fruitless, and the continuous hum of the big -80°C freezers was giving both of them a ringing in their ears. The Sample Management staff were in and out of various freezers all the time, it was almost choreographed. Mostly they were taking boxes out, all marked with tape, which were then given to analysts collecting their samples to check against a request sheet, fascinating. They were about to head back to the station when a young shipping technician arrived with about fifteen large boxes piled high on a stainless steel cart, a new delivery.

Thompson and Banks watched as the tech wheeled the cart through the room and parked it next to a stainless steel work top. One of the sample management techs broke off from what they were doing, took all the paper work and set about opening the boxes one by one to check the contents. The shipping tech collected another cart that had presumably been used for a previous delivery and started to head back to shipping, beeping his card and heading through the access door that led to the Shipping Bay.

The inspiration that Thompson had been seeking had happened there and then, but only just, another few minutes and they would have been on their way, now he had his phone out and was calling the Circus back into town.

Within the hour, scene of crime were back on site and checking out the carts, four in total. They'd been told that none of them should have been to the equipment wash recently, it was only done monthly and so they hoped that there would be something on one of the carts that might be helpful. A complication might be eliminating the other users although, in theory at least, user contamination would be limited. GLP demanded the use of protective clothing and, especially gloves. If the killer had dumped Marie-Eve on a cart and wheeled her into the freezer, they might not have had GLP uppermost in their thoughts. Unless, that is, GLP had been ingrained into their psyche!

Thompson and Banks discarded their protective coats and gloves and sat with Reid in his office, the door shut. He didn't seem too worried, he just sat in his chair while they sat opposite like a couple of interviewees hoping for a career taking samples out of one box and putting them into another, but, of course, they weren't.

They went through the sample delivery process again, not wanting to lead Reid. It was best that he did the thing from start to finish on paper, which they could then take away with them. There may be something in the process that they'd missed and they wanted to see how Reid described the process, especially the parts he included that others might not hear, such as those GLP aspects he'd been quick to make them obey on the day of discovery.

Reid wasn't exactly impatient, but he certainly wasn't enthusiastic, perhaps a symptom of being in a job that wasn't very fulfilling. It was clear he was brighter than the average Sample Management technician, that was why he was the Team Leader, but it still didn't seem to fill in the corners of his mind, so what did?

"So", said Reid, "the samples arrive. A shipping tech brings them through to Sample Management".

Banks stopped him. "How"?

Reid looked blank, then he realised what she was after "Multiple boxes would be on a cart, of course".

"Every time? Multiple carts, same carts?"

Reid explained that they swapped one for one as they'd seen earlier, he didn't pay much attention as to which cart was used and, now that their hazmat-suited friends were busy with them, they wouldn't have any at all for a while. Thompson assured him that they'd get them back as quickly as possible and asked whether the carts were always used for every delivery.

"Single boxes will get carried through unless too heavy, but mostly Shipping will wait until they have a cart full, less effort".

Obviously it had not occurred to Reid that the use of carts was relevant. For Thompson and Banks it was a game changer, it meant that the transportation of a limp Marie-Eve Legault was much simpler than they had thought. It might not have needed very much strength at all, thereby bringing Orinoco Smith and Mills into play.

Banks had a thought. "Would Mr. Shepherd have used a cart for the transportation of boxes delivered on the night of Legault's death?"

"Yes, certainly he would, it was multiple boxes, as you know" said Reid with a trace of impatience in his voice. And now another complication arose. Craig Shepherd had a legitimate reason to use a cart, a legitimate reason to have his DNA all over it; this might not be quite the case break that they had hoped for.

Moving on together to the Shipping Department their diminishing joy was finally extinguished. At least two of the carts had been taken to the cage wash to go through the autoclave on the day of discovery, they were sent there to give the slow-witted porter, Alan Bain, something to do. They would have been washed clean of any traces of their recent users. So their chances of finding any forensic evidence on the carts had just been effectively halved.

# FORTY-THREE

Thompson wanted to brief again once he got back to Central Nick, especially in view of the detail about the cart, so he sent out a limited invite stating this would be a quick discussion only.

They'd all got there on time; it was Charnley who poled in ten minutes late, after having to negotiate the vast distance from his office to the briefing area. No apology was offered, nothing, he just cut straight to it. "Where are we now?" Had he even read the damned email?

It was very much the royal 'we', as Charnley had done nothing that anyone could point to. Thompson had organised the interviews, the rest of the team had been digging where it was needed; bank accounts, traffic cameras and CCTV, and Banks had been dealing with NPS in New Jersey. It was clear from her expression after every email or phone call that there would not be a Christmas card crossing the Atlantic for that 'bunch of tossers', as she so exquisitely called them. Jenny Banks was not normally like that, she was a steady-Edith sort. She got on with things, no fuss, no alarms and certainly no surprises. Thompson and the rest had heard the hippy woman call her 'Officer Drabble', and, to be fair, she was a bit drab, although sober would be better, less accusatory as an epithet, but no less unflattering.

Thompson quickly talked through recent progress to very little comment. "Suspects, who are they and in what order at this point in time?" Charnley not so much asked for details as spat out the instruction. Thompson responded in a flat, guarded voice.

"We have a number of potential suspects but the list in the email I sent you is in no particular order because, at present, we have nothing solid to tie any of them to the murder other than circumstantially. Shepherd remains our main person of interest".

The grunt from Charnley was delivered as expected, he rarely disappointed on the grunt front.

Taking the bovine by the head adornments, Thompson decided to recite the email contents, almost verbatim.

"Simon Reid had access, but a weak motive that we know of. He didn't like Legault, had never made a secret of it, has answered all questions apparently truthfully, appears to be laid back and probably is. Has an alibi for the time of death, such as we know it, and doesn't feel right as a killer, more likely to offer a rude insight to all and sundry rather than stuff a woman he barely knew into a freezer. He also pointed the finger at Shepherd with the fling rumour which has turned out to be fact".

"Old news" said Charnley. "Move on, and quickly".

"Moonbeam Orinoco Smith had access, claims to have had a relationship with the deceased but is clearly a complete fantasist, however, could potentially be the killer because, although not physically strong, we have recently discovered that she could have used a cart to place the body where Reid found it".

"Why are we talking about women? Killed by a man, move on".

"Thank you, Sir, but I don't think we should close all doors just yet, at least not until we've had the forensics back on the carts".

Was Thompson getting cocky or just treating Charnley the way everybody felt he should be dealt with, that was indifference bordering on insubordination? There was a glare, not for long, but Charnley looked like he'd added something important to his mental to-do list.

"Craig Shepherd is about as prime a suspect as we have but, he has an alibi for the time of death, or at least if the time of commencement of freezing is when we suspect it to be. He was at home asleep until the call to receive the samples came. Sound asleep according to himself

237

and his wife, and there is no sign of his car on any CCTV outside of the hours he admits to". Thompson drew a breath and continued.

"Andy Mood, the delivery driver is a non-starter. The timing probably rules him out. His onboard Sat-Nav is configured by the depot before setting off, his times are correct and he was only at NPS for little over ten minutes".

"Tracey Mills had access, no real issues known of between the deceased and Mills but we are keeping her on the list because that is right and proper at this stage of the investigation". Now everyone had caught on that Thompson was getting more and more irritated by Charnley and his less than team approach.

From the back of the room, a polite cough announced the presence of Superintendent Perkins who had slipped into the impromptu briefing without anyone knowing. How had he even found out about it? "If I understand it correctly" he said. "How did Mr. Shepherd get to the depot, move the samples to a freezer and fill in the receipt inside the ten minutes indicated on Mr. Mood's schedule? Surely Mr. Shepherd is some twenty minutes away and, given time for dressing, a visit to the toilet first perhaps and then the vagaries of getting to NPS, the times do not seem to correspond". It was like listening to a well-educated voice that belonged to someone who was constantly confused.

DC Liam Prosser started to speak, the room hushed, this very rarely happened when senior officers were present. "The driver has a patch into a pager system that predicts the arrival time, used mainly on holidays and for out-of-hours deliveries. It pages the recipient, in this case the NPS Security station, and gives advance warning of impending delivery. Security personnel are then able to connect with the person on their call-out rota, in this case Shepherd, who then is able to arrive in due time to take the samples, electronically sign the docket and store them, Sir".

Apart from Perkins, everyone else was gobsmacked. Liam rarely said sentences of more than ten words anyway and then good luck if you could even hear him, let alone understand what he'd said. Not for nothing was he known as the 'Hoarse Whisperer' behind his back.

Perkins gave a curt "I see", was about to go and then thought better of it. "Such information would be immensely useful to have included in your intermittent briefing reports. Carry on, Charnley", and he was off, slithering back to his Hibernaculum.

The meeting broke up when Charnley just stomped off to his office and shut the door. The team were slow to break up though, more ideas were clearly circulating and so Thompson took them off the canteen for a pow-wow.

Coffee and biscuits arrived at the table via Laura Knight, it was her turn. They were rigidly democratic about the catering unless it happened to be Dad proffering his fancies, then the catering floor was his.

Thompson gave them a pep-talk. "OK people, I want you to feel the case, get inside the head of the killer, look through his, or her, eyes, experience the death at his, or her, hands. Let's brainstorm this case and find a solution before the advert break - ideas?" Only Dad was confused, the rest just laughed, it was Dave pissing about again to break any tension.

Prosser stayed silent, his earlier loquaciousness leaving him burnt out now and for the next week, probably.

Knight thought they should concentrate on Shepherd. Banks thought they should widen the net to include the security guy, the cleaners and the site manager; Reid was peripheral now. Dad sat quiet, only offering an opinion when pushed by Thompson. "I think we have to narrow it down to the why, rather than opportunity. Killers are rare, most people would never think of killing someone, some are always thinking that way, so do we have one in NPS now, do we need to background check for previous psychopathic behaviour? There is also the problem of the why. Legault was frozen for a reason; there is something that drove the killer to kill, something specific. We must find that now, the rest will follow".

"Right", said Thompson, "we go fishing for reasons".

"What do we tell Charnley?" That was Prosser, being unusually vocal yet again.

"Fuck all" they chorused, even Dad, and nobody could remember him swearing before, ever, although he may have said 'foot', still it was the spirit of the thing that counted.

"Leave Charnley to me", said Thompson. "He wasn't always so shitty to everyone so there must be more to it". The general feeling of the team was 'rather you than me, mate!'

Returning to his work station, Thompson pulled a sheet of vivid yellow paper from his desk and wrote, in large black letters, '#1 Shepherd, Reid, Greenwood, Martin, Mood' Then in smaller letters, '#2 Orinoco, Mills'. After a couple of minutes staring at the sheet he wrote '#3Dooley, Singh. Then in larger letters, he wrote 'delete as applicable'. He went back into the briefing room and pinned the sheet to the dead board, stepped back and admired his handiwork. One of them did it, three groups of suspects, alibis for some, walking on sand for others.

Without him realising it the team had gathered behind him and were staring at the list too. The brainstorming that Thompson had jokingly called for earlier appeared to be happening. Either that or they were wondering what form lunch might take; you never knew what it might be when dealing with the enquiring mind.

# FORTY-FOUR

If the amount of institutionalised racism was much as expected when he joined the force, then Fasildad wouldn't have batted an eyelid. The police were known for it, even if they had taken steps to darken their public face a little bit. That said, he found that much of the racism was done more out of habit than malice, and the feeling in the ranks was less that the other officers hated blacks, Asians or the Chinese but that they hated everybody, whites especially. It was an all-inclusive programme. Knowing that put a different edge to the rare comments he got.

He felt that he was holding his own, forcing his way into a system that had originally been designed only for white men, then that had to adjust for some loud white women and now had to further morph to accommodate 'people of colour' as Superintendent Perkins called them, like pink isn't a colour!

Outside of work was where Dad really felt the ethnic issue, the reaction of his 'own people' verged on savage. The young people told him he'd sold out to 'the man'; why did some Asian kids adopt black language and clothes? He didn't know. The old people told him that the law in Britain, while respected, was not their law and that he would never be accepted in his own community as a representative of that law. Dad knew exactly what they meant but chose to ignore everybody and just get on with it. This wasn't about assimilating into a culture, this wasn't about appeasing minority pressure groups. No, this was all about Dad, all about his desire to be a detective.

Coming from the Pakistani community helped when the PR spin-doctors got involved. Dad was a shining example of the cultural breadth of modern policing. He was a community icon, a role model for all young Asians when it came to representing their culture in their adopted country's modern Police Service. They liked to say 'modern' quite a lot in the modern Police Service.

The case occupying Dad's mind at the moment was a tricky one, but then weren't they all? A dead French-Canadian found in a deep freeze. Maybe she had enemies but more likely they were only work foes and none of those that they'd talked to had seemed mad enough to want to kill her. The possibility of outside interference had crossed Dad's mind, a contract killer from Canada brought in to do a job. He'd mentioned it earlier, a tricky case indeed if mob involvement was a factor.

The team, Dad's team, was a good one, apart from Charnley these days and that would soon change. They were all united in a purpose; unravel the case, pick at the loose ends and tie up the killer in a nice, neat bow, easy. There was just a lot between that had to be done and done right, to get there, to get the conviction.

Dave Thompson was a good lad, straight as a die. A clear thinker, methodical and he followed procedure, but Dad suspected that he didn't take his work home. In his own place he became detached, possibly to retain his sanity, and that might hold him back. He'd have a quiet word, sometime.

After Thompson the team were all of the same rank but not necessarily in alphabetically-sorted pecking order. Dad was the senior Detective Constable through service. Liam Prosser was next followed by Jennifer Banks and then the office junior was Elkie, Laura Knight. That both girls had been fast-tracked and would leave Dad, and Dave, well behind at some point didn't matter, they were both very good and, under Dave, would pick up the right habits. Pity Charnley went odd; he was a good role model at one time.

The thing with this case, or any case, is to take each piece of evidence and put it into sequence. If the killer is amongst the people you have talked to, taken a statement of facts from, then they will have made a mistake somewhere and you, as one of the detectives, need to find it. It may also be that the killer is not amongst the natural suspects, natural by circumstance. Their chief suspect was though, natural by circumstance. A less balanced team might have simply nailed him for it, dumped the file with the Public Prosecutor and moved on, but his team, they would get their killer, whoever it was, male or female, local or foreign, they were starting to get known for it. The cherry pickers would be along at some point, but probably not for everyone.

Dad had the ability to switch everything else off and focus. He didn't know he could do that until he became a detective. His parents had thought him slow, 'touched' even, but he was sharp as a tack, he just took his time getting to the point. While Thompson went methodically and quite correctly through the tried and tested process, Dad thought differently, at a tangent, Thompson encouraged it. The rest of the team had bought into it too, when needed, one team member who would have a duty to reason it out, not get bogged down with too much 'hands on' stuff. It had worked well before and now they were all taking 'thinking time' as a part of the team-motivated training. Other teams had heard what they did and some thought they were all daft, time wasters, but you couldn't argue with the results.

Shepherd might have done it. He could have, so could Reid, so could Martin. Shepherd was there or thereabouts, perhaps. Reid wasn't there at the right time, according to his girlfriend. Martin was there throughout, that should be enough to keep him in mind.

Three obvious candidates then, so who isn't obvious?

The father of the foetus, unknown, has to be an option. The other lover reputed to be in Nottingham, besides Shepherd, was also at present unknown if one ever existed.

The fantasist Moonbeam Orinoco Smith might be an outside bet. Not as the father, obviously, but as the murderer maybe, but perhaps actually killing someone would be a bit too real for her.

One of the cleaners perhaps? No, not likely, they were new unless one had been employed by someone else to do it, something to quietly check.

Tracey Mills, she worked with Shepherd, had a crush on him, was she jealous?

Richard Greenwood, did he feel threatened by Legault, why would he?

Anyone else had access? Bez Dooley, maybe he's the other lover?

The Montreal angle still needs attention, there must be people there who she has rubbed up the wrong way, but enough to follow her here and kill her? This was a long-shot at best.

Realistically, three local suspects plus one in pencil then, all with the means to kill but only one of them with a motive of sorts. Shepherd? No, too easy, although sometimes it is.

# FORTY-FIVE

Jenny Banks was quite annoyed that her colleagues kept calling her 'Officer Drabble'. She knew it was just friendly piss-taking but, all the same, she was not a happy bunny. They knew too and it had eased off a bit for now, but these things had a habit of sticking and she'd end up being 'Officer Drabble' for the rest of her police career if she didn't nip it in the bud now. How would that work for her as Chief Constable? She'd just have to come up with a better nickname for herself, something slightly self-depreciating but not as bad as 'Drabble'.

Sometimes piffling little things like the drabble issue got to her, festered and then came out in a torrent of swearing, the like of which you really needed to be brought up in the valleys of South Wales to appreciate. That made her kind of scary, not a bad thing when aiming for high office or interviewing a mousy type, but it also made people keep her at arm's length, not good, especially when she was aiming for warm and approachable but someone who doesn't take fools lightly.

Her man had got the hang of her now, he'd taken a while though and she'd almost resorted to well-placed hints on Post-it notes before he got down on one knee. She liked being engaged, it was an area of her life almost done and dusted. After the wedding she could file it away and make plans for the child-bearing years. She reckoned on being two years away from the force to have the two kids, one of each, and then back with a vengeance – full steam ahead to the Chief Constable's chair. Luckily, her partner ran his mortgage advisory business from home, so any Chief Constable's chair would do, anywhere.

Cracking the Legault case would look good in her CV; besides, the whole thing was an untidy mess and needed clearing up. Messy was not allowed in Jenny Banks' world; Jenny was not at home to Mr. Chaos.

245

Dave was alright as a sarge, he always let people have their say at any time, he made them all feel like they were valuable team members; they were a team. Jenny had never been a team person much before, unless it was team Jenny, but she had accepted this new working format because it was an area she needed to learn about, embrace. You can't run teams unless you know what it is like to have been in one. She knew that she'd have to be a Dave eventually, but a much better Dave of course. She'd be Dave at some point on her way up, when it suited her. After that, when she was where she intended to be, she'd be a Jenny, the best Jenny there was.

It seemed that the Fish Finger, Legault, wasn't very popular in Nottingham, Jenny had some sympathy there. In Montreal her popularity status was only vaguely known at present, more data needed. She'd only been in Nottingham for a metaphorical five minutes but had already had a relationship with Craig Shepherd, just sex; that appeared to be Legault's way. That had been Jenny's way for a while, at Uni at least, that was what Uni was for, learning, everything. Now sex was taken care of, her man dealt with it.

There was nothing clear-cut about the Legault case and that made it even more annoying for Jenny. No one suspect stood out, someone that they could concentrate on. Of the known suspects, the woman Moonbeam Fuckwit, who was such a waster, was not the one. Jenny had seen wasters before, identified them easily, she knew exactly what they were and there was no need to waste her time with wasters.

The man Reid was a maybe, but unlikely. He'd found the body and then did all the right things until they got there. How did he know what to do? Maybe he got it from the TV or books, or even the Internet, did he like murders? His alibi was strong; his girlfriend was a solid sort, unspectacular, even-keeled. Reid was at the bottom of the list. He did know Marie-Eve from Montreal. They worked together for all of ten days, is that enough to get to know someone biblically? In Marie-Eve Legault's case, it would seem so.

246

The security guard, Martin, was a 'wanna-be'. A shirt with a badge, he'd have carried a gun if they'd let him. He was too helpful, hiding something for sure. Not married at his age, never had been. No girlfriends had come up in conversations despite gentle digging. Gay maybe, so no sexual motivation to kill Legault, he needs checking in detail anyway.

Craig Shepherd, he is a good-looking man in a swarthy, Mediterranean sort of way, Italian ancestry perhaps. He'd had a relationship with Marie-Eve, was it just sex? Why did he do it? Craig is married, with a young child and a seriously cute wife, so why stray? Perhaps he's serial cheap, some men are; they have to keep proving their masculinity via conquests although, from what Jenny was hearing, the conqueror was more likely Legault, with Craig being the conquered party.

Could he have done it? Well, Craig was big enough and strong enough to haul Legault into the freezer if she was killed outside the freezer, strike one. He had history with Legault and had been dumped by her, or so he said, or perhaps it was really the other way around. Whatever, he had a motive of sorts, strike two. Craig had been at the facility that night, although most of his movements were either filmed on their Asda bargain-bin CCTV, where it worked, or tracked via the card readers, again, where they worked. He'd been in Shipping and even to the freezer, and the thinking was that Marie-Eve Legault had been already in there, dying. Could Craig really not notice her when he put the boxes in, was the angle just wrong? Probably, if the procedure was as had been described and they always dumped the boxes just inside the door. Still he would be only feet away from her, for a while, is that strike three or just .5 of a strike?

An outside bet might be Richard Greenwood; yes he just might be their boy. He was yet another dickhead who fancied himself, especially with the ladies, she could tell. He had the means and the opportunity to do it but what motive would he have? His alibi was shaky, on his own at home watching Game of Thrones on Blu-ray. True, he seemed the sort to sit on the sofa waving his cock at Daenerys! They should find time to talk to Joan Bain, get a bit more background on the man and then maybe add him to the pile, somewhere near the top. A good PA knows everything and their impression was that, while she was good, Greenwood wasn't to her liking.

If in doubt then you should always look at the alibis for signs of fraying. Craig had his wife, Jemmy, to vouch for him. He was, she said, at home and in bed until the well-documented site visit. They slept in different rooms when Craig was on-call; Jemmy had the baby alarm with her which made her sleep even lighter. She'd said that she had heard him go and later come back, claimed to be a light sleeper, anyway. Her timings in and out were good for the distance and time spent with the delivery. Too much leans towards Craig to ignore him just yet, though.

What about Reid? He has his girlfriend, Catheryn Selys, backing him up all night. He was out with her for the whole evening, seeing Ricky Gervais at the Theatre Royal. Back 11:30. Check how they bought the tickets, credit card presumably. They had met friends at the gig, prearranged. They were a group of eight of them, all solid, slightly left-leaning sorts if they like Gervais's humour, she expected. They went home after the gig and went to bed. Reid got up at the regular time the next day, everything was normal. Why do I call them Reid and Greenwood but Craig, Craig?

Mo had claimed to be out clubbing but her neighbour said she was in all night as did their CCTV trail. Her neighbour was a neighbourhood-watch type, on duty at the window all night. Her car never moved; it rarely did after she got home, she said, and few people ever visited. Mostly just the one with fluffy hair like an extra from the Village People, she said; that must be Martin. Mo had later admitted she was wrong, mixed the nights up; vodka did that to you sometimes, of course it does.

Neil Martin was on duty so his alibi was essentially all electronic. The card readers showed his entry into the building, then access to some rooms at 9:30pm when he started a round. Nothing more showed up on the activity list until 3am when he did another, incomplete round; then there was more activity when he left the building at 05:00. Why did he only do an incomplete round the second time, was this normal or was he avoiding the freezer?

There must be a patrol schedule, surely more than two full patrols per shift would be done, especially with the busted CCTV and card readers in places? Could he move around in the relevant area without tripping a card reader? He could if the cleaners had lodged the doors open.

Martin was back on-site an hour and a half after his night shift had finished, claiming that he was 'pulling another half-shift'. To do that, he had probably slept all or part of the night in the office. Who'd know? He'd only wake up to let Craig in and check him out, all on the card reader. Martin was top suspect number two, just based on location, although he'd have had no trouble shifting the Fish Finger from point to point. They really needed to know where she died; it would make all it a bit simpler.

Dave had said he wanted some lateral thinking from the team but Jenny just kept coming back to Craig or, less likely, Martin. Sorry Craig, you did it. Sorry Martin, you might have done it but, to be honest, you do come across as a bit of a sad prat.

# FORTY-SIX

Liam Prosser was a pragmatic man, his outlook on life somewhat shaped by being raised during the 'troubles'. While some had a cosy little childhood, football in the streets with jumpers for goalposts, camping trips, fun, Prosser had armoured cars, pipe bombs, kneecapping, mess, always a mess, whether glass or rubble or just rubbish dumped, always a mess. Before the Good Friday Agreement, the only way out was to move and so, when he hit seventeen, he'd moved to Nottingham, leaving the mess and religion, the root cause of the mess, way behind him.

In the scheme of things Nottingham was not a bad choice, not least because he had a sort of cousin there who could put him up for a few weeks. After that he'd got a bedsit in Carrington, worked in a supermarket in Victoria Centre and generally got on with living a quieter life than he'd ever been used to, but one he'd long wished for. Belfast wasn't the place for Liam Prosser to be Liam Prosser, not yet anyway.

At night school he'd done further education and enjoyed it, he was always bright and saw the advantage of having a few bits of paper to put by your name. Then the local police had done a recruitment drive and he thought, 'why not, give it a go, a career if they'll have me', and he got in. Making Detective Constable had been un-taxing and Prosser had it mind to get to at least Detective Inspector, all in good time, and he was happy not to have a regular domestic partner to confuse the issue. His private life consisted of a very small, discreet group of like-minded individuals. Within the group nobody asked questions, nobody was a threat.

The Fish Finger case had kept him awake though. Not at the shock of the murder, when you've seen arms, legs, heads scattered over a road, death is no longer a scary place, just an eventual fact. What bothered Prosser was the why and the wherefore.

Marie-Eve Legault had lived by her own moral code and so she should. Who she shagged was her business and only became relevant to the case if one of the 'shaggees' was the killer. It seemed likely that Shepherd did it, it was hard to look past him, but they should. The pros for charging Shepherd were not rocket science. He had access, a motive, the physical capability and he was recently a lover, a dumped lover. Normally that would do, 'bang to rights' as they say in Wallace and Gromit. He'd always been one to look beyond the obvious though, in all things. He'd heard rumours that it had given him a reputation as a serial skeptic, but he didn't believe it.

The team as a whole were open to ideas but, the longer the case went on, the more those aloft would press for a result, any result. Clearing in-trays was what it was all about to them, not always getting it right, but 'getting it right' was the team's unofficial motto.

Prosser thought that they should widen the interview range. Call in partners, sit them in an interview room and take them outside of their comfort zone. Mo would be the hardest. Prosser had seen her before, years ago, when he was just another punter buying shots and joking with her, but that was a long time back and she hadn't look quite so raddled then. She obviously didn't remember him, why would she? Just another face to serve, a thirty-second relationship ending in a tip. Tracking down her significant others might be the problem, although it just might be that she was just a lonely old woman who had nothing and no one.

Maybe Marie-Eve had spurned Mo's advances? Would that be enough to make her kill Marie-Eve, did Marie-Eve bat for both sides, too?

Martin was a different matter altogether. It was another face that he knew but not from clubs. He'd seen it on a web site that had been set up by vigilantes trying to stop the cottaging and drug trade around

Colwick Park. The web site had since been taken down after the threat of legal action, but for a couple of weeks, every night it had shown grainy photos of men coming and going to one spot, the pictures probably taken by a low-cost trail cam. Prosser had seen Martin's photo on there once, he was sure, on the day before the site came down, in fact. He might not even know that he'd been Internet famous for a very short while.

Reid didn't do it. He was just an ordinary guy in a job he variously enjoyed and despised, working for a company that had a tendency to treat everyone like sheep. At least that was the impression he gave. He had the means, although, as far as they knew, he had no way to get into the building without wafting his card at the reader. He and Martin could have teamed up though, but why would they? Reid seemed to treat Martin as a sort of joke, which, to be fair, he was. Reid didn't like Marie-Eve Legault at all though, but that is not a crime. Prosser didn't like a lot of people but there were only a handful that he'd kill without thinking about it, and most of those were back home anyway.

So who was outside the box? Martin's partner/s maybe for reasons not yet known. Shepherd's wife, Jemmy, maybe, but she would only have a motive if she knew about her husband and Marie-Eve and the signs were that she didn't. Mo's associates; Prosser remembered some of the scene's denizens were dodgy as fuck and she'd known them all. Did she have a friend to help her do this? Again Martin might fit that bill; they appeared to be close but not in a physical sense. Reid's girlfriend? She was just a nice woman, worked in Boots as an admin. They were close, you could see that, and there is no suggestion that Reid had any relationship with Marie-Eve other than an occasionally fraught working one.

Reid had been to Montreal, so perhaps he had a different take on Legault, perhaps he'd heard something that might be helpful. He would be Prosser's recommendation for the next round of enquiries, then Jemmy Shepherd, then anyone that they could dig up with a close association with either Martin or Orinoco Smith.

252

While he'd been brainstorming, Prosser had been scribbling on the A4 pad where he kept his link notes, not for public consumption, just bits to help him pull the strands of the case together. Craig Shepherd was written in capitals and circled several times, was his subconscious seeing things that he'd not yet noticed? Maybe, but not really admissible in court!

# FORTY-SEVEN

When Dave came up with Elkie (LK) as her nickname, Laura just didn't get it at first. Not great for a detective really, but then she'd never been one for such conundrums; she was more what she thought of as an intuitive thinker. She knew people in general, her time as an army daughter had seen her travel to live in distant lands, meet strange and interesting people and had made her more worldly-wise than many of her age. Academically she was good and her later years at Nottingham High School for Girls had set her up with a solid social life, a few interesting boyfriends but not someone who she'd want to come home to daily. Her exam results, and likely her mixed parentage, mummy was from The Gambia, had been good enough to put her onto the fast-track programme to be a detective, so that was what she'd wanted to be.

The team was unusual in that there was no animosity. Other deployments had shown her what the rank and file thought of fast-tracking and, in some cases, a 'touch of the tar brush' as they called it. On the surface there was appeasement but it was underlain with a seething resentment at someone seen to be cutting corners. Not from everybody, mainly from the men who'd never had what it takes to get any higher, the dead-necks who were 'old school' sexist, racist and particularly homophobic. Things were changing though; the detritus of the old-guard were slowly being filtered out to anonymity while the bright, modern thinking decent people were slowly taking over the asylum.

She'd long ago accepted her role in precipitating that sea change, even if there might be some discomfort for herself from time to time.

Dave had asked them all to go away from the briefing room and take time to think about the Fish Finger case. He wanted some fresh thoughts and, rather than have a verbal melee where the loudest makes the biggest impression, never her forté, he wanted measured thoughts, alternative perspectives, something they could use to take the case forwards. Dave was good like that, and he listened.

The thinking was that Shepherd did it but Elkie wasn't so sure. He had a young baby, oddly just called 'Small', that demanded lots of him emotionally, and he had a wife who he obviously cared about. Sure, he slipped up with Legault, but she was a predator, that much was clear, while Shepherd, despite his physique, was just prey, that was clear too. He was attractive, that couldn't be denied, and he'd be popular with the straight gals, so was that how Jemmy Shepherd had got him, she wondered, was Jemmy a predator too?

It was hard to hide from facts and it was facts that would put this case to bed, sooner or later. The facts were not stacked too high against Craig Shepherd that he'd couldn't be seen over them, but they needed to see what facts the other suspects had accumulated in the 'for' and 'against' columns.

Martin was creepy and Elkie hadn't liked him at all. There was something about the way he moved, almost insinuated himself into conversations. She could see that others felt the same way and chatting groups soon disbanded when he became a part of them. Only Orinoco Smith seemed to be OK with him, friendly even, there was something there but it was not obvious exactly what it was. Martin could have done it or at least aided and abetted. They needed to know what he was all about before pressuring him and simply disliking him was not going to helpful, so Elkie decided to 'fess up when they all got together, 'fess up so that she would be kept away from the Martin part of the inquiry as much as possible, or, if not, then at least her antipathy could be taken into account.

Reid seemed OK. There was nothing that they had found in his past to mark him out as a potential murderer. There'd been a fight at school once, rough stuff with an injury to one of the kids involved, enough for a police visit. Whether Reid had been responsible for the injury was largely hearsay and not of much use. He'd had a speeding ticket and a credit card debt that was now being paid off on monthly terms. He had a live-in girlfriend, no kids. No real worries there as far as they could see; Reid was last on Elkie's list of possible suspects.

Orinoco Smith was a dilemma. Elkie had met people like her before, usually men, squaddies who liked to pad their resume with tales of derring-do in the Falklands, or Afghanistan. They were always, to a man, making it up. True, they had served there but more often than not the action they claimed to be involved in was mess stories, recycled and embellished. Elkie knew this because she knew people who had seen that kind of action and they didn't talk about it in public, usually not even in private, but sometimes they did and Elkie had a good ear and, with squaddies, a pair of tits helped, too.

Elkie wondered about Richard Greenwood. He'd been under the radar for now. He had the means, he had the opportunity as far as they knew and he often worked late enough to have the place more or less to himself. He was also a smug bastard who thought every woman wanted him. She could imagine him as the touchy-feely type, the sort the office girls would be sure to avoid or at least make sure they had an escape route available. He was the man in charge though, the new man really; he was a NPS CEO appointee, so why would he do anything to upset the apple cart like killing a colleague, especially a temporary one?

Or perhaps there was something there and the case against him was stronger than it appeared. The more she thought, the more Richard 'Dick' Greenwood was the one to have a deeper look at, check his background. She wondered whether he understood the nickname the others had used for him, 'Dick'. It made her smile.

There was also the Montreal angle and Elkie thought Reid might have something more there for them. They could also do with a little extra personal background view of the Fish Finger's life there; friends and lovers, and enemies, especially enemies. She made a note to suggest a teleconference with someone in the Montreal Police Force, someone that might be able to fill in a few blanks on Marie-Eve Legault.

The other name she'd typed into her laptop's 'The Strange Case of The Frozen Fish Finger' file was Bez Dooley. He was technically in the same position as Legault at NPS, the technical manager. Did he feel threatened by her, might she have been after moving in and taking his job or was she likely to become the NPS technical director, his boss, the boss of all technical managers? Worth checking. Dooley seemed a grounded sort. Married, kids, steady. Just a list-padder really, but she'd not be thinking about this case in-depth if she missed him out.

Dave's list had Ranjit Singh on it. No chance, HR couldn't tie their own shoe laces, let along do a murder carefully enough to not get caught straight away. It was a prejudice against all HR staff she knew, but Elkie had met enough of them to form a firm opinion. 'If you can do it, then just do it, if you can't do it then be an HR person'.

She re-read her list and conclusions and sent it to print, eight copies. She'd be able to give one to everyone before they next got their heads together; she very much hoped that that would make Dave happy.

# FORTY-EIGHT

Another day, another set of people to talk to. The Fish Finger took time to thaw, as expected and my gut feeling was right. What killed her was being frozen, brought about by being incapacitated following a blow, or blows to the head. Whether the injuries were acquired by slipping in the freezer or a good, solid set of whacks remains to be seen but, given the floor cleaner dumped on her, a whack was most likely.

Charnley is keeping at arms-length for now; Perkins is nosing around though, spooking everyone. The team have their tasks, interviews, where were the people and what were they doing? The leg-work we all have to do.

Prime is Shepherd, he was intimate with her, had access and may have been around when it happened. The downside seems to be that he is a bit soft.

Reid is a non-starter. Cocky through nerves, it's commonplace. We need to know exactly why he disliked her though. There may also be a Montreal connection; if she was up to something then the Montreal Mafia might be involved, although this doesn't seem to be a very professional job.

Something he was talking about might be relevant, or at least interesting for me as a plot line. The clinical study they have, a big one, is iffy according to Reid. I need to get my head around this more, it might have something to do with the Fish Finger too. If she found something out, something bad, then her death is linked. As I understand it there seems to have been corners cut, but no solid evidence of cheating, however that might be done. Not sure whether I can legitimately get more from Reid on this unless it develops, case-wise.

Moonbeam is an odd one. Not a killer in my book but she has fingers in pies. I caught her looking at Prosser too, an odd look, maybe she knows him but where from? He's open about his leanings so maybe there, I'll have a word.

A definite murder weapon is missing so far, we need to chase. We do have the potentials, a couple of heel bars but both wiped. How was she persuaded into the freezer, carried or walked?

Something is shifty about the site manager. He has a few bits on record, not murder but shady enough. No convictions but 'smoke and fire' as Charnley always says. Gossip has him down as a fanny-chaser, looks the sort, maybe he chased Marie-Eve's and she put him right, or welcomed him, possible both ways.

Something about Martin is shouting at me and I can't think what. We checked him, nothing, not even a parking ticket. The trouble is that he has a face you want to slap and I'm sure I've thought that before, so when?

Day two didn't get us anywhere really. Shepherd needs a bit more of a push but I don't expect anything there, really.

# FORTY-NINE

## Tuesday 20 September

Moonbeam Orinoco Smith sat alone in her little house, a starter home but plenty big enough for just her. She'd always believed that it would be just her from an early age and had been right so far. She couldn't see any upsides to sharing her life, either her real one or the one she was convinced that she lived.

She finished off the family sized bag of cheese & onion crisps and reached for the second bag. She was going to smell like her Grandma all next day, she knew it. Still, who'd care?

Dead Marie-Eve was bothering her, lots. Mo had liked her and thought Marie-Eve had felt the same, a spark. Two fish out of water, one in a strange city, the other stuck in the wrong life, the life of a middle-aged, getting fatter, woman who struggled to keep track of what stories she'd told people. When she was out at clubs, when she was pulling shots with the great, the good and especially the beautiful, it had been so easy, because that was real. She should have let it go when it went of its own accord, not strung it out in desperation.

The drink was never a problem; she could take it or leave it. The coke though, she'd been careful with that shit, she'd seen too many end up sinking into a pit of despair, a deeper pit than the one that she was sat at the bottom of now and that had seemed deep enough.

Something about the guys at the club, the late night gang was bothering her. A face, she knew it, different though, dressed differently, less formal, more relaxed with people of the same tastes, mostly. It had bugged her since the first dead Marie-Eve day. Losing Marie-Eve was bad enough in its way, but also vicariously exciting, the most exciting thing that had happened to her for some time.

260

A thought struck her; perhaps the photo album would help. Most of the photos were rough, taken by others on low-res pocket cameras, before phone cameras. Perhaps it was a sign of her age but she had printed them all, no matter how bad. She still preferred prints, even if they did fade like everything else.

She only kept the photos to cheer herself up now and then, although they almost always upset her these days. She often felt that she should have gone out like a rock star, before the weight came, before the looks went but she'd never had the nerve, she'd just hoped that it would all turn out good again, fun again. Instead it was the treadmill. Work, eat, sleep, pay bills, work, not even enjoyable work, not even work that she could sink herself into, wrap around her like a protective shield, excel at, be the best, the star.

The album pages looked worn. The photos had been pulled out too often, some had curled and others had become damaged as they'd been ripped out having been stuck to the page. Five pages in, a low-light scene from the club, people laughing, dancers behind her and a man, happy, smiling, not looking at her but at another man, a man he was dancing with, both happy, relaxed, being who they really were.

Mo fetched her stronger glasses, the ones she needed for really small print. She never wore them at work. The old photo was bad, blurred. The colours not true, the edges ill-defined but it was him, she was sure. The angle of the nose looked familiar but the eyes seemed different, they were older now, more worn out. It was him though, she knew, did everyone else know though?

Work came around as it always did. Get up; go in, same coffee, same act. She chatted to the girl in the cafeteria; it was the same conversation, more or less, great weekend, out late, sleep all day, living the dream. Mo wondered whether they still believed her, she wouldn't. Was she being totally self-delusional? Did her girls laugh behind her back? Reid did, he laughed to her front, in her face once even, or did he? She wasn't sure, she knew that he saw the real picture though; did that make them allies at work?

It was late morning and she couldn't settle, work held no attraction today, or any day for that matter. The police had been in, tying up loose ends they said. Checking facts, asking for more information, any more gossip. Prosser had seen her in the cafeteria and broke off from Officer Drabble to come over. Were people watching this, jumping to conclusions? He asked to sit with her; he'd like a chat, informal. "It's a free world".

He was silent, more nervous than she was, so she jumped right in "still go to the club, man?" Boom!

"I wondered if you recognised me. It was some time ago, a lot of vodka has flowed under the bridge since then".

"I knew it was you, are you still keeping secrets?"

He laughed. "No secrets, the people I work with know who I am, sometimes they joke too hard and sometimes I do. Times have changed".

"So you remember me, in my pomp?"

"I remember you then, but I don't recognise you now, who you have become. This place doesn't seem very like you at all, not the Mo that I remember. When did you leave the scene?"

Now it was Mo's turn to be uncomfortable. She blustered about still hanging in there, living the life but Prosser knew better and said so. She'd started her well-worn routine, as he'd expected her to, but soon gave up. There was no lying to this guy, he was paid to see through them, to deliver the truth, so she shrugged, "we all get older, the price of life".

Prosser nodded. Then they started to chat like old friends which, in a way, they were. When she laid her current life out like that, she despised herself. She'd become all the things she'd tried not to be, apart from living with someone, that would never happen. She could see that Prosser was different, happy, settled. He lived a life of his own choosing.

The conversation seemed mostly to be about history, past lives, but Prosser slipped in bits of the present day, work people; what were they like? Any real animosity towards Marie-Eve? What was she really like? Building a picture of a woman he'd never met and, by the sound of it, wouldn't have wanted to, anyway.

It was not too hard for Prosser to sift the wheat from the chaff of Mo's subsequent monologue. Most people, it seemed, were indifferent to Marie-Eve. A foreign head, nothing more, and she'd be gone back to Canada soon enough anyway. There appeared to be little warmth from the female side of her colleagues. The men were harder to read. Some liked her at a physical level, she wasn't unattractive. Others resented her power over them but they were the sort to resent the power of any woman. The people Marie-Eve seemed to have any sort of relationship with, a visible one at work at least, were limited. Reid was in the 'very much disliked-her' camp. Shepherd? Mo had no real idea there; she didn't think she'd seen them in the same room even. Martin, well he was just a big softie and Prosser thought he'd picked up a hint, was Martin gay too?

Marie-Eve and Marco was raised, "anything there?" Mo thought about it. "Maybe. Marco had always seemed eager to please her, even though he could be a complete arse to others, childish even, but for Marie-Eve he did as he was asked, and she always asked, never told him, bluntly, like she did with Reid".

Prosser hadn't made any notes and Banks was motioning by the exit for them to go, this had supposed to have been a quick fact-checker. He smiled warmly at Mo and told her to take care of herself, even gave her his business card if she thought of anything else, no personal number though. The tenuous link that gave them a bond of sorts remained just that, tenuous.

As they drove back to base Prosser's phone pinged, a short text from Mo. *'Marie-Eve and Greenwood, I forgot to say, they always seemed friendly. Hope that's of use, Mo'*.

# FIFTY

## Wednesday 21 September

Reid had opted for 'popping' into Central Nick as they'd called the thing, like mates dropping by to discuss the match or who should be bought and sold in the next transfer window. He was greeted by Dave Thompson who led him to a comfortable interview room.

"Simon, this is DC Jenny Banks who I'm sure you remember". The look Jenny Banks shot Thompson was interesting, Reid noticed it and wondered whether something was going on there. Thompson had smiled at her which seemed to diffuse the situation, it was over in an instant so perhaps there was nothing at all. Thompson continued, "this is DC Fasildad, another team member who I've asked to sit in while we chat. I'll reiterate, you are not considered of interest to us, at present, but you may have insights that could seem trivial to you but useful to us. Jenny will make any notes she thinks relevant and will, if you wish, go through them with you after, just so you know that what she jots down is what you meant, OK?"

Thompson had covered everything although not being of interest was a bit economical with the truth. Until whoever deep-froze Marie-Eve was under lock and key, nobody was out of their sights yet, as Reid knew full-well.

"Since our last conversation Simon, things have moved on apace. We'd like to talk to you about Ms. Legault, specifically about her situation in Montreal. We understand that you spent three weeks over there and worked with Ms. Legault, and with her colleagues and staff, and it occurred to us that our investigation may benefit from any personal insights that you may have about her relationship with her staff there, gossip even, that you would be willing to share".

Ah, thought Reid, so I'm not being locked up, banged-to-rights, good. He said though, "of course, officers, anything to help but just one thing, I was only there for two weeks, nine days in the facility due to an administrative mix-up involving their HR".

Dad and Banks exchanged glances that said, 'I hate it when they say that anything to help crap!' Not that they didn't usually want to help, it's just that the baddie on TV is always a smarmy 'happy to help' type, As far as they knew, Reid wasn't the baddie, but he was a bit smarmy though, nerves maybe.

The informal chat soon turned into a question and answer session as something specific occurred to each officer, a blank that needed filling. Everyone, it seemed, wanted to know whether Legault was popular in Montreal? Reid was a bit surprised by this; surely they had been on the phone or exchanged emails with both the Montreal Police and the relevant people at NPS Montreal. What did they expect from him after ten days there? Should he mention the flirting, or had he imagined that?

He answered anyway. Yes, she was popular amongst the Francophones, not so much amongst the Anglophones, and then he had to launch into a lengthy explanation of the whole French – English thing in Quebec, at least as far as he knew and understood it himself, quoting 'a number of people I spoke to' rather than admitting his entire knowledge of the Quebec separation question came from a stumpy redhead called Paula, who got more talkative the lower the beer was in the pitcher.

"Had he heard any adverse rumours regarding her, at work or socially?"

Reid thought about leaving it out, but felt that the mysterious return to NPS Montreal that others had been surprised by was now worth a mention. The suggestion was that she might 'have something' on the management, perhaps something historical involving their work. The phrase, which he duly repeated 'she knew where the bodies were buried', sounded more apposite now than when Paula had used it.

'Did Reid know much about her socially, did he meet her socially while in Montreal perhaps – in her role as Technical Manager of course, nothing else, unless...'

No, nothing socially and not too much professionally really. Most of Reid's time had been spent learning the system, being showed it by one of the other Sample Management techs, Lewis something. He had been on the end of her ire over a disciplinary matter though; it would be in his file.

"Yes, we've seen that, not relevant, funny but not relevant".

Then they asked had he heard whether Legault was involved with anyone 'romantically' at NPS Montreal?'

At this Reid held his hands up and wondered out loud whether the Nottinghamshire Police worked on hearsay and rumour, did they even do fact checking as routine because this was a strange thing to ask someone who has already indicated the limits of his relationship with the deceased. He realised he sounded like someone off Crown Court, but passing on vague and possibly spiteful tittle-tattle wasn't going to catch Marie-Eve's killer and he told them that he wanted no further part in it, if they were just after low-brow gossip.

Banks explained that of course they checked everything but, short of sending someone to Montreal, they were hitting a bit of a brick wall as far as personal information at that end was concerned. Rumour and gossip, while having no place in due process, could sometimes offer leads to areas as yet undiscovered.

Reid felt like applauding and saying 'and there rests the case for the prosecution, Your Honour!' he didn't though.

In the end they found some middle ground. Marie-Eve had no regular, open boyfriend as far as he'd heard but word was she was seeing someone – on and off. It seemed she preferred that type of relationship, no ties or expectations. The man was rumoured to be a business client of NPS but no name had been mentioned to him, neither the client's name nor an individual's.

Reid was thanked for taking time to 'chat', as they kept on calling it, and was also asked not to discuss their conversation with anyone for fear of prejudicing the enquiry. They felt that they had to say that, despite having formed the opinion that Reid wasn't the sort to run around yacking out of turn, quite a private guy and, as far as they could tell, honest.

"Oh, by the way, did Dominique Yip get talked to?" Reid asked. "She was with us here in Nottingham for a short while but left to go back to Canada. She didn't think much of Marie-Eve or NPS from what I heard; she might know something at the Montreal end though, having worked with Marie-Eve there".

Thompson was first to speak. "We have a number of leads to follow, obviously I can't discuss individuals".

'No, then', thought Reid. Well, that was fun!

On the dead board, Reid's photo was given a blue sticker, not involved, but red stickers remained on ten others. They really had to get the 'maybe' list down to a manageable level.

All of the team met to discuss Reid's contribution; all were in agreement that it was minimal. There was something though, Dominique Yip, who the hell was Dominique Yip? "Elkie, another little job for you", said Thompson.

The team got their thinking heads on, each taking an independent look and coming back with their ideas. A new element was another person now in Montreal but who had been in Nottingham and whom nobody had seen fit to mention before, Dominique Yip. I rather like this shifting of emphasis; it is something I can use as a device.

We still keep coming back to Craig Shepherd but I continue to have my doubts and I suspect he is just currently the path of least resistance. There is more to this case than meets the eye but, as yet it is dodging our steely gaze.

I think Jenny thought I was taking the piss and reacted; that is something I can build into a story to get some friction going between characters, even when there isn't any.

# FIFTY-ONE

Richard Greenwood sat in his big chair in his big office, looking out of his big window over the car park where his big car was parked, his big company Porsche SUV. Like many small men, Greenwood stood just 5'1" in his pedicured feet, he overcompensated. It was one of the reasons why he was so out of his depth in his previous two clinical research incarnations. Normally, he'd have been marked as a failure for life but in such an incestuous industry as Pharmaceuticals, you always got another chance eventually and so now he was here, site manager for the recently acquired Nash Pharmaceutical Solutions. He'd arrived at the big time at last, and nobody was more surprised than him.

While being the CEO of NPS Nottingham was really great, it actually didn't require a great deal of input from the actual CEO, or site manager as they had taken to calling the post. The company was like one of those huge tankers that are run mostly by computer. The course had been set, the ship was at full steam ahead and the Captain only had to stand around looking as intelligent as possible while all about ran smoothly.

He opened his email account; there was one with a red flag from Jim Duggan himself. There was link to a piece and the message was to read it; when Jim Duggan says 'read', you read. It also said that Jim would like to find the person responsible for the piece which appeared via a fake account on Linked-In after the NPS rif in Montreal. Clearly the author worked, or had worked, for NPS and the company lawyers were currently trying to see whether the wordsmith might have broken the non-disclosure agreement, applicable during and after employment by

NPS, in some way. All NPS site heads were in the cc list, so it wasn't just Greenwood and Nottingham that they were looking at.

He clicked on the link, when Jim commands, I obey.

*The Captain*

*The big ship is rocking and the old Captain has left, taking some important crew members with him and leaving the ship floundering on choppy seas. By good fortune, calm returns just as a new, and more importantly, available, Captain takes over. The new Captain brings in a new First Mate and the ship resumes its course. Over time the shipping magnate that owns the fleet thinks the new Captain is responsible for the resumption of stability. He's wrong and really should pay more attention to detail.*

*Now that the ship is running true, the Captain and his senior matelot crew (SMC) decide that they can start chopping out the dead wood and, at regular intervals, throw the dead wood over the side. To assuage consciences, those cast over are given varying lengths of rope still tied to the ship. Some cut the ropes and swim away to find a better ship, the rest hang on until the inevitable happens and the crew pulls them back in when they need them again. This has happened several times before and usually to the same people, but they, much like many of those doing the tossing, know nothing else and are truly, dead wood.*

*The shipping magnate decides to reward the Captain for his unwitting installation of stability on the ship by giving him his own, personal lifeboat, the MV Corporate. In the event of disaster, the MV Corporate can be used to escape to the soulless, but safe waters of the corporate sea. The Captain's First Mate is assured that, as always, there will be some room in the lifeboat for him, should the need arise.*

*Changes in tides mean that the ship is now cruising with a full load, but the Captain thinks it could go better, after all, there has to be a reason to justify him being the Captain in the first place. He instructs his SMC to review the ship's processes, as many are out of date, lack*

271

*imagination or are just woefully inefficient and always have been. To do this, his SMC decide to form a sub-committee to conduct a review.*

*The sub-committee will contain all those existing senior crew members whose very processes are now in question and who have steadfastly maintained the same inefficient processes because 'that is how we always do it'. It does not seem to occur to anyone currently sailing on the Corporate Sea, that those charged with change don't have any outside experience to inspire, just what they have always known and done and some have even been responsible for instigating on the very same ship, more as a scent-mark denoting their elevation from the ranks rather than an innovation.*

*The ship is made up of lots of sections. Some make it go, some keep it going and others make it float. The Captain probably knew all of this once, but delusions of grandeur can drive rationality away to a dark place. He and his SMC decide that, to go even faster, it needs to be lighter still. To achieve this, more dead wood must go and his committee members for the new project, christened 'Refloat' ('Rehash' was rejected), are once again the ones who always decide what dead wood can be tossed overboard.*

*The names are duly selected and the secret of the clean-out kept until the day that the latest batch of dead wood is pitched over the side. This time the choices are not just from the regular ranks but higher up, and more important in the overall running of a smooth ship. The ship carries a precious cargo, paid for by the cargo's owners. Every section of the ship's crew is geared to taking care of part or all of a particular owner's cargo, and they do. It is not always an easy task. The SMC, most of whom have no idea what the cargo is, let alone how to look after it, hinder rather than help, it is almost as if their sole mandate is to throw banana skins under the feet of the crew, all of the time.*

*Every time there has been a clearing of dead wood, nobody knows who has actually gone until there is a gap that needs to be filled, usually by people inexperienced in that role, but they learn through their costly mistakes, mostly. The ship still steams on smoothly on the*

272

surface, but below there are fires and each one needs to have time spent being fought. Some do get extinguished, others just smoulder on. From his lofty perch, the Captain sees none of this. From his Ivory Tower, the shipping magnate neither sees anything, nor cares.

All previous clearing of dead wood had involved the removal of mostly small sticks, alone not that important, collectively though, more effective than the SMC realised. This latest clearing included some logs, big logs; important logs, logs that made the ship go, steer and, most importantly, float. The dead wood goes and the ship sails on, it takes a while for any change of course to take effect because it's a big ship, but it is no longer a happy ship, not that it ever truly was.

Mutterings from below are heard and so the Captain decides it is time to teach people a lesson. They may be the most experienced mariners around, but a dose of humility is needed and so, a role reversal. The qualified crew are told to report to the waiters and washers, those whose peak of education was getting a question right on 'Deal or no Deal'. Realising that this is not a 'Just for Laughs' sketch after all, surreptitious ship to ship messages attract other vessels in need of a quality crew and one by one they leave. Meanwhile the owners of the various cargoes, once all very much in the dark but now hearing strange rumours, are wondering just how a group of waiters and washers ever ended up in charge, and is there anywhere else that they can place their precious cargo.

A (very) little way along the line, the volatile seas of commerce get choppy again and the ship starts to list alarmingly. The Captain has seen this before, in fact it has happened on every ship he's ever commanded, and so he takes to his lifeboat. His First Mate, always with him in these difficult times before, is towed behind in a small coracle attached to a rope, a rope that can be severed by The Captain at any time if needs be, should it become dead wood. The ship eventually goes down with all remaining hands, including the SMC, all of them end up in the water without a rope to hang on to. Who would have thought that removing pieces of wood could sink a ship!

273

The shipping magnate hears the news, he's lost a ship but he has plenty more, besides, he'd never liked the ocean that particular ship sailed on and had always resented having to visit the ship to tell them that they are all doing very well. His other ships will now have to pull in the slack; some will no doubt sail on blissfully ignorant of reality, other ships will probably sink. Again it doesn't matter to the shipping magnate as he lives on dry land, hardly ever goes to sea anyway and when he does it is in a big and expensive, not to mention unsinkable, ship.

Our story ends, like all stories, with an ending. The latest bundle of dead wood makes good, well away from the sinking ship and is all the happier for it. The majority of the sunk ship's crew are able to find other ships in the same sea but carrying different cargo. Since they'd had no real buy-in to any particular cargo anyway, it doesn't matter much to them whose cargo they handle.

The one-paced SMC, so important when the ship sailed true, had to fall back on their limited experience to try to find another ship, so they were thankful for all those crew barbeques where they had learnt to flip burgers, a skill that would now come in very handy in their new life roles.

And the moral of the story? If your steerage, engine and flotation are messed with when they work well, and you put the running of your ship in dangerously incapable hands, then down you go.

The Patient Watcher

He'd actually quite enjoyed it, the writing was clever, amusing even. Nobody was named but he could see the underlying meaning, he was quite sure that it had been written by a Brit and he quite liked the idea of recruiting a First Mate, a deputy who could carry the can when the inevitable happened. He'd give Glen a call, see if he fancied it, he'd always responded to the call before and he was an ideal 'yes-man'. Greenwood might have been out of his depth, but he was nothing if not a realist.

He quickly sent an email back, dropping in a few 'deplorables' and 'a disgrace' here and there, and even a bit of 'no stone unturned'. That should mollify our glorious leader.

Technically Greenwood was on trial at NPS for a six month period; that was the company policy with all new employees. Realistically, though, he felt that he was asbestos, untouchable, and, while they hadn't actually chased him down and forced him to take the job, they had been keen enough in their pursuit of him to give him that warm and fuzzy feeling. Greenwood felt that his talents, which he never for a moment doubted, even in the darkest hours, were finally being appreciated. He was in the job for as long as he wanted this time, but he'd still make sure that he had someone around in case of disaster. After all, somebody has to stay with the ship when it sinks.

All at NPS had been progressing fairly well so far, but now there was a fly in the ointment, a dead one, Marie-Eve Legault, luckless Marie-Eve. He'd met her of course, just some blonde-haired woman from Québec who chirped up at meetings from time to time, hoping to be noticed, trying to be important. Greenwood wasn't even sure what she actually did; well he knew what she was supposed to be doing, integrating the Nottingham site at technical level and ensuring that the company practices were understood and implemented. It said that on the first page of the file in front of him, but what was she actually doing? He was certain that she was a spy; she had a long history with the Montreal facility although that too was a relatively recent acquisition by NPS.

Well whatever she had been up to, including the detailed report on his staff, had been stopped now and for good.

The file he was reading told Greenwood little else, he was trying to cram for what he expected would be a searching oral exam by the police. He was the Site Head, he had to know his people and be able to confidently talk about Marie-Eve in the right way. As to who killed her,

Greenwood decided not to pay too much attention to that one. No point in sticking your head up over the parapet.

The newly-deposited pile of papers and files in his in-tray was not really work, just stuff for him to glance at, see whether there was anything he should be in on, claim influence with, be known for. That was how he'd always worked. Be aware and step in when the time was ripe. Make sure your name appeared as co-author, even if you only contributed a review. Be published, that was where you built your reputation, that was where you found the respect you were due. As site manager there would be plenty of opportunities to ride on whoever's coattails suited him best.

One folder was marked 'Strictly Confidential'. How stupid was that? It would be the first thing anyone would read, whether they were allowed to or not, and there it was sitting out in the open, staring at him. He had to remind himself that he was authorised to see everything, he was the Site Head after all.

The file was from big Jim Duggan himself, from their holiest of holies in New Jersey. Greenwood hoped he'd get the chance to go out to America to meet him, share a beer and ideas; he'd never been to the US, not even on holiday, but he knew that, if he got the chance, he'd find a way to contribute, become a player, get on Jim Duggan's radar.

The contents of the file were simple, just a short memo. The Saviour study was his first priority and the value of the business to the company could not be understated. NPS would perform outstanding service to Saviour at all times, dissent would not be tolerated and Greenwood had a free hand in deciding whether individuals would stay or leave – all scientists would be required sign a study specific non-disclosure document before seeing the study details and starting work on the analysis.

Between the lines reading suggested that Duggan had many pennies invested here, interesting.

Weekly updates were required by conference call, they would be at 16:30 eastern standard time every Thursday, the relevant senior scientists to attend; this was not negotiable. Well fuck that, thought Greenwood, I'm not calling anyone at 9:30 at night, I'll get Joan to schedule a morning call; that would suit us much better, and he scribbled a note in the email margin. Then he added, 'check on who has access to study details?'

He re-read the memo, just in case, but he'd missed nothing. Then he blacked out the question about study access. Only the scientists would know what it was all about, and they would be tied up legally with the disclaimer. Anyone else involved, fetchers and carriers, would be too thick to understand the science-speak, he struggled with it most of the time himself!

There was nothing else of note in the pile. A few disciplinary items, nothing serious, nothing the brown guy in HR couldn't sort out. There was also a report on site security from Neil Martin, the bouffant lickspittle who fawned all over him when he came in. He'd had it in his tray since just after he'd started the job. It was just a lot of moaning about 'broken' this and 'insecure' that. Another note in the file from the building guy, Reg, or Cliff, or whatever, said that all would be fixed when the whole system was updated in six weeks, less than a month now; it wasn't worth spending money on repairs only to have the new system replace everything soon.

He probably should have read this file earlier.

After a quick sort of the files into two piles, action and ignore, he called Joan for coffee and biscuits and fired off a few emails to make it look like he was doing something. One was to Joan telling her to sort out the scheduling of the Duggan – Saviour weekly conference call thing. An answer came back from Joan in moments, a simple 'no'. Greenwood smiled, he'd half expected that, do keep nailing that lid shut, lovely Joan, I'll soon have someone worth looking at sitting in that chair.

Greenwood had no intention of straying too far from his office today, what with the police roaming around the building, asking questions, disrupting the flow. He'd have to talk to them at some point, he'd find out when, but when it happened they could come to him; he was the mountain after all.

He felt that he ought to feel sad about Marie-Eve being dead and everything, but he didn't. He really didn't give a shit. He'd only spoken to her a handful of times, he didn't like her, not at all, not his type, too in control, too aware of herself and, he'd noticed, a bit light up top, tits not intelligence. He might have to write something though, for the company on-line newsletter, an obituary. Joan could do it. She seemed efficient enough but he'd already decided that she didn't like him. Her being the previous incumbent's PA since the beginning didn't help her cause, that and the fact that his PA really had to know how to cross her long legs provocatively and mustn't look like a Maiden Aunt.

Greenwood liked the idea of sitting in what was once Clive Gerrard's chair, the famous Clive, genial Clive, well-liked Clive. They had no real history, in fact Clive had messaged him with condolences after the last disaster, a message sent before the details hit the fan, painting a brown scene for everyone involved. Now he was Clive's replacement. Poor Clive, pensioned off for good.

He'd already had Gerrard's photo removed from the reception and the on-line magazine. In time, he'd make sure that all memory of Clive Gerrard at NPS faded away.

Greenwood then scribbled a note to see just how much Clive Gerrard had been paid, the brown guy in HR should know. He really ought to make a chart of names under his blotter, something he could flip up and refer to. Some people get touchy if you refer to them as the brown guy all the time. It helped smooth your way in if you remembered names. Greenwood never could though, it was one of his failings, that and the science.

There was knock and Joan came in with another bunch of paper for him, why she couldn't just get on with it was beyond Greenwood, what the fuck did she do all day?

More files, more useless bits of boring paper. Finance had sent another sheet with a chart showing the Marie-Eve death-affected losses to the company, including, and especially, the delayed analysis of the Saviour study samples, the break-down was by the hour. Most of the stuff in the pile could have been sent electronically but Greenwood was not generally a fan of electronic, everything had to be on paper for him by preference. He didn't have the concentration for stuff on a screen, unless it was moving flesh.

And that was another thing for him to sort out with IT. His browser kept saying that his favourite site was blocked, he was the boss; nobody blocked him.

The chart from finance showed big numbers being lost due to the closure, however temporary. He'd have to act, get one of the department managers to talk to the police, get a time when they could resume business. Maybe someone in technical, that manager guy who was not a scientist but clearly switched on, he'd do.

There was also a bunch of envelopes, sealed and addressed to him personally, although one just said 'to the Site Manager'. What now?

He could buzz Joan through, give them to her and get her to deal with them, it was probably just people trying it on, taking him for a mug as the new boy, asking for things they'd never dared ask Clive Gerrard for. There was always a few chancers around, seeing what they thought was an opportunity to exploit the system, but he was not as wet behind the ears as they thought he was, he'd show them, right then.

The first envelope contained a letter, hand written, neat writing. 'I am writing to inform you that I have tended my notice and will be leaving Nash Pharmaceutical Solutions on...' It was the head of LCMS, his main analytical department. He'd met him briefly, Tim something or other, he couldn't quite make out the surname. Bonser? Bonner, perhaps?

The next one was from Sheila Pitt, typed and signed, the same thing. Sheila, a tall woman and yet another with no tits, Clinical Labs or something, maybe Immunochemistry, that was it. Greenwood ripped open the rest. Sarri Tong, Daniel Ameobi, Lissa Goodchild, Kay Daniels and, finally, Joan Bain. All going with just two weeks' notice; can they do that?

Greenwood called HR straight away. He'd picked up the name now, Ranji. There was no nice talk, just "Greenwood here, what the fuck is going on?"

A short silence was followed by "you've seen the mail this morning then? I have copies too, plenty there to keep us busy".

Greenwood was incandescent. "Fix this, offer them more money, an extra week of holiday, anything, we can't bleed this many people now, right in the middle of the biggest NPS study ever, we can't, just fix it", and the phone was slammed home. The bastards are after me already, somebody is behind this and I'll fuck them good and proper when I find out who it is.

Greenwood's cell phone pinged with a text, he was part through it when the phone buzzed and Joan, Greenwood's soon to be not Personal Assistant, announced the arrival of a couple of police officers who wanted half an hour. Hilarious, thought Greenwood, they could have all day if they liked, at least this would be actually doing something instead of sitting in meetings, sagely nodding despite having no idea what anyone was talking about.

The heads-up text was about their imminent arrival just before Joan's buzz. That golf club subscription, and showing interest in the other stuff was worth its weight in gold sometimes. It was certainly worth its weight in 95 grand a year plus shares and options, plus private medical. He'd never have got to interview stage based on his CV without a golf chum whispering in the right ear. Now he was in and it was very unlikely that anyone would chase up and check his first degree and PhD, just as well, really. Once he'd got his feet under the table he'd have another go at getting in properly, the new job and elevated social position was bound to help.

Before he had time to do his breathing exercises, a cursory knock was followed by the door being opened by Joan. Greenwood welcomed the two officers, DS Thompson and DC Banks, very nice. Joan was dispatched to bring refreshments but the officers declined. Just as well, Greenwood was quite sure Joan had every intention of ignoring him, anyway.

After thanking Greenwood for taking the time out of his busy schedule (the comment delivered dead-pan so they actually meant it!), Thompson started to ask questions, the intriguing, but not pretty DC Banks started to take notes. The gap between the buttons on her blouse opened a little showing skin and the edge of a navy coloured bra, was that police issue? Greenwood knew that he'd not be able to concentrate, so quickly changed the angle until the view, if not his mind, were more decent.

The first bunch of questions revolved around Marie-Eve's duties, responsibilities, whether she was popular, had she been responsible for sacking anybody or upset someone and they'd left the company. Greenwood explained about the need to assimilate, Marie-Eve was an executive management-driven secondment and so reported above the current Technical Manager, Ben Dooley.

Thompson corrected him, "I believe that is Bez Dooley, Mr. Greenwood".

Greenwood shrugged, "so many new names to learn."

Getting back to Marie-Eve quickly, Greenwood was sure that nobody had complained about her at all. She was quietly efficient, mostly observing at first; then advising as departmental procedures were

281

brought into line with the NPS company protocol for each aspect of the operation.

Greenwood then began to outline the NPS policy on firing employees. They were never fired but their jobs may be rationalised and so they were always laid off with benefits. The company preferred the term reduction in force, a rif, and they were to occur annually if needed, usually in October, the timing at the behest of the marketing and finances department. They'd had one not long before he joined the team. When Banks asked whether there was an active union at NPS and whether the rif, as Greenwood had called it, was actually legal under UK employment legislation, Greenwood tried to explain the outline of the total contract system operated throughout the NPS family, as far as he understood it.

"Since the arrival of NPS employees were all employed on new personal contracts which they are required to sign before their employment begins. There is a non-disclosure clause included, something essential and standard throughout the pharmaceutical industry, and employees, in signing their new contracts, accept to be bound by the same rights across the board, effectively adopting the policies as applied at head office, in New Jersey, that is in the USA".

Thompson and Banks exchanged the briefest of glances, while Greenwood ploughed on, he'd done well so far he thought, remembering all of the corporate gobbledegook almost correctly, and he wasn't going to stop until he'd spat it all out.

"The work-force is effectively divided into two sections. Professional staff, who are all on the new contracts, and technical staff, the majority of whom are now on zero-hours contracts, which they actually seem to prefer as their new work practices offer a greater degree of flexibility in their lives".

Thomson and Banks exchanged brief glances again and it wasn't hard to see what they thought of an annual firing spree with no rights because you'd signed them away. Banks started to say something along the lines of UK law taking precedent over anything from the good old US of A, so Greenwood jumped back in, outlining all the employee benefits and the way departing employees were generously compensated. Staff reductions were only ever contemplated when driven by market forces; "we are just much more up front about it than other employers". So far there had only been one rif at NPS in Nottingham and they had been able to meet the quota with mostly voluntary redundancy and natural wastage.

Picking up on the angle of questioning, Greenwood assured Thompson and Banks that all those who had completed their tenure with NPS, fired, effectively, had been well looked after and there had been no recriminations.

Thompson moved on the conversation on a bit, he had to; his blood was starting to boil a bit at the thought of Yanks imposing their arcane employment practices on UK citizens and this slime-ball apparently buying into it all. He pulled a sheet of paper from a file he'd been carrying, "this is a crime report regarding some minor vandalism at the NPS site. The events were just after the rif, as you call it. We didn't investigate; it was put down as the sort of vandalism we all have to tolerate these days, petty, mindless. Was it"?

Greenwood shrugged again. "The site in general has events as you call them, it is an industry problem and we were just one of a few. At the time they didn't consider it likely that a former employee would have been responsible, it was a random act of mischief was the final conclusion I believe, I wasn't here then".

They asked about site security, CCTV. Greenwood remembered the contents of one of his files and spoke about the ongoing re-vamp, high-tech everywhere. "You have seen our entry system, state of the art; even I have to have a card to enter every time, provided I remember to pick up my card when I come in that is", and he laughed at his own wit.

"Does that happen often, what happens if you don't have your card?"

"Everyone here knows me now; I made a point of going to every department to personally meet all of my new charges. The people in Security have the power to issue a temporary card for those who forget their registered card, I've done it myself two or three times, my current card, and he beckoned towards a key-card on the desk, is a temporary one for management level".

They moved on to Marie-Eve's friends in Nottingham; who did she mix with socially, confide in perhaps? It was a while before Greenwood fully grasped the question. He'd always had colleagues, but they certainly were not friends and he definitely would not confide anything to any of them that was not to his benefit. He went for saying that Marie-Eve seemed to be well-liked, got on very well with her colleagues but, as she was only in Nottingham for a short period of time, he didn't think she'd made any friends outside of her work colleagues and that their relationship would likely be work-based only.

This seemed to satisfy the police and they started to pack up their things, Greenwood glanced at the clock, eighteen minutes gone since they walked in.

Seeing that Greenwood had taken the bait and that he clearly had more to say by virtue of his obvious impatience and relief, Thompson and Banks sat down again. Greenwood was clearly a bit shaken by this but, as yet, they didn't really know which buttons to push for an answer; they decided to let him go at his own pace. It didn't take long. From nowhere Greenwood launched into a detailed explanation of pharmaceuticals and how you progress through the ranks, emphasising the value of publication and how it improved your standing within the scientific community, even if you'd never penned a word in your life.

Their expressions were unchanged but they were somewhat taken aback at what to them was clear plagiarism or even parasitism. Greenwood talked about how it was perfectly normal for colleagues to

284

be included as co-authors on publications and how, the more senior you became; the more publications would bear your name until it was just your name the author wanted as a sort of validation of the paper.

"Did Marie-Eve Legault ever co-author a paper of any sort do you know, take the credit for someone else's work, upset them, might that be why she was killed?"

Greenwood called up 'Pubmed' on his PC and scrolled the author list under Legault. Yes, she had published but obviously not a scientific paper, more a Quality Assurance thing, a kind of overseer's guide. Greenwood beamed as he sent a file to the printer, handing the fresh sheets over to the officers and almost expecting a reward.

After a bit more inconsequential rambling they had clearly reached the end of the interview unless they could provoke another reaction. "Ok, we're done here then", said the woman, but Thompson looked up and went all Columbo. "One more thing, Mr. Greenwood, as you said, you are fairly new here yourself. Where were you before?"

Ever since he could remember, Greenwood had had a tendency to blurt under pressure, so his machine-gun delivery of a list of previous employers must have caught the officers unawares; they asked him to repeat it while one of them wrote it down. "Why do you want to know that?" he asked, then calmed a bit. "It's all in my CV, I can get you a copy. I just updated it to include the NPS position."

"That would be great, thank you, Mr. Greenwood. This is nothing to worry about, just background checking, building a bigger picture, you know. Someone killed Marie-Eve Legault, probably somebody who works for NPS now and so is still here in this building. By accumulating information and then cross-checking we slowly weed out those less than truthful statements about where people were and what they were doing, when an unconscious Marie-Eve Legault was drenched in water inside your big freezer then left to freeze to death".

Thompson left it there hanging, Greenwood realised that they were looking to trip up liars, then they'd work through the liars until they found the right fit for the murderer, but who would be the last piece of an unwelcome jigsaw. Not him, he hoped.

"By the way, what time did you leave yesterday?"

So that was where this was going.

"I worked later. I had a morning thing so got in late. Actually it was a long-standing golf appointment with one of your senior officers. I left between eight and nine in the evening, the Security people should have the information".

"Thanks, we'll check with them then. Did you have your own access card or a temporary one?"

"I honestly can't remember, officer, Security will know though. Now, if there is nothing else I can do for you, I do have a pile of things to work through, NPS Nottingham doesn't run itself". Behind him the printer coughed out his nine page CV which he presented to them as if it were an Olympic gold medal.

Once they'd gone, Greenwood turned his attention back to the letters of resignation. He had calls to make, contacts to tap up, who was behind this coordinated assault on his kingdom? Whatever else might be going on, this deliberate poaching of his staff would not be ignored, somebody would suffer, he'd see to it personally.

*He couldn't be sure whether Lucinda had meant it or was just messing around, the way she used to when they first got together and found out that he like to be dominated. It had looked innocent enough, she said she'd thrown it so the handle was forward and that it was just bad luck that his briefcase had spun mid-air, catching him with the little brass corner protectors which he now knew to be razor sharp. She was concerned enough to dress his wound, she seemed genuine enough. He'd be OK but it did sting a bit. He'd got it looked at, some of his staff*

286

*called themselves Doctor, you'd think they'd know about this sort of thing but it was Joan who'd patched him up in the end.*

He wondered whether the police had noticed his injury, no; probably not; they didn't come over as all that bright.

As they reached the car, Thompson and Banks went through her notes. They'd parked in full view of Greenwood's office, sort of deliberately. Thompson pulled out his jotter and started to scribble, equally visibly. From his office, Richard Greenwood had watched them walk over to their car, where they sat for a while. Why?

Greenwood was, as expected, shifty. He was obviously eyeing Jenny's tits, as we expected he would, you have to applaud the talent to make an accurately lined-up gap in a blouse look so innocent! I think Jenny is something of a Mata Hari on the quiet; that was her idea on the fly after all.

Whether this dickhead could have killed the Fish Finger, probably not, but he might know someone who could have though, and for that reason alone he is a suspect.

Interesting to see that he'd got a dressing on his writing hand, nearly invisible but something happened there. We'll think about maybe getting his DNA, with his permission of course, heats up the baddies nicely that process.

No wriggling about leaving late, that is interesting, although how late? He might have still been at NPS around the time of death. We'll need something more precise though, to see whether he had the opportunity.

If I use Greenwood as a character for anything I'll need to tone down it down a bit and make him less obnoxious!

Banks asked for a look so he showed her. "Better Mata Hari than Officer Drabble, thank you very much", but she knew that Drabble would stick and, when she wasn't around, where's Drabble? Would be the Central Nick version of 'Where's Wally', for a while at least.

While Richard Greenwood was sat sweating in his big chair at Nash Pharmaceutical Solutions, across town, Unit Six in Netherfield industrial park was hastily being re-decorated with fresh 'For Let' signs. The posters saying 'Coming soon, New Blue Sky Solutions – We're Hiring' and a phone number, were being unceremoniously torn down and stuffed into black plastic rubbish bags.

# FIFTY-TWO

Although shaken by the police visit, Greenwood had soon rallied and was busy with his to-do list. He still had contacts and, if he was going to lose all of his top scientific heads then he'd replace them with others, people who would be more than willing to accept a step up and all that came with it. But first he pulled out his mobile; there was another little thing he had to do.

Opening the encrypted app on his phone, he scrolled down to 'Daddy's Girl'. The things you could get apps for these days were amazing, where were these women when he was younger and full of testosterone?

He ended the call with a smile. The image she'd sent, while not being explicit, certainly dropped a heavy hint. He was nearly there and this time the woman was welcoming him with open legs. He knew his reputation and did nothing to dispel the rumour; the truth however was much more grounded in fact. Greenwood was never really the 'ladies' man that he liked to portray, he'd just got lucky once or twice, the twice being thanks to his little blue chemical friend. Now the wife of someone who worked somewhere within the facility was positively hurling herself at him, lucky him.

Jemmy hung up and took great pains to try to wipe the phone's call history 'forever' but it kept coming back again. Greenwood had sounded flustered; she had that effect on men. Well, she used to before Small arrived.

She still wasn't sure whether what she was doing was that good an idea but she needed a bit of stimulation, something to nullify the tiredness caused by a combination of the new baby, Small, and Craig. For all his good points Craig was a shit liar. She knew he'd played an away fixture while she was still feeling delicate post-birth, actually quite a long way post-birth. She also knew who it was with. This new line of enquiry might garner more information on the issue from a different angle.

She was quite confident that she could mess the dick Greenwood around, manipulate him even without actually doing anything more sordid than sending a bikini shot. Besides, having a bit of leverage there might help her, or even Craig, later on.

When Greenwood's PC started to bleat out a strange ring, he knew who was trying to Skype him. He accepted and the face of Lucinda, his significant other, filled the screen. "Why are you so red?" she demanded, using that brusque, 'you're a twat' voice.

"Just ran up the stairs, I had a feeling that you might call and didn't want to miss it".

She seemed mollified by this but it was really hard to tell, she had a cat's bum of a face and it probably wasn't going to improve with age, good job she had money. "Don't be late tonight, we are going out, remember".

"Yes dear, looking forward to it, where are we off to this time?"

"You'd forgotten hadn't you? Dinner with mummy and daddy, Jesus, you really are fucking useless sometimes! Had you also forgotten my little dinner party at the weekend?"

"No dear, it's in my diary and starred as a special occasion".

The silence on the end of the phone told Greenwood that Lucinda was just taking a breather before going off at him again. When it came it wasn't nearly as bad as he'd expected. "I want to get help in so that the house is spotless, ready for the weekend. I've got a contact number of a cleaning firm, not cheap but highly recommended, no arguing".

"No problem my sweet, you get all the help you need, after all, we can afford it. Look, I'm just heading out to another meeting, busy day again, nose to the grindstone, you know how it is. I'll be there later; do I need to pick up anything on the way home?"

"No, just be on time".

"One last thing, my dear, did you say who would be coming to the dinner party at all? I don't recall, what with my head full of the new job and everything and now this incident at work".

"No, I didn't, but one of the guests works in the same place as you, Craig Shepherd, do you know him?"

Greenwood thought on his feet, the name seemed familiar but not that familiar that he could place it. "No dear, but I can look him up. This is a couples' dinner, am I right?"

You really do have shit for brains, Richard". And the phone went dead, there was no warm goodbye, Lucinda didn't do warm at all.

Greenwood went to the company internal directory. It had been called 'Valued Members' when he had his orientation, making it sound like some sort of dick web site. Now it had been relaunched as the sickly sweet 'Our Family'. He quickly found Shepherd; he was in Shipping, wherever that was. A vague memory of being walked through various departments and having to be interested bubbled up, part of his introduction when he first took the job. The staff photo showed a slightly swarthy man, nothing special, so why was the name familiar?

His company biog told Greenwood that he was a company man since leaving school, married with a newish child, lived in West Bridgford. He supported Nottingham Forest and was a keen angler.

In much the same way that a power-saving light bulb comes on, slowly the truth dawned, this was Jemmy's husband. Jemmy, his potential leg-over project. Oh fuckity-fuck. Greenwood's mind went into overdrive.

How had Lucinda come into contact with Shepherd and then it clicked, when she went maggot-drowning, her very weird hobby of fishing. She must have met him at some fish-torturing club thing.

A second revelation hit him involving the police. They might not like potential suspects getting together to fix their alibis. Greenwood didn't really think he was in the frame but this Shepherd guy was the man who was in the freezer on the night when Marie-Eve was slip-sliding away. He had to be high on their suspect list.

He hit redial and went through the situation slowly with Lucinda, without pointing any fingers but with heavy emphasis on the police aspect. She was less than chuffed but in the end she agreed to call Craig later and suggest another time, citing unforeseen issues. Shit, she'd have to cancel the whole shindig and she'd rather liked Craig, he'd even offered her the use of his caravan, should she ever go Carp fishing.

# FIFTY-THREE

## Wednesday 21 September

The location for the meeting had been chosen with care by Mo. It was a very public coffee house in Castle Marina, near enough to the shops for anyone seeing them to not be suspicious; just two girls out shopping together, stopping for a coffee before resuming the assault on their credit cards. Mo also wanted the security of other people, even strangers. Since Marie-Eve had died, she'd become nervous, almost paranoid. Then when Jemmy suggested they meet up, after all this time and with her now being married and with a baby, it just had the effect of heightening the paranoia. What if Craig had set her up to get her alone?

Jemmy was all smiles and carrying the baby in a chair thing with ease. They hugged and exchanged 'lovely to see yous' and 'why did we leave it so longs' before taking their seats. Mo had already bought in coffee, she knew what to order. Jemmy led the conversation, mummy chatter, the sort you get from previously interesting friends that then think having a baby is something everyone that wants to know about in excruciating detail. Mo half listened, in that polite way that people listen to stuff they have no interest in, when it occurred to her she had no idea of the child's name, or even whether she'd been told one. She'd got the basic stuff from Craig at work. Jemmy had had a baby, baby and mother OK. Mo suddenly realised that she didn't even know whether it was a boy or a girl.

In a short period of respite from the enrapturing tales of eating, spewing and shitting, Mo asked first what the baby's name was. "Oh, Small, just a casual Small for now. I read that children can be defined by their names so we want the baby to have the opportunity to self-define. If baby decides to be called something that pleases baby, then that is what it will be, no pressure".

"You don't think being known as Small might be a definition, speaking as one carrying Moonbeam Orinoco around for life?"

"No, baby will laugh when we explain". It was a statement rather than an expectation.

"And gender?"

"Neutral, another life choice to be made later, we've got books on it".

Mo didn't know what to say, although part of her screamed 'yes' when thinking of the years she'd carried around her peculiar moniker. Had her mother not been so stoned when she was being named, she might have done a bit better. She could have just about managed to live with Moonbeam, shortened to Mo it wasn't so bad, but Orinoco and then Smith! The thing is she just couldn't bring herself to change it. She always thought she might hire someone, one day, to find out what her real surname was, her father's surname, but she always lost her nerve when push came to shove. She might well have just been a plain Smith all along and the reality of that wouldn't do at all, not for Mo, not after a lifetime of being called Moonbeam Orinoco Smith.

It was a good twenty minutes before the conversation veered back around to real life again. Jemmy said she wanted to catch up on what Mo had been doing and where she was living now, surely not still in the manky old bedsit on Forest Road, the one with all the prostitutes and pimps and strange men knocking on her door at all times? Mo said no, now she had a nice little rented house quite near the manky flat, still in an edgy area but that suited her. It wasn't too far for work and was close enough to walk into town when she wanted.

Jemmy still kept digging and Mo was unsure exactly what she was after. It had been Jemmy who'd married and abandoned most of her friends, not her.

She didn't much feel like playing the Mo act any more so told it like it was. "After you got married and left, I had a few flings, drank a bit too much and burned away a lot of candles from both ends. These days though, I am just happy to kick back in my little house. I miss my old dog and might get another, just for the motivation to walk. That's me now, a simple quiet life with nothing else to tell". That little diatribe had the effect of killing the unwelcome line of enquiry dead because, to Mo, that was exactly what it appeared to be.

Jemmy then started talking about all the fun they used to have together, as if she'd not understood Mo's comments about being abandoned. She went on about stuff they'd tried, mostly drink but they'd dabbled in the hard stuff, pills, coke even. These days Mo's clean living lifestyle, if that is what you could call it, meant that her extravagances were limited to the occasional snifter of alcohol. It hadn't always been like that though and she wasn't best pleased that Jemmy had mentioned it. True, in the days of her youth, when she'd been trying hard to find herself, she'd tried most things. Luckily her body didn't do addiction, well chocolate but that didn't count. It would be true to say that while Mo had had a good go at Chasing the Dragon, well certainly ambling briskly after it for a while, she'd come out the other side largely disappointed with drugs.

From out of nowhere and with an almost hysterical tone, Jemmy asked about the murder of Marie-Eve and did she think that Craig had done it and should she tell the police of her fears. Talk about wifely support! Mo had known that this little catch-up would go this way, the killing was dominating the lives of everyone who was a suspect at the moment and Jemmy was bound to be curious, nervous even. She probably only ever got to know anything about it from the papers and Craig and, if he was involved or even the killer, what might he have told her?

Mo had thought about it and decided Craig was too wet to do anything like murder; to be fair everyone she spoke to thought the same. Cheating on his wife? Now that was another thing and there had been rumours before, should she tell Jemmy though? Instead she just patted her hand and reassured her. "Of course Craig didn't do it; in all probability he was at home with you when the body was put in the freezer. He is a gentle man, caring, he loves you", she said, "and he loves the baby".

It was hard for Mo to know whether this was what Jemmy was seeking this time. She'd always been a bit obvious back in the day; that was how they'd ended up in bed together for a night. Jemmy had wanted to try a woman, she said, before committing to Craig, before being sure. Mo had thought that she didn't much care for being the only available bi-sexual woman on offer and so Jemmy had had to make do, but the shots had lowered her sensibility threshold and she'd let it happen. Jemmy realised that she wasn't a lesbian the next day and begged Mo to be discreet, and she had been, this time.

They talked about the murder some more, like a couple of ancient lady detectives trying to see who fits the bill. Mo didn't really have much idea at that point; she never felt that any of her colleagues, even Reid when he was being a complete arse, had it in them to kill someone, not really. Oddly, she told Jemmy that she thought Neil was the nearest thing to a killer out of all the choices. He valued his standing and his 'lifestyle', as she put it, could compromise that, so perhaps Marie-Eve had found this out and threatened him in some way.

Jemmy had listened intently, asking the odd question, mostly about detail but, as Mo had said, she'd only picked up gossip here and there and didn't believe much of it was true. A couple of times Mo wondered whether Tracey had been pumped for information too, but didn't ask. Jemmy was obviously putting pieces together in her head. Judging from the way she framed her questions, it sounded like she now had a good idea of what had happened, well in her own mind she did.

Jemmy asked whether Craig had shown anyone, a woman, any woman, special attention at work. "Come on Mo, you know what I am asking, how my mind is working. Do you think Craig has been cheating on me

296

with anyone?" Mo said 'no' quickly, perhaps a bit too quickly and perhaps in a way that meant she was hiding something. Jemmy hadn't missed it. "Spit it out, Mo".

"Him and Tracey are a bit embarrassing sometimes, like 'get a room, guys'. Sorry, Jemmy".

Jemmy laughed, "I know all about that one, Tracey told me she was winding him up and was it alright? I said go ahead, if he bangs you though I want to know, I'll give him such a whack".

"Well, that is a relief, I wasn't sure whether to say. You know how obvious Tracey can be sometimes".

"What about this Marie-Eve woman? What was she like, attractive, looking to get laid? Do you think Craig liked her, did they have private meetings with the door closed or anything like that?"

"Not that I'm aware of but she was a bit difficult. I don't think she would be Craig's type, very manipulative; mind you I quite liked her". Jemmy didn't seem to pick up on those comments in the same way and Mo could see that she was genuinely worried about Craig and his possible involvement, else why would she be fishing?

Eventually the conversation returned to less tense themes and the time flew by. Mo had actually enjoyed some of the girly, child-free parts of their chat; she'd forgotten that Jemmy was fun at times. She'd have preferred to have been able to be bit more like her old self for a while but that Mo was long gone. At times Jemmy had twisted the topic of conversation this way and that, and Mo had had trouble following the thread. Later, it occurred to Mo that the thread was mostly the murder and that Jemmy genuinely thought that Craig had been shagging Marie-Eve and had then killed her for whatever reason. In some lights it was quite a compelling argument, but still Mo thought that surely the Craig she knew was too much of a pussy to kill.

They parted with hugs and were almost to the door when Jemmy realised she was one baby light. They both laughed about it in the car park but Mo thought 'how the hell do you forget your own child like that?' It was very disconcerting and Mo wondered whether Jemmy was suffering post-natal depression or some other such baby-bearing related shit. Maybe she'd ask Craig next time she saw him unless, of course, he was banged up and on remand!

# FIFTY-FOUR

Nash Pharmaceutical Services – 'We Make Blue Sky Fly' - looked on the surface like a modern and well-equipped operation, but, as always, corners were cut when it came to some equipment and property maintenance. Staff complained about heaters or air conditioning not working, some doors no longer worked on their access cards. The lift from the basement frequently scared passengers with sudden shudders and the boys in the cage wash rooms were a bit cavalier at times. They'd only recently narrowly avoided wheeling a cart containing expensive test article for one of the studies into the cage wash one time, and then only because a passing tech involved in the study had recognized the container and had been able to stop them.

Management had decided that the next, more targeted rif would see to the problem of what they considered to be reckless technicians, while the company trainers reacted with a typical knee-jerk and the standard operating procedure had to be updated, again. Such updates could take months sometimes, but the cage-wash protocol had been rushed through, meaning that a few other issues had fallen behind the 'get-fixed' pecking order.

It was Elkie who, using her particular people skills, had come back to Central Nick with some very interesting information. In the course of her chatting informally to people, she'd had her ear bent by one of the girls in Shipping about poor working conditions and how anyone could get in the shipping bay door during the day, and did, often using it as a short cut after heading out for a lunch time walk or more likely a smoke. Frequently the door was left open and the rooms they worked in, just off from the bay, got cold and draughty as a result. It didn't help that people would wedge doors open sometimes inside the facility too, that would throw the air conditioning out of kilter and they never knew whether they'd need to be working in a thick freezer coat or in a T-shirt and shorts, often both on the same day.

Of particular interest was the fact that some of the card readers and even the CCTV in the area was not working. All you needed to get in from the outside, if the shipping bay door was locked, was the right key!

Now the team reckoned that they had the answer as to the how the killer had entered the building, if they hadn't already been inside. They'd also suspected early on that Marie-Eve had been in contact with one of the shipping carts, annoyingly one of the ones already washed. At autopsy there had been slight marks noted on her legs and they seemed to match the general shape of the carts. This meant that the killer had probably moved Marie-Eve from one point to another using a cart, which added two complications. Marie-Eve had been moved, presumably already unconscious, from elsewhere in the facility, Shipping for choice, and, in using a cart, the killer didn't need to have the strength to move a limp body any real distance to the freezer; the killer might not have needed to be a particularly strong person after all.

Thompson had the makings of an idea and so had one of the recently washed shipping carts collected from NPS and brought up to Central Nick. In terms of weight, Elkie was not dissimilar to Marie-Eve, so she was selected to feature in a role play, in the privacy of the station; that would allow them all to visualise what happened. Dad would film it and they'd use it in the next case brief.

"Do I have to shag Craig Shepherd first for realism?" Elkie wanted to know.

"Always willing to go the extra six-inches for the team is our Elkie", said a disapproving Jenny Banks, mostly because she'd not thought of the joke first. "It was a joke, right?"

"A joke, of course", said Thompson. "While he's a suspect he's off limits, and that includes you, Liam".

Prosser hadn't been paying attention and so thought he'd missed an instruction. "What do you want me to do?"

Thompson clapped his hands together, "enough, let's get this little show on the road and no more cracks about cracks, especially yours, Elkie".

"Yes master" she said, demurely.

It all worked out pretty well, Dad, the smallest of the guys on the team, did the lifting and placing. Elkie played the corpse well, offering no extra help when it came to the lifting and transporting. They shunted the cart around the non-public area of the station, roughly taking it the distance from the NPS Shipping area to the walk-in freezer. The only fly on the ointment was Perkins' voice asking "what the fuck they were up to?" Thompson explained and Perkins went off shaking his head. They didn't feel the need to edit out the comment on the final video clip.

As they were watching the limp Elkie being ferried around, they had something of a break via a message from Reid at NPS. He called to say that a cart that might have been used around the time of the murder had avoided the cage wash after all. According to Tracey Mills, when Alan Bain had taken everything down to the cage wash, he'd had a little accident and a wheel had become disengaged. He'd not been able to fix it and so had carried each piece of material on the cart that needed washing into the wash manually. Everything had gone in the wash except the cart.

Thompson asked that the cart be placed to one side and not touched by anyone else; they would have it collected shortly. Reid confirmed that it had already been done; it was locked away in his office. They all realised that this might be the cart used to convey Marie-Eve from Shipping to the freezer and, if so, it had avoided being cleaned of any prints and DNA from all users unless the killer had wiped it down.

Thompson gave instructions for Bain to be included in the investigation, specifically so that they could take his DNA. It would have to be done with the permission of his mum, Joan, and discreetly at NPS, if at all possible. "Talk to her first and assure her that it is for elimination purposes only. Don't mention that her son will be added to the suspect list, perhaps only in pencil for now".

Once back at the facility, DCs Prosser and Banks checked on the security of the cart. It was just as Reid had said and it was all neatly bagged up. Then, on Thompson's instructions, they asked for a full tour of the crime scene, including Shipping, with the Buildings Manager. They would also need a detailed list of all faults outstanding, including any repairs made post Marie-Eve Legault's death.

Nobody was going to admit to leaving doors wedged open, but it was obviously still happening as they were able to go from Shipping to the Freezer Room without the need to use a temporary access card, much to the Buildings Manager's embarrassment. Prosser needed to check with the night cleaners again whether they'd left doors open on the night as had been suggested. He'd get Dad to call them, the cleaners where all Bangladeshi but it was probably the same language as Dad's native tongue, more or less.

During the visit, Prosser made a point of pacing the route from the shipping door through to the freezer. It could be covered, wheeling a laden cart, in about 45 seconds with the doors all open. Then he was taken to Marie-Eve's office and did the same thing with the route through to the Shipping Room where the murder, or at least the rendering of Marie-Eve Legault incapacitated, was now thought to have taken place.

Some of the corridors had cameras but, according the buildings guy, only six of them in the facility were operational and none of them worked along the route from Shipping to Sample Management. They were in luck with one still working in the main admin area where Marie-Eve's office was located, and so they should be able to pull the footage off it, if it hadn't already been deleted by IT. It seems that one of the IT guys was super keen on what he called a 'clean systems' policy, which meant deleting anything unnecessary such as CCTV, before uploading the operational daily data to the NPS central database system.

The detectives next met with Lin Ti, a junior in the IT department. They could see that he was a nervy sort straight away but perhaps with good reason. The company was planning on overhauling IT and he fully expected that he wouldn't be a part of the new format. He seemed very switched on to Banks, more so than some of the other staff she'd had the pleasure of meeting, such as Marco Baggio. He'd seemed very detached from the job and he, like some of the other longer-serving employees around NPS, were actively canvassing to be included in the next rif. The compensation package appealed to them more than the job, nowadays.

It only took Lin Ti moments to retrieve what was left of the video. "Sorry", he said, "I was lucky to get this, it was being deleted when I hit 'cancel'". Prosser and Banks watched the CCTV with interest. The rescued tape ran from around 8pm onwards, showing a fuzzy looking Marie-Eve Legault returning to her office, possibly from the bathroom. Little later they saw her get a drink from the vending machine and then head out towards the direction of Shipping, her last walk anywhere. The tape ended there in even more of a fuzzy mess although there was a vague suggestion of a shadow entering the admin area not long after Legault had left.

"Can that be cleaned up? Do you think that is someone?" asked Banks.

Lin Ti was non-committal, "it isn't a great system in the first place, as you've already seen. It may be something or nothing but you are welcome to take a copy and give it a try". Apologising profusely he reached into the desk; he produced a naff USB with the NPS logo and byline on it and loaded the file up for them. "Unwanted gifts from a sales show" he said, noticing their surprise that he had a drawer full.

"No need to return it either, as you can see. Help yourselves if you want a few", so they did.

As a final look-over, they went out of the shipping door and walked around the delivery compound. It had a rather flimsy entry barrier that was opened remotely by Security; it appeared to be stuck up at present. The bay was just big enough for a large van to turn around; anything bigger would need to reverse in. The rear of the compound backed on to the Wilford Clay Pits nature reserve and there was a gap in the bushes where people clearly went through. It was, Buildings Maintenance said, a popular lunch spot on fine days but they did have plans to complete the fence and put in a gate with a Security link.

Prosser and Banks headed back to the ops room. They had both reached the same conclusions and were confident about how the killer got inside, if they'd had to, and the route taken from Shipping to the freezer and then back. They had an estimate of the length of time that the killer had spent doing the deed, and they also thought that they knew how the facility had been been entered and from where. Now all they needed was a traffic cam on the main road between Silverdale and the playing fields by the old railway line and they might have something meaningful to look at. Banks texted Thompson with the CCTV location request and time period, things were moving a bit now.

Back at base, Thompson got the Lego box out. It might look daft but it really was the most practical way to recreate the scenes on the desk in the ops room. Dad was left with the task, using Google Earth to get the shapes right. In the next briefing they would able to go through what they suspected had happened with the wider team, including Charnley; if he fancied dropping by and staying for five minutes.

The Silverdale CCTV arrived and Dad managed to get a very grainy video-grab image of a dark figure on a bike, emerging from the subway and heading towards the railway bed which served as a trail. The same figure returned approximately 12 minutes later. No details could be seen, the camera was on the adjacent ring road and the image was in the periphery of its view, but it must have been the killer arriving and departing, it was too coincidental. Another little problem was that the time stamp made no sense, another little technological glitch to hold them up.

After a few calls the bad news was that the system had malfunctioned and every traffic cam on the ring-road system had the wrong time stamp for the whole evening. Even if they could ID the shadowy figure on the bike, a court wouldn't accept the tape as evidence, it had been accidentally corrupted.

Next morning the short briefing went very well and everyone was engaged by the new details. Dad got a small round of applause for the NPS Lego simulation. The only figures they had to use as killer and victim substitutes were of Xena – Warrior Princess and a Monopoly set so Xena ended up being the killer and Marie-Eve Legault was represented by the boot. It was all a bit surreal.

## FIFTY-FIVE

We thought we'd got a break with the cart thing, they use them to shift boxes around, certainly one was used to ship the Fish Finger from the Shipping Department, where we are sure she was assaulted, to the freezer, where she died. The cart opens up new possibilities but also brings shipping people into play.

We got the electronic tracking file on the sample delivery driver, Andy Mood. He never left his route, tracked via his phone and he only handed boxes to Shepherd at the door. They could have done it together but there is absolutely no connection between the two that we can find, other than occasional meetings to swap a signature for samples. Mood was eliminated officially.

The rota for late deliveries told us nothing. Only Reid and Shepherd were on it, both needed the money. Mills was on it at one time but her new man was proving demanding, so she'd taken a break.

The Montreal end is not producing much except that there is a rumour that Legault was planning for the future. We all do that, but she seems to have been to Panama twice in the past year, done as cheap trips using a Panama all-inclusive holiday as cover. Her apartment had no clues but Panama, twice, was interesting and something to follow up.

The team is working well but how do you take their characters and disguise them so they don't see themselves in the book?

This plot needs more players who are pulling different strings. Jilted lover is so cliché, angry staff overlooked for promotion or even let go, they have a savage method for that, doesn't ring very true, not strong enough.

This might be money, outside influences perhaps. I feel two thousand words coming on just sorting out the suspects' different motives.

## Fifty-Six

Thompson was already on his mobile when he had another call with some interesting news. The results from forensics were in on blood contamination at several keys spots in and around the Legault murder scene. Iain Lynch, who'd been burdened with trying to explain the results, was a bit understated on the phone, he thought that the findings might just muddy the waters but he'd tried to present them in a way that made sense, he'd send them through immediately. "I am presuming that they should go to you as a cc on the email, the main recipient still DI Charnley?" Thompson was happy to confirm that that was the case.

Charnley may not be an active participant in the on-going investigation as such but Thompson wasn't going to allow any disrespect to creep in, no matter how obvious it was that he was running the show now.

Lynch was quite right, the results were somewhat complicated. Almost as complicated as it had been getting the DNA from the suspects in the first place, with Greenwood, Mills and, most vociferously, Martin, not happy about it. They took some convincing that it was in their best interests although it was only when they were informed that others involved had no objections that they relented.

The unwashed cart had some blood on it, none of it Legault's but traces of both Simon Reid's and Craig Shepherd's. There was also an unidentified hit which may belong to someone in shipping or it could be from the killer. They would need to widen the DNA testing sweep to include everyone even remotely associated. He'd have to go through the list and draw up a new set of targets.

The freezer door handle also had blood on it. Reid's and Shepherd's but also Tracey Mills', this was to be expected although the term GLP plopped into Thompson's mind, surely all people accessing the freezers

308

would wear gloves at all times? The report also stated that there were traces of another chemical on the handle which they hadn't yet managed to isolate; it may just be a Sample Management product.

The doors from Shipping through to Sample Management also had blood traces, what did those cleaners do these days? Again, and not unexpected, were traces from Shepherd, Mills, Neil Martin, Alan Bain and, on the entrance to Shipping, from Marie-Eve Legault, which was interesting. The door to Sample Management, the main door and the door through to the Freezer Room had traces from Legault, Reid and Martin. The really odd one was Legault who, according to Reid, didn't spend much time in Sample Management. How had her blood got there and did she have any recent hand injuries?

Perhaps the most interesting result was from Legault's office door handle and her desk drawers. Naturally she had left traces, she must have nicked her hand or something. The other sample from the door came up with the name Richard Greenwood. So the big boss had been poking around in her office, was she there when he was making free with her drawers? Thompson knew from experience that Greenwood did have a hand injury; he'd subconsciously tried to conceal it when they met him at NPS. How and when had he got it would be a part of their next line of questioning. Very intriguing.

Now there appeared to be a very good reason to move Greenwood up the leader board a bit, to at least second, maybe he was going to make a last minute bid for the winning post, he'd be fun to arrest.

Looking at results, Thompson added a short summary of his thoughts and forwarded the information to the rest of the team. Dad would summarise for Charnley anyway, not that it might affect what conclusions Charnley drew. If he had his head on, his insights should be worthy of consideration, if not, well they had other and more reliable brains working the case.

Thompson had just scribbled the word 'samples' on his rough pad; that was something they hadn't factored in. The samples of Sample Management fame were made up of a variety of types including blood or blood derivatives and so contamination was possible, did samples ever migrate to exterior surfaces? The whole blood thing had just become potentially more difficult.

A little bell rang in Thompson's head, something Reid had kept banging on about, GLP again.

Despite it being quite late in the afternoon Reid picked up. "Sorry to bother you, Mr. Reid. You mentioned GLP and I forgot to jot down the term in full and its ramifications. Could I trouble you for the abridged version, please?"

Reid was only too happy to help. "Good Laboratory Practice is an industry standard that basically means all actions are done to the highest standard. That meant the wearing of masks, lab coats and shoe covers as appropriate". Thompson apologised for butting in "and gloves, especially gloves?" Reid confirmed, "especially gloves".

Over the next twenty minutes or so Reid covered every area. He agreed that traces of sample could be found to contaminate sites but that the practice of GLP, which he never let up on, should limit it. The sites inside the Freezer Room at least should not have any blood traces, gloves are mandatory and the rule is pretty well kept.

Picking up on this Thompson asked Reid whether, hand on heart, gloves were worn 100% of the time when accessing the freezer room. Reid laughed, "no, Detective Sergeant, they are not. Even I lapse when rushed. I wouldn't like to put a percentage on it, but there are lapses, quite frequent lapses".

Thompson moved on, he was quite interested in the process of GLP; it was much more like he expected science to be, disciplined and everyone working carefully. Reid was able to answer a few more questions, never pausing, he clearly knew his stuff. Finally Thompson played his last card. "One last thing, Mr. Reid, did you cut yourself recently?" Reid confirmed that he had and explained about snagging his hand on a rosebush while fishing out his dropped keys. Again there was no hesitation in answering, the actions of an innocent man, or just a cool customer?

By the time the phone was back in its cradle Thompson felt he had a little more clarity on the situation.

# FIFTY-SEVEN

## Sunday 18 September

The pile of SOPs on her desk seemed to be getting higher. Marie-Eve wasn't quite sure why she was even wading through them on a Sunday evening, what were minions for, after all? She picked up the phone and dialled the number, knowing it would be late but needing to chat. When a voice answered in French it took her a second to get her mind into gear; that was what working in English all day did to you. Soon the office was full of French chatter as Marie-Eve and her best friend, Genevieve, caught up on recent events.

It was mostly 'he said, she said' stuff; they didn't talk in too much detail. Marie-Eve knew the company well enough not to trust a work line with anything other than harmless gossip and shameless praise for her real bosses back in New Jersey. Whether they were bright enough in HR to know what she was doing was anyone's guess. One item of interest was a fact-finding visit to Head Office from the FDA. They'd shown particular interest in the Saviour study but had left satisfied, or so they had said. Marie-Eve tried to keep a calm voice. Keeping track of the Saviour stuff was getting harder and every portal access she did would have her electronic name on it.

Once Genevieve had hung up, Marie-Eve contemplated calling it a day, but there was stuff she should wrap up, if only to keep up the pretence. In a few days it wouldn't matter, either way, but her work ethic, wherever that had come from, meant that she still cared at some level how she was thought about, professionally at least.

And there was the other thing to stay late for, too. What was that all about?

Deciding it was time for a break she headed out to the machine, past the stragglers of the weekend admin group, all just finishing their day too. Nobody acknowledged her, but then she'd set out how she operated in her first week on secondment when she'd had the old lady removed. She'd felt a pang of guilt and there was no doubt that Gladys knew her stuff and, if not respected as such, had engendered a healthy fear amongst her staff. The trouble was that Marie-Eve needed a sacrificial lamb to mark her arrival and Gladys getting the boot, as they called it locally, had served her purpose well.

The machine made lousy coffee but the candy was better, way better than back home. If she lived in England she'd be the size of a house in two years, it was for the best that she was going home very soon.

Back in the office, she untangled her iPod and ran lesson six of 'Learn Portuguese' again. She was definitely getting better; she just hoped that Ben was trying as hard as she was. Really she knew that the staff they would hire, domestics, would be bilingual, French and Portuguese, maybe English too, but she felt that, if going to live in Brazil was one of their options, or perhaps just a scent trail, then she really ought to have an idea about the language. It would help give her a start and she'd surely pick it up better once she heard and used it daily. The effort might be wasted if they ended up in Australia, or she ended up in Panama, but it was a welcome distraction sometimes.

Her break over, Marie-Eve logged onto the system, into the portal and started dropping files onto her encrypted USB. While she was waiting for the thing to finish she had another pick at the scab on the back of her hand. It had annoyed her intensely that she'd snagged her hand on Craig's stupid fish hook. It was taking weeks to heal, and every time it looked to be getting a bit better she caught it again.

Her ringing phone made her jump, now was supposed to be quiet time, she'd made it clear that she was not to be disturbed when she was trying to get her work done for the day but now everyone had gone, the calls came in directly. Her phone automatically displayed the caller's name, Greenwood. Great, what did he want?

"Marie-Eve, still here I see, still slaving away for the man, eh?"

"I'm surprised to see you here on a Sunday Mr. Greenwood, I thought you usually headed off to the golf course at the weekend".

"Things to catch up on I'm afraid, Marie-Eve, and I wanted to touch base about a few things seeing as you are leaving us soon and heading off back to Canada, at the end of next week, I think. I do hope that you have enjoyed your time here. We've certainly appreciated your input and learned a lot about the ways of our new Lords and Masters".

"It has been an experience, Mr. Greenwood and you can't beat adding experience to your CV. I've been mostly satisfied with the NPS Nottingham staff's efforts at getting up to speed. There have been a couple of exceptions; it will be all in my report under 'deliverables'".

"Excellent, excellent. Perhaps we could go through your report together, just to give me the heads-up, before you file it with New Jersey?"

"I'm afraid that won't be possible, Mr. Greenwood. My report is almost completed and the most recent chapter will be sent to Mr. Duggan and my manager in Montreal later, perhaps even this evening. I have to act impartially at all times and retain objectivity in all situations, as I am sure you understand".

"Oh, of course, Marie-Eve, heaven forbid that you might think that I was trying to influence your report findings. I am sure your report is very even-handed and that you appreciate, and have considered, that a transition from one system to another, more alien system, will always include a few bumps that need ironing out".

"Was there anything else, Mr. Greenwood? I am very busy and I have other things I need to get done this evening. I need them ready for the appropriate desk in Montreal tomorrow morning; I still have a department there to run too. I also have three serious disciplinary reports to complete for members of staff here so that HR can action them tomorrow, once their action is approved as appropriate, of course".

"No, I was just checking in with a friendly greeting and offering help if needed, I'll let you get on now. Incidentally, who do the disciplinary actions involve?"

"Craig Shepherd in Shipping, Karen Armstrong in Lab Sciences and Paul Sturrock in Finance. HR have been fully briefed and are ready to act. Under data protection these are classified files so I can't discuss the issues too broadly and your approval to HR for action in these instances is really just a formality, I'm sure you understand, Mr. Greenwood".

"I see. Thank you, Marie-Eve, I'll leave you to it then. Good night".

"Good night, Mr. Greenwood".

Once the phone was back in its cradle, Marie-Eve allowed herself a small smile as she thought 'oh gosh, silly me, and you, Mr. Greenwood. I forgot to mention, you are the subject of a disciplinary too, already approved by HR in New Jersey, how silly of me to forget!' Marie-Eve was quite proud of her dipsy English admin impression.

In his office, Greenwood pushed the USB into the machine. He might not be a great scientist but he did have contacts who knew how to do things, computer things and his one-off payment for the latest little job may well pay dividends later. In the background the printer whirred. Following the instructions before him he found the PC on the system and scrolled down to the files. They were named in French, which was a pain. He managed to find the ones marked 'Disciplinaire'. Another read 'Le Compte Rendu', even he could figure that one out! It all made for interesting reading. So the whispers were true, she was a wrecking ball and he was one of those who would be getting the full weight of

315

her ire. Now that was a problem but not one that couldn't be solved, one way or another. Greenwood knew that he needed to stick a spoke in that particular wheel, and, if he did enough damage, then she might not bother too much doing a full re-write, what with being so close to going back to Canada. He rose from his desk, time to get more 'hands-on', he thought.

# FIFTY-EIGHT

## Wednesday 21 September

While it had never been allowed to enter Jemmy's head that Craig could be involved in the murder of Marie-Eve Legault, there were others, she was knew, who had thought differently. The police naturally suspected all the men in Marie-Eve's sphere and quite right too, all men were bastards.

One of her magazines had recently had a piece about a woman who hadn't suspected anything but her husband had turned out to be an infamous serial killer. He was caught when she'd noticed that he was always acting strangely around the time that women and men had gone missing. Craig had been shifty at times too, sloping off to that caravan and going fishing, or claiming he was going fishing. What was so fascinating about fish anyway, were fish more interesting than her and Small?

There were other things too. The general lack of a foreign scent on his work clothes when she knew that Tracey Mills toyed with him to make him 'go red'. Tracey had already cleared it with Jemmy before winding him up. When she'd asked, Jemmy had laughed and said "go ahead", making out it was a great girly hoot but actually she was not very pleased with Tracey, not pleased at all. Technically, what Tracey planned was sexual harassment but whoever heard of a woman sexually harassing a man? It was always the other way around, in Jemmy's experience.

Perhaps she should talk to the police about her fears. They would sort it out and, if Craig was a killer, then he'd be carted off to prison to become somebody's bitch. If he wasn't, then she could feel safe again with that police-confirmed knowledge.

The card hadn't moved from where DC Knight had put it on that first visit. 'Officer Drabble', nice one Mo! She called and it went straight to voice mail. 'Hi, it's Jemmy Shepherd, I was wondering whether you would want to talk to me again, go through Craig's movements and such. I'd be happy to chat without him around, in confidence, call me back, thanks".

Satisfied that she had at least been a good citizen, she fired up YouTube and loaded her favourite Yoga video. Small was fast off, that stuff was good. She'd have nothing to disturb her now for at least an hour, maybe two if she'd been heavy handed. She closed the curtains, stripped off and followed the moves the people on-screen were doing. Yoga naked, it just seemed so natural.

She was only half-way through the routines for the second time when the phone rang. It was DC Prosser, she'd hoped for Drabble. Would she be in for the next hour, they were local and would drop by. Perhaps Drabble was driving. At first she couldn't place Prosser; perhaps she'd not met him yet, he sounded Irish, exotic, then she remembered that he wasn't exotic at all and that Drabble was the dull one Mo had mentioned, it was Laura that she liked. Laura that she could be friends with.

She put coffee on and arranged a plate of cake fancies. Small slept on, that was good; there'd be no interruptions for a while. She stopped casting YouTube to the TV, got dressed and opened the curtains. They arrived ten minutes later.

Welcoming them at the door, opening it before they knocked, she ushered them into the living room, Small slept on. They accepted coffee and cake, she wasn't sure that they would after last time but it was polite to offer and the visual temptation of a well laid-out plate is what the style magazines recommended. It obviously worked because they demolished all the fancies between them. She was pretty sure that there was nothing spiked in that batch.

318

Once the polite bit was over they started to ask questions, just small things but mostly about Craig and his movements and how sure she was of her version of the events of the night of Legault's death. Of course she was sure, she heard Craig's pager go and coming back she heard a car outside but Craig had obviously tiptoed in quietly so as not to disturb her, and especially Small. They both nodded and the woman scribbled away. She'd said her name was Laura, a pretty name and it suited her, but Prosser had called her Elkie, a nickname perhaps. Jemmy liked that, she sensed that they liked similar things, were on the same wavelength, not everyone was. Perhaps they'd really could become friends when all this was cleared up and Jemmy could also call her Elkie?

Prosser, who said his name was Liam, a strong name, a nice name, continued to ask the questions, always basically the same question as far as Jemmy could see.

How was Craig generally in himself? Was he pre-occupied, evasive, relaxed, or happy? Plenty of emotions there to choose from, surely he could only be one or two at a time, though. Generally, she said, he was happy but Craig was always happy, after a fashion. He sort of rode along on a wave of, not apathy but not raging enthusiasm either. The only time he got excited was when he watched his football or went fishing. He had a caravan at Calverton, did you know? Yes they knew about that, Craig had told them. Then they wanted to know whether she had been to the caravan herself?

"Not with Craig", she said, "but I did take a look at where it was, one time when I was out that way visiting a friend, just to get the image of his hidey-hole in my minds-eye, for peace of mind". More nodding and scribbling took place.

Had there been any personal problems between her and Craig, was he faithful, was she? Jemmy flushed and snapped "of course we're faithful; we are a classic love story, unbreakable". Prosser apologised for the question but they had to ask, often crimes were committed

319

because of infidelity and, if there had been a history, even suspected, then it was worth following up on it.

Out of the blue Jemmy launched into the history of their relationship. Her own confusions regarding her sexual preferences until Craig came along. How Craig had been dating someone else when they met, she wasn't. How she'd planned to date him having seen him around and how they'd fallen for each other across a cafeteria table. It was all a bit disturbing in many ways. Craig had clearly been played for and caught just like one of the Carp, or was it Tench?, that he fished for. Jemmy had been angler and bait and had caught her Tench easily. Craig would be a Tench thought Prosser; they don't fight much once hooked!

Suddenly Jemmy tearfully said, "I think Craig was seeing that Marie-Eve woman, cheating on me and Small. I never asked him because she died and it didn't seem right. I don't know whether he was going to leave us for her but something must have happened because he became sullen, uncommunicative and angry. It seemed that he didn't want to be with Small and me, he wasn't interested in me anymore, you know, physically".

She thought she'd been quite convincing, she always was good at tearful. She thought Laura especially might chip in with some comforting words but she didn't, neither of the officers reacted so she calmed down and waited for the next question.

Elkie scribbled some more notes but Prosser was so transparent that Jemmy could see the questions bubbling up through his system and out of his mouth. "What made you think that Craig and Marie-Eve Legault were seeing each other?"

Jemmy shrugged, "I know Craig. Strong women can manipulate him".

"Right," said Prosser. "Thanks for the coffee and cakes, much appreciated and we'd appreciate it even more if you kept them as our little secret from the rest of the team, we don't want to foment discontent". Jemmy just nodded, she wasn't really sure what he'd said apart from not letting on about the cakes, but it was another secret that she could keep if they wanted her to.

"Will you need to talk to me further? Only I have planned a visit to a friend's outside Nottingham. I'm taking Small too, and I'll be gone for a couple of days perhaps. I can leave a number I can be contacted on". Prosser saw no reason for her to stick around and so told her a temporary absence wouldn't be an issue, taking the number she offered.

In the car Prosser and Elkie looked at each other. What had they just witnessed and was there enough in the ramblings of Jemmy Shepherd to pull Craig in for a bit more of a chat in more severe circumstances? If they did, it sounded like he was the sort that would cave at the first suggestion of involvement, maybe worth a try. The bit about Jemmy not being 100% sure about Craig's return time, even though she didn't put it that way, was food for thought. Time to report back and see what Dave thought they should do.

# FIFTY-NINE

Thompson re-read the sheet in front of him. The info from the various items of evidence had been fed through piecemeal and most had been quickly discarded as irrelevant. So many people had contaminated various items and the general crime scene as to render the forensic information next to useless. One thought, more in hope than expectation, was that Craig Shepherd's phone would have information on it that would incriminate or exonerate. He'd already had word that they were having some difficulties with it, as most of the internal works had effectively fused when it had been placed in water.

There was also something odd about the sim card, it had not been used for about six weeks, all it contained was old, fragmented data. The phone was a Pay-As-You-Go and so getting anything from the service provider was problematical. It did however seem that the card provided with the broken phone (and copious quantities of baby sick, thanks!) had not been used during the period before Legault had died.

Craig Shepherd had been entirely up front regarding his phone, just as an innocent man would be, so what was going on here?

Setting his own phone to record he called Craig Shepherd, no time like the present.

"Mr. Shepherd, DS. Thompson here. I have a question about your broken phone. It is a Pay-As-You-Go, care to explain?"

"Quite simple, I can't afford a smart phone and that is the third phone our baby has destroyed in the past three months. After the first demolition, maybe six weeks ago, I bought two from Asda, activated one, which lasted a few weeks before destruction this time, then about a week before Marie-Eve died I activated the second. I know that is what you are looking for. You have the remnants of that phone now, I

322

have since bought another two, one I have activated, one for if, or when, Small destroys it".

"Do you load the phone with important numbers after every loss or do you just swap the sim card?"

"I swap the card normally but since you have my old card I've had to do it manually this time, missing one or two obvious numbers off, I should say in advance, to save the question later".

"OK, thanks for the information, you've been very helpful. By the way, where are you now?"

"Just having a late breakfast officer. Full English in a transport café, is that OK?"

"Fine, full English you say? Lovely, enjoy".

Thompson considered the option of going out himself and finding a greasy spoon for a full-English of his own. In his drawer the haslet sandwiches that comprised his lunch lived a life of their own. Dismissing the late breakfast idea, he peeled off a yellow post-it, wrote a short sentence and stuck it onto the dead board next to the photo of Craig Shepherd. Another small piece of the jigsaw found and this one not just a piece of blue sky. Somewhere out there was a more interesting sim card than the one that had been supplied.

# SIXTY

As usual, the little transport café in the pull-in opposite Clumber Park was busy. Craig liked it there, it was anonymous and he could think. True, for some people, the sound of hairy-arsed ex-Miners calling everyone 'my love' or 'my darling' might have been off-putting, but it was a perfectly normal way of talking in their community. Now, up and down the country, similar rough-hewn men were busy forging a new career, a forced life-change for those whose lot had changed enormously since the mines had been closed by Thatcher all those years ago.

Craig was learning to live with being the prime suspect; he saw it on everyone's face at work. If he'd been a detective he'd have gone after him, too. He knew well that he'd had the opportunity but what about a motive? That was complicated. He hadn't really been interested in Marie-Eve but she'd been interested in him and it just sort of happened. It was as stupid as you could get, he knew that, but was at a loss how to adequately explain the whole thing.

The breakfast in front of him beckoned. That was another reason for coming here, a proper greasy spoon breakfast and plenty of it. While he might have a certain swarthiness associated with those of southern European descent, something from his mother's side apparently, Craig was as English as the next John Bull when it came to a cooked breakfast.

He felt his mobile phone buzz, not a number he knew but he answered anyway. More questions from the police. He spoke quietly into the phone so as to not bother any of the other diners, quickly answering what seemed to him to be an odd question, something he'd need to think about. Hanging up, he decided to try to do his own detective work while he could. Soon enough he'd be back at work and the demands on his time wouldn't leave much time for reflection.

He pulled his fishing notebook out of his pocket, his current one went everywhere with him, not just to write down the where, when and especially the weight of a fish caught, but also to jot down his every day thoughts, especially on bait concoctions. Craig loved fishing; that was why he bought the caravan in the first place; it was even fishing that brought him to this very café the first time. He'd been doing a three-day Carp session on Bellmoor Lakes near Retford. Sneaking in on a mate's permit, he'd had word that one of the club bailiffs was on his way round and the Bailiff knew his mate's face. Legging it smartly, the local bailiffs had a bit of a lively reputation when dealing with transgressors, he'd headed home and just followed his nose and the rumble in his belly when he saw their sign. He'd been a regular ever since.

On a fresh page he wrote down the pros and cons of his situation. Nothing incriminating because they might yet see his notebook, and he wanted to make sure what was written down was objective.

If the police were going to target him as the killer, as he firmly believed, then they were probably not going to go hard looking for whoever really did it. That was only natural and, while circumstantial would never stand up in court, Craig knew enough about the police to know that he'd need some sort of insurance policy. Having an alternative suspect and the information to back up the claim just might be the additional layer that he needed, on top of his natural honesty and lack of guilt, but he'd have to try to work it out first.

It occurred to Craig that he felt as well as he had for some time, since just after Small had arrived. Clear-headed; focused even, keen to figure this out. He was missing Jemmy and Small, obviously, but it was her idea that she should go south to see her friend for a few days while everything got sorted out. She'd be annoyed to know that her lovely and highly nutritional meals had been dumped in the bin as soon as her car had left the drive. If you have to live like a single man while your wife was away, you might as well eat like one, too.

The page in the notebook was still blank.

A pro to start with first, then see where we go.

Pro, he hadn't murdered Marie-Eve Legault. He scrubbed that out, not having done it was a given. So he wrote down that he was asleep early on the evening when Marie-Eve had presumably been overpowered and then placed in the freezer. Then he thought 'presumably', he'd assumed that he was asleep when she died, he didn't actually know. It was half a pro at best, and he marked it up as so.

Con: Craig had been sleeping with Marie-Eve, she had dumped him. A bit of a heavy con there. It had been a relief that day when she'd told him they were done, she'd beat him to it and that was always better where women were concerned. If the dumping is their idea, you can still be friends after.

Pro: he'd admitted everything to the police; it had not ended in acrimony, just fizzled out. He should have told them the full details though, that he was planning to end it but then she did, been more transparent. He hadn't hidden the detail; it just hadn't poked its head out at the right time.

Con: Craig might benefit from Marie-Eve being gone. Since her arrival, his relationship with Bez Dooley had become a little fraught. He wondered whether Marie-Eve had precipitated this, once they had stopped seeing each other, unprofessionally, so to speak! He knew that Bez got frustrated with him and he'd tried hard to get back into gear, but his head just seemed to slow down sometimes and mistakes were inevitable.

Why would Bez go down that route though? True, they weren't best friends but they didn't despise each other either. Bez was one of the people he thought he got on reasonably well with; well, one of the male people, true.

This was getting him nowhere. He just seemed to be adding an extra layer of complication, so he started a new line, suspects and why.

Reid despised Marie-Eve. He was up himself big time, especially after being sent for training in Montreal. Possibly up for the chop at the next rif, or so the rumour had it; a rumour that he will surely have heard. If so, would Reid react that badly? Obviously the police didn't rate Reid a suspect, they seemed to be less demanding of him. Was he telling the police things, rumours about him, information without substance, something incriminating to cover his own arse?

Craig realised that his thoughts were running away with themselves, and his heart was racing, fast. Reid was what he was, not his choice of friend but not his enemy either.

What about Mo? Delusional, certainly, she thought that Marie-Eve fancied her, maybe she did, maybe they were a thing, maybe Mo was his replacement? The thought that Marie-Eve might have switched her affection from him to Mo made him smile, Mo, surely everyone knew, was not a full shilling. Besides, hadn't Marie-Eve mentioned Mo as a figure of fun at one time? He wished he'd listened more intently to her when she was yapping, after.

Neil Martin, had they considered him? Not only was he on-site throughout the time that she was put in cold storage (stop it, he thought), but he had a thing about Marie-Eve. Her Montreal chic was something of an obsession with him, but there was also the question mark over whether he was gay, it had been hinted. There was certainly something about Martin that Craig couldn't put his finger on.

What about the cleaners? No, harmless the lot of them unless one was a hired gun from the Montreal Mafia. No, daft idea, he was sounding like Jemmy now. He'd not even thought that someone from Montreal might have a grudge until she raised the possibility, her and her vivid imagination.

Andy Mood, the delivery guy? No. He had no opportunity unless he was working with Neil Martin. He'd not been allowed around to the loading bay until Craig had arrived and opened up, as far as he knew anyway. No, not Andy, he was such a nice, helpful guy, so not Andy.

Who else?

Alan Bain? He was a sandwich and cheese course short of a picnic but he never appeared aggressive, just a sad case, ignore Bain.

Bez Dooley then, seriously, why not? He didn't like having his nose put out of joint when Marie-Eve effectively took over in Nottingham. He was the head of his own tech department and then she'd waltzed over here from Canada and just nudged him aside at the first meeting they'd had with staff, temporarily perhaps but still he was miffed. Bez knew the layout of both the delivery bay in Shipping and the Sample Management room and equipment. Not many people would have been aware of the minus 20°C freezer or even know how to work the shelves and everything, but Bez does. Maybe Bez, then.

What about Greenwood? He fawned all over Marie-Eve at the Senior Management Committee meetings, or so Craig had heard. True, he was a bit worse for wear after a rumoured boozy lunch but everyone knew he was keen. He had a reputation for being over-friendly with the female members of staff and didn't Julie Miller, the Immunology Scientist, get a verbal-written warning for threatening to cut his balls off with a rusty scalpel? Great line! Maybe Ranji could help him out there. Maybe Ranji should make the list too come to think of it. He must know what Marie-Eve was like; HR people do talk to each other, surely.

Perhaps he should call Lucinda, she seemed keen to fish for Carp. He could take her to Calverton, show her the ropes and slip the odd question about good old Dick Greenwood into the conversation. She

328

seemed to hate her husband and, unfortunately, find Craig himself physically appealing. She was attractive in some ways, she went fishing for one, but Craig had decided that, after Marie-Eve, he would no longer let himself get cornered by another woman.

The egg yolks on his breakfast were starting to congeal so Craig mopped them up with his slice of fried and pressed on eating. He felt that, at last, he was thinking along the right lines.

The last of the tea went down well and Craig said his goodbye to 'mi-duck, mi-darlin' as he thought of the guys at the till. Odd that he never knew any of the ex-miners' real names.

He was half-way to the car when another name flashed in to his mind, Marco, the IT guy who Marie-Eve worked with closely. He might be worth a punt too, slimy, mardy twat that he is.

Having found the time to rationalise everything, Craig felt a little better, certainly clearer of thought. He almost wanted to drive down to Central Nick and go through everything with Dave, Liam and Laura, he quite liked Laura.

The run down the A614 was easy, although Mapperley Top through to West Bridgford was busy as always. The cars outside the house were an ominous sign. He we go, he thought, a chance to offer up my opinion.

He pulled onto the drive and was just letting himself in when Thompson and a female officer door-stepped him, asking to come in. "Of course they could", he said, "more questions then?"

He'd just remembered that Jemmy and Small had gone off visiting her friend and was about to explain when Thompson's tone changed. "Craig Shepherd, I am arresting you on suspicion of the murder of..."

# SIXTY-ONE

It was just like on TV where the cops arrive and trot out the caution, all that 'things you say may be used later' stuff. To be honest, it just washes over you, and of course you say you understand but it is doubtful that many do, not the first time they hear it.

There were no cuffs, although the neighbours could see he was being arrested, they didn't know why although some might have guessed. They knew where he worked and the freezer murder had been all over the local press. It had even made a couple of the nationals; they must have been short of London-centric stories the day the press release went out.

The police station seemed familiar; it had only been a few days since he'd been there voluntarily to make a statement. They went to a different interview room this time, unremarkable, just a place to sit, a place to talk and, judging by the blinking red light in the corner, a place to appear on police reality TV.

The Duty Solicitor was wheeled in and he asked whether Margaret Bough, who had been in with him last time, was available, she wasn't but they could wait. To Craig there was no advantage in a delay and so he allowed the new solicitor to offer a few sage comments before the interview began.

Introductions were made, for the tape, he knew the names that matched the faces and the formal interview, under caution, began. Like a chess match, the opening gambit was the only one available, did he kill Marie-Eve Legault on or about the night of Sunday 18 September?

"No".

Did he aid and abet another individual in the killing of Marie-Eve Legault on or about the night of Sunday 18 September?

"No".

The Duty Solicitor was whispering about not answering if he didn't want to, but he didn't think it was helpful or cooperative to refuse to answer like they do on TV. True, they have to defend the accused but if the accused is a scumbag, how can they advise them to make 'no comment' with such obvious glee?

Craig was happy to answer all questions. He had no part in the murder of Marie-Eve and had no real idea who might have done it. He'd answer honestly and trust British justice to do right by him; "you have to have some faith in the judicial process", he said.

He assumed that next up there would be photos on the screen or things in bags, labelled as exhibits, evidence of guilt. He resolved to go one piece at a time, give a thorough explanation if he could and ride it out, he was not guilty; there was no hard evidence to say that he was.

Item NP-LGT1002 was a key to the NPS shipping bay at the Wilford site. The only fingerprints and DNA on it were his. Explain about the key.

He told them the key was his, he was one of six key holders and that they would normally sign in electronically into Shipping with our cards, then unlock the door. That way Security would record them arriving and would monitor the out-of-hours activity in shipping via the shipping bay CCTV.

Which also didn't work, did he know this?

"Correct, it doesn't work and, yes, I am aware".

"Does anyone else have this information?" asked Thompson.

"Yes, it is public knowledge around NPS technical and of course the Security people and senior management all know about the system frailties too".

They told him that they knew why the card reader and CCTV inside Shipping and the area didn't function, which saved him trying to explain further. He felt that he had to chip in though. He had reported the faults daily by email, until he was told that the 'pending security update would cost-effectively correct the minor security issues relating to the non-functioning card reader and internal CCTV', to quote the management. It was on record with building maintenance and the emails were on the back-up server; please check.

He got a slight smirk back. "We already have", he was told. While it was true that the repeated complaints had been made by him, maybe a killer would already be preparing the ground in advance.

Maybe, but he wasn't a killer.

The photo they showed him was of a shipping cart. "Tracey had a name for each one," he said, "but they all looked the same to him".

Can he explain how his DNA and blood were found on a shipping cart believed to be the one used in the murder of Marie-Eve Legault?

Yes, he used all of the carts from time to time, including the night, or at least evening or morning of the murder. If his blood was on the cart it came from one of the cuts everybody in Shipping got from time to time, his most recent being from retractable bladed knife and, no, he wasn't being clever; he didn't kill her and so didn't know whether she'd died late the day before she was found or early on the day of discovery.

Then he was asked to go through his movements between 9 pm when Marie-Eve Legault had last been seen alive and 7:10 am when Simon Reid had discovered the body; this despite having already done this several times. Nothing had changed so he virtually recited his previous statement, word-for-word. He got no reaction from the police, no comments or a clarification were asked for.

Then they asked him about the night cleaners and their schedule. Interesting, was one of them a suspect after all? If so, why was he now under caution?

He said he'd seen them about when working late or after having been called in to receive a delivery, as had the other people on the late delivery rota. The rota changed every six-months and, obviously, when someone was on long-term sick, or had resigned or been fired.

This got their attention. A whispered conversation between the police and note made, surely they knew that there was more than one person on the call-out rota, and that if the one at the top wasn't available, they would just call the next number in sequence!

They asked him about cleaning materials and the gunk they use to mop the floor with. He said if it was the same gunk they had for cleaning spills in Shipping, then there was some in the shipping room cabinet, along with the usual cloths, mops, thick rubber gloves, not disposable but the sort used when washing dishes. This too was visibly jotted down, was that all for show to get him to open up?

They asked about the cleaners' schedule again, how did they work? He told them that he didn't really know the intricate details, although the new ones did have a habit of wedging doors open to save fiddling with their access cards. The new people were with a different contractor, presumably somebody even cheaper than the last one. He explained that before NPS took over, they'd had the same cleaners for years, they all knew them by name and they were always open to doing extra if you needed a deep clean done somewhere and that type of thing. They went in the last rif, cost-cutting. This provoked some furious scribbling. He thought that they were on the verge of asking him to repeat everything, slowly; he'd been talking very fast, deliberately, small victories and all that. Besides, it was all on the tape anyway.

They asked him about the rumours of another rif, one driven by Marie-Eve Legault. Had he heard whether his name was on it? Yes, he'd heard the rumours but that is what they all were, and why should she target him? His particular company cog was so generic that it would make no sense to ditch someone who already knew the job, in spite or anything else. Even HR wouldn't allow that.

They then wanted more details about Marie-Eve and the affair. They'd had it all before in detail and so he just repeated the whole timeline, making a point to show regret, calling it a mistake, it should never have happened.

Did he know that Marie-Eve Legault had been in the early stages of pregnancy when she died?

"Shit, no, was it mine?"

That one had hit Craig firmly between the eyes. Marie-Eve pregnant!

No answer.

He asked again, "Was it mine? You took my DNA so you know, right?"

No, they said, it wasn't his.

"Oh". No point in asking who was the father, but if it wasn't him as they said, then who? Was there another set of trousers that she'd been plundering in Nottingham?

They asked how things were at home, was the marriage happy? A fairly new baby, new mum, lots to do.

"Yes, we are happy, but we are having to deal with a new baby. I'm sure that you've checked out our finances already and can see that things are very tight on only one salary?"

"Why hasn't your wife gone back to work?"

Craig thought 'none of your fucking business, matey', but said that they had been trying for a second child and that she would probably try to find work after the second child had started nursery, hopefully at NPS.

'A plan, then?"

"Jemmy's plan," he said. "I wanted to wait a few years, get better off financially before thinking about a second child".

"Did Jemmy know about Marie-Eve?"

"No, how could she? Nobody knew apart from me. Marie-Eve said she'd told nobody either, she barely knew anyone here except at work and, as far as I know, not socially. I doubt that anything had been said to any of her friends in Montreal but I can't be sure, she never mentioned any. If you think that any of the Montreal people know anything, go and ask them".

"It's being done".

There was then a pause, so Craig asked whether they were going to charge him properly?

"We have 36 hours to formally charge you although we can ask for an extension", said Thompson. "You are cooperating, or so it seems. Because of all the circumstances, you are obviously our main suspect so you can expect to be here for the duration, your solicitor can advise you further".

And with that they finished the interview and Craig was taken to a room with no view.

The solicitor stayed in the cell for five minutes, he reckoned they had nothing but circumstantial and were just taking a punt, did he do it?

For the first time in a long time Craig wanted to hit someone and it was close to being the anonymous solicitor but he reined it in. No, he didn't do it. Then he asked whether Jemmy would be told that he'd been arrested but the solicitor told him that she already knew. The police had been in touch and she was heading back home.

"How was she when she found out that I'd been arrested?"

"No idea I'm afraid. Look, there is nothing I can do here so I'm off but you can call me or Margaret if you need us. My professional opinion is that you will spend the night stewing in the cell and then they will probably just let you go".

"And the world and his wife will now know that I am enough of a suspect to be arrested and therefore no smoke without fire, yes?"

"Again, probably yes, sorry".

Craig watched the door shut, loudly; he wondered whether they might add sound effects to make it more chilling, if he was in charge he would. Well, he'd wanted time to reflect and now he'd got it. It wasn't too bad, peaceful even, although he thought that the guilty wouldn't feel that way. He looked at his feet and drifted away with his thoughts for a while until the door opened and a tray with a cup of tea and sandwich appeared.

He apologised for not having any change to tip room service, it didn't even get a smile.

# SIXTY-TWO

The dead Marie-Eve thing had really shaken Tracey Mills, but that didn't stop her from telling everyone that she was still planning to 'get' Craig, just to cheer him up. She'd decided that she'd wind him up and get Jemmy back, even though she had her blessing. The idea had germinated at the staff Christmas party when they'd danced, close, and she'd seen the look on Jemmy's face. She didn't need to go after Craig; she already had a nice boyfriend, Chris, a relief after Gary: there'd be no need to get a restraining order with this one. She even thought that Chris might be 'the one'. She always said she'd know him when he showed up, and Chris was the first real contender.

Craig was alright and interesting enough to be different. He was just a little project and having him dancing along would slap Jemmy on her pretty little face, nicely. Tracey bore a grudge for a long time and she bore it with venom, while smiling.

To get to the root of the issue you had to go back to pre-NPS and pre-baby, when Jemmy was a Lab Analyst and Tracey was in the same position as now, second-in-command in Shipping. At the time, lab work was slow and so lab staff were deployed to other departments. In part, they were used simply as an extra pair of hands, there to help out, but also as an in-work learning event. The management thought that the processes each department used could be improved by better understanding of the system. In reality, this only applied to the supposed higher-ups roughing it with the equally supposed lower-downs. Nobody in their right mind would let the likes of Tracey Mills loose in a lab!

Jemmy had been assigned to shipping and they had a large shipment in to verify, this was before Sample Management had become a sole-purpose department and took over the role. The study was clinical and

337

typically messy; the checks had to be done with care, matching a manifest against a bar code on the sample, easy enough. At first Jemmy kept on wanting to change the way they did things but Tracey had insisted that she follow the Standard Operating Procedure, as they all had to. When the samples had all been done Jemmy had said loudly, but mostly to Tracey who seemed to have found a way to get under her skin without trying, "well that was easy. Isn't it interesting that we analysts can come here and do your job for you so easily but you people", yes, she said 'you people', "could never do ours. That is why we are more valued by the company".

Tracey was livid, there was no need for insults but with Craig and Jemmy now being a pair there was nobody to go to, to complain. Craig tried to be conciliatory, but Jemmy was dismissive of him too, calling him a jumped-up clerk. It must have been fun at home that night but, knowing Craig, he'd let her walk all over him. From that point on she had decided to wind Craig up through flirting, simply because she believed she could, her real target was Jemmy, though. She might have been a mate but sometimes you had to stand your ground, even with a mate.

Her work dress had always been practical, but she started going for something a little more provocative, she took on the persona of a femme fatale and quite enjoyed it. She'd confided her intentions to the young girls in Shipping, mostly students working part-time, and they had thought it a scream and insisted on getting all the details. There was no thought for Craig though, they reckoned he deserved it for not backing Tracey up, even the seventeen year-olds knew how wet he was.

Over the course of a few weeks after the snub from Jemmy, Tracey had made it quite clear to Craig that she was his for the taking. Craig, to be fair, did have a bit more backbone than it appeared and managed to keep his distance. Tracey was starting to get bored with it after a while and, besides, Chris, her new and exclusive boyfriend, was beginning to mean a lot to her, so she decided to drop it. Then they had a team picture taken for the company magazine.

They had to do it three times because Tracey had draped herself all over Craig, making it look like they were intimate. She'd laughed it off after, but one of the girls had got copies and sent them around the department, including one to Craig. He deleted it after he'd got it, but threatened Tracey with a disciplinary if she didn't behave. Tracey was pissed off because she hadn't sent the photo, but promised to behave from then on and she had recently been as good as her word.

She later found out that Mo had been shown the photos; one of her girlies was in Shipping and it had been she who'd encouraged them to send the photo out. Tracey thought about going to Craig and telling him, but Mo was known to have contacts within the company - how else would she have survived so long? Besides, she'd been a big mate of Jemmy's at one time, so perhaps she should tell Jemmy it was her big mate who was stirring it up. This made more sense than Craig getting caught out, so she texted Jemmy with the picture and said it was only larking about and she was sorry if she'd upset her. At least that way she was being nice and getting her own back, even if only a little bit.

Out of the blue, Jemmy texted Tracey asking whether they could meet. Tracey was a bit flustered by it, she hadn't gone too far overboard with the Craig thing, the photo was the nearest they got to anything physical, but she knew how she'd feel if it was Jemmy with Chris and she really didn't want a cat fight, well not in public.

They arranged to meet in the café at Nottingham train station, very 'Brief Encounter'.

Tracey was early, picking up the special birthday cake had taken less time than she'd expected and she was half way through her second latte when Jemmy arrived. She greeted Tracey like a dear friend, hugs and kisses and the smell of baby wipes. Tracey was uncomfortable and, once Jemmy was sat with her own coffee concoction, had started to apologise again but Jemmy waved it away. "I knew you were pissing around and it was because I was an arse that time in Shipping. I owe you an apology, besides; you are really not Craig's type".

Tracey wasn't sure whether to be insulted by the last bit. She was tempted to throw down a challenge, 'knickers off' the winner takes all, but thought better of it because, obviously, Jemmy had already won that particular argument, resulting in Small. In the course of the conversation Jemmy started asking questions about the dead girl, Marie-Eve. Of course, Jemmy would have known that there had been an attractive and powerful new girl around NPS but had she felt threatened by her?

Tracey said that she knew that there was a rumour that Craig had been up to something with Legault.

Jemmy was, at first, rattled by the news, tearful, then she was looking for the inside scoop on her husband's infidelity, believing that Tracey, who worked so closely with Craig, would be the person to supply full details.

Tracey denied knowing much more than the rumour, so Jemmy started talking about trysts in a caravan. Tracey said she had no idea about a caravan at Calverton. No, Craig was just Craig, he was the sort of good-looking bloke that would generate rumours amongst the girls; maybe it was just that, a rumour?

Jemmy seemed to accept this, even though Tracey hadn't been very explicit, when she perhaps could have been. This wasn't teasing anymore. There was a silence while both women sipped their coffee, then Tracey asked "did he kill Marie-Eve?" It was a thought that she'd been struggling to shift.

Jemmy laughed, "Craig? No, I'm sure of that but he might know who did, there were some strange things going on at NPS recently". Craig had spoken about them one night but Jemmy had been occupied with

Small and the new bathroom design. Jemmy told Tracey that she was genuinely worried that Marie-Eve might have been killed for some work-related thing and that Craig might be next.

Tracey felt out of her depth. Murder and intrigue were stuff of the TV, not sample shippers at NPS. Somebody killed Marie-Eve for some reason that we might never know. She wasn't popular, ruthless even, but she had clearly liked Craig.

Over Jemmy's shoulder Tracey saw a face that surprised her and shrunk back in the chair, had she been seen? Jemmy noticed the change and asked "what's wrong?", but Tracey just pointed to the cake and said "surprise party later and I've just seen the birthday boy. He mustn't see me or the cake". When Tracey looked back, he was walking out of the station, as if going downtown.

"Shit", said Tracey, "look at the time. I've got to dash. Look, I'm really sorry about the tease, I'll keep an eye on Craig and report back and when they get the killer, and soon, we can all get back to our lives. Did Craig tell you about Chris, my new man? I think he might be the one", and then she was gone, heading for the platform and home.

The train was coming, it was lurching around the bend and soon they'd all be crammed onto it. The usual jostling for position was now taking place, it was only a Sprinter going to Radcliffe-on-Trent and the seating was limited, certainly not enough for this time of day. It was always the same, the train would stop, the doors open and those that wanted to get off would have to fight the tide of sweaty commuters flooding on.

Tracey wasn't really thinking of much at all. She had the hand-made birthday cake in a box being carefully held the right way up and she was determined that she was going to get a seat. It would have been tricky to hold on for balance and to keep the cake from damage if she couldn't sit and there was no guarantee that there would be a kind gentleman offering a damsel-in-distress his seat, no matter how much leg she showed.

The crush seemed a bit heavier than usual this afternoon; perhaps one of the earlier trains had been cancelled. It happened on these rural lines all the time, you got used to being treated like cattle. The train had started to brake noisily and the people around her were like sprinters in blocks. The train was then perhaps only thirty feet away when Tracey suddenly lurched forwards, stumbling while trying to keep hold of the cake. Then she fell onto the rail. There was no time for the train to stop.

There was panic on the platform. Some were being sick, some just sat down where they previously stood, a few looked at their watches and muttered, a dead woman was going to spoil their evening, now, they'd probably have to try to get the bus home or something. A few others just stood with their mobile phones out, videoing the whole thing, planning their YouTube party for later. You couldn't see the body, they all presumed she was dead, but the railway staff running around like headless chickens was quite funny, that would get the video lots of hits.

The British Transport Police were there very quickly and tried to contain the scene. They ushered the passengers to one side to give them air. A relief driver had to back the train up, they hoped that she might have gone under the train and got between the tracks. It was possible; they'd seen it happen before.

Once the train had backed up it was clear that it needed police involvement. The train had done its damage, but the most poignant thing from the scene was the cake by the rail. Through the clear cellophane of the box top it was strangely undamaged, with a cheery 'Happy Birthday' looking as if it had only just been iced on.

The problem of shutting down the station and keeping everybody there as witnesses was too big and many simply left or headed to another platform, seeking anonymity. When the police did get there, only 30 or so passengers remained and the statement process began.

Back in the café, Jemmy had brooded over her coffee for a few minutes but she too had to get back once she'd done her little chore. The neighbour was looking after Small, but she didn't really like leaving her baby with anyone; this was the time of bonding and she'd read that the more time they were able to spend together, the closer they would become.

A short while later, as she walked back from the record store to the car park, the sound of sirens began to fill the air, police and ambulance. She walked briskly along, dodging the oncoming pedestrian traffic, trying, like quite a few other people, to beat any rush. Whatever the din was all about, she didn't want to hang around and find out, nor did she want to get held up by it. Craig would be expecting his dinner when he got home and she was trying a new vegan recipe tonight, just in case she became vegan.

It was a bit later in the afternoon when Thompson got the call from Superintendent Perkins. Tracey Mills had died under a train in potentially suspicious circumstances. Thompson already knew from the radio coverage on the late local news that there had been an incident; he didn't know who had been involved though. She was an NPS employee in the Shipping Department, a suspect in the Marie-Eve Legault case, and so Tracey Mills was his now, too.

Perkins had indicated that this might just be a coincidental death, although detail was sketchy. It also might be linked to the Marie-Eve Legault case, look into it and see, he added "don't worry about Charnley, I'll deal with him". Thompson pinged out a text to the team. If they had already gone a-wandering then they'd have a heads-up, if not, they might call for more details, but he didn't have any for now.

Tracey Mills, he tried to remember her. The only thing that came to mind was a slightly flirty, slightly Mother Hen sort. He'd put Prosser onto taking her statement when the Fish Finger had been found, it was a deliberate choice; she wasn't going to side-track him. He could have used Banks or Knight but suspected that she'd be more responsive to a

343

man and he had just the man who definitely wouldn't be responsive to her.

# SIXTY-THREE

## Monday 19 September

Although quite burly, Bez Dooley, the technical staff manager at NPS had never been known to throw his considerable weight around. He'd never even been known to raise his voice, even when faced with a ranting scientist, a ranting technician or his ranting wife, Wendy. To be fair, she didn't rant too much but, because she had been the shop steward when it was Blue Sky, sometimes she had to be forceful with management like Bez when protecting her members. That had changed quite radically when NPS bought the business and the union had slunk out the door like a scalded cat.

Some people wondered whether it was healthy for them to lunch together, work together and then expect their relationship to contain those nuggets of surprise that come from living in another life stream, if only for the working day. Bez just got on with it. Wendy was very likeable unless she had her dander up, they seemed very well suited.

Dead Marie-Eve was the only topic of conversation around their usual table. The mixture of techs, analysts, Bez and a couple of scientists were thought of as the 'lunch club'. Always the same faces, always the same table. Most of the time the topic would be a soap, the football or who in one of their departments was up to something naughty, very rarely politics, never religion. They did like tittle-tattle though, dead Marie-Eve had monopolised the recent conversational theme, and of course they all had their own thoughts on 'who done it'.

Unlike the police, the lunch club were not bound by the facts and so were free to speculate wildly. Whether it was spite or wishful thinking, the chief suspect they all agreed on was Richard Greenwood, and the rude affectation 'Dick' that they always used when referring to him, made them titter without fail.

345

The consensus was that dead Marie-Eve was banging Greenwood, surely not the other way around because Greenwood couldn't bang a front door on his own. Word was that she'd dumped him for someone else, another someone, her third or maybe fourth in the short time she'd been in Nottingham, although Bez took this with a pinch of salt, as one who would know better than to accept gossip at face value should. Greenwood had taken the dumping very badly, it was said; he'd been head-over-heels for Legault and just couldn't let it go, so that was that, he was guilty of all charges.

In reaching the verdict, at least three of the group had had Mo as their reliable source for details of the affair but, like top scoop journalists, nobody would ever betray their source. And once again Mo's fantasy world tended to find traction on many subjects where, all too often, there should have been none.

Bez tended to sit out these discussions but his wife loved to dig deeper. That suited him because a good manager has a finger on so many pulses, preferably without the owners of said pulse realising it. Whose finger he used for the job didn't really matter, just as long as vital and sometimes important information got fed back to him. Oddly enough, nobody had figured this out, he was just Bez, good old Bez, but Bez was ambitious. Quiet and undemonstrative it was true, but effective and fiercely ambitious.

Lunch broke up with 'Dick' well and truly sitting in the electric chair waiting for someone to wet the sponge and throw the switch; they just had to draw lots for who got to pull it.

After lunch, Bez sat in his office, the door closed and his thinking cap on. So Marie-Eve was dead, how did he feel about that? Nobody had made any connections to him, even though they'd seen her breeze into his office and almost dismiss him with that familiar derisory wave of her hand several times. At first it was just irritating to be so undermined, later the inner Bez had reached out, his strong hands closing around her neck, thumbs on her windpipe, and he'd squeezed and kept squeezing. The outer, more public Bez had been patient, unruffled, a sea of tranquility when a retaliatory typhoon might have been more in order.

So far the police had not been to see him, they surely would. How deep would they look, would he be a suspect or just need to be eliminated from the investigation? There had certainly been enough witnesses to Marie-Eve's behaviour towards him to give them a reason to at least ask the right questions. He was confident that nobody would bad-mouth him, they all knew him, mild-mannered Bez, so they would never suspect him, nor suggest anything to the police. Not Bez, no, never.

The was a noise on the door, not a knock as such, more the sort of tap you do when you go to a close friend's house and let yourself in but announce your arrival with a brief tap, just in case they were up to something interesting. It was Wendy clutching her little travel lap-top. "Well Bez, dead Marie-Eve, it looks pretty bad for those who found themselves the wrong side of her, belittled by her, did you off her?"

Bez smiled, he knew she was messing around, chucking in some gangsta-type dialogue, there was no true question in her voice. Wendy knew people, she could tell what they were like and she reckoned she'd know a killer if she met one and Bez didn't fit the bill.

"I suppose you have been making notes for your next little piece on Linked-In?"

Now it was Wendy's turn to smile. "You know me, Bez, I always like a good story and the dead woman has given me an idea. I'll wait until the killer gets banged up though, I don't want to get put in the firing line, even if I do use a pseudonym that I'm sure only you know about".

Bez swivelled his monitor her direction and showed her the rant about 'The Captain' from Greenwood, and the selected text he particularly objected to.

"Heavily edited, I see", she said. "Almost like it was too close to the truth".

"A good manager lets their people manage. They share the credit, play by the rules and look after their people. This lot", and Bez pointed to the company logo, "are only interested in money. True, they flap their arms around in indignation when they read stuff like 'The Captain' but, at the end of the day, all they want is the money. It helps to know what you work for. A job is a necessity, how you discharge your duties to the company employing you is up to you".

"Well said, that man" said Wendy. "Can I quote you for the forthcoming tale of the virtual healer?"

"Chapter and verse, if you like".

"You know that the police will be along to talk to you later. I'll let you know if I see them, I can see all from my little pigeon hole". Later the same day, Bez got the call and knew that the police were heading his way, he readied to greet them.

His office door was open as always and the two officers entered. "Detective Constables Prosser and Knight, am I right?"

"Bez Dooley?" the Irishman said. "Have you been expecting us?"

"Of course, I expect to be a person of interest as I had access and an apparent motive in the form of a dislike for Marie-Eve Legault, so of course you are here".

"Did you have enough of a dislike to kill her, slowly?" asked Prosser.

"No officer, I didn't particularly like her, she didn't want to be liked, as far as I could see. She was here on a mission, which I think was self-advancement. I found her indifferent to me, we met a few times to discuss how to work the NPS way, something I believe my people already do, and we attended a few meetings. Not together, but as two individuals".

"There is talk of an impending reduction in force that she was to be responsible for; did you know anything about it?"

"She wanted rid of Simon Reid in Sample Management but I don't, and I think that I persuaded her to change her mind. She wasn't aware of his technical qualities, not many are, but I am and he is to be the LIMS Administrator for NPS in Nottingham in due course. Incidentally, he doesn't know about that, it hasn't actually been approved, yet".

"Did Reid know he was on a rif list?"

"Yes, I told him and I also told him not to worry, we have a good working relationship".

"What about Craig Shepherd, do you have a good relationship there, was he on the list?"

"Yes he was, I don't know why, but it was possibly personal. I don't much like Craig Shepherd and recently he has become distracted, making mistakes and making me like him even less. I am the manager and mistakes stop at my door".

"Were you on the rif list?"

"That I can't answer and I doubt that anyone here could, although it will be in her personal files I expect. To remove me she'd have to advance a good, written case. I suspect HR would have tipped me off if I had been a rif candidate but there is also the possibility that a removal at my level would need to be approved by a higher authority".

'Richard Greenwood?"

"I doubt that Dick would be in the loop, you may need to ask Head Office in New Jersey. However, I don't think she looked at me too much and I don't think she had me down as a rif candidate, but that's just a hunch".

"Do you know anything about the whereabouts of her laptop?"

"No, sorry, can't help you there. I presume it's missing then?" Bez continued without a pause. "In anticipation of your visit, I thought to write out my schedule for the relevant period. You can see that I was not here late on the evening of Marie-Eve's demise, it was, after all, a Sunday. There is also a list of people, with details, who can verify my whereabouts for the times given".

"Very organised, premeditated even".

"Organised is what I do for a living, premeditated is something else entirely".

Prosser went through a few more details, mostly duties and whether Bez felt emasculated by his boss being a woman? "She wasn't my boss, we were of equal stature within the company. However, she had a certain arrogance that made her feel that she was superior to everyone, I saw that early and dismissed it as irrelevant. I felt that, in Nottingham at least, she was somewhat ephemeral. I was right as it turned out although I had expected her to leave the normal way and not feet first."

Knight had been quiet but something had been bothering her. "You seem untroubled by her death, serene even, like you don't care".

"That is because I don't. My capacity for caring is limited to friends and loved ones; anything else that people claim is just playing an emotional game, such as when Princess Di died. I didn't find it troubling at all, why would I, we had no connection. I save my emotions for those important to me. Is that cold?"

Prosser answered quickly "No Mr. Dooley, to me that makes perfect sense".

Elkie was a bit taken aback, she thought she knew people and here were two men who were able to compartmentalise compassion, she couldn't. She'd have cried all night if she'd been around when Princess Diana had died. She welled up just thinking about it, it was probably the whole fairy-tale Princess thing.

"One last thing" said Prosser. "Bez, what is it short for?"

"Steven".

"OK, well thanks, Mr. Dooley, if we need anything else we'll get in touch".

Well, that went well, thought Bez.

# SIXTY-FOUR

## Wednesday 14 September

It wasn't unusual for Mo to spend upwards of an hour a day on her work phone, just chatting. It annoyed the rest of the Sample Management team, well those who paid attention, because she didn't pull her weight at the best of times. It annoyed the hell out of Reid too, because he'd tried to do something about it with Bez Dooley and was effectively told to leave it. While he could do nothing about her through official channels, there was nothing to stop him pouring oil on the situation locally at every opportunity.

In an attempt to make a case, Reid had even downloaded her call log, just to see whether there was anything even the untouchable Mo couldn't shrug off, but they were all either in-house and to other staff, mostly her 'girls', to Neil Martin in Security or to three outside numbers, two unknown. One was familiar though; it was Craig Shepherd's number. Instantly ruling out Craig and Mo in any sort of amorous relationship, it seemed likely that Jemmy was still one of Mo's girls, despite having left to have the baby many months previously.

The Saviour study was now rolling in unabated and the team had all become involved; well, all except Mo, who'd freaked out the first time she was asked to sort out her share of the patient list and freaking out just wouldn't work with this study, it needed clear heads. So Reid had picked five of the most competent in the team and they'd been working almost exclusively on the study since it got transferred from Canada. It must be getting boring, not just the same study all the time but the daily challenge of getting it right. Thankfully, they now had a system that was fairly watertight. If there were going to be problems ahead on this study, and there certainly would be, then the Sample Management aspect of it would not be a contributory factor.

Mo was yacking down the phone again. Reid could see her work station from his; he rarely used the office, preferring to be 'visible and available' as he called it. She wasn't her usual faux-hip self though. Whoever she was talking to, it wasn't a casual conversation. Mo was frowning and, because she couldn't help it, being very expressive with her arms. The call ended with a loud 'no', the pause in sound in the room was brief but there, something was not making Mo happy, not that Reid cared. He'd long ago thought it best that Mo should be happy, or sad, somewhere else.

When he looked back over, Mo had gone, another toilet break, she had upwards of ten a day but Reid didn't say anything about that. You can't have a go at someone for a weak bladder.

From the way the Sample Management room was buzzing, you would not have thought that Marie-Eve Legault had been in earlier, threatening to fire the lot of them if they didn't get their collective fingers out on the Saviour study. It had been a typical piece of anti-motivation and the casual observer might even think it calculated to annoy, rather than encourage people.

Marie-Eve's uncalled for rant, which to be fair went over the heads of most of the group and was, he suspected, aimed mainly at him anyway, was filed under 'other reasons to dislike her' and he got back to his PC. True, nobody had really got to know Marie-Eve after her arrival in Nottingham, although not through want of trying. She'd been invited to Sample Management group meals for birthdays and had declined, in fact the cheesy group ritual of buying a cake for one of the team's birthdays, and taking a five minute break to eat it together, hadn't found favour either. She'd been positively annoyed by it, refusing the invite with a snarky "so that's how you spend work time is it, how many staff, times five minutes have we lost, you do the math!" Way to make friends and influence people again, Madam.

It had become fairly clear to Reid that Marie-Eve Legault had an agenda of some sort in Nottingham. Reid knew about her rumoured

Montreal Cabal but in England it had to be different, there was something else going on here that made her distant, frosty even. Once he'd seen how she intended to behave, he'd decided to ignore her as best he could. He'd ride whatever storm she brought with her and just get on with the job in-hand. She would be returning to Montreal in due course anyway and their paths would be unlikely to cross again.

The room may have been busy, but most of the staff in there just functioned rather than thought about the job and, while some of them often exasperated him with their lack of understanding of the basic science of what they did, in many ways he was quite proud of his team. They might not always understand the nuances of drug research but they got the job done and a couple of them always stuck their hands up when asked to do impromptu overtime, not that Bez was ever happy to sign the sheets. Every time anyone did overtime there was a Spanish Inquisition, and for that reason Reid rarely bothered to log it if he'd only done an hour or so extra. It might not have been noticed, more like it was expected, but not claiming it meant he spent less time in Bez's office, and to be frank, Bez was a bit of a pedant at times. Reid supposed he had to be, in that job.

The end of day ritual for Reid was to go into Clousseau and check that everything was hunky-dory. It didn't take too long normally, not now that the system was better understood, by him at least, and it was only a few clicks to see who'd cocked up electronically. Mostly the team 'fessed up when they had a mishap, he'd drummed it into them how easy it was for him fix things when they did their Clousseau training and, unless someone had been exceptionally dumb, or just had an awful day, things generally ran smoothly.

The Saviour study was now the most time-consuming check and Reid was part-way through the latest batch when he noticed that a patient that had been retired, that is, had previously withdrawn from the study, had then reappeared in the sample listing. Thinking that it was nothing more than an admin error, he checked the hard-copy delivery sheets against the physical sample. No, there it was on the delivery sheet, patient 007 from Tashkent was very much alive and well, and back in the game.

Pulling the box of frozen samples from the freezer, he skipped through the 81 spaces to where he knew the new set of samples for the patient began. Something was wrong. The labels were different and had been overlaid on the original set at the Mexico City clearing house. The new labels gave nil chance of getting a look at what was underneath.

In Clousseau, Reid deactivated the samples and scribbled a post-it, sticking it to his monitor for the next day. The most likely thing was that the clinical collection site had used the wrong patient's tubes and forgotten to do a correction, easy enough to fix, just annoying. He had some more bits and pieces to do in Clousseau but would soon be on his way home, it had been another long day at the ice face.

Marie-Eve peered at the computer screen, wading through the numbers. Even the dumb management in Nottingham could see that most of their Sample Management and a fair proportion of the analytical staff were spending most of their time on the Saviour study – at least on their electronic timesheets they were - leaving little else to charge against. This could cause premature problems for her and Saviour and would have to be addressed. As would a couple of little technical problems she'd recently decided to create.

She realised that she was probably seeing Gremlins where none existed but there was no time like the present. She had doubted that anyone would be around at 7:30 in the evening and so was a bit surprised to see Reid still at his PC. "Milking it for everything you can, Reid?" she said, using a deliberately accusatory tone as she looked over his shoulder at his PC screen.

Reid ignored her at first, clearly into something he didn't want to be distracted from. She bridled and was about to call him out for insubordination in ignoring her, when he looked up, smiled and

355

apologised, explaining that he was engaged in a sequence of operations that he couldn't leave, and asking if he could help.

He always did this, was always nice and unruffled, no matter how spiky her barbs were. She liked him for it, in a way. He was one of the few men she'd met in the business who'd stood up to her when she'd had to discipline him in Montreal. Still, she had a role to fulfil and warming to someone so junior wasn't a part of that role.

"Simon, I've been going through the departmental time sheets, another of those time-consuming little jobs I've been given to make sure that you are all on the straight and narrow. Your department seems to be very study-centric in terms of where the staff working time is being placed, that study being the Saviour project".

"Well, it is a huge study and it is very time-consuming for us, Marie-Eve. Whilst some of my staff may have booked much of their working week to it, I've kept a close eye on them and find that it is entirely justified. You will have also noted that no overtime has been claimed against the Saviour study by my staff, nor by me, although here I sit with my head in that very same study, way past my knocking-off time".

"As the uncelebrated head of your little department I would expect that from you, Simon. The company does not reward for nine-to-five but for dedication to the cause and a willingness to go the extra mile, to quote Mr. Duggan".

Reid laughed, "if the unpaid extra miles I do were to be converted to Air Miles, I'd have enough for a return trip to Honolulu by now. As it is, I can barely stand the price of an off-peak return to Derby".

"Humour again, Simon, I remember the fun we had with that ridiculous verbal-written warning. Did I ever apologise for that? Probably not, I don't generally. You no doubt realised at the time that Ria Sullamane was behind it and that her boyfriend, who just happened to be Head of the facility, always backed her up. My hands were pretty much tied and, while some might enjoy sort of thing, I did not".

356

"I see our ironic humour is even affecting you. Are we going to get around to the purpose of your visit, presumably you'd like a little less time booking to the Saviour study, spread the load as it were?"

"Simon, I'm not asking you to do anything underhand, I would just be happy to know that you are making sure that your people are correct with their timesheet entries and not slipping in an hour here and there on to the Saviour study where they think it won't be found because, as I said, I've been looking and it certainly will. Do we understand each other?"

"Certainly, I'll be making sure that my people account for their weekly toil correctly at all times. We strive for honesty and greatness, as they say, in this department at least".

Marie-Eve failed to pick up the mockery of the glorious leader, nodded and went to leave, pausing only to casually ask Reid whether he was aware how fast things could change at NPS. Also, did he report everything to Bez Dooley? Reid said he understand that NPS had a fluid policy towards employment and promotion, and that he had a good working relationship with his manager, Bez, and hoped he would continue to have, what he considered to be a good working relationship with her. He sounded like a politician!

Changing tack, she suddenly changed her demeanour. "Simon, are you ogling my breasts? That would be so politically incorrect you know, tantamount to sexual harassment and you know we don't stand for that at NPS".

Reid didn't flinch, "no, Marie-Eve, I'm actually admiring your pendant, I don't remember seeing you wear it before. I'd say that your breasts were incidental but that could be taken the wrong way, so I'll stick with the pendant. Is it new?"

Another change saw Marie-Eve dismiss the pendant as a mere trinket, just something a friend had given her, then she smiled and put on a faux French accent. "Oh meester reeed, you are confusing mee wiiith your cleveur Eenglish, I am jurst a siiimpul French gurl, tell me, what is incidental to my breasts, nothing I assure you". Reid laughed politely, Marie-Eve laughed too but the moment was brief and she was soon back to being the Ice Queen, pretty pendant or not.

As she left he got an 'I'll be watching' over her shoulder. Me too, thought Reid.

Once he was sure that she'd gone, she had a habit of suddenly appearing silently and he was sure that she kept a pair of flat shoes in her office just for that purpose, he tapped a little aide-memoir into his phone; time and date and a rough outline of the conversation. Pity he hadn't had the thing recording, but the underlying message was clear, she wanted him to lay off the Saviour study, time-wise, so as to not draw too much attention to it. He'd have to tell Bez tomorrow, for now though he'd better get out of there before she came back and dealt him a few more barely subtle innuendos. What the fuck was that all about?

The following day, Reid tried to pick up where he'd left off. The reason he left himself notes was because he was usually able to clear his mind of work irritations once home, putting them on hold by completely forgetting the minor details until he was back at work. The Saviour retired patient had kept popping into his thoughts though, and he would never settle until he'd ironed out what was the latest in a long line of issues for that study.

The trouble was, he couldn't remember the specific sample issue. His note containing barely legible scribble must have been cleaned up by over-zealous night cleaners; maybe it had become detached from the PC and ended up on the floor, understandable. The only thing for it was for him to retrace his steps through Clousseau until he got a hit. It took a disturbed hour, but he found it - patient 007, so it was 'fingers in dry-ice time' for a while now, at least until he got to the bottom of it.

The first issue was that the freezer didn't hold the sample box, or at least it wasn't where he'd left it the evening before and where the inventory told him it should be. This happened from time to time, as some staff, especially the part-time people or seconded helpers, had a habit of putting boxes on different shelves when searching for their samples, so he'd have to clear each shelf in order and repopulate as per the inventory. He did, and there was no box.

He went back to the PC and checked the Clousseau sample pull lists, the samples for patient 007 hadn't been requested and transferred to the lab. He went back to the freezer and went section by section again, still not finding his patient 007 box. This was getting weirder by the minute.

Somebody was playing clearly silly buggers, so he set to doing a few random checks, especially featuring the Tashkent facility. By sheer fluke, the boxes had been double-numbered, he found three more anomalous sets of older samples where the patients had left the study and then miraculously returned. Next he went back through the sample information sheets that had come from the facility, using the copies he made when he was in Montreal. The patients were marked with a cross symbol, the patients were dead.

Digging deeper and it was clear that Tashkent was an interesting place. In total he found a further twelve patients from there who had either died or, according to a collection sheet footnote, had left the study sick enough not to be allowed to return. Right, he thought, first things first, who has been sneaking into our freezers and what have they done with the missing samples?

In the Security station one of the newer guys was sitting at the monitors. "Jeff, I need a bit of information, can you tell me who logged into the Freezer Room between 18:00 yesterday and 07:00 today, please?" Jeff pulled up the details easily, without asking the sort of questions Neil Martin might have. "Could you print it for me, please?"

Next it was into Clousseau as an Administrator. A few clicks and he had the logon details for the previous day. It didn't take long to see who had been playing at 'Bull in a China Shop'. Armed with his tracking records and a set of suspicions, he made for Bez Dooley's office. Bez was in, he said, unless it was to moan about Mo again. Reid sat and took a deep breath, this was going to sound like sour grapes. Bez knew of Reid's antipathy towards Legault, he very much had the same feeling. "Problem?" he said.

"I think that Marie-Eve has been tampering with samples, sample labels and has been going into Clousseau to alter information".

"Go on".

"I've uncovered some serious discrepancies involving some patients returning to the study, sometimes after shuffling off the mortal coil. Well, according to the study paperwork they did".

"Simon, just to be sure that I understand, I suggest you go through this, item by item, and show me your evidence. I'm presuming that is the file that you are clutching to your chest?"

"Sorry, Bez, I'm just a bit taken aback by this". Reid went through each of his suspicions and confirmed each round with the relevant printout. The case looked worth following up. If what was indicated was true, Legault was deliberately tampering with samples, altering sample information and changing the Clousseau data for reasons unknown, but probably not good. She was presumably also the person responsible for the missing samples, he'd have to check the incinerator card log, just in case. What Reid was suggesting was very serious falsification.

Bez seemed to grasp the seriousness of the situation. "Do you think she might be doing this under orders? Perhaps it was why she was sent here in the first place, after all. I'm sure you thought it odd that, after Dominique Yip had been with us, they then felt the need to send someone else along to do the almost exactly the same thing".

Reid shook his head, "I don't think NPS management would sanction this, they might be shoddy at times but falsification is the worst thing you can do in contract research, and that is what this is". Reid went on to tell Dooley a few of the things that he'd heard about in Montreal, things that didn't feature in his debriefing report.

"I'll have to go higher", said Dooley.

Reid nodded, "actually, Bez, if you are talking about involving Greenwood then you'll be going lower, in more than one sense". Was Dooley going to appreciate the joke?

"Simon Reid, I didn't think you'd stoop so low as to resort to sarcasm!" he said with a grin.

Dooley asked for photocopies of everything, the issue's timeline in simplified form and a written list of the 70 affected patients so far detected. He'd need to go through it himself first, on paper at least, he didn't understand Clousseau as well as he'd like. Then he'd talk to someone, not Greenwood though, but someone at Head Office, in New Jersey.

# SIXTY-FIVE

## Friday 09 September

The car pulled up around seven in the morning, black, nothing very fancy, nothing very cheap though either. Ben went to get in the passenger seat but the muscle driving the car waved him into the back, where more muscle sat quietly. Ben nodded to them as he entered, neither muscle acknowledged him. So, it was like that.

The car drove into town on the decaying highway before turning off, taking a back route of unremarkable streets before climbing the hill towards Summit Park. As they rose higher, the city of Montreal spread away in all directions, dominated by Mont Royal, as always. The house was insignificant, neither grand nor shabby, and the car drove straight into the garage. Unusually for Canadians, the garage was completely empty. Whoever lived here, permanently or more likely temporarily, really didn't get the genre.

Once the automatic door had closed, Ben was let out, noting that the child locks had been previously employed, perhaps for his own safety. He was led, and followed, through a short passageway and into a kitchen. Coffee was on the go, it smelt like toast had been previously enjoyed there, too.

A little further on and the room opened up with vaulted ceilings, beams, lots of wood. He was directed to a comfortable couch; on a small table was a folder. He was asked whether he wanted a drink and accepted coffee, one part of the muscle left to get it, the other muscle stood by, silently.

The coffee arrived on a small tray, carrying it was a wiry man with a trim goatee. Ben knew the face only vaguely, but knew the name well, the face belonged to Richard Pointer.

Ben made to rise, but Pointer motioned him to remain seated and raised a hand to the muscle who was already bristling, as if he were a guard dog ready to defend his master, which in many ways was exactly what he was. Ben waited for the conversation to begin. What little he knew of Pointer suggested that that was the correct protocol. He wasn't exactly nervous, Carrie had been in the house and making a video of the car as he left, hopefully getting something of the driver at least, and he still had his cell switched on, so he could be tracked. Perhaps his imagination had taken over his senses but, well 'belts and braces' where some people were involved. At least they might find his body.

Pointer smiled and the pleasantries began. He was actually quite warm, little jokes were interspersed into the casual conversation but the expected main topic, the only real topic pending, was Ben's compound and the opportunity for investment in thereof, although his was not broached immediately. Ben knew it would be, soon though, but was this particular fish the species he really wanted to hook? It was like catching a shark when you were only aiming for a few greedy bottom feeders.

A laptop appeared and on it were some files that Ben recognised, because they were his own. Various pages came up, projections, percentages, time periods, the operation, everything that Ben had placed where it could be found, if you had the knowhow and someone on the inside. Ben mocked a little surprise. Too much might have been overdoing it, he was in the water with the shark now and he had no intention of becoming the bait. He was the one doing the fishing and, when the shark was all played out, he was the one that would walk away.

Another man appeared, professional, a money man. He tapped keys and went through more of the file. Looking directly at Ben he started firing questions. "How many investors were there, including the ones not included in the files?" So they knew that much. "What was the timescale for the project to the next phase, were the predictions correct?" Check that one, too. The end question was the one Ben had been waiting for; how it would be put was the most important question he'd face, perhaps even the last.

"Ballpark, to market, what was the projection for the sale?"

Now Ben was nervous but he didn't show it, instead he smiled a little, not a giveaway grin but what he hoped was an understanding smile, a smile of comprehension. He launched into his 'volatility of the industry' speech. The lack of certainty was stressed. The success ratio laid bare, no embellishment because both the men opposite would know and the outcome might not be favourable for him. He told it like it was; all except the last bit, only he and Carrie knew what the last bit would be. Marie-Eve knew some but only what he'd needed to tell her to get this far.

The two men rose and Ben went to rise as well but the nearest muscle moved forward and he saw that rising was not an option. Pointer smiled and waved the muscle back, but Ben stayed put. "Please wait there, Ben, I just need to talk in private with my colleague. I'll return momentarily, meanwhile if you need more coffee or would like something to eat just ask" and they were gone. Ben looked at the muscle and asked for more coffee, cookies would be nice too. One went and fetched the order, the other stood silently, imposing his menace on the room without trying too hard.

Ben had just inserted a rather nice piece of Scottish shortbread into his mouth when Pointer returned and started speaking. Coughing slightly as he forced down the crumbs and taking a quick slurp of the coffee to smooth the operation, Ben apologised and they got down to the detail. How to play this?

Ben took the position of being flattered by Pointer's interest and intrigued as to how his project information had been obtained, but Pointer waved away the latter point as being unimportant. He wanted numbers and he wanted to know how the whole thing would pan out, going forward.

Pointer wanted to invest in the next stage. He knew that Ben was moving in that direction, he had information from the ongoing research that even Ben hadn't got yet. He wanted to be a major investor; anonymously of course, if his interest became known, it would upset the pharmaceutical applecart. He wanted to be in for 60%, did that work for Ben? Ben did the math mentally, no need for exact figures when that sort of money was being talked about and it would mean that the others currently investing would have to come up with substantially less for the next, and last, phase, if it happened. Or, he could just take the lot and run.

He continued his delivery with his poker face and then left a pause to give himself a bit of thinking time. He leaned forwards and shook Pointer's hand, deal! Pointer looked, not happy, perhaps slightly smug. He knew this was an offer that could not be refused, that was how he did things. "Now", he said. "You will deal with my associate in all matters regarding this. I will expect you to give her the details required for the investment transfer and I expect you to keep nothing from me. If you do then I will know". The last sentence made it perfectly clear where Ben was now, with a simple handshake he lived or died.

Ben knew all about giving investors a lack of processing time, that was his tactic and it had worked very well for him in the past. Just when he thought that they were all done, Marie-Eve Legault walked in. Pointer smiled, "no introduction needed I believe. I will leave you in the capable hands of Marie-Eve, once again".

Marie-Eve sat down opposite, very businesslike. "Right, Ben, now we both know where we are, let's proceed".

Ben's charm kicked in before his sense of betrayal. "OK, to business then" and they settled back to add Richard Pointer to the deal. For Ben, this wasn't an issue. He did, however, feel that he had to rule

Marie-Eve Legault out of the role he'd hoped that she would have later in the enterprise. Now they would meet only to talk shop, nothing else was on the table.

"So Ben, how do we proceed?"

"I need to consolidate funds and set everything up for a surgical excision. Once that is done I'll be in touch and you will need to wrap things up in Nottingham quickly. Have your exit strategy in place and just vanish".

"And after?"

"I don't honestly know".

# SIXTY-SIX

## Thursday 15 September

Marie-Eve's phone barked, she'd set her alert sound to a bark for her Whatsapp account, that would mean only one person was trying to get her attention. She knew, if asked, that she could laugh it off as something a friend did to her phone for a joke and she'd never bothered to reset it. Sometimes it was even an ice-breaker, besides most people these days found nothing unusual in a phone that woof-woofed.

She decided that the bathroom was the best place to go and read it. She was reluctant to shut the office door again during the main part of the day, partly because the moron Greenwood had pulled her up about it. "Marie-Eve, you do know that we have an open-door policy in the company and that we follow it rigidly here in Nottingham?" Greenwood had told her in rebuke. Of course she fucking did. She also didn't want to attract undue attention from the pool of admins outside; they saw all and would welcome any excuse to go telling tales indiscriminately.

The executive bathroom was empty, it usually was, so she slipped inside, sat on the toilet seat and opened up the app to see what Ben wanted. She'd known this bathroom well these past couple of days, always a refuge for the nauseous. She knew the whys of it but that could wait a little longer, until she could see which way the wind blew.

The text just said 'update'. This meant that there had been developments and that the plan and its component parts, fluid as it was, would require an element of steerage.

She responded with 'send', their code was simple enough unless there were complications; that was where the Whatsapp encryption came in useful, nobody could stumble upon anything incriminating.

'Phase three accelerated, run interference across the board, especially TK, five days and counting'.

She replied 'D -05 confirmed'.

A wave of tiredness swept over her, five days and she'd be out of there, well four really, she didn't want to be around any longer than she needed to be. She opened up her Air Canada app and booked the return flight, first class this time, the expense was not going to be an issue and anyway, before questions were asked she'd be long gone.

Once back in the office, she fired up the PC and went to have a look at the system, to see if anything obvious stuck out. In Clousseau she found the samples and the site. They'd been marked with a comment to 'hold pending investigation', this was Reid's doing. Pity she'd not got Reid in her pocket rather than Shepherd, that had been an error of judgement but she might still be able to use her leverage.

For the time-being, she needed to drop a few tacks on the road to analysis, so she deleted the 'hold' text from all samples. There were so many marked 'hold' that she was confident that her creativity with certain samples would go unnoticed for long enough. Besides, she had a way to muddy the tracks.

In the Shipping Office, Craig Shepherd was going through the new deliveries and populating the online Incoming Shipment file with the relevant information. It passed the time. It was only when his door clicked shut that he looked up and saw Marie-Eve. Whatever it was that she wanted this time, it was probably not good for him.

"Look Craig, I realise I was brusque but we were a mistake. I was missing my boyfriend in Montreal, we were going to break-up and I was confused and, besides, you didn't put up much of a fight so I thought, why not?'

Craig was a bit taken aback; this wasn't the hard-nosed bitch that he'd expected her to be this time. Perhaps that was coming along later, once he'd found out what it was she wanted and he'd refused.

Craig heard himself speaking the words but was surprised at how hard he sounded. "Just get to it, Marie-Eve, I'm busy, you're supposed to be, too. You now obviously want something from me and I am not inclined to be helpful, whatever it is".

She smiled that humourless smile that everyone had learned to dislike. "I want your Clousseau log-in user name and password. I want to see what you have been up to in there. I have been getting disturbing reports about discrepancies and as, for some unknown reason, you are a full user, I am investigating you and your actions personally. While you might not believe this, it is in your interests to be 'helpful', as you say, because if I find that you have fucked something up, I can get it fixed".

Talk about a double-edged sword. She was telling him he'd possibly messed up their shiny new system and that she wanted to stop him getting into trouble for it. This didn't make much sense.

Then she switched her manner from icy-cold to pleasantly warm. "How are Jemmy and the baby? You never did tell me its name."

Was that a threat or a genuine, as far as Marie-Eve Legault could manage, question? He knew it could be both.

Two minutes later and she was on her way out of the office, a yellow Post-it holding the salient details.

Craig didn't much care that he'd deviated from the straight and true course of GLP by giving away his Clousseau log-in. He'd only ever done the induction course. He hadn't been signed off by Reid as trained,

369

meaning that he had little idea of how to actually do anything in it, and why would he? Shipping was an Excel-based department; he'd never need to learn Clousseau. There was nothing there that she might find, although the subtext was that someone had been into the system and had messed up, he wondered who. He also wondered how come he had full access, what with being untrained, and how she'd known.

Tracey came in not long after, "what did Cat's Bum-Face want?"

Craig wasn't really in the mood but Tracey had been a bit of a pest so now it was his turn. "Oh, just rif stuff; she is compiling a list for the next one and wanted to know if I had any names for her list. You know, was there anyone I thought we could lose off the full-time staff?"

Tracey bit like a pellet-fed Trout. "You wouldn't do that to me, would you Craig? I know we lark about a bit but we always get the work done, and you and me is just a bit of boy-girl flirting. Jemmy knows, I asked her if it was OK to flirt with you, honestly I did, and she was OK but told me not to go too far. I promised not to, this time and I've kept my promise, you know I have".

She was looking nervous, a bit tearful even. Craig knew he couldn't keep her dangling too far. She could be a bit fragile after her treatment by her last bloke; he had been something of a monster. "Tracey, as if I'd get rid of my best person, and you with such perky tits, too".

Her demeanour changed in an instant and she looked like she'd just won a goldfish at the fair. "That Mr. Shepherd, Sir, is sexual harassment and I may have to report you to my boss", she said, smiling.

"Oh, I'm so sorry Miss Mills, please take this pile of Shipping receipts and enter them into the spreadsheet as compensation for my stating the obvious".

"Perky eh? I like perky".

"Careful, Tracey, you know how nicknames can stick".

"Better 'Perky Tits' than 'Cat's Bum-Face' any day", she said and gathered up the pile of inventories before walking out with an exaggerated wiggling walk.

When she was gone and he'd had time to process, he was vaguely troubled by the thought of Jemmy giving Tracey permission to flirt with him. That wasn't like her at all but then Tracey was an old mate of sorts and she obviously trusted her to be as good as her word. He wondered whether the whole thing was Jemmy's way of seeing how well-behaved he was under the sort of suggestive barrage that Tracey was capable of, interesting.

# SIXTY-SEVEN

## Wednesday 21 September

"Do sit down, Detective Inspector. Would you like a tea or coffee? It really is no trouble".

So that was how he was going to play it, the devious bastard. Charnley never had liked Chalky Perkins and not just because of the funny handshake and dubious list of acquaintances within the force. Poker-face and a firm 'no' would do here. In Charnley's world, each scenario had more meaning than was visible above the surface. Perkins inviting him into his, what did he call it? , 'the inner sanctum', was yet another ruse to get behind his carefully constructed defences. They were not going to get him before his last case was done, nothing would work.

"Detective Inspector?"

With a start, Charnley returned to the ongoing situation. "Sorry, Sir, I had drifted off, it's this case, lots to think about and I tend to get rather absorbed. More so as it is my last case before retirement and I want a good conclusion".

"Yes, quite. Well it is your impending departure from the department that I wanted to speak to you about. It is normal in these situations to canvas the senior officer of any team regarding their successor and, while nothing is certain in these matters, the continuity of a successful team is much to the benefit of the service and, of course, reflects well on the chain of command".

"Meaning you?"

"Meaning all who are a part of the whole, Jock".

"I would recommend Thompson without a second's thought, Sir. A fine and considerate officer who delegates well, is a confident and incisive thinker and who has the respect of his colleagues".

"That is the answer I expected. However, as always, external forces may cloud the issue. External forces well beyond my control, that is certain. There are officers in teams elsewhere in the service who are also looking to shin up the greasy pole and I feel it only fair to tell you that your man Thompson will have his work cut out. He will be a runner in a large field and equality constraints will only add to the hurdles to be faced. The times are a long way behind us when promotion was granted almost on the nod, these are competitive times, Jock".

"Of course, Sir and I have every confidence that Thompson has the talent to succeed. However, I think to refer to him as 'my boy' is a little disrespectful. Thompson is very much his own man and I have grown to appreciate that in the years we have been colleagues. I understand the changes that have taken place and the new nature of the Force and recruitment but, on merit, you will not be disappointed in Thompson if he is selected to fill my cooling shoes".

'What on earth happened, Jock? We used to be friends of a sort, back in the day. These past 18 months we've become like an old couple who can't stand each other but feel stuck for eternity. The warmth has gone and I don't know why, and it troubles me".

The switch caught Charnley by surprise. They'd never been mates, ever, but colleagues, yes; close in times of difficulty, yes. You had to circle the wagons sometimes, and you had to know that someone you could trust had your back. Perkins was waiting for an answer, his face leaning towards concern but with a background of his trademark sneer that everyone who worked under him knew and loved.

"To be honest, Leroy, I don't know myself. You changed orbit, I didn't, and we both had to focus on different things. My team is my life, you have a wider brush with which to paint; it was inevitable that a drift would occur. It's par for the course, I suppose".

Perkins snapped back into officious mode and Charnley knew it had been a device, a clam knife to open his shell and disgorge the contents there in the office. It hadn't worked and they both knew it. The short but resigned silence was soon filled with Perkins stating the bleeding obvious about the Legault case. Did he really want a team of egg-sucking Grannies?

Perkins ended with an oily "thank you for your time, Detective Inspector" and Charnley knew it was the undisguised instruction to go. He hoped that he'd not harmed Thompson's chances of stepping up, he really was ready, but he didn't trust Perkins or his ilk not to spike the promotion out of spite or, more likely, to bump up another pinny-flapper to consolidate their hold on the realm, bastards.

On his way back to his own office Charnley caught Thompson's eye as he passed through. A slight beckoning nod, reminiscent of the good old days before Charnley went weird, was enough to reassure Thompson that all was not yet lost there, not for a while anyway. Deciding to grasp the bull by the balls, Thompson went for it.

The door to Charnley's office was always shut, a 'fuck off and don't bother me' policy, it's called. Thompson felt the need to talk to his boss. Not because he thought he'd get much positivity from him, this was his swan song before he took his pension and didn't look back. He wasn't always like this, just these past few years, but because things were moving and, whether Thompson liked it or not, Charnley was still the boss.

There was no answer to the knock but Thompson went in anyway. Charnley looked up but said nothing, then carried on fiddling with a box of files on his desk.

"I want to talk to you about the Legault case". With Charnley, Thompson had long ago learned to use as few words as possible.

"Go on".

Thompson started talking, offering up the events sequentially and adding bits of fluff picked up when the sticky sweet of temptation had been placed in front of eager mouths. It wasn't clear whether Charnley was listening; the box file seemed to hold his attention. Thompson continued until he reached a point where he expected a return for his spent breath.

Charnley stopped fiddling and put the file on the floor next to a dozen or more similar box files. He looked at Thompson like he was an irritation, not at all welcome. "And that little monologue couldn't have been in the daily written case report? Oh, wait, most of it has been. What's your point, Thompson?"

Thompson felt his cheeks flush and his fists tighten. Charnley noticed but didn't seem worried, but then why should he be? Thompson knew Charnley had been a hard bruiser, if needs be, during his long career. If he started swinging, not only would he be trying to assault a senior officer, he'd probably also get his head kicked in and he wasn't sure that Charnley would stop punching, even if he'd beaten the crap out of him.

"Go on, son", Charnley said, a flicker of a smile soon lost when the scowl returned.

"Permission to talk bluntly, Sir?"

"I said 'go on', what did you think I meant?"

"What the fuck is it with you? When I started you were a normal DI, a team player who worked with everyone, went to the pub, stood a round, patted backs when they deserved it and kicked arses for the same reason. You are of no use to me hiding in here like an old man, appearing at briefings, scowling at everyone and being a general shithead, Sir".

Charnley stood up sharply. Oh shit, thought Thompson, here goes my nose! But he didn't launch into him; instead he raised his finger to his lips then scribbled a Post-it with the name of a pub in Widmerpool on it, and 'GO THERE NOW' in capitals. Widmerpool was a very long way out in the sticks, interesting choice.

Thompson looked up as Charnley started to bellow like a randy Moose. Lots of 'how dare you talk to me like that, you little shit, I should have your badge' and so on, all delivered as Charnley slowly shook his head. The sham tirade ended with "now fuck off and don't ever come into my office and talk to me like that again, got it?"

"Yes, Sir", said Thompson, but no 'sorry' was offered.

Widmerpool took about 40 minutes to get to, sat as it was on the edge of the Vale of Belvoir. The pub was nice enough, a bit twee and obviously more food than drink-orientated. Thompson didn't think he'd ever been there before; it was tucked away a bit. You had to be deliberately going there to find it, unless you'd managed to get lost in the maze of lanes in the vale and just came across it by chance.

The bar, such as it was, had a few people in it. One table held two couples chatting, the boys sipping beer, only one of the girls with wine, the other being the designated driver. You needed one out here; you'd be too far from civilisation to try to sneak home over the limit, too much road to cover and eager traffic cops waiting in strategic spots. Thompson knew, he done a bit himself.

Thompson bought a half of a beer he'd never heard of and pitched down on the window bench seat. It was a quiet enough spot but with the bonus of a view of the car park. After ten minutes of checking his watch and thinking he'd been stupid to even play the game, lights appeared in the car park and Charnley got out of his old Fiat. He parked in the far corner, under some trees, and made a show of crossing to the pub slowly. Once inside, he swept the room quickly, efficiently, skimming past Thompson who thought to wave. WTF, no, this meeting was clearly incognito.

Charnley went for a mineral water and walked over to join Thompson, sat down and took a deep breath. "Do you think anyone followed you?" he said, not quite what Thompson had expected but then sharing a cosy corner in a rural pub with his nutty DI had also not figured in his to-do list that evening.

"No, not followed. I stopped part-way here, nobody behind me, then I chose to sit here so that I could see the car park, nobody came before you, nobody has come since".

"Good". This wasn't the office Charnley, this was a different man altogether. "Sorry, Dave, but I had to know I could trust you. I had to get you to go out on a limb, make you have a go at me and do it for real; not staged, because I'd have known. They'd have known" and he started peering around the room in case 'they' were watching him from some hidden nook.

"Right". Thompson had no idea what he was talking about, and who was this man actually talking to him and calling him 'Dave', for fuck's sake?

"Dave, we are being watched at work. There are people who would be happy to kick me out without a pension, and they have been looking for ways to do it for a while now, I know this as immutable fact. The same people have a stake in the Legault inquiry I believe, I don't know what it is yet, though. I thought that, by taking a back seat, I'd be less obvious, less of a target, just some miserable old has-been marking time to pension day while you and the team pulled away at the case".

"Right". What else could Thompson say, he was beginning to wish he'd asked Rebecca to call him with a false alarm at a pre-set time, at least he'd have an exit strategy then.

"I think my office and the briefing room are bugged. I've heard things, bit and pieces repeated to me by individuals who weren't there when the things were said and they didn't appear in writing anywhere. I think they are going after me because I know something damaging to them".

"What?"

"I don't know precisely but it has something to do with a scammer who is now involved in the pharmaceutical industry. It is somebody I thought I had nailed to a tree ten years ago but who managed to wriggle free, aided and abetted by senior police officers and with the help of one of my old team members".

"Perkins?"

"I'm not sure, but I think so. I can't stand the slimy git and I've heard things from previous DIs, people who I trust as straight and true, well at least within the spirit of the law. Perkins always has some sort of agenda, they reckon it is apron-based and the Masonic influence can't be underestimated. There is a network of them at all levels but especially at superintendent level, an area of control".

Thompson felt that he wasn't getting the full picture. "Who in the pharmaceutical industry were you after? One of the players now or someone we don't know? I need to know this stuff otherwise I have one hand tied behind my back".

"It was Clive Gerrard, the founder of Blue Sky Research, recently bought out by NPS. He was a scientist with no obvious finance but had set up the Contract Research and Manufacturing Company almost overnight. They had a good reputation in the trade, one of the reasons why NPS bought them, but they had areas of 'manufacturing' that we wanted to know about. We were sure that they had a crystal meth lab in the best place to hide one, inside a legitimate manufacturing lab".

"You think Gerrard financed the legit business with drug money?"

378

"No. Initially, I suspect, the money came from Canada – now do you see a link? We thought that a secret investor was expanding their business interests, selling meth into Europe, so to do that they set up Blue Sky, put enough in to make it legit, a shining light in the industry even. Then they set up the meth lab and had people assigned to the 'project'. Whoever put the money in, and it may have been more than one investor, had political muscle that we couldn't easily beat. Gerrard didn't get talked to, no search was done, we were just told it was an expensive dead end and to move on. So we did".

"Silly question, but surely the case would be one for the drug squad and not a murder investigation team".

"A minor pusher had been killed, probably an accident, but then we joined up some more dots and eventually found Gerrard at the end of them. We passed it on, of course, and that was when the stop order came. Nothing more happened, as far I could find out".

"And Perkins, how does he fit?"

"He was a DS in drugs and the contact who we told about Gerrard. Shortly after, he became our DI, but only very briefly. It was two plus two maths and nothing was very clear. Perkins then left the area, I got DI later, then he came back as Detective Chief Inspector, then Superintendent and now here we all are".

Thompson considered the revelation. "I don't see NPS, or Legault, involved in drugs, well not illegal drugs obviously. I can see that the secrets, 'where the bodies are buried' as it was put, could be some narcotic information that got Legault back into NPS in Montreal but surely, if she was a threat, the Montreal end would not have shoved her unconscious into a freezer in Nottingham. They don't mess about with niceties over there, she'd have been concreted into the bridge support like the rest, eliminating her being the whip that keeps the other people in line".

"I'm not saying that is the case but it is an angle you might not have found without being told. I hope that this turns out to be a simple case of revenge for some misdeed against someone; a rif victim, somebody snubbed or slighted, an angry lover".

"Like Shepherd?"

"Shepherd, or maybe his wife, a woman scorned and all that".

The discourse over, the two men sat for a while in silence looking at their drinks. One thinking 'this is nuts', the other brooding in a pit of dark despair, brought about by an all-encompassing conspiracy evolving around him. Could he even trust Thompson? Too late to think that, now.

Thompson spoke first. "The Legault murder smacks of something more personal, and dumped Craig Shepherd still fits the bill, or is as good as we have right now. Legault was sharp with people she had no time for, so perhaps she had belittled someone, Martin maybe? He strikes me as the sort with a shoulder chip, not to mention a secret. Maybe she found out something about him, something as simple as being asleep on the job. He seems to rake in the shifts so how does he keep awake if he doesn't kip a bit on nights? I get the impression that Shepherd was a reluctant lover, I think he is just a mouse who couldn't say no and Legault was a predator who delighted in playing with her prey. Having said that, I can't see him being emotionally capable of murder and hiding it; unless there is a hidden side, very well hidden. His wife, Jemmy would know. I should talk to her again although I don't see her bopping Legault one and chucking her in a freezer".

Charnley had been listening intently but, when Thompson had done, he went off again talking about a contract killer and Legault being party to dangerous knowledge, or even a double-cross and getting caught. None of that made any sense at any level and Thompson got more and more frustrated by his superior's continuing detachment from the known facts.

"I hear that people are still using the 'Fish Finger' when they refer to Legault".

This was easier ground for Thompson to navigate, he could deal with facts. "Yes, sorry about that, Sir, I'll remind them again".

"No, don't bother, the PC bluster is all for show, they can call her what they like, I've come up with a few myself in the past. I've often wondered, when I had my run-in with Ray Frost, and I know it would have been discussed in detail and at length, what did they call me?"

This had the potential to be another 'Tumbleweed' moment but Thompson decide to go for it anyway, the nickname wasn't derogatory, more respectful. "Well, Sir, they called you 'Old Harry'."

Charnley looked surprised, "as in The Devil, Old Harry?"

Thompson grinned, "well, sometimes that would fit but no. 'Old Harry' meant Harry Houdini, the great escapologist". There was no change of expression so Thompson simply couldn't read how Charnley had taken it. To be fair, it was pretty respectful, it could have been much worse. It seemed to take a few seconds more for Charnley to find the words, then he told Thompson that if he ever found out who'd come up with that one they would find themselves helping muggers cross the road in St-Ann's for the next three months. The slight grin told Thompson that Charnley was still in there and that this was yet another joke. Nobody back in the Nick would believe him if he told them.

Without any obvious full-stop to the proceedings, Charnley got up to go. He was halfway to the door when he looked back, all traces of any humour erased from his face and said "this is strictly between you and me, Dave; the others cannot be trusted until thoroughly tested, agreed?" Thompson just nodded; again, what else could he possibly have done?

# SIXTY-EIGHT

## Thursday 22 September

After the buzz of the initial body find, there followed the laborious process of sifting through everything; checking and double-checking and generally making sure that all the bases had been well and truly covered. Police work was always shown as glamorous; dashing about, pinning snouts up against the wall until they squealed the word on the street, or having roof-top chases and last ditch victories. Nobody in the team had ever had a roof-top chase. The few times any of them had chased a suspect, they'd invariably got away, generally having more motivation to run that extra mile all the quicker.

Early in the day, Thompson called a short briefing, just to keep everyone in the loop. Charnley didn't attend. In fact, when Thompson had stuck his head through his office door to tell him about it, he'd just shook his head and waved him out, fair enough then.

The briefing went along quickly, they all had stuff to do and the Legault case wasn't really making much headway, so the meeting didn't have too much new information to cover. They'd just wrapped up when Thompson's phone rang; they had another body associated with NPS, Neil Martin from their Security Department. Looked like a hit-and-run on the Colwick Loop Road.

The main morning, nose-to-tail, rush-hour traffic had just about cleared and it was easy enough for Thompson and the team to get out to Colwick quickly. Two cars of detectives arrived at the scene, pulling onto a cycle track to keep out of the way of the steady flow of traffic. They might have to shut the road for forensics and scene-of-crime people to do their stuff, thought Thompson, but the uniform standing over the scene pointed out that the incident had taken place on a park access road just along from the Starting Gate Pub and not on the

Colwick Loop Road as they'd first thought. That was a relief for all, shutting the Loop Road would result in chaos but it still had to be considered, initially at least.

Thompson decided to use field judgement; the apparent scene was isolated and shutting the road would just make everyone's life that bit more difficult including theirs. The Racecourse had an access road with a locked gate that they could use so as not to further contaminate the scene with their vehicles. Ten minutes later, the barrier was opened up from the inside by a grumpy Head Groundsman, so the cars were all parked inside while the team got stuck into the details.

The uniform filled them in. The body was found just off the access road and before a now-open barrier, along an overgrown walking trail. It looked like the impact had been enough to move the body down the trail a way, no sign that it was carried, and there was blood and bits of a headlamp lens on the road. The body was found by the park staff while opening that section of the park, killing time by collecting litter from the trail before a brew.

The finder was a Mr. John Fraser, a park ranger, and he could be located in the ranger's lodge at the park's main entrance off Mile End Road. The car behind them, the one parked just inside the entrance and half on the verge, matched one that Martin was registered as owning. The car had been cordoned off with tape, pending their arrival. Hurrah, a uniform with a brain! Thompson made a point of noting her collar number.

"Anything on him, cash, credit cards, phone?"

"His wallet is in his pocket, so not a robbery; we also found a bag that might belong to him, a satchel type".

Thompson went over to look, the SOCO team were busy but let him have a peek at the brown, old-style satchel. "Was there anything interesting inside the bag?"

383

"Actually, yes", said one of the SOCO team, "a mouse, for a computer".

"Thompson held up the transparent bag containing the cord-less mouse. "Prints and DNA on that should be very interesting".

Over the next couple of hours they tried to piece together Neil Martin's activity. He'd left work around 6:30 am. He lived in nearby Netherfield. The park was on his way home so perhaps he'd decided to go for a walk? He'd parked on the Candle Meadow entrance car park access road, the park gates would have been locked at night, opening around 07:00 am, although usually about 40 minutes or so later, and remaining open until dusk.

There was nothing suspicious about Martin's car; local doors were already being knocked on to find out if anyone saw anything odd but the park at this entrance was well-hidden from prying eyes. Thompson expected nothing and reckoned they needed list of dog walkers and the like, there might be one or two emptying Lassie before going off to work.

Back at the scene, another uniform had been put on road duty out of necessity. A surprising number of people seemed to use this bit of the park and they were causing congestion problems when, after pulling in unawares, they were panicking when faced with the might of the Nottinghamshire Police!

Thompson went to talk to Fraser. The lodge turned out to be a steel container with windows and a door that, when locked, you'd not get through even when using Semtex. Fraser was drinking tea and doing the Telegraph crossword, the only other occupant was an old, ruddy-looking guy who appeared to be selling tickets to anglers and tutting.

Ever the hospitable host, Fraser offered Thompson a brew which he gratefully accepted.

"Was the park gate opened and closed at the same time every day?"

"Yes, give or take, depending on park priorities, such as needing to shift a dumped, stolen car or reporting the daily vandalism". Fraser was pretty off-hand and Thompson soon realised that, far from being shocked by finding a body, Fraser just took it in his stride. It wasn't his first on the site.

Over the next 30 minutes or so, Fraser gave an account of the discovery on Neil Martin, dropping in the occasional comment about how dangerous the park could be and how difficult it was to get coppers to support a warden when there was an incident. The impression was that Fraser didn't think much of the police, or it could just be like most of the general public, frustration at thinking they'd been short-changed when it came to policing in general.

Thompson had closed his notebook when Fraser asked them how they were going to trace the rest of the poofs and junkies. Of course, it came back to him, Colwick; rent boys, gay pick-ups, drugs. He remembered hearing that there had been a problem on the park but couldn't pull the detail back. Martin was gay perhaps, or a junkie and possibly the person who killed him was too; a tiff, a pick up or a drug sale gone wrong? "You might be surprised at the hour but, to be honest officer, that area has a reputation as a 24 hour pleasure stop. It even has pages on a web site dedicated to specialist interests!" said Fraser.

Whether the death was an accident or deliberate would be an important part of the puzzle, Thompson realised. Whatever had caused Martin to end up in a crumpled and bloody heap in a shrubbery, the Legault investigation had just become a lot more complicated.

"Thank you for the statement, Mr. Fraser and the interesting tea. I may need to speak to you and your colleagues again but, just a word of warning, calling members of the gay community 'poofs' is not on, especially when talking to a police officer, even if they are. Please remember to use the term 'members of the LGBT community' in future".

Fraser looked at Thompson as if he'd fallen out the back of an Alsatian. "These are not members of the gay community as such, officer. These are married men and junkies who turn my park into a no-go area for everybody else, including members of the LGBT community. If they want to be gay, or stuff their veins with drugs, then let them get on with it in the right places, not in the undergrowth of my country park, thank you". And with that he donned his wax jacket, ready to patrol the park, the newspaper with the completed crossword cast aside.

The ruddy-looking man on the desk then decided to join in the debate, ranting something about Poles and Slovaks stealing Pike and Carp to eat. "It's illegal but do the police do anything? No they bloody well do not, what are you going to do about that, son, eh?"

Thompson looked the old curmudgeon straight in the eye and said "if you can give me a description of the stolen fish, identifying features and the like, I'll send an officer around later this morning to pick it up".

Ruddy-face looked amazed and pulled a pad out of his drawer and started writing, "give me an hour, will you, and it'll be ready then".

Thompson face broke into a wry smile as he walked back to his car. That would be a nice little job for Liam.

Back at the scene, the CSI people had been very quick, the body had gone to the mortuary and a handful of investigators were clipping back vegetation to collect bits of car. Arc lights were being set up as some areas of the trail were heavily shaded. The SOCO boss reckoned it wouldn't be a long job; the incident was restricted to a very small area.

Thompson hated to do it but a field brief was needed. "Listen up everyone. This whole area is a drug pitch and gay pick-up place. I want every condom within 200 m collected, bagged and the DNA run through the database. Watch out for needles, pick them up too". It was not a happy groan that came from the crime scene people, not a happy one at all. As it transpired, the area was fairly trash free, it seemed that everything obvious was picked up daily by the wardens, including condoms.

Heading back to the warden's lodge to ask about the litter bags, the ruddy-faced man, still beavering away at his list, just told them to help themselves and pointed to an elderly Landrover in the car park. Today's Starting Gate pickings were in one bin bag and the needles had been placed in a sharps container. The only problem was that the sharps container contained a couple of weeks-worth of needles from all around the park. Oh, well.

Thompson had the team reconvene at the station where the debate was whether the death of Martin was an isolated incident or related to the death of Legault. Thompson's rule of thumb was, if the word 'coincidence' made it into the conversation more than six times, it wasn't a coincidence. As rules of thumb went, it was possibly not the best, certainly not the most logical, but it was something. The main thing now was to find the car that hit Martin and whoever was driving it, but Charnley had indicated by email that overtime was a no-no on this one.

Soon bodies would be on phones, following up on the fragmentary clues they had. The car was blue; that they knew, and it might be an SUV, the bits of light cluster looked vaguely SUV-ish. Not an exact science; that was being done elsewhere now, too.

Calls showed that none of the regular body shops had had anything blue in for repair in the past day, so perceived wisdom was that it was parked somewhere with a sodding big dent in it and perhaps the odd scrap of flesh; that would be a nice and easy tie-in if they could find it. As was Thompson's way, something bubbled away at the back of his mind, not quite there but taking a shape he could interpret. Thinking hard didn't work; you had to come at these vague thoughts from an angle, like seeing something out of the corner of your eye, something that you couldn't look at directly but had to piece together from scraps.

It was getting late in the day and a lot of conversations were underway. The dead board had been updated, ready for tomorrow. Stood, hands on hips and staring at the board, like an amateur woodworker checking to see whether the shelves he's just put up were level, Thompson was startled by Superintendent Perkins.

"Still here I see, Thompson. Any developments you can tell me about in advance of DI Charnley's report tomorrow?"

"Another death Sir, hit-and-run, the victim works for NPS. A tenuous link, but we can't rule out that the victim, Neil Martin, was involved in the death of Marie-Eve Legault. He is, or was, a suspect".

Perkins stood too for a moment, then he noticed that Colwick Park was involved. "Yes, Sir, one of the entrances off the loop road. Do you know the park, Sir?" said Thompson, hoping he wasn't inferring that Perkins had been a visitor to the crime scene, 'out of hours'.

Perkins picked up the innuendo straight away and laughed. Then he explained that, a couple of years ago, he'd been on his way in when a dumped car was called in. Normally they are insurance jobs but this one was dumped in the main lake there and the possibility that someone might still be inside had not been fully eliminated. "So I called by, just as they were about to take one of their little boats out to attach a hook of some sort, then use their Landrover to winch out the car".

Thompson frowned, asking whether, if it was a potential crime scene, shouldn't they have had a team in attendance? Again Perkins laughed again, "they have a different attitude on that park and a car was not going to be left polluting their lake longer than necessary. I got there just as one of the chaps was launching the little boat, so I introduced myself, it meant nothing to them; I could have been PC Plod! Then I asked if I might come out in the boat to observe? The boat was launched and we were in the process of heading over to the sunken car when a crescendo of swearing erupted. It seemed that, in their haste

388

to get the boat out onto the water, the bung that stops the boat filling up with water had been omitted and we were sinking".

Trying not to laugh, Thompson went for earnest in expression but only got amused. "To cut a good story short, DS Thompson, we sped back to shore, grabbed the bung, and another chap in green bailed the water out while we went back out, hooked the car by the door frame and hauled it out in one almighty rip".

"And was there a body, Sir?" "Sadly not. The little shits who had nicked the car had just dumped it in the lake instead of burning it as usual. Still, it brightened up a very dull day somewhat. Carry on". And he was away, back to his office.

Fraser had mentioned dumped cars on the park, and Thompson now went off home with a fully formed idea fashioned out of an irritating notion. Tomorrow they would go back to Colwick Park and check the lake. No sooner had the thought passed through his mind than the mobile phone rang. It was Colwick Park, a different ranger this time but they were still open and would Thompson be interested to know that their boat had just sheared a propeller after hitting a submerged object where none had previously resided?

Stopping in a convenient spot, Thompson roused some of the weary troops, arranging for Elkie and Prosser to head back to the park for a look. He called Dad, who was still in the station and busy updating Charnley's briefing, telling him to include the new information, then he texted home saying he'd be a bit late again, and sorry.

When Thompson got to the park, the others were already stood on the bank side as the park Landrover winch hauled away at a length of rope. The otherwise calm lake seethed as the blue Hyundai Tucson edged slowly up the bank. All the windows had been left down; presumably to make the thing sink quicker. There was also obvious damage to the nearside wing at the front. The car was almost clear of the water when a loud thwack signaled the rope snapping and it sailed off away and into the dull green yonder to a chorus of 'fucks'! This was going to take even longer than expected!

Two hours and not a little more colourful language later, the SUV was on the back of a flatbed tow truck and being taken from the park, leaving a muddy trail as it went. Whoever had dumped it had probably also nicked it, judging by the steering column damage and the nest of wires on show. It didn't always do to jump to conclusions, but this might just be a stolen car, driven by idiots who whacked a lurking Martin, panicked and dumped the car in the lake under the cover of the early morning. Fraser had mentioned vandalism, how had they got into the park, clipped a barrier lock perhaps? On the other hand it might also be a not-so-sophisticated way of trying to cover up a crime, only time and the attention of the forensics bods would tell.

The delay in going home wasn't too bad; at least the traffic would be lighter. On the way out of the park, Thompson had to nip into the lodge to tell the desk warden to let him out. Outside, a warden he'd not met before was bolting a chain to a lock on the night barrier. "Problems?"

"Hacked off last night. Usually the shits get in when someone in the Marina comes in at night and can't be arsed to shut the barrier but this time someone took a bolt cropper to it".

"How many keys are there for this night barrier?" asked Thompson, expecting the answer to be perhaps ten or so

"About 320 at the last count, most are with boat owners, the rest are for us, the ground staff and a few odd ones allowed on discretion to people we trust".

"Is there a list?"

"Of the boat owners, yes; the others, sort of. The keys are security stamped with a number and issued to specific individuals; unfortunately the odd one does wander. If it helps, I'd say your car dumpers chopped the lock and dumped the car. They would have another one to take them away from the scene, unless they are local shits, of which there is abundance, then they might just walk away".

"We'll need a copy of that list please, as accurate as you can make it. Someone will call by tomorrow".

The warden had finished the repairs and was heading back to their tin hut, shouting "no problem, son" over his shoulder. "No need to call by, we have your card, I'll email it." Thompson reckoned that they were not far off the same age so where the 'son' business came from, who knows. Years of dealing with a difficult public, probably.

# SIXTY-NINE

Well, that was interesting! Neil Martin dead, seems to be a hit and run although why he was where he was we don't know yet. There may be a link to the Legault case but it is probably coincidence. Let's hope so, there is enough muddy water swilling around the Fish Finger for now.

Side note, the uniform who took control at the Martin scene at Colwick; Carla Adams, mention in dispatches. She did a good job on her own initiative, one to note for the future.

Somewhere there is a bunch of twoccers who will be shitting themselves. One will crack and drop his mates in it, we'll need to nudge a few people to put the word around that we have prints, DNA etc., see who jumps first. Expand on twoccers, taking without consent and the whole car nicking thing – the devil is in the detail for crime novels.

I'm getting a feeling that we might be barking up the wrong tree in the Legault case. The alibis are water-tight and we need to find one that is leaky. Not easy with the bunch we've been thinking about mainly, a bigger net needed.

I think that there is a lot in the pharmaceutical industry to play about with, scenarios within scenarios. It seems that the scientists see themselves separate from the technical, which is fair enough, they studied for it, but some of them definitely have a poor opinion on the lower classes. There is plenty of inspiration there for various sub-plots although I grudgingly think Charnley was right about the Legault killer, not from the scientific side at all.

On top of everything else we might have another couple of hundred people with boats in Colwick Marina to talk to, although we can perhaps whittle that down to those with any pharmaceutical connection. All boats have to be licenced, another job for Dad. Meanwhile we'll go back to NPS and rattle some cages big-time. This is sounding more like 'The Sweeney' every day.

# SEVENTY

Thompson sat in the small waiting area at NPS waiting for Ranji to find time for him. He suspected that the HR man was pissing him about. Banks whispered "three more minutes and I'm pulling him for obstruction" but Thompson did the calming sign with both hands. He wanted to work with Ranji; he thought he had information that wasn't being freely released. True, they could get warrants and dig but that only gave you the cold facts; the impressions could give you just as much, if the story came out voluntarily.

Ranji appeared and apologised, he was quite rotund but sharply dressed and looked every inch the professional. Thompson and Banks followed him into his pleasant office and settled into the chairs opposite his desk. How many people have sat here hearing that they are being let go, thought Banks, all their plans and responsibilities hammered for reasons that they'd never actually know. She didn't like the way companies like NPS treated people, very much.

Ranji started shooting rambling questions at them and bumbling about nervously, as some people do in the presence of the police, so Thompson cut him short and took control. He was asking the questions, the interview, such as it was, would be conducted to Thompson's tune whether Ranji liked it or not, and in a place of Thompson's choosing if he felt that the expected cooperation was lacking. "Please understand, Mr. Singh, a young woman died and we will find the killer. You will play your part in full and you will not obstruct, obfuscate or impede us, otherwise you will find out the hard way, understood?" No direct threats were issued but they were certainly implied, that was one of Charnley's little tricks that Thompson thought worth keeping.

"Mr. Singh".

"Ranji, please".

"Ranji, I've spoken to just about everyone involved with Marie-Eve Legault around the company. Law enforcement officers in Montreal have also been asking questions, as we try to build two pictures of her life but we are still lacking important details". Ranji drew breath as if filling a set of bagpipes ready to start that awful squealing noise they make. He'd decided to tough things out with bluster but Thompson quickly deflated him with a sharp comment. "Please wait until I've said what I need to say, then you can respond".

"OK, sorry Inspector, sorry". Ranji looked contrite but sounded a little like he was annoyed, probably because, as an HR professional - as he kept describing himself – he was used to controlling the conversation, and therefore the employees, whenever they had cause to speak to them.

Thompson reminded him that he was a Detective Sergeant and not an Inspector. He felt sure he'd already made this point clear, was the HR man getting flustered?

"Marie-Eve", Thompson said, "is something of an enigma. She worked for NPS, and then left. Then came back and that was considered unusual, not company policy but nobody in Montreal is giving a satisfactory answer. This is where you come in".

Singh looked nervous and slightly astonished. He wriggled a bit in his seat, his body language betraying his discomfort. He seemed to reach a conclusion and began to talk. Banks had her notebook ready but couldn't keep up because his words came as a bit of an incoherent torrent. Thompson let him run a while then reined him in. "Right Ranji, now you've burst the dam, let's go back a bit and deal with your statement, such as it is, in manageable slices".

Thompson led once more, itemising, as he went, the things he felt relevant, his enviable memory taking the disjointed deluge and examining each piece before placing it in context. Banks smiled,

Thompson was good at this, he had the sort of memory that worked like a Dictaphone, every detail retained and, for Thompson at least, easily retrieved. That was, she hoped, what gave Thompson an outside chance to be their next DI, once Charnley had been put out to grass, or better, glue!

"So", said Thompson. "Marie-Eve came back because she was the best in her field, technical management and because the new head of the Montreal facility wanted her to, really?" He waited while Ranji composed himself, he had another bit of the question to go yet and whatever Ranji said now decided how, or even whether he'd need to ask it.

Ranji now talked in a more measured pace. "Clients loved her, her staff were loyal, well those in senior posts were, and NPS wanted to use her expertise across the company to use the Montreal technical model as the company model. Who better to do that than the designer of that model, Marie-Eve Legault?"

For the look of it, Thompson leaned in close to Banks, judging that Ranji wouldn't be able to hear him. "Nice shoes, Jenny, are they new? Just scribble a bit, look like I am giving you something to write down".

Thompson paused a while then asked why, if Marie-Eve Legault's previous Montreal position with NPS was in the area of Quality Control, she was then considered just right for the role of Technical Manager?

Singh had no answer to that one, citing it to be Montreal business and suggesting that they ask them. It was what Thompson had expected but worth a try, now he went back to the earlier incoherent statement offering bite-sized pieces of it back to Ranji for confirmation or clarification. After an hour, Singh asked for a brief pause while he arranged coffee and had a toilet break, he was sweating profusely although he suspected an HR professional would refer to it as perspiring.

While he was away, Thompson and Banks talked quietly about how it was going. So far Singh, despite the initial diatribe dressed up as fluster, had sung the company song loud and true but both officers felt that a couple of verses were still missing, the sort they didn't sing any more, that didn't go with the new image. Thompson decided to rattle him a bit more vigorously; to see whether he could shake anything else out of his tree.

Coffee came, they sipped and talked politely. Singh wondered whether the police had an HR department similar to the one at NPS, "they must have", he said. He fancied he might apply if a job came up, always looking to advance.

At this Thompson wondered aloud who was the current head of HR in NPS, Nottingham was? Ranji said that he was, he'd taken over when the previous head had moved on after the NPS takeover; left, not as a part of a rif. He'd been head-hunted from Boots. Thompson asked about the HR recruiting process and Ranji wondered why this was relevant, but Thompson just shrugged and suggested that he was making a mental picture of everything.

So Ranji explained that they had 12 HR people, he was the head, he had a deputy then there were six senior HR staff and then two below them then two below them. "On the bottom rung?" asked Thompson.

"Yes, the bottom rung, but with prospects".

"And how did promotion work? Did HR people go when the company had the rifs that he'd heard mentioned?"

"No, HR never lost people that way. The only time HR people left was when those keen to rise more quickly than was on offer at NPS chose to move elsewhere and to a higher post, as had happened with his predecessor".

"Do all vacant HR posts get advertised?"

"No", said Singh, "we are almost always able to fill the posts from within. Our current people already know our system and so any new people come in at the bottom and work their way up".

"Presumably unless they are coming in at a senior level, say head of the department, but surely such a senior position would be advertised?"

"Normally but, as I say, I was head-hunted from my previous position in HR at Boots".

"Head of HR at Boots or lower down? If so, where?"

"Not head, senior-junior".

Thompson nodded and then thought for about thirty seconds or so, before asking who actually hired new HR staff.

"We do", said Singh, "our own HR department", his eyes showing that he could see where this train of thought was going and really didn't like the destination.

Thompson kept him simmering nicely. "So, all new HR staff are hired by HR staff?" he continued. "Yes, I see, and people only get promoted if a gap appears above them and not because they show ability?"

"No", said Singh.

"Now, and please correct me if I am wrong", said Thompson, "but every time HR hires someone for lower HR posts, the candidate is not hired because they will improve the quality of the HR department but more because they are not good enough to challenge the position of those above them?"

"It really doesn't work that way", barked Singh, indignantly, but Thompson was on a roll and continued.

"From the outside it looks like those above them have put in place a protectionist policy that actively stops themselves being challenged by more talented and competent HR people from outside. In other words, they always hire the worst HR people on offer who, via the process of automatically filling empty shoes as people move on, eventually move higher and higher until those at the pinnacle are the same people who were not good enough in the first place, am I right?"

"No", said Singh more loudly than he'd intended, "you make it sound like a conspiracy, but it is tried and tested practice".

"Devised by HR the world over and resulting in a compound lowering of departmental competency?"

"No, really, I must protest. You have no idea how we work, the things we have to deal with. Thefts, rumours, fights, infidelity, we get everything thrown at us every day and nobody appreciates us. We are able to offer a restrained face to a disorganised world; we keep everything going, we are the most important part of the company machinery".

"Really?" said Thompson. "I thought NPS was a science company?"

Singh once again filled his chest with air and not just a little indignation, then deflated like a cheap party balloon when Thompson said, "now you can tell me all about Marie-Eve's Legault's 'infidelities', as you call them". So Singh did, the facts, the rumours and a few names they didn't have yet.

During the entire exchange, Jenny Banks had been diligently taking notes, details of spoken words and unspoken reactions. Once they got back out to the car she had to ask. "OK, so what was that all about?"

Thompson laughed. "I've been waiting for years to do that. I once worked for one of the supermarkets while at college. I had a girlfriend there and she worked in the delicatessen. She had to haul huge cheeses around so I asked why they hadn't got a cart. The Supervisor, who didn't like me much, took me to HR who decided I was being disrespectful to her and fired me. I've had something of a bad place for HR staff since that day and, I can safely say that they have never disappointed me."

"Any other highly trained professionals I should keep you away from?"

"Well don't get me started on Elfin Safety!"

The case got a bit murkier when we found out that Legault was involved with a Montreal wide-boy (their description). Something is up with the drug company and there are links between Nottingham and Montreal via a company called Saviour. The wide-boy, Ben Arjah, runs Saviour, not a bricks-and-mortar place but virtual. Legault was a known associate but they were reported to have split up during a visit home. We are getting DNA info on Arjah, looks like we might have found the daddy.

The Montreal boys have a back-story involving their Mafia, who make our baddies look like Girl-Guides. Big money seems to be sloshing around. NPS in Nottingham are not giving any financial details yet but confirmed that the study is the biggest they have ever had. I used back-channels to ask Simon Reid and he told me, off the record, that the sheer number of samples they are getting is unlike anything he'd ever seen and that there is quote 'an air of confusion over the whole study'. Interestingly, the samples that came on the night of her death were also for the Saviour study. That whole concept needs fleshing out a bit; I need to know some pharma procedural stuff for accuracy.

My gut says Shepherd is less in the frame now, Smith and Reid are not contenders either. This might be something from the outside, possibly International. I bloody hope not!

The pharmaceutical angle is an interesting sub-plot that might make it to the main theme. Time to talk to players in the pharma world, the old owner of Blue Sky Solutions might be interesting, if we can find him.

# SEVENTY-ONE

## Sunday 11 September

The red-eye was always a pain, or so Marie-Eve had always been told. She'd never been to England before she'd started her standardisation project though, so it had all been new to her. Now she knew exactly what they meant and sleep deprivation was just a part of the job. At least this time would be her last before things come to a conclusion.

The flight from Montreal to Heathrow wasn't too bad, cattle-class but with enough room to push back a bit and relax. She'd spent part of the flight, as usual, reviewing more of the NPS Nottingham standard operating procedures, this bunch would all have to be changed to bring Nottingham up to spec and to standardise the technical staff operating procedures across the company.

It was boring work, reading SOPs written by people who were basically stupid. Montreal had them in abundance, people who had risen two or three places above where they should be, intellectually, and who had then been charged with changing their departmental SOPs. Often there was no actual need to change one radically but they did so anyway, as much to scent-mark their territory after getting a promotion as anything. Nottingham seemed to have more staff stability *for now* and fewer SOPs, albeit ones in a slightly different style. There was still the need for change, to what extent was still unknown but she was getting close.

Reading work documents took Marie-Eve's mind off things, stuff she really didn't want bothering her at the moment. Her always reliable period going absent without leave was one, the main one, and she really didn't know how she felt about that. Maybe it was just a biological glitch, it had happened before once or twice, but the dates meant that there was the possibility of a problem, something to monitor but not for too long, not if a decision was required.

Heathrow was much bigger than Pierre Elliot Trudeau Airport in Montreal; she still called it Dorval just like everyone else. Heathrow was a city in itself, very much like the other International hubs she'd passed through, a vast and unwieldy creature occupying its own space in time. The queue to get through customs was long and slow at first, but soon picked up pace. Eventually she'd had her passport stamped and been on her way for her baggage, adrenaline keeping the tiredness at bay, for now.

Her journey was fairly straightforward. A tube train ride to St-Pancras, a direct train to Nottingham and she'd be met at the train station. She hoped to be back in her hotel in Nottingham by 2 pm, but perhaps that was optimistic. It all seemed a bit of a slog and she still couldn't understand why someone from the company wasn't collecting her from London every time, she was Head of Technical Services in Montreal, after all.

Oddly enough, her journey had all worked out despite her reservations about the UK transport system. Seeing England for the first time was stimulating but it had soon lost its novelty, now she just suffered it. London was impersonal, difficult to understand and so spread out. Once on the train they went out through dull suburbia that could have been anywhere. Then the train passed through a place called Luton, it looked far worse by train than it did seeing it on that first trip when she'd been picked up by Craig Shepherd and driven to Nottingham. Now here they were again slowing down to pass through and the thought occurred to her that she'd been lied to, where on earth did Luton fit into that 'green and pleasant land' description?

Pulling into Nottingham Station seemed to be such a long and drawn out affair, involving miles and miles of seemingly endless railroad tracks. Once she'd cleared the station, found her ride – an impersonal pre-booked cab - she was on her way back to Wilford and her hotel.

The first time she'd arrived her spirits had brightened a bit and she'd started thinking of the whole secondment to Nottingham stint as more of an adventure than a chore, not any more.

The traffic around Nottingham was heavy and on the wrong side of the road, something she'd had to adapt to. She'd been expected to drive, a rental had been arranged and she'd just needed a bit of practice before venturing out alone. She had hoped that one of her new work colleagues would have taken her out for a quick lesson, she'd been sure that she'd find a nice guy to help out a Madam in distress, she didn't.

Thinking back, she'd only had one day to acclimate and then it was down to work. Her meeting with Richard Greenwood, the site manager, was on the Wednesday morning after she'd been shown around her department. She couldn't think of a technical support department in NPS as anything other than belonging to her, no matter where it was. It only took her a few days to be lording it, or was that 'ladying it' over her Nottingham contingent.

The hotel had turned out to be very near NPS, walking distance even, if you were so inclined. True the place was a bit shabby, a cheap and cheerless chain staffed by plastic grins and a whiff of illicit cigarette smoke everywhere, even though it was a no smoking place. There was at least a real English pub next door that did food, but no self-catering option. She should have to watch that, she was already feeling a bit bloated.

The view from the room was leafy but also included a main road stuffed with traffic that fair roared past the window. The cars seemed endless and fast, and she had no idea where the road went, or even exactly where she was, maybe she'd been a bit jet-lagged. She'd later checked Google for her exact location, once she'd paid the day rate for the Internet of course. Who pays for Internet in a hotel these days?

She was put there because it was close and cheap, and very much the way NPS operated nowadays. In the old days, when attending conferences in the USA, she'd always had a suite. Maybe they just didn't have hotels with suites in England.

Dinner alone at the pub was always interesting, not terrible as she'd been warned about but not something to mark up as memorable. Nobody ever paid her any attention. There was always soccer on the big screens and some yobs at the bar would be cheering when one of the teams scored a corner or something. She'd have to stick to Pepsi for a while now, alcohol wasn't an option until something had been decided one way or another, but it wasn't an issue. True, a light French white wine was a nice and refreshing drink but she'd never been a slave to the stuff and never would be, unlike some she'd had to deal with.

The hotel and the new room now seemed smaller than it had been just a few days ago. A small table, a lamp and an uncomfortable chair were her companions for the duration, again. She had considered making a fuss until they moved her somewhere more fitting, but decided to tough it out. It would have been too easy to wallow in self-pity, but that was not Marie-Eve.

She dumped her stuff and pulled out her laptop, she knew that there would still be people in Montreal working so she fired off a couple of emails, read a few more and then settled in to rest. Sleep came quickly enough but she awoke at 4:30 am when a door slammed and a car started. Outside there was still traffic using the road, did it ever stop?

After breakfast, of a sort, she went for a short run, just down the old lane to the business park and past NPS. It was just over 1.5km to the site, according to her Fitbit, an easy distance if the weather was OK. Back in her room there was a text. This time she was being met at the hotel by Richard Greenwood, the erstwhile site manager. The message curtly told her to please be ready for a 9 am pick-up. The phone told her she had seventeen minutes to get ready, merde!

405

She thought about texting to say she'd make her own way in but that would take time and Greenwood was probably already on his way if not there already. He had a way of trying to get you off-balance.

Greenwood sat impatiently in his BMW, he'd decided to use the other car today; it looked good and he always wanted to make an impression. In her recent absence he'd been told all about Marie-Eve's report and how, with her influence within the company, it would be in his best interests to stay on the right side of her. He checked his watch, it was nearly nine and she was nowhere. Exactly on time Marie-Eve Legault crossed the car park and checked that the guy waving at her was indeed Richard Greenwood. She'd dressed to be noticed as usual, business-like with an edge, classy; she too always liked to give the right impression.

Greenwood's diminutive status made Marie-Eve aware that her five-nine plus heels, might be intimidating, but Greenwood had just greeted her with a plastic set of 'hellos' and 'nice to see you agains' and then he said something trite about the weather.

Mercifully, the trip to NPS was very quick by car and they barely had time to cover anything more than the flight being ok, the room being ok and her meal being, ok. She was aware of his eyes straying to her legs again but shrugged it off, it happened a lot; it probably meant that he wasn't gay.

At the facility she had stuff to do for security, again, and a crisply uniformed Neil with the lightly permed hair, like someone from a seventies band with a YMCA moustache, took her into the office and did what was needed to give her a temporary pass card. She really didn't understand why she had to do this little charade every damn time.

Her third real card in Nottingham, the one with her new photo on it, would be available later; Martin said that someone would drop it by her office to save her coming back for it. She pulled him up on that, saying she'd collect it herself; she didn't want her card being used by anyone or anywhere but her, and what sort of security guard wouldn't insist on cards being collected personally? Martin seemed a bit upset by this, she knew he was only trying to be nice but she wasn't in the mood. Not surprisingly, he turned colder towards her immediately. Way to go Marie-Eve, your first victim on your return to Nottingham and in record time!

The fatigue of travel, and probably her suspect condition, caught up with her a couple of times and she even got lost at one point when trying to find her way to the cafeteria. The food there was actually ok; it had a home-cooked element to it unlike in Montreal, where it was bland. The coffee here was always good too; she'd been told before she'd left Montreal the first time that Brits couldn't do coffee at all, how wrong they were.

Most of the middle of the day was spent with her Nottingham counterpart, of sorts, Bez Dooley, just catching up on progress. He was a bit more matter-of-fact than usual she thought, maybe he still felt threatened by her. Now that he knew her a little bit at least, he should do. She then had an hour in her office before a runner, whose name she knew but had temporarily forgotten, knocked on the door. Could she drop by Mr. Greenwood's office as soon as was convenient?

On the way, she decided against small talk. The runner introduced himself as Glen Coffey, one of the juniors in sales, and she remembered him as one of the people she'd had five minutes with earlier in her stay. He didn't mind being forgotten; he said it always happened, in that polite, self-depreciating British way that was both endearing and annoying in equal measures.

She was deposited at Greenwood's P A, Joan Bain's, desk. She only remembered the name because she'd got a little name thing on the desk, announcing it to the world. She had been instantly forgettable the first time she'd seen her and would be ever more. Joan was busy with something; she glanced up and gave a thin smile "I won't be a moment". Marie-Eve didn't answer verbally but 'well, fuck you, madam' went on a loop in her head for a minute or two. When important matters of state had been completed, "Joan, is it?" showed Marie-Eve in to Greenwood's office.

Although she'd been in there a couple of times before it had not been for long, by choice. Greenwood rarely conducted business in there, he preferred Conference Room One where he could sit at the head of the table. The office was a nothing place, really. No reference books in a bookcase, always useful for giving a good impression even if you never actually opened one. The desk was clean; the in-tray had a couple of sheets in it, the out tray was empty. Greenwood sat dwarfed by his large office chair, there was no sign of a white cat to be stroked, anywhere.

Marie-Eve's mind couldn't help it, Greenwood had become 'Mini-Me' immediately she'd met him and that was never, ever going to change.

Pleasantries over, Greenwood launched into the tight-ship speech he'd obviously rehearsed, hoping to make a good impression and still not entirely sure whether he was dealing with a spy or a liaison, even though she'd been around a while now, off and on. Reading the situation perfectly, Marie-Eve thanked Greenwood for his kind welcome back, dropping in the 'don't worry, I told you before, I'm not a spy or anything, I'm here to offer my help and expertise to our British friends and colleagues to aid the transition' line; she'd been rehearsing too, but her delivery was much slicker.

Greenwood's phone buzzed and he apologised before answering. It must have been something important within the scheme of things because he left the room immediately, telling her he'd only be a few minutes. While he was gone she browsed the wall of certificates, he had everything up there including his first-aid course certificate from years ago. She whipped her phone out and photographed each one for later perusal. By the time he re-entered, she was back in her chair demurely awaiting the resumption of the meeting.

The meeting as such was more of a fishing expedition and Greenwood rambled on a bit about various scientific issues without actually getting to the point, which Marie-Eve knew was her report. She managed to steer the conversation away from the report and towards the importance of Good Laboratory Practice and, to her surprise, it seemed he wasn't really sure what he was talking about. Marie-Eve put it down to nerves, she had that effect on some men and it had proved useful from time to time. As far as she could see, Greenwood would always be a minor player at NPS, if he kept his job that is. He was just a figure-head who would do as he was told by Jim Duggan. For her, he was an irrelevance; he wasn't a part of her plan.

# SEVENTY-TWO

## Monday 12 September

Marie-Eve read the 'Whatsapp' message with interest. So, our dear, beloved boss, Dick Greenwood is a big, fat liar. She'd sent her phone images of Greenwood's main qualifications to a 'friend' who would be able to double-check on their veracity. It seemed that both his degree and his PhD were obtained from the University of Lying Bugger, actually supplied by a guy somewhere in the US who'd set up a business selling certificates. They were quite realistic, but neither claimed educational establishment had admitted to taking on Greenwood as a student, so it looked like he'd lied his way into NPS.

Having the information was one thing, but finding a use for it was another. Her plans for the foreseeable didn't really mean that she was looking to go higher in NPS but her mandate from Ben was to get noticed and what better way than taking down the relatively new head of their UK branch, along with the idiots who hired him without checking. She smiled, that would be that supercilious Ranji then, too.

She decided that she needed some additional input, so she sent off an email to one of her more trusted friends at NPS in Montreal. Had she thought about it, sending the information in a company email might not have been sensible. It was too late to do anything when she realised that they still archived every email, in or out of the company by everyone unfiltered. That was one of their little local policies that was probably worth keeping and rolling out throughout NPS, were she intending to remain in their employ. That must amount to thousands of emails every day she assured herself, nobody important would ever see it in time.

A few days later she was in Ranji's office. He was playing the serious man, peering at what was obviously her file, initiated when she first arrived in Nottingham, she assumed. It looked quite thick, probably full of complaints but also holding copies of her reports, or at least the ones she'd allowed them to see, including reports on those NPS staff who were the next rif material.

Singh began with the standard "you're probably wondering why I called you here, Marie-Eve", to which she answered "no, not at all, I'm here because you saw my email to a colleague which reveals that Mr. Greenwood got his job under false pretenses."

Singh was taken aback; this was supposed to be under his control. All he could manage was "yes, that's right".

Marie-Eve launched into a lecture about how her remit included the assessment of all NPS personnel up to, and including, the head of Nottingham and that, of course, included all those below that position such as staff in Human Resources. While she was happy for Ranji to be aware of this and the processes that might follow, she reported elsewhere and higher up in the company than just to a site head. The email contents are confidential to a point and that point would be decided by her, and not Greenwood or a local HR manager.

Had she gone too far? Singh looked like he was going to explode but he managed to rein it in and, with that irritating way they have, countered with "of course, and what an excellent job you have done, but I would have preferred you to have come to me first. You have exposed a serious issue, one we cannot take lightly and one that I will have to raise with Mr. Greenwood, personally, when he comes in here. Yes, he is waiting outside now. Had you come to me first we could have navigated this in a more professional manner, now I have to spend time fire-fighting as much as anything. I happen to know that Mr. Greenwood's credentials, his real credentials, are sound. I investigated them myself".

Marie-Eve sat calmly, taking in this new information, not actually believing it having seen that Singh had everything to gain by watching

Greenwood's back. It was a level of control over Greenwood that Singh could exercise when needed, she was mildly impressed. Indeed, it was a process that she'd used to her advantage in Montreal from time to time.

Sitting back and looking very relaxed, she smiled. "I'll tell you what; we'll call this round a draw although I would like to see the hiring details for Greenwood myself. You know, CV, how much you actually researched him and, of course, who interviewed him".

Now it was Singh's turn to smile. "That information is covered by our data protection laws I'm afraid. I will though be informing Mr. Duggan personally of your interest and findings. I think we're done here, Ms. Legault".

Keeping her composure, because now she was the one approaching boiling point, she left the room, barely acknowledging the waiting Greenwood as she breezed past. This wasn't over, she thought, not by some way.

She had to wait ten minutes before she got connected to Jim Duggan. "Ah, Marie-Eve, I see that you have been making waves in Nottingham".

"That is why I was sent, I believe, just doing my job, Jim". Now we'd see whether the company first-name policy worked too, none of this stuffy Doctor this and Doctor that at NPS, no, we are all equal!

"I appreciate the job you have done, Marie-Eve, and we need to proceed with caution, particularly as the Pharmaceutical industry can be quite reactionary when senior staff have issues. Please leave this with me for now, don't press the subject anywhere and be assured that action will be taken at the appropriate time. Again, well done, Marie-Eve, your reputation is well justified and this work will stand you in good stead when bigger and better things are on offer. Oh, and give my regards to Ben when you see him". And he hung up.

What? How did he know about Ben, did he suspect they were still an item? Even after their acrimonious split, engineered, true, but still convincing. She'd need to let Ben know, there may be deeper issues now, had 'call me Jim' found out about Marie-Eve's involvement in the Saviour study?

# SEVENTY-THREE

## Friday 23 September

In Central Nick, people were in early, knowing that another body was going to add to the mountain of checking and cross-checking they had been doing for first, Marie-Eve Legault, then Tracey Mills and now Neil Martin.

The dead board was filling up. Legault took up most of the available space but Mills had her space and now Martin had his own corner, just like he'd had in real life.

Information about Tracey was still being accumulated. She wasn't known to them for any criminal activity but she had been involved in a domestic a couple of times that had been resolved on site on each occasion and not followed up. They were waiting for more information from the HR people at NPS and also from other departments within the Nottinghamshire Police.

The scene of death photo for Mills was colourful, to say the least, plus they had a selfie from another passenger who had captured a part of Mills in the background at around about just before she fell onto the rail and in front of the approaching train. 'Fell' meant coincidence, 'pushed' meant something much deeper, something they were all not really wanting to consider yet. It was too soon, but, given the NPS link between the three deaths, each officer knew that 'serial killer' was on everyone's lips.

The CCTV from the station had been useful to a point. It had shown Mills in the café earlier talking to someone, as yet unidentified but a woman, a friend perhaps. It had also showed the scrum on the platform as the train had approached. Unfortunately, the camera angle meant that the sheer number of bodies between Mills and the camera made it hard to see exactly what happened but the way that Mills fell, carefully keeping the cake in her right hand level, suggested that it was not a suicide. But was it an accident or did one of the other passengers deliberately push her?

Elsewhere within the Police Station, others were busily working through the CCTV, isolating faces, checking them against the list of people known to be involved, if only by virtue of waiting for their train home and then they could be eliminated from the enquiry. It was a fairly quick process as most of the people on the day had allowed a phone-photo of their faces and their contact details to be taken for just this process. Only about eight were missing, presumed to have left the scene quickly for whatever reason, and the station entrance CCTV should help there. It was unlikely that a killer would allow their photo to be taken, so it was fair to think that one of the eight was of interest.

Lack of space in the room meant that the team had to view the most relevant bits of the CCTV on a single TV monitor. While watching the section containing Mills and the unknown woman, Elkie almost immediately called her 'Jemmy Shepherd'. Three minutes and a phone call later it was confirmed, that Jemmy Shepherd had been there, had coffee with Mills, an old friend, and had left before the incident. They also had car park CCTV nearby that had her getting into her car about fifteen minutes after the death of Mills. Just a coincidence, then.

The CCTV reviewers had also isolated seven people in or around the café who were also on the platform at the time of death. Not unusual, and just a process of elimination for each individual. At the end of the café clip, Knight again chirped up. A man in the café was familiar from a previous case she'd read about but she couldn't recall which case or who he was. Like a poorly-remembered pop tune whose name you couldn't dredge up, the idea of who he was kept hiding within her brain.

The platform footage was hard work, as expected. They had mere glimpses of faces, people turning and moving, a bit of shoving and some strong language but really just the normal hurley-burley of catching a commuter train. Suddenly Knight yelled 'there', and they hit 'pause' then went back, frame by frame. The same face from the café was there, on the platform, and now three bodies away from Mills. Who the fuck was he?

Thompson sorted Prosser and Knight to follow up and visit Jemmy Shepherd again, to get more details. Maybe there was something in the girlie chat that was useful and they needed to know where she was, after leaving the station and before getting to the car park. On the way to Jemmy Shepherd's house, Prosser kept quiet. He could see that Elkie was desperately trying to sift the detritus of her pretty sharp memory to isolate the platform man, the man who might be responsible for the death of Tracey Mills, the 'Pizza Express'. Who came up with that? Banks he thought, it sounds right up her gallows-humour street.

As they arrived, Jemmy was just getting home from a jog around the local streets, with the baby in the buggy. She was a bit flustered, mostly because she was sweaty and didn't look her best but also because Craig had called about dead Tracey, just before she'd set off. She had been the unnamed woman on last night's news, and so she'd expected the police to show up. They'd have seen her on their CCTV video clips and she felt sure that they would want chapter and verse on the conversation she'd had with Tracey, yesterday afternoon.

Once they were all inside and Small was ensconced in the playpen, Jemmy made tea first, served it with Hobnobs then left them for a few minutes to change. She'd been thinking about the conversation she was about to have all through her run. She had nothing to hide here, it was just a girlie conversation of sorts, but there were bits that were not the business of the police, so she mentally edited her anticipated responses accordingly. She then dug into her handbag for the receipt for the Radiohead CD she'd bought on her way back to the car, knowing full-well that she'd need to justify her time between leaving Tracey and getting into her car. It helped that she'd read everything

Ann Cleeves had ever written, it was a pity that Prosser didn't match her minds-eye image of Jimmy Perez.

Once settled, Jemmy waited for the police to initiate the interview, well chat, really, or so they said. First they passed on their condolences for the loss of her friend, how close were they? And then they were off. The questions were simple enough to answer, 'was Tracey agitated or did she seem normal? Was she bothered by anything, did the recent death of Marie-Eve Legault bother her or didn't she know her? Who'd arranged the meet-up? How close was Craig to his staff and to his number two Tracey, in particular?'

Jemmy saw where the emphasis was swinging. Craig had been at work and so was not 'in the frame', as they say, but perhaps they thought that the murders were the actions of more than one person, two people on a killing spree for some reason unknown, perhaps a 'Bonnie and Clyde' type of glamorous couple?

Nothing Jemmy said really shed light on the situation, apart from her insistence that Tracey would not have killed herself. Suddenly a phone rang, not the usual 'bring-bring', but Gloria Gaynor telling the world she'd survive. Prosser turned an odd shade, but rose to answer, deftly changing rooms to be out of earshot.

Elkie made small talk, switching to baby, how was she getting on? How exiting, being a new mum. She was very good at putting people at their ease but, at this point, it would have taken a heavy sedative to calm the inner Jemmy, perhaps one of her 'specials'...

Prosser came back in and sat down. "Does the name 'Gary Coutts' mean anything to you?"

Now it was Jemmy's turn to be confused "he's inside isn't he, GBH or something?"

"Out last week, not a happy bunny we are told. You obviously know the name".

"Yes, he was Tracey's ex, not a happy split that one. She had to get a court order to keep him away. Why, was it him, did he kill Tracey?"

"He is a person of interest to us based on his history with Tracey, obviously. Is there anything else you can tell us about him? Have you met him perhaps, did Tracey still see him despite the court order? It happens, sparks can take a long time to fade".

Jemmy confirmed that she had met him, disliked him and told Tracey he was trouble, it gave her no pleasure to be right. As far as she knew, Tracey had not seen Coutts since the court order. Her impression was that there never was much of a spark from her side and that it was Coutts who did all the pursuing.

Knight scribbled notes as she spoke. They asked if she knew where he lived. "Hucknall somewhere I think, he had a rougher accent than most, like people from pit villages".

Prosser could see that Jemmy wasn't going to offer any more, even if she did know something. He asked the perfunctory 'If she thought of anything else no matter how insignificant, could she please call them?' Knight then gave her a card to add to her growing collection.

Prosser and Elkie got up to go; they never asked for the receipt of anything, their thoughts must have been elsewhere. She got curt thanks for the drinks and biscuits, and they were off. After a couple of minutes Jemmy went over and checked the street, apart from the usual cars it was clear, nobody loitering with intent. She'd have to be cautious though, Gary out, shit!

# SEVENTY-FOUR

Now it is getting silly. Three bodies in the mortuary, all were working for NPS. I'm pretty sure Martin pegging it is coincidental, a drugs thing going by his addiction as per the autopsy but still, we could have done without it. There are bits and pieces falling into place though. Interestingly we have bits of blood from several locations around NPS, including on the shipping cart. The ID might be enough to get stuck into someone a bit more but, as the cart is in general use; the blood could be anybody and everybody's.

With Mills and Martin dying, it is getting more and more complicated. Her death might even have two edges to it. Primary has to be her ex, on a court order and violent. Secondary is Shepherd, again! Known to be flirty with Mills, according to gossip, thanks Elkie, your naturally easy-going disposition is an excellent tool when it comes to loosening tongues unwittingly.

The people in Montreal are going to speak to this Ben Arjah character tomorrow, so we might get a bit more about Legault's involvement with Saviour and him, but surely that is just boyfriend and girlfriend stuff.

If this goes like a typical detective story, we'll have another murder and a rescue, pity we don't have guns for everyone here in Nottingham but why spoil a good plotline! Thinking about it, they do in Montreal, perhaps the Mounties will shoot their man after getting him to confess; that would make a good ending.

# SEVENTY-FIVE

## Tuesday 13 September

The weekly management committee meeting started when the last of the scientific heads rolled up. Most were there just to show willing; Greenwood was there because, as de-facto head, he needed to be. Besides, why spoil things by being unduly lazy when everything was going so swimmingly?

The finance guy sat quietly, not catching any eyes and slumping down in his chair slightly, he looked like a mouse surrounded by cats! Still, having a mouse in finance was better than a smoothie that smiles all the time and says how good things are, whilst squirrelling away cash into their own secret accounts. Greenwood had experience of a few of them in past lives, he'd even split the proceeds of creative bookkeeping with one although, to be fair, the lass had no choice once she'd been found out.

They took ten minutes or so to go through the tedium of various study updates. It was all gobbledygook to Greenwood, but he always tried to seem attentive. They could normally whack through a meeting in twenty minutes or so, sometimes they had to add another five for a serious disciplinary before firing whoever they were talking about. Mr. Finance had looked worried throughout though, now what?

Under 'any other business', the mouse raised the issue of Saviour and their unpaid bills, that old chestnut. The department heads were not in the least interested, unless they were told to suspend analysis, which meant that they then had to find a whole load of people something to do, and quickly. The finance for the study had been raised during several previous meetings, ever since the blasted thing had arrived in Nottingham with minimum notice. This time it was a bit more serious, or so the mouse claimed.

Mr. Finance announced that he'd checked with Montreal's finance department, Saviour had not yet paid a single invoice anywhere for storage and analysis. Were it any other contract, then they would have suspended all activity until the finances had been straightened out. The sum owed to NPS across the board was substantial, six figures substantial.

Marie-Eve Legault, who Greenwood had forgotten all about, chirped in with the news that this happened a lot with bigger studies. Saviour were very important to NPS and that this would almost certainly be an administrative error at one end, or the other, before tossing a venomous look in the direction of Mr. Finance.

As a murmur developed, Greenwood cut in quickly. If they weren't careful this would degenerate into a long discussion that would end up going in circles and he'd had enough for today, besides he had an errand to run. "Please present the actual money owed at the next management committee meeting, let me know how much it is as soon as you have it. I will conference with Mr. Duggan in New Jersey and we will decide what is the best way of going forwards. As you know, Mr. Duggan has taken a close interest in our relationship with Saviour. Right, if that is all, meeting adjourned, minutes to be circulated tomorrow, thank you everyone".

Nobody argued, only Mr. Finance was in a continued state of bother. Greenwood glanced at him accusingly, so he slunk out of the conference room. Greenwood was last to leave, whoever it was that tidied up could get on with it. As a sop to the rumours he said loudly, "I trust that you gentlemen heard everything clearly and appreciated the positive way I handled the meeting?" He flicked the lights off, closed the door and headed home. In the darkness of the empty room there was a barely audible 'click'.

In the corridor Marie-Eve was in conversation with Mr. Finance, who appeared to be waiting for Greenwood. Her voice was not particularly loud, but it had the cutting edge of a band saw. She was strongly

421

advising the hapless accountant about the 'whens and wherefores' of presenting such information and how dare he drop it into an SMC meeting unannounced and then leave it on Dick Greenwood's shoulders, disgraceful!

Mr. Finance fled, but Greenwood had appreciated the show of loyalty and said so. By this time, Marie-Eve was again bursting for a pee, otherwise she might have offered something more conciliatory than barking "I'm thinking about the company, not you" in his general direction. Greenwood had no opportunity to say anything, as she disappeared into the nearby loo.

He considered waiting, but he had things to attend to and, besides, when he'd run his little errand she might not be so high and mighty, afterwards.

# SEVENTY-SIX

## Sunday 18 September

Marie-Eve sat at her computer, her eyes had begun to water a bit; it had been another long day. The thought of the rewards to come were no longer such a motivating factor; she was tired, no, exhausted, and didn't have a great deal left in the tank. 'Two days to go', she kept telling herself, she'd rest then.

For the whole scenario to work, she'd realised early on, there were no shortcuts. Reports had to be read, more reports written. Standard Operating Procedures had to be updated properly, otherwise she could be found out. Now was not the time to be cavalier.

For the past two hours she'd been doing her final report, nothing was going to change significantly in the next few days. Her rif recommendations covered the dead wood and what she considered the idiots with a couple of spiteful inclusions, just because she could. What they did with the report when she'd disappeared didn't concern her; the writing of it had been cathartic, especially where Greenwood and Craig Shepherd had been concerned.

She was about to go out to the vending machine and get a cup of sludge to see her through the last hour or so when her phone pinged, somebody was texting her, Ben surely. She was genuinely confused by the number that came up, it was familiar but not in her contacts list. It was local, too. She felt that she should remember who it was, but her normal razor-sharp memory was having a bit of an off-day, hormonally speaking.

Wondering how she might find out who the text was from, mysterious as it was, she thought that the most obvious source would be a company employee, it had to be for them to be inside the building, so

423

she logged into 'Our Family'. The company directory, and did a search. She was more than surprised at the number that came up. What did he want at this time of night?

Feeling both confused and angry, she got her cup of sludge but found she had to do another bathroom dash before she could savour it. When she got back, the cup had gone and the cleaners were doing the offices. She asked them where it was but they had no idea what she wanted, they didn't speak any English, or French, making communication impossible. The irony was lost on her.

Heading back to her office with another cup of something, this time hot chocolate for the sugar, she had her second surprise of the evening when she saw Neil Martin as he was checking that doors around her were locked. He must have seen her, but there was no acknowledgment and he was quickly out of sight as he followed the retreating line of cleaners who were heading for their break. Marie-Eve knew this because she'd drawn up their schedule, more as a way of showing who held the power than an abiding interest in what a bunch of cleaners did.

She'd had never had a blood pressure problem before but she felt herself getting angry and tense for no reason that she could readily think of. She just might add the prancing pony, Martin, to the rif list for ignoring her, illogical but satisfying. The text was also bothering her, why did he want to meet her? That was done with; she'd made it very clear. Was he going to plead with her? Him on his knees, telling her he couldn't live without her, that would be fun. She wondered whether this was a chance to at least tell him, face to face, that she thought she might be pregnant. She was fairly sure it wasn't his, but only fairly sure.

At least it would be quiet everywhere, nobody overhearing their private and, she would make very clear, final conversation, beyond work. Slipping into her silent flats, she set off for the Shipping department, leaving her office door ajar. This would only take moments, besides, nobody else but the cleaners were around at this late hour.

Shipping was dark, except for the dim night-lights that people used to navigate the room before hitting the main lights. Where was he? Was this just a wind-up, a way of making her look silly? If it was, he'd be out of the building before he got his coat off in the morning. Then she remembered that he was in London for the day tomorrow, training. Well, one more day doesn't make any difference.

The door had silently shut behind her, the damper designed to stop it from banging.

"Hello, Marie-Eve". The voice came from behind her, surprised her, then she felt everything swim and she was falling, her legs had gone, not now, not now!

# SEVENTY-SEVEN

Slipping quietly around the back roads of Silverdale on the bike was quite easy. It was late enough that the pubs had just about shut and most of the identical bungalows were now in darkness, just the night owls were still up, watching re-runs of old standards on Dave.

Nobody would think twice about a late-night cyclist heading home after a long day, or heading out for a late shift, hoodie up against the wind, head down, anonymous. At this time of night, there wouldn't be anybody in the subways either. The coterie of wanna-be thugs that made them such an unsavoury proposition earlier in the evening were now away to their beds too, just the old coffee cups and chip trays left to blow back and forth in their own private, complicated, dance.

Crossing the main road, over the field and onto the old railway bed was easy too, although a yelping Fox flushed from its meal on the bank caused a brief alarm. From the cover of the thick hawthorns and elderberries, the Shipping bay door was maybe 25 yards away, time to put the gloves on. The distance was covered silently, but not without incident. Hawthorn is not a very forgiving bush at the best of times. Once the expanse of the paved area was crossed, the short protrusion of the loading bay was useful as cover. The approach light didn't work, that had been very fortuitous, but not as useful as the knowledge that the shipping door was waiting for Buildings Maintenance to get to it. The card entry pad was broken, had been for ten days now, and the only thing stopping anyone getting in was the locked door of course. It would be locked though, wouldn't it?

The side door opened easily enough, it would with the right key, though. Inside, the Shipping department was quiet, dead even. The CCTV camera bracket and the nest of wires that would have given the dozing security guard a lovely picture of the sudden and unexpected activity, was now just an untidy mess in the corner of the room. There were no more cameras to worry about, NPS hadn't yet arranged for the security overhaul to start – too busy making money to spend it.

The door from the corridor to the Shipping Room opened and Marie-Eve walked in, as expected. From behind, a totally unexpected voice greeted her. "Hello, Marie-Eve".

Marie-Eve's legs just went from under her. Shock, surprise, the last voice she expected to hear, maybe, but a stroke of luck too, no need to crack her head with the heel bar, after all, but she got a good hit anyway. There was no telling how long she'd be in dream world without a bit of ferrous encouragement. She was totally and utterly limp, passed out. She got another, just in case.

Putting the heel bar back in its rack, after a good wipe down of course, it was time to act quickly. This should sort the bitch out.

Marie-Eve was lighter than expected and not at all difficult to drape over the shipping cart, it had paid to work out, especially now. Seconds later and the whole assemblage was pushing on through to the Freezer Room. You could always rely on cleaners to not quite grasp security issues and to leave all the doors open so that the floors could dry. They'd all be on their synchronised meal break now, good plan Marie-Eve, thanks.

The walk-in freezer door opened, the retaining clip clicking quietly into place. Pushing Marie-Eve up the ramp and into the freezer was the hardest bit and needed a run up. Inside, the shelves were already wound across to one end, too obvious. It was easy enough to wind the shelves the opposite way to make a gap, aisle six; right at the back would do nicely.

The floor was slightly slippery. 'Be careful, don't slip now and knock yourself out too, how ironic would that be?'

'Phone, where is her phone?' Shit, it must be in her office. This was going to be a complication, did she delete messages? Of course she did, no evidence for anything that was how Marie-Eve worked. Oh well 'c'est la vie', for those of us who still have one.

There was a heavy thud as Marie-Eve left the cart a bit quicker than intended. "Aw, did you bang your head there, Marie-Eve? Good".

Frost was already forming on the stiffening, soon to be stiff, Marie-Eve Legault.

The door closed quietly, the temperature had held so no alarms were going off in Security. It took no time to get back to Shipping, line the cart up with the rest and find the cleaning stuff.

The bucket and cloths were where they'd always been, a half-full container of economy cleaning fluid on the same shelf. Time to give the cart a quick flash over.

How quickly would she freeze, quick enough? Perhaps a bit of encouragement was needed. Warm water freezes much quicker than cold water at extreme temperatures, worth knowing, thanks QI. A convenient bucket had been left in-situ by the cleaning staff, right by the Shipping Room door; that would do nicely.

Going back down the corridor, the tension was mounting. Breathe and relax, it will be worth it.

In the freezer, Marie-Eve hadn't moved but then she couldn't, not easily, what with being in the land of nod still! Suits me.

It was a bit of a squeeze but the water in the bucket was slowly poured over the inert body, the blue of the cleaning fluid giving Marie-Eve an odd, ethereal look. Was she already dead? Had the hits been that hard? Hope so.

There was an overriding temptation to go back in and pee on her face but no, you could probably get DNA from pee. Nothing like a good spray session to mark your territory though.

Closing the door again, another idea came. Fumbling nervously in the pockets of the freezer coats hung by the door for a pen it took three goes to find one. It was a slack fit in the door mechanism but it would do, can't have Marie-Eve waking up and going walkies now, can we?

Three minutes later and it was back on the bike, through the subway and down to the car. Bike stowed, a careful drive home and savour a job well done.

Half-way home the shakes started, convulsions, oh my god I did it. I killed Marie-Eve, I hope.

The house was quiet, no lights were on in any of the houses nearby; all was quiet, all was peaceful.

The shakes eventually eased off a bit. Nobody was going to find her until the morning, by then she'd be deep frozen. Then it hit, a late delivery. What if samples came and they found her and she woke up? She could tell them who'd tried to kill her. Oh fuck, not so clever after all, maybe a few more extra clouts from the heel bar would have been insurance.

Slipping inside home it was as planned, silent. Bed beckoned as the adrenaline started to ebb away. Sleep came, for now, and with it the certainty that nobody else was going to find her, even if there was a late delivery of samples. She'd be there undisturbed until they opened up Sample Management in the morning, then they'd find her, then she'd be dead. Who'd find her, which lucky Sample Management tech? Who cares, tomorrow was another day, a better day for some at least, but not for Marie-Eve. Oh no, not for Marie-Eve, sainted daughter of Eve.

# SEVENTY-EIGHT

The night, well early morning now, was quiet, just the nocturnal noises to be expected but no owls, he rarely heard owls at night, it made him laugh, every TV show or movie always inserted an owl into a night scene, just to define it but in real life you rarely heard anything at night but traffic and sirens. The best way to define night was that it mostly contained the normal bangs and rattles that our noisy world constantly threw up.

Although it was dark, it wasn't pitch and it had been easy to park the car and nip through to the lake. The bank was a bit muddy but so what, with all these ducks plodding around it all the time there would be no possibility of footprints remaining. Besides, it was probably going to rain soon.

The water here was deep, he thought, surely they would sink, they usually do, and nobody will find them unless they drain the lake, and, even if they do, then time and water will have erased anything he didn't want anybody to see.

He threw them one at a time and the laptop skimmed like a large stone before sinking with a faint gurgle, maybe only 20 feet out. It wasn't a very good throw.

He hoped that he was right and that nothing was backed-up on their servers. It was a stand-alone, after all and she'd refused a company one, well a Nottingham one, citing her French keyboard as the reason. She'd claimed that she didn't know how to use an English keyboard and, as she'd be writing reports, it was important not to have unnecessary distractions, such as hunting a keyboard for the right key.

He'd had the server searched thoroughly and he'd looked for a USB in the obvious places. No, he had to be right, everything she'd written was now settling into the silt at the bottom of the lake. She was going to have to start from scratch on that final report and that would buy some time.

The phone was just a bit of spite, a little something to mess her about, make her life inconvenient for a while at least.

# SEVENTY-NINE

## Wednesday 21 September

Carrie, Ben's personal assistant, was getting more and more frustrated. Every time she rang Ben, it cut to voice mail and had done so for the past three hours. He'd always made himself available to her in the past, if only to flip a quick text saying 'busy, ten minutes'. Then he'd call for a break in whatever he was involved in and call her. He knew she would only try to contact him if it was important, so where was he?

Ben sat in the back of the car, knowing full-well that the doors wouldn't open even if he tried them. He'd been told to empty his pockets and his phone had been opened and the sim card removed, it was unceremoniously tossed from the car as they drove. They ran one of those hand-scanner things over him and seemed satisfied that he wasn't carrying any hardware. He never did, that sort of thing was not his style at all.

They were heading out of Montreal and he suspected that they'd be arriving soon at the small airfield at St-Hubert. There, he would be encouraged to climb aboard a light aircraft which would take off quickly. Once airborne he'd find out exactly how this was going to go. He was calm; calmer than he had any right to be, because he'd recognised the driver who had invited him into the car, an invitation that really only had one good outcome, and one very bad one!

He'd rightly guessed that Richard Pointer had, somehow, discovered the extent of Ben's duplicity. Now perhaps the best he could expect was to make an unscheduled exit from the plane, the large guys who flanked him would no doubt facilitate that. Then there would be a short period of descent followed by a longer period of nothing. Was it even worth speaking?

"I'd have been happy to drive over to see Mr. Pointer", he said, trying to break the ice. Amazingly one of them told him that Mr. Pointer had limited time available and so had arranged for Mr. Arjah to go to him, as efficiently as possible. Not going to die just yet then, thought Ben.

They'd been aloft for about forty minutes or so when the plane began to descend. The airfield was more of a simple landing strip in the middle of what appeared to be a single, monoculture crop. The landing was a bit bumpy but, given the location and Ben's delight to at least be back on terra firma, he wasn't about to complain.

A Toyota Landcruiser met them and they all sat in silence as they bumped along a track which was, in places, actually better paved than many of Montreal's main roads. They arrived at the farm inside fifteen minutes, which suggested that it was a part of the large property on which they'd just landed. Ben locked this information away for later use, if there was a later.

He was ushered into a pleasant kitchen, warm and fragrant - a fresh baked bread smell. He was offered refreshments, which he accepted in case it was a while before he ate or drank again. Coffee and a slice of farm bread, toasted and buttered, was brought through, and very nice it was too.

After a couple of minutes, a guy Ben recognised as a senior minion entered the kitchen, followed by Richard Pointer. He looked smart but casual, almost at home, maybe he was.

He apologised for what he called the 'cloak and dagger' extraction of Ben from his office, but it was necessary. Elements within the industry had become aware of Ben's 'little scheme' and were shaping to become inextricably involved, this was bad for everyone, especially Ben. He, on the other hand, would be considered to be a victim and as angry as they were about the scam of all scams.

433

At this, Ben carefully considered his first question. He could see Pointer waiting for the right question, or what he would consider was the right question. The wrong one would surely see him dead. "Carrie?"

Pointer smiled. "She's fine, she is another one of mine but she has taken a real shine to you so you can keep her if that is what she wants".

Ben shrugged slightly, that explained a lot, still, so far so good. Should he apologise or brazen it out. Again one response would be frowned upon, maybe not fatally but perhaps painfully. He went for a simple "thank you". Pointer smiled again, it seemed genuine.

Pointer added, "I was sorry to hear about Marie-Eve Legault, you two were close and I greatly valued her skill-set". Ben made noises about her death being circumstances beyond his control and not linked to his project, as far as he knew. At that, Pointer assured Ben that he too had had nothing to do with it and his agents hadn't found who had yet, either, but he was confident that they would. She was one of his and, when they did find the killer, there would be a price to pay. A short nod of acknowledgement from Ben was his only response, what could he say?

"Your scheme was brilliant", said Pointer, "but one small element let you down and we'll discuss that at length, sometime. But for now, however I'd like you to consider yourself my guest. We will stay here for a while then move to another, more self-contained location. My organisation can use thinkers like you and, following a little establishment of company policy, you will be a part of my machine. I should point out that this is non-negotiable on all levels and that, were I not to offer you this opportunity in this way, then those elements whom have recently developed an interest in your project would be given enough information to effectively retire you, unless I choose to have it done myself".

Ben understood, but the gravity of the whole situation suddenly sat heavy with him. At first it was more like a dare, a game, now people had died, people he'd actually cared about, had Marie-Eve cared the same way? There were others too, people who had been involved but who didn't know anything about the actual plan. "Gavin and Grant?" asked Ben.

"Alas, my capability for intervention and overall feeling of responsibility does have certain limitations".

"Ah".

One of the associates, as Pointer called them, handed Ben a phone. "Now, please talk to Carrie, she's taken quite a shine to you to the point that I am not at all sure where her loyalties truly lie. Assure her that all is well, use your code words if you must. Tell her that you will be well taken care of and that she should just follow my instructions to the letter, despite whatever you and her might have arranged. Then we will all be much the happier".

Ben nodded again; his capability to talk coherently seemed to have deserted him. He dialled the pre-loaded number and she picked up on three rings, a guarded "Hello" on seeing a number displayed that she didn't recognise. Ben simply said "Case Two" and hung up. Elsewhere and beyond Ben's control, computers were being wiped and any public trace of Saviour would be gone, virtually.

He gave the phone back to one of the minions and waited for a response from Pointer. Again he smiled and said "a prearranged code, with all parameters previously discussed and understood, I like it. I knew I was right about you. Would you like me to explain what 'Case Two' is, Ben? I have all the details right here".

Ben just shook his head, knowing that it was 'game, set and match' really. "When will I see Carrie again?"

"Soon enough".

"Will we be staying in Quebec?"

"No, we'll discuss options at some future date although they are somewhat limited". Pointer stood to go but then paused opposite Ben and held out his hand. "Welcome to your new family". A brisk, firm shake and he was off and Ben resumed breathing. It looked like the lavish retirement that Ben had planned was not going to happen, well not just yet, anyway.

After a couple of days, Ben was taken back to the airstrip. A few plane changes later and he found out exactly where he would be for the foreseeable future.

Richard Pointer and his money man sat looking into the computer screen, while the man on the other end presented the verbal-only report. Everything had been done as requested. There was a pause while the money man tapped his keyboard, scrolled a file and showed it to Pointer.

Pointer gave an unspoken signal that the deal was to be finalised and then money was moving electronically between points, untraceable and unknown to all but a few. The deal hadn't made much money for Pointer, not in the scheme of things, but at this stage of his career it wasn't the money, it was the respect. Word would spread out in discreet circles that someone had tried, and failed, to steal from him and that the outcome was the same as always, the scheme had failed. They all knew what that meant, failure was considered somewhat final.

Elsewhere in a very pleasant house in a nice area of Panama, Ben relaxed. Carrie was lounging in the hammock doing a conversational Spanish course, speaking to the disembodied voice appearing in her posh Bluetooth headphones. Anonymity, he was told, was assured. Think of it as employment with perks and a very binding contract.

It could have been worse, far worse, but this would do, at least until the real 'Case Two' was initiated. Yes, for now, this would do very nicely.

# EIGHTY

## Friday 23 September

Mo sat in the living room while Small got busy with whatever it is was kids did with piles of seemingly identical toys. She could hear Craig nearby but, not being totally familiar with the house, she was not sure which room he was in. It was only later, when Jemmy told her he was watching the football, again, that Mo figured they had a TV room where he could at least escape from Jemmy and Small.

Climbing into Mo's little car, they eased off, Jemmy chattering and, as usual, not really waiting for any sort of participation from Mo. That was fine, all was fine. This would be a bit like the old days when they worked together and partied together, just at a more mature level now.

Topics of conversation revolved mainly around Small again. Mo didn't mind too much this time, she'd heard most of it before but she let it wash over her. They were about half-way to the gastro-pub when, out of the blue, Jemmy said something odd, totally out of context and so unexpected that Mo threw in a "what? Didn't hear you", just to clarify.

Jemmy did a hand shuffle to indicate that it was just a throw-away thing, nothing worth repeating but Mo had heard right and Jemmy's comment seemed to be designed to drop Craig from a great height into the pool of steaming poo that was the Marie-Eve Legault murder investigation. It really didn't make sense because what Jemmy said did not match up with what Mo knew as fact.

Filing the information under 'WTF', Mo tried to move the conversation into the bland, and certainly away from babies, but Jemmy kept on telling her all about Small's latest achievement, and, surprise, surprise, it largely involved successful bowel movements in the right place. It was going to be a very long night.

The gastro-pub was OK but perhaps a bit fancy for a girly night out. The food was on the restricted side, and made more of the presentation than actual substance. Jemmy seemed well pleased though, and even started to be a bit like her old pre-Craig self, making risqué jokes and sort of flirting with both her and the waiter. Mo had seen this stuff before and kept her at a bit of a distance, complications were not welcome for Mo for the time being.

The evening meandered along with Mo feeling a bit detached, what with her being sober, and Jemmy letting her hair down and making some very odd comments, most of which probably meant nothing. As Mo was driving she stayed sensible, just sipping fizzies, even if she'd pay later when the gas made its way out. Jemmy slurped a few interesting concoctions down, stuff that even former barmaid Mo had never heard of. They were having quite a loosening effect on Jemmy.

Mo had almost switched off when she realised Jemmy was talking about the murder again. She was asking stuff, detailed stuff; curious stuff. Then she came right out with Craig and Marie-Eve, the caravan and everything. Mo tried to look surprised but wasn't, rumours got around, some of them were even true. Jemmy was getting up a head of steam, not a rant but a calculating explanation of what followed; then she said that she'd shagged Greenwood!

This last nugget of information had Mo coughing, "what?" Then Jemmy started through the whole 'getting Craig back for being a bad boy' thing and how he could be violent, often scaring her, making threats, even to kill her if she ever cheated on him. Then she started on the night Marie-Eve died, stunned with a couple of blows from a crow bar and then dumped in a freezer and then the evil bastard had covered her in warm water to make her freeze quicker. She even said Craig was out of the house longer than he'd told the police and she'd not told them about the lie, part out of loyalty but mostly out of fear.

Mo was shocked and shaken. Now she wanted nothing more than to get home, lock the door and hide. How could someone she had worked with do that to Marie-Eve? Feigning a migraine, Mo said that she'd need to cut short their night. Jemmy didn't seem to mind at all, she'd got what was bothering her off her chest and had passed the burden onto Mo.

Dropping Jemmy off, Mo didn't hang around despite the offer of coffee. Her head was feeling thick, it was almost as if the migraine story was becoming a reality, which was odd; she'd never had a migraine in her life. As Jemmy gave a final wave Mo did a double-take. She was sure that she'd missed something, a piece of jewellery she'd noticed on Jemmy, a nice thing, she'd commented on it and Jemmy had said it had been a gift from Craig but she wasn't wearing it now. Where did it go?

That night Mo turned the whole thing over in her mind a hundred times, now she thought that she had the answer to who had killed Marie-Eve. There was no arguing; lies had been told to cover the tracks, this was not something she could sit on despite her best instincts; she had to call the cops.

## EIGHTY-ONE

"Not writing tonight?" Rebecca sounded concerned. She encouraged Dave Thompson to write, it was good for his mind, relaxing even, and, when she was allowed to read it, it gave her a little insight into the more complicated parts of his personality that often stayed hidden from her.

"I think I'm having a bit of a writer's block. This case isn't moving like it should, even though we have been asking the right questions, they just don't seem to be going to the right person".

"Look, Dave, I know you try to shelter me from your job and I understand why. The world isn't a very lovely place at times and you are being protective, that's natural, but I am quite a good objective thinker. I was even school Cluedo champion back in the day, so talk to me in minimal detail".

So Thompson went through all of the case characters, the possible killers, starting with Shepherd and moving through the field, ending with Greenwood. Then he made some hot chocolate and waited while she was thinking about what he'd said, fidgeting and shifting position on the sofa for a more comfortable position. Their next sofa would be better quality, and possibly designed for at least two full-grown adults to sit on. Thinking about it there would have to be an element of stain resistance about it too, at least until their kids were house-trained.

Dave thought about that. Kids, plural, yes there had to be two, one as insurance. He chided himself for thinking like a policeman but knew that it was unavoidable; he'd always see the darker side of any situation first.

Rebecca asked about female suspects and so Thompson talked about the obvious. Mo, who had been potentially spurned as a lover. Mills, who had been loyal to Craig Shepherd, protective even, and finally Jemmy Shepherd, but the team had thought that all were peripheral, unlikely to have either the strength to overcome Legault or the motivation to kill her.

"Except Jemmy".

"But she was at home asleep when the murder took place and, even though her alibi is Craig and she is his, and they have not faltered, what they say rings true. Craig Shepherd was at home, not far from heading for his pit, at the time of the murder. Jemmy backs this up and, although we haven't asked her directly whether she killed Legault, Craig's story backs her up and he is, as I said, 100% with it, despite our little tricks".

"OK, so motive first. The Orinoco Smith thing is garbage. From the snippets I've heard from you, she isn't capable and she was at home, witnesses confirm – in the bin with Moonbeam Orinoco Smith, agreed?"

"Agreed, but the men...",

"Ignore the men; we'll get there if we need to".

"Well they are all suspects, legitimate suspects".

"Suspects with alibis, you said so yourself, although out of all of them, Greenwood, I think is most likely. He was there at the time and Martin seems to be his alibi and vice versa. So, Tracey Mills. Killer?"

"No, flirty and might been carrying a torch for Craig, but no killer and now dead too, of course".

"A torch, what is this 'Brief Encounter'?" Thompson smiled.

"Now, Craig".

"But you said men later."

Rebecca just shrugged off Thompson's indignation at her changing tack. "Did Craig Shepherd do it, gut feeling, enough non-circumstantial evidence, yes, no?"

"No".

She continued. "Simon Reid, yes, no?"

"No".

OK, Neil Martin, dead now, of course, but not a complication that affects his being a suspect, yes, no?"

"No".

"Bez Dooley, what's his real name, is it Bez?"

"No", said Thompson "it's Steven".

"Is Steven Dooley the killer, yes, no?"

"No".

"Richard Greenwood and Ranji Singh, both peripheral you say, so, are they killers, yes, no?"

"No".

"We'll come back to Greenwood I think."

"OK".

Thompson was quite enjoying the exchange and Rebecca was getting into her stride.

"Now, more peripheral characters still, Alan Bain and Andy Mood, killers, yes, no?"

"Look Rebecca, thanks for your help and everything but you are just telling me what I already know".

"Humour me, I'll take it they are a no, so, one to go".

"Jemmy Shepherd".

"Jemmy Shepherd. Now, here is a little insight for you, women don't like their men to mess around. Some women forgive, others don't. With the don'ts, you know that the guilt will be there forever, with the forgive types you have to ask why. Does Jemmy Shepherd seem the confident type, does she love Craig?"

"Yes, confident, modern, a new mum. Yes, I think she loves Craig, they have a baby".

"If she wanted to, could she dump Craig over his cheating and attract another man, even with a baby in tow?"

"Yes".

"So what does that tell you?"

Thompson sat there looking confused. True, he was a modern man, feminist, equalitarian, a humanist and even thought that girls could play football, but the female psyche had dark areas that even Luke with his Lightsabre wouldn't go into. He tried anyway.

"She didn't dump him because she loves him".

Rebecca asked, "and what is he to her?"

"Husband, partner, friend, how am I doing?"

"You are getting warm. Did you know that a male Polar Bear can be up to four feet bigger and nearly double the weight of the female but that the female will fight the male to the death if he tries to take her cubs?

Now, substitute cubs for partner, baby, lifestyle, life and what do you have?"

"Jemmy Shepherd found out that her husband had shagged the Fish Finger, sorry Legault, and then, rather than simply forgive him or leave him, she chose to defend her family in the best and most complete way that she could. But really, she doesn't seem the type".

Rebecca sat back, the bump was lively again; she was getting very close to time. "Obviously, these are only the uncluttered thoughts of a heavily pregnant woman on the matter, but it was Jemmy Shepherd, in the Shipping Room, with the Crowbar – do I win the game?"

Thompson was already head-down over his jotter scribbling. Taking this hypothesis further would wait until tomorrow. Rebecca was right; it was time to look at the case in another way. If it worked out, great, if not then, well, at least they tried it. He paused, looked at Rebecca and asked "If it was me cheating and you found out - forgive, leave, fight, which would it be?"

"Mummy always told me to keep an air of mystery, it helps a relationship along. Besides, you aren't the type; I know, I kept Gerbils when I was little".

Thompson, even with his incisive detective's brain, didn't know what to make of that one so he just said "OK", kissed her carefully on the forehead and went back to his notes on the latest plot twist.

Sometimes you get bogged down in detail and going the traditional route – note to self, step back regularly and look at the bigger picture. We should have had Jemmy Shepherd higher up on the leader board. I think we had a degree of sympathy for her, mostly because her man was playing away but also because she had a new baby and men find thinking of a shiny new mum as a suspect to something quite grim, disturbing.

We'll talk to her but, from what I understand, she is quite mentally agile. I would expect her to dump Craig in it if she thinks we are getting too close. There are parts of Jemmy Shepherd that we don't understand at all.

# EIGHTY-TWO

## Saturday 24 September

Driving in, Thompson had more of a spring in his step even though he was sitting down. He'd been turning Rebecca's reasoning over and over, and had decided that this was an angle not yet covered and very much worth exploring. He also realised that it was an angle that had occurred to him previously but one that he'd been consciously avoiding. Was it the baby that was clouding his judgement?

Once in, he called the main team together and went through his discussion with Rebecca. The response was universal, they agreed. Knight said that she had a feeling about Jemmy before but nothing they'd asked anyone pointed to her. Now they were going with a very raw motive but what else was there?

Prosser then revealed to all that he knew Mo from way back, just as a bar worker, but had seen her before the years had been delivered in bulk. Thompson thought that Prosser should exploit the link and the fact that Mo and Jemmy were friends. "Just some judicial pumping for information, give her specific questions, perhaps something only the killer might know. Jenny help him out, you have a devious mind".

She frowned, "true, the only reason I haven't bumped you off for your job is that you are too nice and I can't think of a polite way of doing it".

"Good manners cost nothing" said Thompson.

Dad asked for a quiet word, so Thompson led him away from the rest, "I'm all ears".

"Boss, I've looked at this angle and the evidence is thin but logic points firmly in the direction of Jemmy Shepherd. We might need to manufacture a set of circumstances in order to catch her, if it turns out to be her. Conventional interviewing will get nowhere, we need it from her. There could be accusations of entrapment".

"OK, leave the details to me, I have to talk to Charnley on this one, he is all we have. I don't fancy going to Perkins, if it goes wrong he'd think nothing of dropping us all in the shit".

Dad wandered off; satisfied he'd made his point. Thompson headed over to the closed door of Charnley's office, knocked and, this time, waited for the grunted invitation to enter.

Charnley was reading various reports; Thompson assumed he'd been in the process of wrapping up the details where he could. Soon, hopefully, he'd be out of there but first he had to buy in to what Thompson had in mind.

Charnley listened with something approaching his former intensity. When Thompson had finished, and he'd not had a single interruption from Charnley, he saw the smile on his boss's face. "Well done, Dave, great minds think alike, and all that".

Ignoring the comment, Thompson went on. "Sir, I'm concerned about being accused of entrapment".

"Don't worry, Dave, we are not encouraging Jemmy Shepherd to commit a crime, we are seeking to clear her name unless she acts in a way that suggests guilt or she confesses. How the confession is obtained is a grey area. I like your plan but nobody must be coerced into taking part, that has to be clear, and you have to ensure the safety of everyone. If you can't, then it is a no go. If you are satisfied, and I leave it to your judgement because, despite occasional appearances, I do trust your judgement, Dave, then it is very much a go. I will need the risk assessment, come and see me when it's ready".

"And what if it isn't Jemmy Shepherd and she incriminates Craig?"

"Win-win as I see it, time to put this one to bed, Dave".

Thompson was a bit taken aback. His old boss had finally returned to them, and as good as new, and he'd given consent. It was time to get the ball rolling.

# EIGHTY-THREE

Back in the office, the group involved were talking through the details. Prosser broke away from the chatter and picked his vibrating phone out of his jacket pocket. He did a double-take before realising it was a recent addition to his limited contacts list, Mo. The office was noisy and so he had to shield his ears to get what she was saying, she sounded scared.

He told her to jump in her car and head for Arnold town centre where they could meet up. She agreed immediately, hung up and Prosser was left to wonder what this was going to be, fantasy or fact. You never really knew which you'd get from Mo at any one time, sometimes both in one sentence.

He went back to the group and interrupted, telling them what he'd just heard, as sketchy as it was. Thompson just said "go", so he pocketed his Dictaphone, not sure whether to slip it into his top pocket hidden or sit it right out on the table. He decided he'd be up front if he needed it. He headed up Mansfield Road, rehearsing what Thompson had told him they needed. Would she go for it? Not if her story was a fantasy, she wouldn't.

The greasy spoon café was pretty undistinguished and Mo was sat there nursing a tea. The remnants of a scone, and whatever she'd spread on it, were scattered all over the table top. He could see that she was very wound up; this was for real, whatever it was. Their greeting was brief, no slang, no cockiness, just a middle-aged woman and a weathered-looking man meeting up.

Prosser let Mo settle a bit before asking why she wanted to talk, she wasn't one to be chivvied along and whatever she had would all come out at her own pace. She started, incoherently at first, then went off into something of a long ramble; the only problem was she seemed to be telling her story from the middle. He called a halt and suggested she wound back a bit, just so he could catch the details again. Taking the hint she took a deep breath and started from the beginning, beginning with the phrase, "I think I know who murdered Marie-Eve".

Over the next twenty minutes or so, Mo went through what she knew and what she suspected. Surprisingly, after a few minutes, she had calmed down considerably and was able to deliver her information sequentially. When she had finished, Prosser sat back, looking for signs that there was fabrication but she was genuine, she'd told him two things that were not public knowledge. She truly believed that she knew who had killed Legault and her measured delivery of facts and supposition added up.

Unless she was the killer herself, then she'd know the non-public facts anyway.

Her story over, she sat there, looking like a kid waiting to be told she'd done well and it was hard for Prosser not to do just that, but check, 'check and check again' was the mantra. He pulled out the Dictaphone and asked her to repeat everything, right from the beginning.

Mo looked a little hurt, not surprisingly, but when he explained why, that he'd have to let the rest of the team hear it before there could be any action and that he wanted to make sure he got everything right, however trivial, she got it straight away and then delivered the exact same information into the tiny recorder.

"What now, do I need protection?"

It was a good question. To Prosser her story made sense and it filled in gaps that the team had been wrestling with.

"I need to talk to my DS now, and probably even my DI about this, but I don't think you are at risk at the moment. If the killer gets wind of your suspicions then, yes, protection, but for now act normally, be Mo for me, I know you can do that".

She answered with a simple "of course".

"I also need to know that you are willing to participate if we have to set up a sting?"

Mo looked surprised. "What exactly would I be doing, what would be my role in a sting?"

"You'd be the bait, Mo, pure and simple".

She nodded silently. Inside she still wondered whether this was the right thing to do but someone who had killed once, at least, was too dangerous to ignore.

Prosser rose to go, but before he did he thanked her and she was shaken by the honesty of his thanks, this was real and it felt fulfilling. He told her he'd be in touch, very soon, and was lost from sight in moments as a crowd of student types entered the café, all noisy and carefree and certainly not carrying the weight of the knowledge that a calculating killer was someone they knew, and thought they knew well.

Once he was back in the car, Prosser called Thompson and told him to listen. He set the Dictaphone going, laid it next to the phone and set off back to Central. Things were going to move pretty quickly now.

Game on! Thanks to the fantasist we have something, a strong line too. Fuck it, no; we have the killer, I'm sure. This is going to be dodgy, it will sound like a fiction if it plays out the way we think it will but it seems the only way. Charnley needs to sign off on it first, but I think he will. This is it, we're closing in. The story might have a hero, or maybe another victim, we'll see how it all plays out.

# EIGHTY-FOUR

Thompson walked into Charnley's office, he didn't seem to mind, it was almost as if he expected it. He pushed a yellow Post-it over to Thompson 'work only!' it said. Thompson nodded and told Charnley they had a lead and needed his permission for the set up to catch the killer. Charnley nodded back, "do it, Dave, finish this one off neat and tidy. This will go well on your record, they have to replace me and I'll be recommending you. You might not get it, though, what with the current climate", and then he looked around the room as if expecting hidden figures to appear.

Thompson presumed that it was his turn to speak. "Thank you, Sir, I very much appreciate it".

"I'll need a written plan before you do the set up, but take it as read; you have a go".

"Yes, Sir, as we said a little earlier, here is the risk assessment".

Charnley looked it over and said "very good". And that was that.

Back in the ops room, Thompson called the team together just as Prosser got back. He kept it to within the group and made sure they knew that there would be an element of danger. Laying out a paper map of the sting site, Thompson highlighted three places. Prosser and Banks would be in location one, Thompson and Elkie at location two and Dad would be in location three. "Any questions?" Nobody had any.

Prosser called Mo and arranged for her to meet the team the following morning, when they'd go through the plan, set her going and catch the baddie. It all sounded pretty simple, but Mo was feeling a distinct dislike for reality at this point. She also had to make the call to set up the meeting, could she do that now and then let them know? "Yes", she said, and hung up. Fifteen minutes later and she was back on the end of the phone. She sounded perkier, more Mo-like or at least like the image she liked to project. "Game on tomorrow, boys and girls".

Next they had to set up with the location, Colwick Park. John Fraser was quite happy to help; a cool customer, a result, no doubt, of his previous service in the Military Police that he kept banging on about, or perhaps he just liked the cloak and dagger of it all. It must get boring stuck on Colwick Park all day with just the ducks and grebes for entertainment.

The plan was simple. Mo would be wired; she'd agreed, wasn't coerced and had almost insisted. They needed some confirmation, a confession. Prosser and Banks would be on the main lake in a small boat, concealed by dense overhanging trees; that would put them very near the rendezvous spot, moments away.

Dad would be observing Mo through binoculars, while hidden opposite the sting site.

Thompson and Elkie would be behind Mo as she made her way to the rendezvous spot, once they were sure the killer wasn't in the car park, watching. To anyone looking they'd just be a couple 'using' the park for their own purposes, as many did.

Most of the time, being a Police Officer was boring but when they went for the kill; when they were really going for it; that was the time that they all felt alive.

# EIGHTY-FIVE

## Sunday 25 September

The house was quiet when Craig got in, no Jemmy, no Small. He was feeling worn and ready to do whatever was needed to put things right. He wasn't being noble, just facing up to his responsibilities. At times he despised himself for not having a backbone but this time he was ready to stand up and be counted.

There was no note but he wasn't worried, her car had gone, the buggy too, she was probably out tightening her pelvic floor again, not that he got near it that often these days. He wondered who had actually changed. He was just Craig but she'd become Mum and was working hard at developing her life-long relationship with Small, as she called it. After a day at work, all Craig wanted was dinner, football and a beer. Was this conflict what the rest of his life was going to be like?

Marie-Eve was never going to go away now and he might as well face it, they had him in their sights. So, what could he expect for manslaughter, or could he make up an accident? She'd slipped and banged her head, she was dead and he'd put her in the freezer in panic. She'd tried to blackmail him but it was an accident, just manslaughter, five years, ten years, would they both wait for him?

He realised he was crying, well snivelling. In his head everything added up, he could do this thing, take whatever came and make sure that Small and mother stayed together. For some reason he thought to look around the house, tried all the rooms in case she'd dozed off somewhere, Small lying on her chest, having an afternoon kip, but no car, they must be out.

In the nursery, Small was fast asleep, the sort of deep sleep that this baby seemed to manage where others screamed the house down day or night. He checked for the rise and fall, there was breathing there, he always made sure. He plucked the drinking cup from the crib, it was just about empty. Small was probably sleeping off a good dose of milk.

Once back downstairs he made a hot chocolate and pulled the Hobnobs out; a little feast, he could always hide the packet. It seemed odd being home mid-afternoon but he just couldn't settle at work; he wasn't sure that he ever would again.

In the TV room the set was still playing, casting a YouTube video of yoga, it looked like hard work. He found a Forest video, the glory European Cup team; he'd watch that a bit, sound down in the unlikely event that Small howled.

He drained the hot chocolate and managed only four biscuits before he felt dozy. He'd have five minutes, Jemmy couldn't have gone far, not leaving Small like that. Where was she?

## EIGHTY-SIX

Where the fuck were they? Prosser and Banks sat uncomfortably in the little boat as it bobbed about, tight to the trees in the sheltered bay on Colwick Lake, two fishing rods poked out as they pretended to be fishing, very apt. Prosser could run through a brick wall, fight a Pit Bull and possibly beat Frank Bruno now he was getting on a bit, but water and boats were not for him. He was sure his poorly-chosen lunch of a biryani would become decorative objet-d'art on them both, very shortly, and then there would be another death. Banks would kill him.

The earpiece wasn't working too well at all, fizzing and popping and making parts of the message sound like someone speaking Klingon in a light wind. The wildlife was noisy too. Prosser had never really noticed it before but, when you were trying to listen, really listen, ducks and geese can sound like a right racket. Surely there had to be a better way to be in proximity of the sting, but Thompson had wanted someone on the water, ready in case the killer jumped in. There was a sort of logic to it, if you really wanted to find it. Prosser just wanted to find a bucket.

There were always a few cars in the secluded car park by the Nottingham Racecourse, a back entrance into the park and quiet. Most afternoon users were courting couples getting out of the way of prying eyes, although the spot was far from romantic. Other cars might belong to dog walkers. The little shit machines had to be emptied twice a day and where better than the open spaces of Colwick Park? Especially in the Nature Reserve, where there were few people around to shame you into picking up nature's little gift.

As the afternoon wore on, and anonymity was almost guaranteed, more cars would show up, cars containing people with a more nefarious intentions. Doggers were not unknown. Prostitutes, too, popped in and out, so to speak, liberally decorating the car park each night with enough rubber to make a set of tyres. It was also a gay meeting place and a drug wholesale operation, all activities not covered in the multi-use description of the park. There had been a time when car thieves would have been a real issue too but, since the placing of the average speed cameras along Racecourse Road, an overkill of course, given its length, car thieves seemed reluctant to make the drive down as often these days.

Just one car was in the car park when Mo got there, she didn't recognise it but then it was a car. She was nervous, in fact Tena Pad nervous! She pulled alongside the rustic fence and waited. Her phone pinged. 'Take the gate in the corner, go straight to the open area, go left around the lake and, in the bay before the main public car park walk the lake edge to the bench at the end. I'm watching'. No caller ID.

As she got out of the car, another car pulled into the car park but as far away from Mo as was physically possible; two business types in it, a man and a woman. The seats went flat almost before the car had stopped. It looked like they were a couple of enthusiastic shaggers, fresh out of some nearby office for a quickie. It was hard for Mo not to stare, they were very engaged.

The paths were soft, gritty and muddy in places. Mo crossed a bank with a thin lake to her right and then came out of a tunnel of smaller trees into an open area. She'd been to the park many times before to walk her little dog before she'd died.

She took the better path to the left, the main lake appeared on her right, trees to the left. Nobody was visible anywhere near, just a distant jogger bouncing away and some even more distant dog walkers on the far bank. She could see some cars opposite, across the lake, in the Marina, she thought.

It took a while to get to where she thought she was supposed to be. It was a dull day and getting a bit darker but she was able to find her way ok, she knew that she'd be easily seen by someone hiding in the bushes. A noise was approaching but it was just the jogger again, feet scrunching on the path, rhythmic, breathing heavily, looking stupid in skinny leggings and a hoodie top, going past at a rate of knots and accelerating off along the path.

Mo turned to her right, now she was walking on grass, short cropped. It had recently been cut and bits stuck to her shoes, it was still wet following a brief shower, earlier. The lake seemed much bigger from this angle. She pressed on, walking along a spit of land that jutted out into the lake, to a bench at the end, hidden from the view of everyone unless they were opposite or on the lake, hidden from everyone but the killer.

There was a kind of peace to it all, the gentle lapping of the lake against the rocky shore. The chatter of birds was almost a background noise. She could hear different sorts, perhaps some were on one of the islands or out in the lake, ducks maybe or geese.

The bench was empty but a small bunch of flowers were tied to it, as people were wont to do these days, the flapping cellophane making a slight rustle, the flowers looking fresh, recently placed. Mo walked towards the bench and sat down. The flowers had a card, more instructions? 'Poor Marie-Eve', it said. Mo froze.

Back in the car park Thompson climbed off Elkie, blushing. "Do you think we were convincing?" he asked.

"Fuck, yes", said Elkie, as she rearranged her park shagging gear, as she'd been calling it all day. She was laughing at Thompson's discomfort, but then any signs she had that she'd rather enjoyed their theatrical embrace wouldn't be so obvious on her.

They moved quickly into the park and along the old horse trail that ran parallel to the main path. Stealth was the order of the day; nobody used these trails much now. There was just a newly cut path down the middle, just wide enough for one person at a time. There was less visibility than they'd expected but they had to be cautious and not be seen, or it would all be a waste of time.

In the Marina, Dad was sitting on his friend's boat, he'd always promised to drop by and see it, well now was the time. Through binoculars he could see that Mo had arrived at the bench, alone, but she couldn't see him. He relayed the message to both parts of the team. 'Mo had arrived, she was alone'.

Thompson tapped Elkie on the shoulder, gave her the thumbs up. They slipped back into a plantation by the main path, hidden. Mo was behind the bushes on a wooded peninsula 200 yards away. They waited.

Mo shuffled uneasily. This was a stupid idea, she should have just ignored her thoughts, not told the police about it, just packed up and gone away for a bit, maybe her brother in San Francisco; wouldn't that be a nice surprise for him. But the Mo that had once lived on the edge had won out, besides she felt more alive now than she had for years, well for now at least.

Her natural instinct was to flee and she felt poised to spring, to run off away from the bench, run without any style, no poise, just run and keep running.

"How did you know it was me, Mo?"

Mo's body tightened so much she thought she was having a heart attack. For what seemed an age, words were just stuck in her throat.

There was a slight rustle and the jogger was standing next to Mo, hood still up, steaming slightly, breathing heavily but controlled.

"Hi Jemmy, how's it going?"

"How did you know, Mo?"

"You were just too keen to drop Craig in it and you knew too much detail. I thought I knew you but when you left Small in the café that time, I started to suspect that you knew all about Craig and Marie-Eve and that incident showed me that you had problems. A new mother doesn't leave their kid like that. Then, when we went out, I was sure, the way you behaved after a few drinks, comments you made, questions you asked, stuff you knew that wasn't public knowledge, stuff I didn't know then. It had to either be you or someone you'd got to do it for you, but not Craig".

"Oh, fair enough, Mo the sleuth, a regular little Miss Marple aren't you. I have to make a decision now Mo, a life or death decision for us both. Do I kill myself here, drown myself out in the deep lake and put an end to all this? Or, and a good 'or' this one, Mo-and I think you know the answer but I'll tell you anyway-or do I kill you here, now, then slip away from here and keep playing the game a bit longer? I have to say, the latter option is much more attractive".

Mo answered "Whatever option you choose, Jemmy, you're in complete control". *Just like they'd rehearsed.* "But I don't want to believe it, Jemmy. I know you, well I thought I did. Can you at least tell me why?"

"Why is easy, Mo, he's mine, he was from the first time I saw him. He's mine and I'll kill anyone who messes with him. You don't mess with me, Mo. Marie-fucking-Eve Legault doesn't mess with me, nobody messes with me anymore, nobody".

Prosser thought he caught the word 'go' from Thompson, so go it was, then. Slipping out from the cover of the bankside trees, Prosser and Banks headed for the peninsula, quietly. Neither of them complained when they'd got their feet wet getting out of the boat, kept just off the bank to stop any noise. They pushed it off and let it drift out and away; the park staff could recover it later. If Jemmy jumped in the lake now, Banks could rescue her.

460

Edging along the narrow path through the plantation silently, the same path the killer had used to get in behind Mo but they didn't know that, they held their collective breaths, ready for the take. They could now see part of the bench. Mo sat to the right, a hooded figure to her left standing still and talking, although too far away for any audible detail. Should they wait for the signal, when Mo would run and they would move in, or should they just go for it?

Prosser slipped his hand into his pocket, found the thick webbing and wound it around his left hand. You always had to have an edge.

As soon as Mo had sat down, Dad left the Marina on his bike, no lights, no pale clothing. He might be visible to anyone really looking hard but that was unlikely. Inside a couple of minutes he was in place by the track out of the park. "Ready".

"How did you know he was having an affair with Marie-Eve?" Mo was buying time and, besides, she wanted all the details in a morbid 'confession and redemption before death' sort of way, although death was not a part the plan. Hopefully!

"Luck really, just dumb luck. I knew he kept the caravan at Calverton, the one I was not supposed to know about. I thought it was for sex but it wasn't, or at least not at first. On the handful of occasions that I was able to follow him he was alone. He went fishing, I'd satisfied myself that nothing was happening there. Then one evening I caught just a whiff of perfume on him. I tried to get a better smell of it, got close, sexy, but it was a trace, nothing more. So I followed him one more time, it was going to be the last time because I thought I had to drop it or go mad, and there they were, together. I wasn't sure who she was at first, but Craig did always like to talk shop at home. I remember he mentioned a Marie-Eve, told me she was a stuck up, bossy French cow and I just knew then that it was her".

"And then?"

461

"I lightly spiked Craig's drink one night with the stuff I use to settle Small, so he'd go to bed early and while he slept, I took his keys. I drove to Silverdale and biked into the back of NPS, you remember my little fold-away bike that I got to get my shape back after having Small, I always keep in the boot? I knew how to get in through the delivery bay; the card reader was broken so I got in with just the key".

"That easy", said Mo.

"I knew she was working late, Craig said that she was winding up her big, bad report before she left for Montreal and that there would be a rif, he might even be let go. Once ready, I texted her using Craig's phone, a phone I had to destroy later because I couldn't find out how to delete the bloody history forever. I told her to meet me in Shipping. I knew she'd come if the message came from him, and she did".

"And you intended to kill her; that was your plan?"

"I was going to smash her face in with the bar that they use for opening packing cases and see how it went but she fainted on me. So, after a few whacks for good measure, I had a bright idea and took her to the freezer on a cart thing, threw a bucket of warm water over her that the cleaners had left propping a door open and the rest you know. I went home, to bed and slept. I heard Craig go out to receive samples and then come back. He'd have woken me if he'd found her, but he didn't and she died. I was fine with that".

"So that was it, you could have just let her go home to Montreal, forget about her, forgiven Craig and got on with your life, you idiot". Jemmy didn't like that at all but it was true. "Right, and now, Jemmy, who lives and who dies? You always did like to be in control". Mo started to applaud sarcastically, tensing to sprint.

"Sorry, Mo, me live, you, die, I think" and a knife was just suddenly there, then so too were the police.

Mo dived forwards and Jemmy hit the floor running, squirming out of one of the officers' grasp, swinging the blade as she went.

There was blood, wet and sticky all over Mo's face. "Am I stabbed, will I die?"

Nobody answered her, there was just noise, shouting, screaming and then there was just her and Prosser alone. He was clutching his hand, holding it up and asking very calmly to people she couldn't see for a medic. He never even said 'officer down'.

Thompson and Elkie went too late. Jemmy saw them and accelerated away in the opposite direction, trying to ditch the knife in an old cut of the River Trent but only managing to reach a dense plantation with her throw. Only one of the cops who'd tried to grab her was following her now, but too slowly, way too slowly. She tore up a small hill, the park entrance was only maybe a hundred yards away now, then she had the possibility to get lost in the local roads and houses, get back over the footbridge to her car and then she'd be gone.

Running down the other side of the hill she had less control. She was sprinting hard now, stupid police, they'd never catch her. The last thing she heard sounded like 'whoops' as a bike slid into view and she crashed over it and into the gritty path, arm first then face down, ploughing into the rough surface. The skin stripping off her, hurting. Then she couldn't move; someone was holding her down expertly.

She sat in the ambulance, quiet, she felt like she'd been roughly grated, like cheese. Her arm felt odd, dull, aching, it had been strapped up. Her good arm was handcuffed to the stretcher. An officer, Elkie, sat next to her on the stretcher, close. Her legs and face did hurt, lots, everywhere hurt. Opposite was another police officer, his hand bandaged, bloodied and raised, packed in ice. He looked like he would kill her here, now. Please do.

She grinned at him, "hey, man, gimme three!"

The punch was fast, a blur, and she felt her nose go, her mouth filled with blood, the back of her head rapped into the side of the Ambulance. Nobody else saw it, nobody saw anything; she'd been injured when she went arse-over-tit over the carelessly-left bike. Jemmy sat very quietly for the rest of the way, too groggy to speak but still smiling, slightly.

# EIGHTY-SEVEN

The loud banging on the front roused the next-door neighbour who called over the fence that he was in, his car was there and she'd seen him go in. She presumed that this was where he got roughly arrested for murdering that girl, she'd never liked him and his sort. "I have a spare key", she said, and she threw it to them, making sure not to move from her ringside seat.

Thompson and Banks raced through the house. Craig was unconscious, sat in front of the TV, they couldn't wake him but he was breathing. Upstairs, in the nursery, Small was barely breathing. Thompson called for an ambulance and they put Small in a recovery position, they'd only ever done it with adults before.

Banks stayed with Small while Thompson went back to Craig. He'd been drinking hot chocolate; the cup was just about empty, the remaining contents congealing slightly. He went to the kitchen and found the hot chocolate tin left out on the counter. He bagged it and did the same with the cup, taking care to keep it upright.

Upstairs, Banks had had a similar thought and Small's tippy drinking cup was bagged too. The ambulance was quick and both Craig and Small were soon getting treatment. They tried to get Craig to vomit as he started to come round, very groggy at first. Small had already woken and was starting to grizzle, neither would die today.

Thompson called the SOCO people who were soon taking the evidence and other bits away. The 'off the cuff' thinking was that the hot chocolate and one of the baby formula tins had been spiked. Both patients would have just slept for a bit longer, although they wanted to keep an eye on Small. SOCO had everything bagged for analysis but the cap to the formula tin wasn't secure and the contents spilled out in the bag. Nestled amongst the white powder was a very distinctive necklace. A small, finely crafted locket, silver, cloisonné, heart shaped.

Soon, Craig was fully awake and asking what they were doing there. Thompson explained about the spiked drinks for both of them, causing a panic in Craig but they assured him that Small was fine, just being checked over. "Jemmy, is she OK too, where is she?"

Now came the difficult bit.

## EIGHTY-EIGHT

The ops room was jubilant. The chatter and general hubbub that you always got at the end of a case never failed to create a bit of a rush for those involved. The uniforms were pleased too, because they'd been patted on the back by most of the team and they had done a good job, digging and probing and finding the information that mattered, or at least would have, had not Moonbeam Orinoco Smith come through the way she had. She might be flakey in some areas, but she held her nerve when it mattered. She'd put herself on the line and helped snap the trap around the neck of Jemmy Shepherd.

The only real casualty was Liam Prosser. He was a bit subdued while all around were wallowing in the glory, but he'd played his part well too. The hand would be a mess for a while but the fingers had been fixed up with a few stitches and he was expected to make a full recovery. He'd been offered sick leave and additional counselling and had turned down both. He'd be mostly a desk jockey for little a while and any reports he typed would be done with one finger. "So, no change there, then", as Thompson had been quick to point out.

Without anyone realising it, Charnley had appeared in the room. It took a moment, but once Banks saw him she shushed the room to silence, not really knowing what to expect. He'd been 'Mr. Bloody Weird' all throughout the case and had no right to share in the glory; fuck, he might even try to steal it.

The room quietened as everyone realised what was going to happen. Once he had their attention, Charnley thanked the whole team for their efforts, an excellent job; a true team effort. He was proud of them and he would be leaving the force on a high. There was a slight groan, audible but hard to find the source of.

Thompson took over. He thanked the team, too, and then pointed to a stack of cream cakes that had appeared in one corner, thanks to a prior arrangement with one of the uniforms. For those that wanted it, there would be a post-case celebration in the pub later, not a piss-up but a toast to a job well done. Then he announced that there would be a leaving do for Charnley at the Saagar Indian Restaurant on Mansfield Road in a week's time, reservation required as they needed to confirm the booking.

Finally he started a round of applause for Charnley. It was muted at first but then it picked up and became rousing, because that is what you do. Charnley had been a good copper in his day and his ovation traded on the past, but not the recent past. Looking suitably embarrassed, Charnley waited for it to subside, thanked the room in general terms and went back to his office.

The celebration wound down as people went back to work, stuff to do before the pub. Thompson chatted to the team for a while, but then sloped off to Charnley's office at the first opportunity. He knocked before he went in again, just like he always used to do. Charnley was stood behind the desk, a couple of boxes on it filled with odds and sods, the detritus of a career encapsulated in a rather sad image. Charnley was tearful, but Thompson made a play of not noticing, chatting lightly about details really; a diversion.

Both men sat down facing each other. Charnley pulled himself together, and for a while seemed to be the old boss, sharp but fair, even handed. "You did well, Dave, you and the team".

"Thanks, boss". Thompson very nearly said 'we couldn't have done it without you', but that would have been wrong and he pulled up in time.

"I know I wasn't involved much in the traditional sense, Dave, but behind the scenes I kept them at bay; gave you the free hand you needed, kept them off your back". Thompson almost asked who exactly had he kept at bay, but he knew that this was a part of the paranoia, a symptom of the PTSD. Knowing that didn't make it any easier to deal with though. Thompson settled for a nod of acknowledgment, non-committal on the subject but Charnley wouldn't know, he'd think he was agreeing with him.

"Did we get anything else on the twoccers who did for Martin?"

"No, Sir, but we think we know who they might be. We might not get them for Martin yet but there'll be a chance down the line if they carry on offending. Of course, killing a man with a stolen car might just end their career in crime, one for the back-burner".

Charnley shrugged. "And why was Martin there in the first place, a little light banditry? He looked the part".

Thompson flinched a little at the non-pc nature of Charnley's remark. "No, Sir, we think he was a user, what you would call speed when you were a lad. His medical showed that he was previously on heroin but got himself clean. We think it was a pick up, gone wrong or just an accident, don't know yet".

Charnley nodded, non-committal himself. "And Mills? I hear that Derbyshire have him, her ex, and we have enough to make him a reservation at one of Her Majesty's less comfortable establishments".

Not registering the joke, Thompson started to add a bit of fill. Yes, they had pulled him while he was on his way to Manchester Airport with a ticket for Spain, one-way. They had sweaty palm prints on Mills' clothing that had his DNA, plenty of detail, he won't wriggle.

"Good, glad to hear it, just a minor distraction in the Legault case then, coincidence". And that was it, out with the old and in with the new, and as yet, unknown.

When both had been quiet for long enough, Thompson got up to go, offering his hand, knowing that he was unlikely to see much of

Charnley again once his police career had been formally 'sent off'. Charnley gripped it firmly, still a strong man in body if not mind. He eased Thompson a bit closer and half-whispered "take care of yourself and the team, Dave, and watch each-others backs all the time, all the time". Message delivered, Charnley went back to his boxes, almost surprised that Thompson was still there, so Thompson left. By now he felt a bit tearful himself.

The atmosphere in the pub was fizzing. Drinks were bought and the team sat around, more relaxed than they'd been since the mysterious case of the Fish Finger had crossed their desks.

Stories were being told of the take, especially by Prosser, one of the injured martyrs, there was always one. All the uniforms in the pub who'd played their parts on the case were keen for the sort of details they didn't know yet, details that would later become legend as well as wildly inaccurate.

Normally, police work was on the dull side and the actual arresting of people often duller. Unless they'd got the edge of a criminal, most offenders simply fell to pieces once the arrest had started. Very rarely did they try to brazen it out, even try to kill the police, the set-up and anyone else who came into their line of fire. In this case Jemmy Shepherd was clearly mad, but even the mad can be calculating if needs be. Her use of Rohypnol was particularly devious, especially on the baby.

The juke box had been playing various retro songs all night but it was only when George Thorogood and the Destroyers came on, singing 'Bad to the Bone' and everyone except Thompson burst out laughing that he paid attention. He was puzzled, what was he missing here? Elkie especially was in stitches. Eventually Prosser took pity on him.

"Sorry, Tommo, we've got a new nick-name for you, courtesy of our Elkie".

470

Still Thompson was confused, "what are you talking about, what new nick-name?"

"I'm afraid they're calling you T-Bone".

They were all looking at him; then Elkie leant forward winked and blew him a kiss. "Oh no, come on, don't do this, even you, Liam, would have reacted. Shit, who else knows?"

Banks patted his hand and said "don't worry, Mr. Lover Man; it can be our not-so-little secret". Thompson looked relieved.

"Thanks everyone, I appreciate it, and you promise that it will stay between just us then and please, be soon forgotten".

"Oh, between us, yes, and Rebecca, of course", said Elkie. "I called her to tell her all about it in case she thought we were having it away while she was 'hors de combat', so to speak, she thought it was such a hoot. I was worried that she might deliver there and then, she was laughing so much".

Prosser patted him on the back with his good hand and said, "don't worry, mate, and, no, I wouldn't have reacted in the same way, she's not my type at all, wrong type of plumbing". Then the jokes really started. "Tommo, what's for dinner? Got to be a T-bone steak". "Come on Tommo, rise and shine!" Someone put 'The Only Way is Up' on the jukebox.

It looked like it would all calm down a bit until Banks put on her best porn-star voice, asking Thompson if, the next time he wanted to do a car park love scene, he'd pick her. Something about the way she said it and the look she gave him, had him feeling slightly uncomfortable. The rest, of course, went bananas, doing Donkey from Shrek and bouncing up and down going 'pick me, pick me', it was actually quite amusing.

While the children were busy wearing themselves out, Thompson slipped away to call home. Rebecca picked up immediately, "Hey, Mr. Lover".

"Don't you start, I'm getting the full treatment here".

"Well, I've got some more news for you, young T-Bone; we'll need a bigger mop. My waters have just broken, it's time".

He raced back inside and told them the garbled news while grabbing his coat. He'd deliberately laid off the pop all night so he could drive, just in case, and even though Prosser was on medication and staying sober himself. Thompson had wanted a clear head for all eventualities.

They were all chanting something obscene that he didn't quite catch as he raced out into the night. He could worry about the nickname thing later, besides, he was pretty sure that it wouldn't take anyway; it was just end-of-case frolics.

The birth had been pretty quick, well as far as Thompson knew how long births took, it was. Rebecca had told him that her family had been breeding stock for generations and that it would be just like 'shelling peas'. Well, it was slightly more complicated than that but, when the crying started, Thompson was presented with his new son and he couldn't be happier.

Now they had to come up with a name and quick, otherwise that would be another line of mickey-taking that his team could inflict on him. Thompson had his own ideas, Bryn he liked, Brian and Peter should be in there somewhere too. He was pretty sure that he was not going to be allowed to use all the names of the Forest Football League Championship winner's squad, 1977-78!

The hospital staff told him to bugger off and get a cup of tea or something while they did whatever it was they did. He went down to the cafeteria and had a coffee and a bun, but was too fidgety to be away too long.

When he got back on the ward Rebecca was her normal self, you'd never have guessed that she'd just ejected a little human from out of her groin.

"Right, young Thompson", she said to the pink, wriggling thing in her arms, "who are you?" The phrase delivered exactly as she'd heard it when Thompson had taken her to the City Ground. They both ended up laughing, the relief of the situation all coming out in a shaking hysteria.

"Go on, Dave, tell me which Garibaldi-clad hero of yours our son will be named after and why; make it good or he will be a Gilles, Justin or Jeremy". So Thompson told her a story that his dad had told him, about a match against Liverpool when the young Forest Centre-Half, Bryn Gunn, had got hold of the Liverpool midfielder enforcer by the throat and near lifted him off his feet, after the so-called hard man had clattered a young Forest debutant once too often.

"Bryn Thompson? No, I really don't think so, try again".

"OK, not Bryn. Being a good detective I have back-up names as you might expect, so pick one from Kris, with a K, Alex, Billy, Guy or Dexter. Nigel will be in there after Nigel Doughty but we can hide it somewhere in the middle!"

"Guy, I like Guy, so Guy Nigel Summers, it has a nice ring to it, unless you are going to give me a nice ring at some point in the future, that is?"

"I think I can manage that. Guy it is then".

# EIGHTY-NINE

A few days after Jemmy Shepherd's arrest and charging, eleven of them went to the Saagar for one of their top curries, Charnley wasn't amongst them. He was OK; Thompson had recently spoken with his sister, who'd spent some time with him 'just to make sure that he was OK'. Thompson knew what she meant; it was the unsaid suicide conversation that they were too polite to come out with. Thompson had already given Charnley's sister the iPod filled with rude messages in the play list called 'sod off'. Whether he liked it, or had even bothered to listen to the messages from each of his colleagues wishing him all the best, Thompson didn't speculate. He might enjoy the music though, they'd been pretty careful with that, making sure to give him plenty to listen to, if he wanted.

The do at the Saagar ended up being an extension of the case-closed celebration, and different parts of the table chipped in with theories, or looked for clarification of a point that they'd not quite got at the time. Unsaid was the fact that, while they had caught the murderer of Marie-Eve Legault, a double murder really as she was about nine weeks pregnant, there was more to the case than just a simple body. They still had a missing ex-CEO to deal with in Clive Gerrard, but Thompson was sure that he was just getting away from it all, whatever that 'all' might be.

They also still had to deal with the Saviour business. Well, Montreal did although, after speaking to them, they didn't really have a deal to offer there. It sounded like they had no real idea how to find Ben Arjah, who, after disappearing off the face of the Earth before they could talk to him, had been confirmed as the father of Marie-Eve's unborn child; loose collection of cells that it was at the time. They had some other missing people at the Montreal end too, people who had been

474

involved in a scam but they didn't want to share and nobody in Nottingham cared very much.

The financially catastrophic Saviour study that had cost its investors so much money, none of it expected to ever be seen again, was not really their problem, although the Nottingham end of NPS was likely to suffer another rif over it to recover something. Big pharma really does not like cutting investor dividends but doesn't think twice about finding more dead wood to exorcise, even where none exists. So they, as an investigating team, had chosen not to dwell too much on the pharmaceutical side of things. They'd dealt with the murder and there were other teams in other departments who'd have to work the alleged corruption case involving Saviour.

As the party broke up, Banks had to poke Thompson who was head down over his jotter. "What do you think, Dave, do we have the next McBride amongst us?" He raised a middle finger, in part as a rebuff to the piss-taking but also because he was just finishing his jottings.

The Fish Finger was killed by a jealous nutcase who very nearly topiaried Prosser's hand at the time of arrest and who would have surely have killed Mo Smith if we'd not been there.

I almost might have expected her to kill Craig and herself, and probably the baby in a 'if I can't have him/them, then nobody can' scenario, it would have been easier than offing Orinoco Smith in a public place like that. Nutty suspects are always the hardest to figure, I suppose you just need to think the same way. Maybe Charnley could have helped there or is that bad taste?

The investors in the virtual company Saviour, will all be out of pocket for a while. A few heads might roll here and there, greedy people wanting more, as usual. Legault was involved in the Saviour sting but we don't know how far, or care. NPS Nottingham has agreed to cooperate without intending to cooperate in the slightest. They'll sacrifice those who they held responsible and, in due course, will find a way to write the whole affair off.

Craig Shepherd has to raise his kid on his own. Mummy will go to some nuthouse for the duration. Mills' killer will get life; there is enough for that so some justice there. Neil Martin's killers, even if not deliberate, might just find themselves back on the straight and narrow from now on, for a while anyway.

For the force this is mostly a success. Two killers caught, hit-and-run twoccers perhaps cured of twoccing so a few less crime numbers to issue, and the country park access roads, railway platforms and walk-in freezers of Nottingham are safe once again.

"I think I have the bones of something here", he said, smiling.

## NINETY

Across town at NPS, another not entirely unexpected scenario had recently been played out.

The day had started in normal fashion but there had been a non-specific buzz that suggested that it would be far from ordinary. Mo had picked up on it straight away, but her contacts were either unable or unwilling to tell her anything about what was going on, although one did tell her to sit back and enjoy the fun.

Expecting her to have her finger on the pulse as usual, Reid went over to Mo and asked the same question, "what the fuck now, Mo?" Outside the room, the sample analysts were coming and going to the collection counter as usual. The Sample Management lot, too, were shuffling between the counter and freezers, all as usual.

By nine-thirty the collection of samples for analysis had quietened down and a few were thinking of taking their break. That was when Bez Dooley appeared.

He entered the room, trying hard to stifle a grin but failing miserably. He looked just like a big, bald Cheshire Cat, as he called for quiet and everyone's attention.

"I'm here to talk about a rif", he said, and immediately there was a wave of panic. Even though they'd only experienced one rif at NPS Nottingham, so far, that had been enough to scare people and they were naturally worried for their jobs.

"First of all, nobody in this department has anything to worry about, far from it. This particular rif is taking aim at the positively dead from-the-neck-up wood, such as that to be found a little higher up in our metaphorical jungle. I'm sure that you will all be disappointed to hear that Dick Greenwood (and he did enunciate very clearly the shortened version of Richard Greenwood's comic first name when saying it) has gone. He was marched off the premises five minutes ago. I hear that he was in tears, oh dear, and what a terrible shame. Any volunteers to start a collection?" He was enjoying this.

Most of the room didn't really know how to react; this was the big boss that they barely knew, talking about getting rid of an even bigger boss who they also barely knew. Mo and Reid knew the score though, and did a fist bump, much to Reid's surprise.

Dooley continued, "Sadly there will be further departures both here and in Montreal. The contract managers and contract liaison staff who were involved in setting up and monitoring the blessed Saviour study have also all gone, including your favourite and mine, Ria Sullamane", and Dooley looked straight at Reid, still grinning. Again the rest of the room were clueless, they'd never heard of her but that didn't matter.

"And there's more. Our glorious leader in New Jersey has decided that we staff have not been well served by Nash Pharmaceutical Solutions, shiny and new as it still is for us here in Nottingham. In his mighty wisdom he has seen that much of the problem lies with those charged to take care of us while we savour being a part of the NPS family. Now, ten points for guessing who from Human Resources is currently taking a walk down Castle Boulevard?"

Reid laughed, "You're showing your age now, Bez, there is no Employment Exchange on Castle Boulevard anymore. You have to go to the Job Centre on Parliament Street, I checked, just in case".

"True, Mr. Reid, true, but I used Castle Boulevard for dramatic effect", said Bez, delighting in using the local pronunciation of Castle as 'Castile'.

Dooley paused, waiting for an answer but, as ever, nobody was going to stick their neck out in front of their technical head, not even Reid or Mo. "Ok, you worked it out of me, my friend and yours, Mr. Ranji Singh has very recently walked the walk of the unrighteous". Message delivered he turned smartly on his heel and left them to it.

Reid gave everyone five minutes to digest the information, not that most of them had been privy to the recent complicated internal machinations brought about by the death of Marie-Eve Legault. Even Reid didn't have the full picture yet, and Mo had been unusually reticent when asked. Seeing that the fun had ended, for now at least, the rest of the Sample Management staff settled down naturally and got on with their day's work. 'So' thought Reid, 'there can be an upside to rifs, after all'.

Back at his work station, his email, now considerably less populous since the Saviour debacle had surfaced and the samples ceased to arrive, had a new message from Dooley. 'My office, ten minutes'. Now what had he done?

The office door was open when Reid got there. "Come in, Simon and welcome to the heady world of supervision". Dooley handed him a new contract and told him to go away, read it thoroughly and then return the signed and dated copy to him.

For once, Reid was less composed than normal. Instead of leaving, he sat down and skimmed the contract; he knew which bits to focus on. Satisfied that this was a promotion and not a sideways shunt dressed up as one, Reid seized the opportunity to ask a few questions.

"Did they find her laptop? It would have been interesting to know what her final report contained".

"No", said Bez, not that I'm aware of. However, they do have some of the contents though because, like a good, GLP-conscious, girl, she'd backed up her data to a Cloud-based server, one set up for her by an IT contact in Montreal. There are some encrypted files on there, but I hear that our best IT brains are currently trying to unpick her defences".

479

"Shouldn't it be the police who are doing that, surely there might be evidence they need to go through?"

"The police have their killer and I doubt whether those who watch over us would like sensitive company information to seep out. I suspect that her Saviour dealings will be on there somewhere, and I would think that our security-conscious bosses would not like too many to know how big a fuck-up they did with that study. Meanwhile, as you know, we have a shit-load of samples in our freezers and nobody to pay for their storage".

Reid had wondered how to broach that particular situation. "That was going to be one of my questions, I suppose we'll need to do a full inventory, and then pack them up in sealed boxes?"

"No need, they are being collected next week and shipped off-site to a storage facility. For your part, just have your people transfer the samples, complete with a copy of the original documentation to our shipping people, and they will go as one lot. No need to be too fussy, once it is out the door it is someone else's problem. Deactivate everything in Clousseau once we have them out of here, and then wash your hands of the study. I know I will".

"Do you think we'll ever know just how badly NPS was burned by Saviour?"

"Simon, this is a new dawn, just forget all about the Saviour study, and Marie-Eve Legault if you can. Concentrate now on your department and be sure that you morph into the company Clousseau expert. I predict a much more interesting career ahead of you, if you focus on the now, rather than the then".

A few minutes later he was walking back to Sample Management with a spring in his step and the fine details of his unexpected promotion bouncing around in his cranium.

Mo saw Reid come back and sidled over to his desk. "We live in very interesting times, Simon, and you look like the cat that got not only the cream but the fish too. Want to tell me all about it, or shall I just tell you what I already know?"

"How do you find this stuff out, Mo? I know you have been around a while but some things are not supposed to be available, even to you. I'll not say just yet what I was summoned to Bez's office for, but let's just say it is entirely within the character of this most interesting day. At some point soon we will talk of it and the ramifications, particularly for you".

Mo realised that it wasn't the 'free ice cream day' that she'd just heard was happening later in the week, as a sort of 'staff appreciation thing' that Reid was referring to. Maybe the rif wasn't quite done with yet, and her personal insurance policy had just expired. Reid read her thoughts.

"Nothing to worry about, Mo, no more rif. Yes, I can see it in your face and, yes, I do know about the ice cream thing and the vast expense that this recently impoverished company of ours has agreed to spend to cheer up the sheep. I'd like that little epithet to stay between you and me, thank you".

# NINETY-ONE

The garb that Jemmy wore looked very plain and ordinary. Normally, she was immaculate or 'well turned out', as Craig's mum would have said. She also looked worn and older than he remembered. He wasn't sure that she'd tried to drop him in it for the murder of Marie-Eve; he did know a few things simply didn't add up but perhaps now was not the time to revise the sums. He'd already decided that this was goodbye, as much for the baby as anything.

Jemmy's eyes were red, she'd obviously been crying. "Craig", she said, "I can't be in here, I can't take it. I didn't do it, not deliberately; it was an accident, a fight. I faced her down about you and her; I knew you'd been together in the caravan and I wanted to give her a beating. It just went too far when she came at me with the bar".

Craig sat impassively. This was going pretty much as he expected.

"The police don't believe me, I only have you now; you have to believe me", and with that, more sobs came but Craig had seen these before. This was practised sobbing, something Jemmy had used once too often with him. He also knew what was coming next.

"They don't believe me and I'm going to get life because they say it was premeditated, but what if you admit to it now, a confession to a crime of passion committed protecting your family. Marie-Eve had threatened me and Small, and you reacted, that would be manslaughter, a few years max and then you'd be out with me and Small, I'd be waiting and we could start again. I'll say I was just going to scare Mo in the park, not hurt her, I wouldn't hurt her, you know that". She never even mentioned nearly lopping a man's fingers off or using a date rape drug to sedate both him and the baby.

Craig could see that he would have gone for it in slightly different circumstances. His confession would have thrown doubt at the case and maybe affected the court outcome, but he knew what had happened was premeditated and that Jemmy was psychotic, she always had been. Besides, her confession had confirmed the details; she wasn't to know that the wire Mo had worn had not been very clear and that a hefty flock of Canada Geese had landed nearby, their honking slightly obscuring Jemmy's conversation with Mo. Can a husband testify against his wife? Not sure, but that was hardly the point. The police had had to convince him of the truth, of Jemmy's guilt, after he'd offered them exactly what Jemmy was asking him for without her knowing it. They'd been right about her.

Jemmy sat shaking, waiting, hoping. Surely Craig would do this for her, he loved her and that is what people who loved you did, they took the blame.

Then she said, quietly and in a more calculating voice "please don't let them make me have our new baby in prison. If I go to prison who will look after Small? You, you who can't say no?"

"I can look after our baby and she has a name now, I decided to call her Eve, do you want to know her middle name, I thought Marie had a nice ring to it, Eve Marie Shepherd."

That stopped all the play-acting, no more tearful Jemmy, now it was the barbs as she launched into a long and rambling tirade about how ineffectual he was at everything, utterly useless. By her saying her piece, and the way she'd delivered it, with spite and bile, she'd shown Craig what she was really like. He'd known all along really, but had tried to avoid admitting it; it didn't make any difference now.

Craig was conscious that he'd barely spoken as Jemmy ranted. He suddenly stood up with such ferocity that not only Jemmy jumped but the two nearby prison officers started too, instinctively reacting. The room seemed to hang until Craig broke the silence. "Goodbye Jemmy", he turned and he was gone. Behind him the screaming had started again; the language and the threats. If they ever let her out he knew he'd have to seriously watch his back.

As he left the prison, heading back to the visitor car park, a familiar figure was coming towards him. "Mr. Shepherd", said Thompson.

"Detective Sergeant".

"Was I right, did she ask you to confess?"

"She did. Is she pregnant? She says she is".

"No, I don't believe she is. Look, I'm sorry; it gives me no pleasure to be right. It must be very hard for you?"

"Not really" said Craig, "until just now I didn't realise quite what she was like".

"What do you mean?" asked Thompson.

"Cold hearted, Detective Sergeant, cold hearted".

Once back in his car, Craig Shepherd gripped the steering wheel tightly and thought, 'it's nearly over'.

Thinking back to the fateful night, he shivered. His utter exhaustion as he drove in to NPS, drugged he now knew, and his total lack of feelings when, as he unloaded the shipping cart of the new boxes of samples, he'd noticed the trail in the slight frost on the floor of the walk-in freezer, as if something had been dragged to the last row. Of course, he'd noticed something wasn't quite right and he'd recognised the shoe poking out. He knew then who he would see if he went to the back of the freezer, but he didn't look, he just turned around and went home.

# EPILOGUE

Reid walked up the corridor to the Sample Management room at NPS; he could hear the god-awful rap music all the way down the hall. At her hutch, Mo looked up, huffed and made to turn off the music.

"Leave it", said Reid. "Time we had a little more of a lively atmosphere in here, a bit of modern beat pop music might just do it".

Mo was astonished but still reached over and wound it down a couple of notches.

"How's it going, Simon?" she asked.

"Better", was all that Reid answered.

Reid put on his lab coat, gloved up and went through to the walk-in -20 freezer. He didn't consciously check for a broken pen on the floor, but, subconsciously he always would. Inside, the shelves were all neatly separated, each line accessible. Just inside the door were two boxes, an overnight delivery. He picked them up and put them on a cart, it was new. A quick glance showed him that the freezer was holding nothing more than boxes and boxes of samples, another little check that he knew he'd always do from now on.

Satisfied that all was well, and aware that the rest of the Sample Management staff were filing in, he wheeled the cart with the sample boxes up to the verification counter, scooped dry ice into a tray and began to unpack the samples.

One of the girls came over, offering to take over, but Reid was having none of it, a good boss was always prepared to roll up their sleeves and help out. He pulled the paperwork from the overnight delivery slot, it was signed by Craig. The poor sod had been dragged out of bed at two in the morning to move two boxes from point 'A' to point 'B'; that was going to have to change. No more night call-outs when Security are on-site, and Bez was on-side with it.

Reid and Mo went about their various daily duties as other techs filled the Sample Management room with inane chatter, as normal, as absolutely normal.

Later that morning, Reid went over to Mo, telling her to read her email.

She opened up his message and began to read. He'd started by raising the whole Orinoco Womble thing again, was he still taking the piss! She was just going to hit delete when she scrolled down and read:

*From Wikipedia -* **Orinoco** *– a shirker who loves sleep and food, (and shots – Reid) and named after the river in South America. Though slothful by nature, Orinoco is capable of some surprising acts of moral and physical courage.*

Mo grinned, "Seems about right!"

# ABOUT THE AUTHOR

Originally from Nottingham but now Canadian and a resident of Nova Scotia, Mark Dennis was ending his 50s when he started his first crime novel, Coldhearted. Now in his early 60s, he has published three novels in the Nottingham series, along with three Nova Scotia-based mysteries, a Sci-Fi novel, birding memoirs and birding guides. He hopes that his main character in the Nottingham series, Dave Thompson, doesn't get shot or killed because that can ruin a day.

Mark lives on Cape Sable Island, a place that gets weather. He shares his home with his scientist wife, editor and moderator Sandra, and their cat, Bubbles, who isn't very bubbly at all.

Influenced by Shakespeare, Tom Holt, Robert Rankin and especially Sir Terry Pratchett, Mark didn't read a crime novel until after Coldhearted had been started. Now he reads lots but not nearly as many as Sandra. He had never realised how cathartic it was to kill, in print only, people who annoyed him!

The characters depicted in this story bear no resemblance to anyone living or dead. Mark used places and procedures he was familiar with, from previous careers as a Country Park Warden and as a Sample Management Technician amongst others, to create, almost from thin air, a set of characters to write about.

For more on Mark's books and other writing, see https://markdennisbooks.wordpress.com.

Follow Mark on Twitter at: MarkDen14868518

Or on Facebook at: https://www.facebook.com/mark.dennis.9212

All titles are available, as ebooks or paperbacks, on Amazon.

# ALSO BY MARK DENNIS

## The DI Thompson Nottingham Mystery Series:

### On The Fly —the second Thompson novel

There is more to becoming DI than being a good cop, which is why Dave Thompson finds he had more than enough tidying up to do when his old boss retires. When a body is discovered on a local nature reserve, is it just the tip of a particularly murky iceberg? This is where Thompson will earn his real DI's spurs.

### Spiked-the third Thompson novel

In this, the eagerly-awaited third Nottingham detective novel, Dave Thompson is feeling the strain. At home he feels cramped, at work he feels put upon, in his head he's struggling to decide what is right and what is wrong in his life and his work-load keeps getting heavier.

When a sports teacher at the private Whitaker School for Boys is found dead, and in rather grizzly circumstances, he gets the case and it turns out to be a pretty tangled web of lies, deceit and intrigue. Things about the case might appear a little complicated, but Thompson is a thinker and, given time, he will get there. It might help if his acting Detective Sergeant stopped saying 'righty-ho' all the time, though.

# The Howey Cross Nova Scotia Birder Mystery series

### The Frigatebird

When a notorious birder is found dead in Nova Scotia, the list of suspects is already available on-line, if you know where to look. Sergeant Howey Cross has to juggle an expanding caseload against a baffling murder, and he has to learn 'birder-speak', otherwise how will he understand what on earth is going on?

### Nor'easter

Howey Cross investigates the disappearance of a number of young women from Queen's County, even though it is outside his jurisdiction. There's a storm coming, the largest ever recorded, but the tail might be even more dangerous, it might bring the dreaded nor'easter.

### Sea Glass

Howey Cross investigates an old case as a favour to his boss, Gordy Cole. Life is changing for Howey, not least because he now has twins to think about, he calls them the 'terrors'. He's also torn about whether to push his career in Halifax, or to take the unknown road and move to King's County. Birds appear with regularity, conundrums too, as Cross finds that life is no longer the simple affair it once was.

## Science-fiction/fantasy

### *The Harvesters*

Kerry Peters lives an ordinary life in Corner Brook, Newfoundland. She likes a beer and sometimes the company of her boyfriend, Gary, although she's sure he's not the one.

After a heavy night of drinking, she wakes up in Transit, naked. The staff there tell her they've sorted out her little problems and she's ready to go on, but go on where, exactly? Kerry didn't know it, but she's one of the Harvested and, after that fateful night, nothing is going to be the same for Kerry, or for anyone.

# Birding Memoirs

## *Going For Broke*

1984 in the UK-'Big Brother', the Libyan Embassy siege, Band Aid, the launch of the Apple Mac and the start of the Miner's Strike. None of it matters when a birding Big Year is in sight. In the days of no mobile phones, no pagers and no dial-up 'Birdline', all rare bird information has to be obtained by phoning little café in Norfolk and hoping one of the customers will pick up...

A young birder on a shoestring finds his way the length and breadth of Britain, finding birds and maxxing out the credit card. He really is 'going for broke'.

## *Twitching Times-a UK Birding Life*

Mark Dennis started birding in the UK as a child, but he really started twitching, going for rare birds, in 1981. From then to 2003, when he left the UK and moved to Canada, he birded his local patch, his county (Nottinghamshire), and the UK, going to see rare birds when he could. Here are his birding memories- lifers, memorable birds, occasions and people; and an entertaining swing through the UK birding scene.

# Birding Guides

## *Cape Sable Island-a Birding Site Guide*

Cape Sable Island juts out into the Atlantic Ocean at the very tip of Nova Scotia. The island is joined to the mainland via a causeway and there the magic begins. For the birder, Cape Island is a must-see place in Canada. Whatever season you choose to visit, there will be birds. During fall migration, there are masses of shorebirds. In winter the wharves are loaded with gulls, and alcids haunt sheltered spots. Spring brings the only Canadian American Oystercatchers and summer, the nesting Piping Plovers. Come when you like and Cape Island's birds will be waiting.

## *Yarmouth Birding-a Site Guide*

The county of Yarmouth offers some of the finest birding in Nova Scotia. Located at the extreme south-west of the province, birds migrating north in spring often make their first land-fall there, while fall birds migrating south can accumulate in considerable numbers at the various birding hotspots found in and around the town of Yarmouth.

This guide is designed to help the visitor find the sites. Finding the birds is a different thing altogether, but if you go to the right places ay the right time you tand every chance.

If you are planning a quick visitor a leisurely weekend of birding, this guide will prove invaluable in making your birding trip a success.

Printed in Great Britain
by Amazon